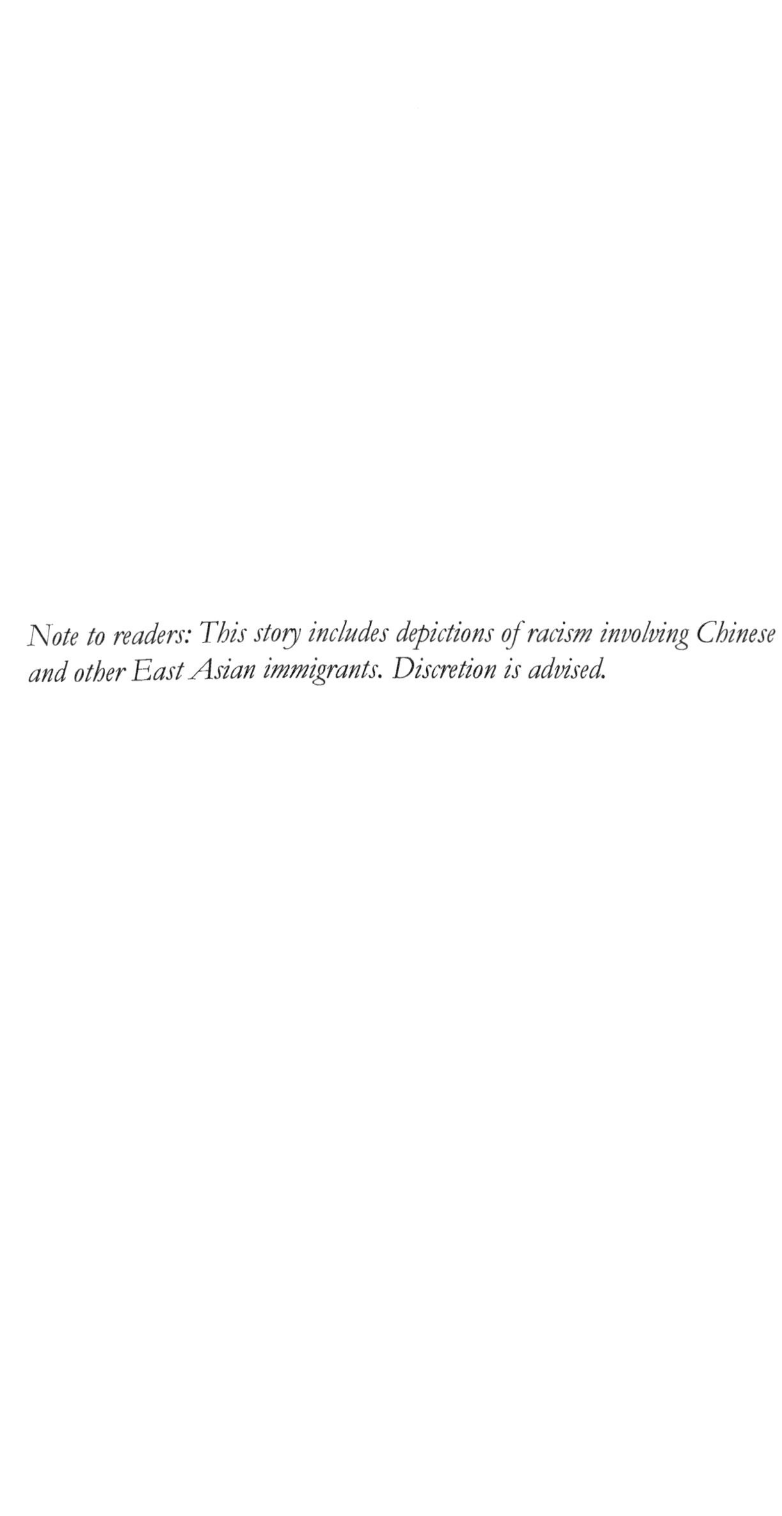

Note to readers: This story includes depictions of racism involving Chinese and other East Asian immigrants. Discretion is advised.

This book is a work of fiction. Names, characters, places, organizations, and incidents are the products of the author's imagination or are used fictitiously. Any resemblance to actual events, locales or persons, living or dead, is purely and entirely coincidental.

Light House Cover Photo by Scott Bufkin
Photo 218880475 / Lime Kiln
© Scott Bufkin | Dreamstime.com

Washington and British Columbia maps obtained from:
https://d-maps.com/carte.php?num_car=7812&lang=en
https://d-maps.com/carte.php?num_car=23532&lang=en

ISBN: 979-8-9886585-1-1

Printed in the United States of America

BOOKS BY D.C. ALEXANDER

Friday Harbor

Blood in the Bluegrass

Chasing the Monkey King

The Shadow Priest: Book Two

The Shadow Priest

The Legend of Devil's Creek

Further information available from:
www.dcalexander.com.

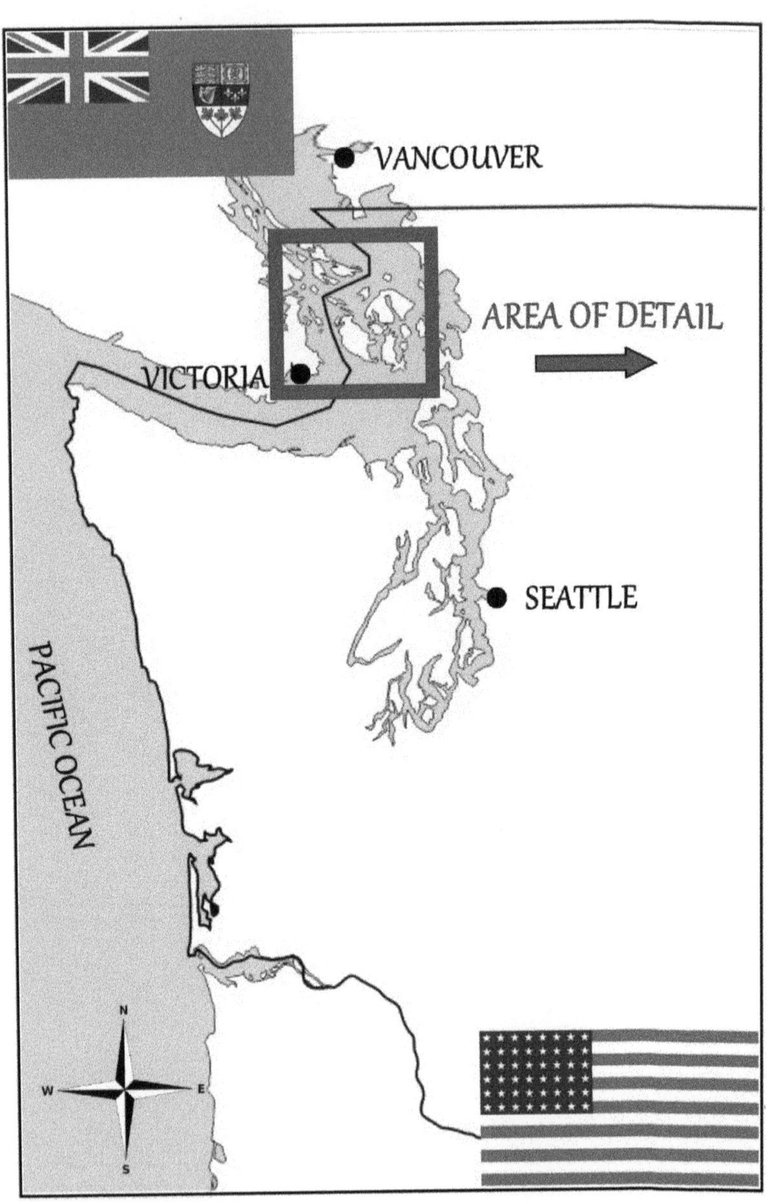
VANCOUVER
AREA OF DETAIL
VICTORIA
SEATTLE
PACIFIC OCEAN
N
W
E
S

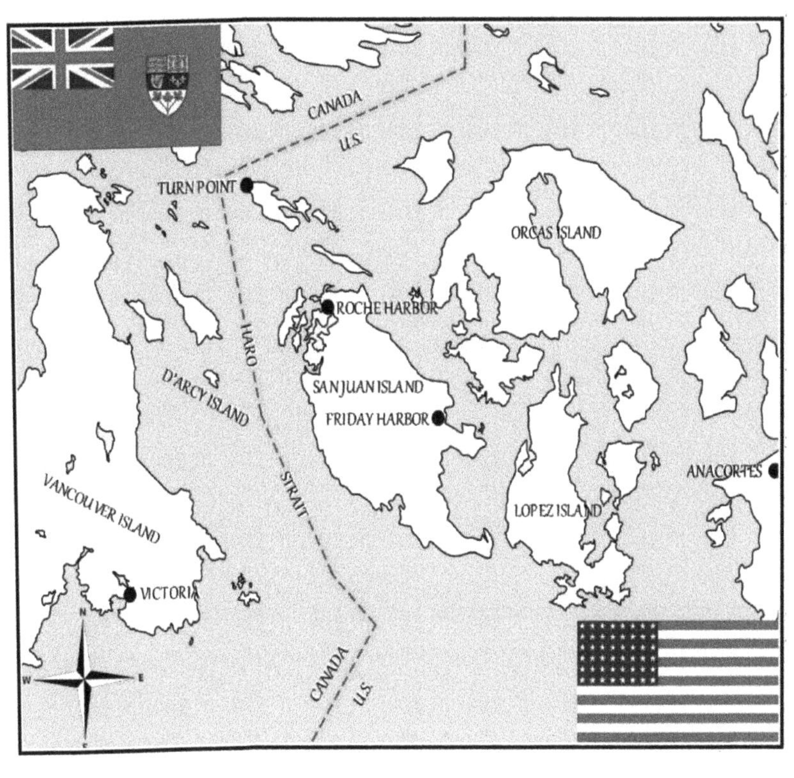

THE SAN JUAN ISLANDS

FRIDAY HARBOR

Inspired by a true story . . .

ONE

Hutouling Village, Guangdong Province
Republic of China
July 1922

When I came inside after fetching water from the river my father was weeping. He tried to hide it, but I saw. I had only ever seen him weep three times in my life. The first time was last spring, when the river flooded the valley and washed away all of our sweet potato fields. The second time was two months ago, when government soldiers came and took my older brothers away to help fight against the Guangxi warlords. This was the third time.

A man had come. A man I did not know. Not from our village. Not a farmer. A city man. I could tell by his clothes and shoes. He sat stone-faced across the table from my father in the front room of our small stone house. They spoke in hushed voices. The conversation was hard to hear. It was something about money. The price of something. Then the city man raised his voice and said 'no.' My father wept harder. It frightened me. My mother, her face like stone, the creases of her tunic stained with sweat, turned from preparing tea and told me to go into the back room and close the door.

The back room was hot and stuffy and dark. The air smelled of dry dirt. Whenever it was hot, the dirt smell seemed to rise up through the gaps between the floorboards. I propped the shutter open just enough to let in a little air and a little light. But not too much light because my little brother, Qiáng, a year and a half old, was napping on his mat in the back corner after again refusing to eat. Our dinner had been rice, mustard greens, and roasted grasshoppers. I hate grasshoppers—especially the big ones with their flavorless, mushy bodies. Qiáng won't eat them even if they're mashed up with rice—even if he hasn't eaten all day. Whenever my mother tries to sneak grasshopper into his mouth, he makes a face, spits, then cries as it dribbles down his chin. He is losing weight.

We have to eat grasshoppers because the soldiers took all of our pigs and chickens the same day they took away my brothers. When we can't catch grasshoppers, my father tries to catch birds and snakes. Most days he can't. Most days we are hungry.

Though I pressed my ear to the door, I could hear nothing of the conversation between my father and the city man. Suddenly, the door swung open. I jumped back hoping nobody would guess that I'd been eavesdropping. There stood my unsmiling mother. Behind her, I could see my father still at the table, his face buried in his hands. "Father, what's wrong?" I called. "Father, why are you weeping?" He refused to answer. Refused, even, to look at me. The city man was now standing. He stared at me from the far side of the front room with no hint of care, then put his hat on.

"Yin, pack your things," my mother said.

"Why? Where am I going?"

"Do as you're told, Yin. Quickly."

"When will I be back?"

"Do as you're told."

My mother watched as I gathered my things, her face hard as ever. It was the face of a woman who had seen too much hardship. A woman who always did what needed to be done without complaint.

"Not that," she said when she saw me taking my late grandmother's old wooden comb—the only thing of hers left to me. "Only necessaries that you can carry." When she turned away, I snatched the comb and slipped it into the inner pocket of my tunic.

"Who will feed Snow while I am away?" I asked, meaning who would go and gather grass seed from the edge of the forest to feed my pet mouse. Snow was almost completely white. That was why I named her Snow. I had never seen actual snow but I knew it was pure white, like a late morning cloud. I had heard stories about it and then dreamt of it falling over the farm. "Who will keep Snow's box clean and give her fresh water?"

My mother didn't answer. She gestured for me to hurry.

I rolled my things up into a bundle inside a piece of old cloth and tied it off with twine. Then I ran to the corner where I kept Snow's box. I took the lid off and reached in and took her in my hands for a moment, holding her up to my nose to smell her fur.

"Quickly now, Yin," said my mother. "You keep everyone waiting."

"Be brave," I whispered to Snow. "I will see you again soon. Don't be messy."

I put Snow back in the box and was closing the lid as she looked up at me with her tiny black eyes. To me, she looked confused. Afraid. I couldn't bring myself to close the lid on her. I began to worry that my mother wouldn't bother to feed her. That she might even get rid of her. My mother never wanted me to have a mouse in our house—just one more useless thing to worry about, she'd said. It was my father who, seeing what joy Snow brought me, convinced my mother to let me keep her.

Snow climbed up onto her back legs and put her little front paws up on the side of the box as she sniffed the air, still looking at me. I think she wanted to come with me. I checked over my shoulder. My mother was no longer in the doorway. I reached into the box, grabbed Snow, and tucked her in the inner pocket of my tunic, next to my grandmother's comb. Then I ran over to where my baby brother slept and put my palm to his forehead and held it there for a second, feeling the softness. I bent down and smelled him. Smelled his hair. He still had a baby smell that I loved. It was a smell of home. Of family. I wanted to remember it just in case I was away for a little while.

TWO

San Juan Island, Washington
September 8, 1922

Sheriff Miles Scott hated the new channel markers. The Coast Guard installed them, in early June, where the narrow San Juan Channel opened into the main shipping lanes of the Strait of Juan de Fuca. Fueled by pressurized acetylene gas, they were far brighter than the old markers. Indeed, their brilliant lights—one red, one green—cut right through the midnight darkness. That was, of course, good for vessels attempting a night passage of the rocky and treacherous mouth of the channel. But to Miles, the new markers attracted far too much attention. All but invited outsiders into the very heart of the San Juan Islands—a sparsely populated archipelago of quiet harbors, forests, pastures, and orchards. A remote, mercifully forgotten corner of the United States. His home.

Miles stood atop an outcropping of rock on the edge of the vast darkness of the shipping lanes, just north of the Navy's new unmanned radio compass station on Cattle Point, powerful binoculars pressed to his eyes as he scanned the approaches to the channel. An unseasonably cold wind was blowing in from the North Pacific, whistling across the open grassland covering this end of the island, carrying with it the faint smell of woodsmoke—probably from one of the isolated cabins that dotted the western shore. But Miles was warm in his heavy wool overcoat—a last souvenir of his time in the Army. The only parts of his broad-shouldered, six-foot-two body that were at all cold were his nose and cheeks, which got him thinking about growing a beard. A thick beard would help keep his chin and cheeks warm in the coming winter. It would also partially hide his baby face, which might help him be taken more seriously as a lawman. Then again, beard or no beard, the locals—many of whom had watched him grow up—would probably still see him as nothing more than an overgrown boy.

Though he'd stood watch for more than an hour, Miles had seen nothing untoward. He hadn't necessarily expected to. Standing lookout was just something he did as a matter of habit whenever he had trouble sleeping, which was often—especially since the war. He called such vigils *night watches.* Sometimes they took him into the small town of Friday Harbor, sometimes down to its docks and cannery, and sometimes to high viewpoints on the wild western shore of the Island where rumrunners could often be seen speeding down Haro Strait under the light of the moon, their cargo holds loaded with illegal liquor picked up just over the border in Canada. But usually his night watches took him to Cattle Point, where he now stood. It was the southernmost tip of San Juan Island. Miles favored the spot because Seattle, Tacoma, and most of the other cities on Puget Sound were to the south. He'd come to believe that cities bred ambition, materialism, and greed—things that always gave rise to corruption and crime. When trouble inevitably came to his simple, peaceful islands, it would come from the cities. He was certain of it.

But on this night, all he had seen were the distant navigational lights of what he guessed was a large cargo ship heading out to the open Pacific. Perhaps it carried wheat from the fertile hills and prairies east of the Cascade Mountains, or coal mined from the foothills outside of Seattle, or locomotive-sized logs from the ancient forests surrounding Puget Sound. Perhaps it was bound for San Francisco, Honolulu, Tokyo or Shanghai. The ship had steamed west, its lights eventually disappearing in the darkness, leaving Miles feeling lonely. Passing ships always made him feel lonely. So did passing trains. He didn't know why.

As he was about to lower his heavy binoculars to give his fatigued arms a break, he thought he saw something. A flicker of light just across the San Juan Channel. He trained his binoculars on the area and stared.

Unable to spot whatever it was no matter how hard he squinted into the darkness, he at last lowered the binoculars. But then, with his naked eye, he saw it again. A brief flash of light.

It was probably just the light of a cabin in amongst swaying trees over on Lopez Island. Then again, it could have been a rumrunner boat signaling to a shore party waiting to help offload liquor. Miles lifted the binoculars once more, his tired arms screaming for mercy. There was indeed a light out there. It was steady now, but he still couldn't tell what it came from. And the longer he gazed at it, the more convinced he was that it was moving.

A boat, then. Definitely a boat.

His arms had had enough. There were no nearby tree branches or other objects upon which he could rest the binoculars, so he sat down on the cold, bare rock and did his best to balance them on his knees. It wasn't a comfortable position. He had to keep his abdomen clenched to stay motionless and upright. Before long, his belly burned with the effort. Still, he watched the light.

After several thoroughly uncomfortable minutes, he realized that he hadn't had to change the aim of the binoculars. Hadn't had to move them at all. Perhaps the light wasn't moving after all. Perhaps his mind was playing tricks on him. *Autokinesis*, they called it in his army training. The longer one stared at a distant but stationary bright spot in a dark environment, the more the bright spot appeared to be moving. The movement was illusory.

He tried to test his theory, looking for some point of reference he could watch vis-à-vis the light. But none were visible in the distant darkness, so he settled for simply watching the light for another few minutes. At last, he convinced himself the light was stationary. A cabin. Not a boat. Not a smuggler caching his opium or liquor on the shore.

You're paranoid, he thought as he was buffeted by the strengthening wind. *For heaven's sake, there's nothing out there.*

But there would be the next night.

THREE

Haro Strait, British Columbia
(near the U.S.-Canada maritime border)
September 9, 1922

"My hands are trembling," eighteen-year-old Leif Jensen said to his father, Hans.

"Come over by the stove."

"It's not from the cold."

The two men sat in the wheelhouse of their wooden, 47-foot commercial fishing boat—the *Lucky Lena*—a stone's throw from the southeast shore of tiny D'Arcy Island. They were in British Columbia, Canada, barely two miles from U.S. waters. It was nearly dark. A cold drizzle rained down from the cast-iron autumn sky as a strengthening northwest wind threatened an eventual gale. But the *Lucky Lena* was anchored in the shelter and relative calm off the island's leeward shore.

Hans sat on a low stool, holding his palms close to a small oil heater mounted near the wall while Leif held one side of a headset to his ear as he tried to tune their radio receiver to a station based in Seattle, 70 miles to the southeast. A single storm lantern filled the wheelhouse with dim yellow light, enveloping the Jensens in its anemic halo on an otherwise gloomy sea.

"Bad weather is brewing," Leif said after a quick glance at the barometer.

"Good. It'll make it harder for anyone to spot us. We'll stay ahead of the worst of it."

A silent moment passed as Leif continued to fiddle with the radio dial, trying to get rid of static. Then he turned and looked at his father. "I don't trust these people," he said.

"They're just people, son."

"We don't know them."

"It's worth the risk."

"If we get caught . . ."

"We won't."

"They almost caught Prosper Graignic last month. He has the fastest boat in the islands."

"He had engine trouble."

"Anyone can have engine trouble."

"That's why we have two engines. That's why we painted the hull gray. They'll never spot us in the darkness and filthy weather. Even if they do, we know every shoal, every cove, every hiding place from here to Anacortes."

A pause.

"Lyle Miller heard a rumor about some new fast patrol boat operating in the area," Leif said.

"There are always rumors. Have you ever seen this supposed new fast patrol boat?"

"No." Leif shook his head. "Still, I have a dark feeling."

"Well, I don't know what else to tell you."

Done tuning the radio, Leif grabbed a pair of binoculars and went out on deck. From the stern of the *Lucky Lena*, he scanned a long stretch of the U.S.-Canada border waters, from the entrance to Spieden Channel, down the western shore of San Juan Island, clear to the southernmost reach of Haro Strait. The only other vessels he could see in the area were a northbound salmon gillnetter that looked to be heading for Boundary Pass and, to their south, the outbound RMS *Empress of Russia*—a 570-foot ocean liner, probably headed from Vancouver to the Far East. As he watched it steam away, Leif pictured it being full of wealthy passengers dressed in gowns and tuxedos, dancing the evening away in a gilded ballroom after a lavish formal dinner with caviar, roasted red meat, and icebox cakes.

He sighed and went back into the wheelhouse.

"Quit your fretting and come over by the stove," his father said as he entered.

Leif inverted one of the ear cups of the radio headset, put it to his ear, turned up the volume, and joined his father, gladly accepting a steaming cup of black tea sweetened with buckwheat honey from their own beehives. The radio played an advertisement for a Seattle shoe store called Wallin & Nordstrom.

"Just think, Leif. After this one last run, you'll be able to pay off the orchard before the twins are even born. You'll be set for life, son. Debt-free. With prime land to hand down to your children."

Leif nodded, staring into his cup of tea, not saying a word.

Hans studied his son's face for a moment, then turned to look at a clock on the console by the helm. "It's time," he said, pulling a notepad and pencil from an inside pocket of his oilskin overalls and pressing the other side of the inverted headset to his own ear. Side-by-side, father and son crouched over the receiver, each pressing half of the headset against an ear. A warm, French-accented female voice invited children of all ages to gather around the radio for today's bedtime episode of *The Adventures of Bear and Badger*. The jingle-jangle title song played for half a minute, then the story began.

"Good day, Bear."

"Good day, Badger."

"What shall we do today, Bear?"

"Let's look for blueberries, Badger. Big and juicy and sweet."

"Bear wants to look for blueberries," Hans muttered, jotting down the phrase on his notepad.

"Shall we invite Fox to join us?" Badger asked.

"No, Badger. Fox is chasing butterflies in the meadow."

Fox . . . butterflies . . . meadow, Hans thought as he again wrote the phrases in his notepad before handing it over to his son. Leif took the pad to the galley table, then drew a large hardcover text called *American Practical Navigator* from a bookshelf and opened it. Inside was a hollowed-out space containing yet another notebook, which Leif took out and flipped through until he found a page labeled *September.* The page was filled, from margin to margin, with codewords. Squinting to read in the inadequate light, he ran his index finger down the list.

"Here it is," he said. "Blueberries means the rendezvous point is Alexander Beach, southwest of Anacortes. The meadow is Mutiny Bay."

Altogether, the words *Fox is chasing butterflies in the meadow* told them that, according to a vast network of watchers and informants, the USRC *Arcata*—supposedly the only U.S. Government revenue cutter currently stationed in Puget Sound—was last reported patrolling near Mutiny Bay, off the west shore of Whidbey Island, well to their south.

Hans wasn't particularly worried about the *Arcata.* It was an old steam-powered tub that could barely make eleven knots and was armed with an obsolete, early model Hotchkiss gun accurate to no more than 500 yards. In stark contrast, and unlike most of the lumbering diesel-powered vessels of her class, the *Lucky Lena* had twin Liberty gasoline engines and could run at nearly 21 knots if she had to. Still, it was reassuring to know that the *Arcata* was many miles to the south and nowhere near their likely route to the rendezvous point at Alexander Beach.

"Alexander Beach is darn near 30 miles from here, even if we take the southern route," Hans said.

"Our special delivery at Mosquito Bay will add a few miles too," Leif said. "These new people better be on time."

"However it goes, we've got a long night ahead of us, son."

"Is it dark enough yet?"

Hans looked out the window. "Yes, I think so. Let's weigh anchor."

As Hans prepared to start the engines, Leif made his way to the hawsehole where the *Lucky Lena's* anchor line met the bow.

But just as he bent over to work the capstan, Leif heard something that made him stand up straight and listen. He strained to hear the sound again, but a gust of wind drowned out whatever it was.

"Did you hear that?" he asked his father.

"I can't hear you out there."

Leif walked to an open wheelhouse window.

"I said, did you hear that?"

"Hear what?"

"I don't know. Maybe an engine."

"You're being jumpy."

"For good reason."

As he said this, the wind died down again, and they both heard the sound. It was a low rumble. Definitely a boat engine, and it was close.

"Turn down the lantern," Hans said quietly.

Leif came into the wheelhouse to deal with the lantern as Hans went out onto the bow with binoculars to try to spot the approaching boat. Leif joined him there a moment later, darkened lantern in hand.

"I see it," Hans said. "Two points off the starboard bow. About six hundred yards out. Making three or four knots. His running lights are off."

"Sneaking up on us from the far side of the island?"

"Probably just a gillnetter looking to drop anchor to ride out the storm."

"With his running lights off?"

"Probably just hasn't thought to turn them on yet. It's just now getting dark."

As he said this, Hans could begin to make out the silhouettes of two men standing on the bow of the approaching vessel.

"Maybe RCMP?" Leif asked, meaning the Royal Canadian Mounted Police—the national police force of Canada. "Or Canadian Customs?"

"Maybe. Hull's about thirty foot, I think."

"Looking for us?"

Hans didn't answer.

"Should I start up the engines?"

Hans still didn't answer. He was focused on the approaching boat, straining to make out its course and its features, hopeful its crew wouldn't notice the *Lucky Lena* in the expanse of deepening darkness. It seemed to be following a course roughly parallel with the shore. But when it got to within about three hundred yards of the *Lucky Lena*, it turned and began motoring directly toward them.

"Father, I asked if I should start up the engines."

"I'm not sure that it's . . ." Hans's voice trailed off as he made out billed caps on the heads of the two men standing on the boat's bow. He couldn't tell whether they were simple fisherman's caps or official uniform caps. Once the boat closed to within a couple hundred feet, he lowered the binoculars. "Turn up the lantern to full."

"Are you sure?"

"Do it, son. Else they'll run right into us."

Leif turned up the lantern.

"Hold it high," his father said.

Leif did, but the vessel still motored straight toward them.

"Vessel, ahoy!" Hans shouted across the water.

The dark figures on deck stood motionless and silent. Maybe they couldn't hear Hans's voice in the wind. Both appeared to be holding objects in their right hands. Hans told himself they were holding lanterns of their own, knowing full well the objects were too small to be lanterns.

"Ahoy!" Hans shouted again. "What vessel is that?"

"I'm starting up," Leif said, dropping the lantern and racing to the wheelhouse. He fired the starboard engine with a whine, a roar, and a cloud of oil smoke.

Just then, one of the dark figures on the bow of the approaching boat shouted, "Heave to," in an authoritative voice.

"Who are you?" Hans shouted back.

"Heave to and prepare to be boarded."

Hans stood in place, staring at the mystery boat as it closed the last few yards and started turning to come alongside.

"Father," Leif called from the wheelhouse. "What should we do?"

FOUR

Turn Point Light Station
Stuart Island, Washington
September 10, 1922

The most disturbing day of Eldon Turley's life began as most others—with a cup of hot black coffee, a plate of crisp applewood smoked bacon, and a slice of toasted brown soda bread smeared with butter and honey. He sat looking out the kitchen window of the keeper's quarters of Turn Point Light Station, on a high, rocky bluff at the western tip of Stuart Island. The sky was a deep blue, clear of any traces of the previous night's storm. A thin fog bank persisted half a mile offshore. But Turley knew it would dissipate within the hour. The inbound tide was sliding around the point, from Haro Strait into Boundary Pass—a stretch of water that separated Canada from the United States, and served as the main shipping route between Vancouver and the Pacific Ocean.

Turley was sipping his coffee, thinking through how he would replace a large gasket on the station's Daboll Trumpet fog horn, when a glint of sunlight caught his eye. He looked out across the water but saw nothing. Perhaps a vessel was running in the fog bank. He watched for another moment, then turned his attention back to his breakfast.

A few minutes later, he was buttoning up his dark blue U.S. Lighthouse Service uniform jacket by the open front door when a glint caught his eye once again. This time, Turley spotted the silhouette of what appeared to be a fishing boat slowly emerging from the hazy edge of the fog bank. It was drifting, its bow slowly coming around as the tide drew the vessel toward Turn Point.

There was nothing terribly unusual about seeing a boat drifting on the tide. The crew had probably shut the engines off to save fuel while plotting a new course or taking care of some other task. Still, given its proximity to the treacherous crag of Turn Point, Turley decided to keep an eye on it.

*****

Ten minutes later, after gathering up tools and checking fuel levels in the oil storage shed, Turley was headed to the fog signal building when he saw that the boat was still out there, still drifting. Only now, it was much closer to Turn Point.

Turley fetched a pair of binoculars from the keeper's quarters and took a closer look. It was definitely a fishing boat—a common seiner. But unlike most fishing boats, which tended to be painted white, this one was painted flat gray. He looked for signs of life onboard, but saw none. It was possible the crew were below decks, working on the engines or perhaps sleeping—unaware that their boat was approaching the dangerous, rocky point.

Turley considered using the fog horn, knowing the thunderous noise would rouse the boat's oblivious crew no matter how hard they might be sleeping—and teach them a lesson they would not soon forget. But there was a good chance the current would smash the boat against the rocks before he could get the horn fired up and running. Instead, he went to a large brass emergency bell mounted on a metal frame in front of the fog signal building and gave it a long, loud ring. The boat was close enough now that even if the crew were below decks, they'd hear it.

Nobody emerged. Stranger still, Turley noticed that the boat didn't have a mandatory registration number painted on its side.

He gave the bell another long ring and kept watch. Then he noticed something that suggested a partial explanation. A slack anchor line dangled from the bow. The boat must have broken loose of its moorings during the previous night's storm.

All at once, dollar signs danced before Turley's eyes. If he recovered the boat, he'd be owed salvage money under maritime law. With this in mind, he ran up the hill to his Ford truck, cranked the motor, and set a speed record racing across the island to Pierre Charlevoix's farm on Prevost Harbor. Charlevoix had a fishing boat with a diesel engine big enough to tow the drifter to a safe moorage.

Charlevoix was in the middle of changing the oil in his Model T. But when Turley told him of the potential reward, and told him there wasn't a moment to lose since the boat was drifting toward the rocks, he wiped his oily hands on his already filthy trousers and smiled. "Let's go get her."

The two men jogged down to the mail boat dock where Charlevoix's boat—the *Susan T*—was tied up. In moments, they had the *Susan T* unmoored and running out into Boundary Pass at top speed, the icy waters of Puget Sound occasionally splashing over the gunwales and raining down upon the men. The *Susan T* wasn't a racer. But they had little more than a mile to go. And after a few minutes, the drifting mystery boat came into view as they rounded Turn Point. They had little time, as the vessel was barely 50 yards from shore, with the strengthening breeze and running tide conspiring to drive it against the rocks.

"Vessel, ahoy!" Turley shouted as they approached. "Ahoy!" Still, there were no signs of crew or passengers aboard. Good.

Turley readied a heavy line while Charlevoix maneuvered to touch *Susan T*'s port side against the drifter. As the boats bumped together, Turley got his line around a cleat on the drifter's bow, then secured it to a stern cleat of the *Susan T*. They slowly towed the drifter a few hundred yards further from shore to give themselves a little more breathing room with which to work.

Repositioned, they spent a few minutes rigging a proper towing line between the two vessels, then motored for home.

*****

Having chained the drifter to a mooring buoy in the sheltered waters of Prevost Harbor, Turley and Charlevoix hopped aboard to examine their prize. Turley was hoping the vessel would have a hold full of fresh halibut or other valuable cargo that would increase the salvage reward. But when he opened the door to the pilot house, he was greeted by warm, stagnant air with an overpowering aroma of wood smoke. There was also a trace of something that reminded him of how new copper pennies smelled. It left a metallic flavor on the back edges of his tongue.

The foul air wasn't the only odd thing. The pilothouse had been ransacked. Drawers were overturned, the contents of shelves swept to the floor, charts and tools strewn about. Then Turley saw something that stopped him in his tracks. At the other end of the wheelhouse, on the floor in front of an open companionway, was a wide smear of dark red blood. It looked as if someone had attempted to mop up a pool of it, then gave up.

"Pierre," he said, pointing at the smear.

The men exchanged glances.

"Is anybody aboard?" Turley shouted. But the only sound he could make out was the lapping of ripples against the wooden hull. He gave Charlevoix another look, then turned and, with a frown, slowly made his way forward toward the dark companionway. Within it, he could see the top of a ladder leading down into the hold. He stepped around the blood smear, paused to mentally prepare himself, then poked his head in.

"Well?" Charlevoix asked.

"I can't see a thing down there."

"You going in?"

He took a deep breath. "Suppose so." He turned around to

descend the ladder backward, took a step through, and slowly made his way down into the blackness below the deck.

"It smells funny down here," he shouted up the ladder.

"Fishing boats always smell funny."

"Not like that. I can't see a damned thing. But I think there's something down here. The floor is slick. Can you find a light?"

"Hang on."

Charlevoix rummaged around the ransacked pilothouse until he found an intact storm lantern. He lit it, turned it up, and passed it down the ladder to Turley's waiting hand. Then he heard Turley gasp.

"What is it?" Charlevoix asked.

"Mercy," Turley muttered as the lantern illuminated the cargo hold.

"What is it? What do you see?"

"Mercy be blessed."

FIVE

"I fail to understand why you won't at least consider taking Sophie Gunderson to the Odd Fellows Dance," said Sheriff Miles Scott's mother, Nellie. They sat at the waxed wooden kitchen table of their tidy clapboard farmhouse, bathed in soft morning sunlight filtered by thin lace curtains. As it always did, the air smelled faintly of the dried apples and cinnamon stored in the pantry.

"Again with this?" Miles said before shoving the last of a buttered, honey-drizzled biscuit into his mouth.

"Sophie adores you. She has a good, respectable family. They're Lutherans, but you can't be picky at your age."

His mother wore an apron over a simple gingham house frock she'd had since Miles was born. It reminded Miles of his childhood. In fact, strangely, whenever Nellie wore it, Miles felt a bit like a child. It was almost as if the frock had a magic power that made him regress at the sight of it. He half suspected that his mother knew this, and that she kept the old frock to remind him of her superior status—or, perhaps more accurately, his *inferior* status—in the mother-child relationship. She wore it to breakfast nearly every day.

"As I've told you before, I have absolutely no feelings for Sophie Gunderson," he said, noticing that his mother's black cat, Monsieur Rousseau, was staring at him from his pillow in the corner of the kitchen, seemingly in judgement. Miles had never liked Monsieur Rousseau. And Monsieur Rousseau had certainly never liked him. He had a scar on his thumb to prove it. "May I please just eat my breakfast in peace?"

"I suppose it's the kiss of death that I even mention her name. I should know better by now. As soon as a mother mentions a girl's name, a son crosses her off his list, right? You could at least shave. You look scruffy."

Miles absentmindedly rubbed at the stubble on his chin without making eye contact with his mother. Sure, he was a bit rough looking—unshaven, hair unwashed, wearing scuffed boots, worn work pants, and a dirty wool shirt. But what was the point of looking dapper?

"Honestly, Miles. You're almost 25 years old. A quarter century. Your stock is dropping fast. You know I'm right."

Miles wasn't about to admit to that. It would only invite further meddling. In lieu of offering a response, he bit into another biscuit. And as he sat there chewing, his mind drifted back to a dream he'd had the night before. In it, he'd been wandering a far corner of their property where years earlier he and his late father had worked for many months to build, in the massive forking branches of an ancient maple, the greatest treehouse the island had ever seen. It was a work of art. The angles perfectly square. The roof sturdy and watertight.

But in his dream, Miles had discovered a long, callused fissure in the great tree's bark—a vertical crevice that revealed core rot. And as he'd approached for a closer look, it became obvious that the rot was extensive and advanced. That the trunk that had looked so sturdy when they were building the treehouse had been decaying from within all along, such that the entire tree—and the beautiful house Miles and his father had worked so hard to build—could very well topple with a splintering crash in the next ordinary storm to roll in off the Pacific.

The dream had unsettled him. He tried to turn his mind to the happy thought of the big platter of bacon waiting for him on the table—crisp, applewood-smoked, sugar-cured bacon.

"Please pass the bacon," he said.

"No, sir. No bacon for you."

"No?"

"No. You've already had double servings of sausage, eggs, potatoes, and biscuits."

"But—"

"I may not be able to dictate who you take to the Odd Fellows Dance. But I can certainly keep you from becoming even less desirable by going to fat."

"For heaven's sake," Miles muttered, reaching across the table for the bacon, prompting his mother to pick up a long wooden serving spoon and whack his knuckles. "Ouch!" Jerking his hand back, he bumped his mug, spilling coffee all over his pants. "Oh!"

"You'll respect my wishes at my table."

"Damnation."

She leaned forward and hit him again.

"Ow!" shouted the six-foot-four, muscular man, half cowering under the threat of his five-foot-nothing, gray-haired mother and her twelve-inch serving spoon.

"And you'll not curse at my table."

"Alright, alright! Jesu—jeepers."

A moment of quiet passed between them.

"You're lonely, Miles."

"Pardon?"

"Especially since you don't keep up with any of your old friends anymore."

He lifted his hands from the table, palms up. "We don't have that many common interests these days."

"You don't make new friends either. You don't socialize."

He shrugged.

"And what about all of your old favorite things to do? You didn't participate in the salmon derby last month."

"I play my saxophone."

"You play it alone, and like a bull moose, without any of the refinement or nuance that makes music beautiful."

"Hey, now. That's a bit—"

"You don't follow your beloved Boston Red Sox anymore."

"The Sox stink this year. And getting back to my saxophone playing, I don't think your description is very—"

"You haven't even touched the Peerless since you got back from the war," she said, referring to an old car Miles and his late father had been refurbishing out in their barn.

He took a breath, then met her stare.

Seeing the sudden anguish in her son's eyes, his mother softened just a touch.

"You miss your father."

He looked away.

"I miss him too, Miles. But life goes on."

He hoped that was the end of their little talk. But, of course, it wasn't.

"You need a girlfriend."

"For heaven's sake," he said again, his voice barely a whisper.

"A girlfriend would be good for you."

"I'm too busy."

"That's ridiculous."

"Then find me one eligible woman on this island who isn't absorbed with frivolity. Needlepointing techniques. How the judges were playing favorites at the strawberry jam competition of this year's county fair. Gossip about whose husband sneaks out to his tool shed to drink bathtub gin."

"So move to the city. There are surely thousands of worldly, sophisticated women in Seattle or Portland or San Francisco."

"I'm needed here."

"Don't be self-important."

"I'm not. Who else is going to protect these people—these simple old fishermen and farmers?"

"Protect them from what, pray tell?"

"From whatever's coming."

She waited for him to explain. He didn't.

"Miles, these old fishermen and farmers, as you call them, did just fine in all the years before you were sworn in. They'll do just fine after you leave."

"Who would take care of *you*?"

"I beg your pardon?"

"Your hip is getting worse."

"I've done fine with it for a quarter century," she said, referring to the 25 years since she'd permanently injured it giving birth to Miles.

"What about the bottom of your foot?" he asked. "Is the nerve damage getting worse? Looks like it to me."

"I'm perfectly fine on my own."

"Really? You nearly fell down the stairs last week, if you'll recall. What if I hadn't been here to catch you and you'd fallen and broken something?"

"I'd have crawled into town on my hands and knees, like a pilgrim at the Basilica of Guadalupe."

"That isn't funny."

"I know. I'm sorry. But look, Miles, you have to live your life. I've lived mine. Your father lived his. It's your turn. That's how life works. It's meant to be filled with wonder and joy and passion." She set her hands flat on the table and looked down at them. "Maybe you really should consider moving to the city."

Miles was quiet for a moment. "Cities aren't good for people."

She huffed. "Theaters? Libraries? The university? Fine restaurants? Clubs where they play your beloved jazz music? These things aren't good? These things aren't elements of an interesting and fulfilling life?"

Miles almost voiced his nascent theory that cities bred greed, and that greed, in turn, led to most human-caused suffering in the world. But experience had taught him that whenever he made such sweeping statements, his mother would call him a dime-store philosopher and offer up a rebuttal that made him feel foolish.

With considerable effort, she rose with the help of her old oak cane and began clearing the dishes.

"Let me get those," Miles said, making to stand up.

"Because I'm a useless old biddy now?"

He sat back down and began rubbing his forehead with his fingertips. He wondered how his mother—one of the few women he'd ever heard of who had a college education, who'd probably read every *Seattle Times* and *Post-Intelligencer* cover-to-cover since the newspapers were founded—could content herself sitting around tables of stale cookies and bad tea, rehashing the same banalities with the same circle of ladies, day after day. Maybe she viewed the islands as he did—as a sort of refuge. Or maybe she just liked always being the smartest person in the room.

"I suppose I'd better get to the station," he said, rising from the table once again, slipping his suspenders over his broad shoulders and grabbing his jacket. He saw the large coffee stain on his pants, considered changing, then decided not to bother. "Thank you for breakfast."

"You think about what I said, Miles," she called as he headed out the door, Monsieur Rousseau watching him go with an expression Miles took as contemptuous. "You aren't getting any younger."

His trusty Graham Brothers pickup truck was parked next to an old weeping willow that stood at the edge of their apple orchard. The orchard—planted by Miles and his late father—was laid out in a perfect square of straight rows running down a gentle slope to the shore of Merrifield Cove. Their property was barely two miles south of Friday Harbor—with just over 500 inhabitants, the biggest town on the island.

Miles checked behind the driver's seat to make sure his saxophone was there. Despite what he'd told his mother, he wasn't planning to go straight to the station. The weather was just too good. And on his idyllic, sparsely populated island, there was rarely any trouble in the morning. Instead, Miles intended to drive out to Pear Point and sit on his favorite secluded outcropping, play a little Sidney Bechet, and watch bald eagles hunt for salmon. It was one of the few things that brought him happiness anymore.

He rolled down his window, fired up the truck, and put it in gear. But as he drove the long gravel driveway from the farmhouse out to the main road, he saw another vehicle racing toward him from the opposite direction, kicking up a long cloud of dust. It was the dented-up Dixie Flyer owned by Bill Shaw, his un-deputized, unofficial aide-de-camp. Both vehicles came to a stop as they drew alongside each other. Bill, whose bland, overlarge face often bore no discernable expression, looked grave. His jaw was clenched and his crooked, yellow teeth were showing—never a good sign. Being ashamed of them, he was usually mindful of keeping them hidden. Unless he was distracted.

"Sheriff, sorry to kick up all the dust. I would have called, but the telephone line is out after last night's storm."

"You're looking a bit harried, Bill."

"Really? I went to the barbershop just three days ago."

"No, *harried*, not hairy."

Bill stared.

"Never mind," Miles said, wishing he'd left for Pear Point just a few minutes earlier. "What's the hubbub? Please don't tell me another one of Eustace Hampton's sheep got out of her pen. I'm not in the mood to go chasing after one of those stinking animals again."

"You might end up wishing it was a sheep. Light keeper from Stuart Island just radioed in, all shook up. Says he towed in a drifter."

"So?"

"He says it's full of blood."

SIX

The late morning air was fresh and crisp as they motored north across calm, dark waters. Despite the beauty of the day, Miles was consumed with dread over what he was going to find. He'd seen plenty of dead and wounded in France during the Great War. But they'd been strangers. This could involve locals—even people he knew. For whatever reason, that made it different.

He and Bill had asked a local fisherman named Riley to run them up from Westcott Bay to Stuart Island in his big troller, knowing they were going to need to tow the drifter back to the state wharf at Friday Harbor for further investigation. Riley was a small man with dirty fingernails and coveralls perpetually stained by fish slime. But he was an expert boatman, and his troller had a powerful diesel engine.

"Blackfish," Riley said, pointing to a pod of killer whales a quarter mile off the starboard bow, running close to the shore of Speiden Island. Their dorsal fins and backs were breaching the surface in intermittent rhythm, drawing fleeting lines of white foam in their wake. Riley turned his wheel a few degrees to port to give the whales a wide berth. They were probably hunting salmon, just as the region's countless eagles, sea lions, and fishermen all did at this time of year. Miles admired them for a minute before returning his gaze to the heavily forested length of Stuart Island, dark and ominous, slowly rising in front of them as they grew closer.

"I expect we should round Turn Point before the tide shift," Riley said.

That, at least, was good news. Running against the powerful

tidal currents at Turn Point could easily add twenty minutes to their journey.

*****

They spotted the drifter, still chained to a mooring buoy, as soon as they entered the dead-calm, forest-lined waters of Prevost Harbor. It was a common fishing boat. But, like Eldon Turley before them, they noted that it was painted an uncommon flat gray and had no registration number on its hull.

"Rumrunner?" Bill asked Miles.

"Maybe. Not one I know."

Turley and Pierre Charlevoix were waiting at the end of the harbor's mail boat dock, mute, staring out at the drifter as they smoked cigarettes. Spotting Riley's boat rounding the point, they flipped their cigarette butts into the water, clambered down into an old rowboat, and shoved off for the obligatory rendezvous. As they all converged on the drifter, Miles could see that Turley and Charlevoix were wide-eyed and looking grim. As Riley brought his boat alongside the drifter, Miles and Bill tossed lines over the drifter's cleats, drew the two vessels together, and stepped aboard as Turley and Charlevoix did the same from the opposite side. A dozen flies were buzzing near the closed door to the wheelhouse.

"Morning, gentlemen," Miles said as they gathered on the aft deck.

"Sheriff," Turley and Charlevoix said in unison, their voices tight.

"Thanks for waiting for us. What's the story here?"

The men glanced at each other, neither looking the least bit eager to talk about what they'd found. Turley swallowed hard and began his account of spotting the vessel drifting toward the rocks of Turn Point and of their recovery efforts. By the time he came to the subject of what they'd discovered below, he was following Miles around the deck while the sheriff took stock.

"One thing that's bound to jump out at you is that she has two huge gasoline engines," Turley said. "And a radio receiver."

"On a humble fishing boat?" Miles said, his implication clear to everyone. He leaned out over the starboard side of the bow. "There's a big dent and fresh scuff mark on the hull up here."

"From a collision with a hijacker?" Turley asked.

"Could be," Miles said.

"Could be from anything," Bill added.

"Do you want to go below?" Turley asked.

Hell no, I don't want to go below, Miles thought. "You gentlemen have a brush or rag or something?" he asked, still leaning out and examining the starboard side of the hull.

"You seeing something?" Bill asked. But Miles didn't answer. Whatever he was focusing on had his full attention. Turley retrieved a stiff scrub brush from the wheelhouse and handed it over to Miles who, getting flat on his belly on the bow, reached over the side and set to work scrubbing at a section of the hull. After less than a minute, he got to his feet.

"Take a look," he said.

The other men leaned to look over the side.

"A registration number," Turley said. It read *M-886*, in large block lettering.

"Someone covered it up with creosote," Miles said.

"Definitely a rumrunner then," Bill said.

"Hey, I know that boat," Riley shouted from the bow of his own vessel. "M-886 is the *Lucky Lena.*"

"Lucky who?" Miles asked.

"*Lucky Lena*. She's owned by a fella named Jensen."

"There are dozens of men named Jensen around here," Miles said.

"Hans Jensen. Deer Harbor. Fishes with his son, Leif. Boat's Canadian built. Didn't recognize her under all this gray paint."

Rumrunner camouflage, Miles thought. "The gray paint is new?"

"Far as I know. Last time I saw her, she was painted white."

"When was that?"

"Oh, maybe a month ago. Out by Sekiu, I think. Hey, look," he added, pointing at the limp line dangling from the hawsehole. "Her anchor's gone. She probably just broke free of her moorings in the storm last night."

"Broke free of moorings in Deer Harbor, and then drifted all the way to Turn Point?" Miles said. "Against the wind?"

"I think you'll discount Riley's theory once you go below decks," Turley muttered under his breath as they made their way to the wheelhouse. Turley handed Miles a kerosene lantern and opened the door for him. "If it's all the same to you, I think I'll stay topside this time."

Stepping into the wheelhouse, Miles was greeted with the same warm, stagnant air and mélange of troubling smells that had greeted Turley earlier in the day. A strong, damp woodsmoke smell, like that of the steaming coals of an extinguished bonfire. And a new copper penny smell that put an unpleasant metal taste on the back of his tongue. *Blood and smoke*, he thought, his mind jumping—against his will—to a particularly terrible wartime memory of a courtyard behind an Army field hospital near the front lines in France. Of an incinerator. Of a crate full of . . .

"Damnation," Miles muttered, squeezing his eyes shut and shaking his head to stop the mental image from taking shape.

"You alright in there, Sheriff?" Turley asked from outside one of the windows.

"Yes, I'm just—yes."

"Looks to me like she was ransacked."

The flies that had been buzzing just outside the door had followed Miles in and were searching the interior in frenzied zigzags. At the front end of the wheelhouse, he saw the dark companionway and large blood smear Turley had described. Strewn about the floor was the usual paraphernalia of the commercial fisherman. Binoculars. Hand tools. Coffee mugs. Nautical texts and charts. A ship's logbook. On the wall, a calendar with an advertisement for engine oil. More notably, in the corner, a hulking, expensive-looking, ultramodern radio receiver—something Miles had surely never seen on a fishing boat.

The closer Miles got to the companionway, the worse the air smelled. At last, he came to it. He bent down, trying not to step in the large blood smear, stuck his head in, and lowered the lantern into the darkness. Like Turley before him, he wasn't able to see much from where he stood aside from a great deal of blood pooled at the foot of the ladder.

Here we go.

He took a deep breath, turned around, backed himself into the companionway, and, rung by rung, descended the ladder into the hold. Reaching the lower deck, he had no choice but to step into the large pool of blood at the base of the ladder. He stepped around the corner of the ladder and into the aft hold, looked up, and froze in place.

Holy smokes.

The lantern illuminated what appeared to be the scene of a slaughter. Dark blood covered most of the deck and was splattered all over the walls and ceiling. Much of it was still wet—especially where it had pooled. There were also what looked like several bullet holes in the wood. Curiously, there were half a dozen rectangular areas on the deck that were nearly blood-free, as though large crates had been removed from the hold in the aftermath of the massacre. In the lowest section of the deck, there was a shallow, roughly three-foot-wide pool of bloody saltwater, upon which floated a few partially burned pieces of scrap wood, rope remnants, and torn paper. The hull wood visible around the periphery of the pool was thoroughly charred.

Stepping around the blood as best he could, Miles made his way toward the stern end of the hold where he found several 50-lb. sacks labeled as *salt*, as well as the broken glass of several smashed bottles. Most of the bottles' labels were still at least partially intact. They had once held Glenfiddich Scotch whiskey, the scent of which cut through that of the blood and smoke as

Miles bent down for a closer look.

"What's it look like, Sheriff?" Bill called down through the companionway.

"It ain't pretty."

"Need an extra set of hands?"

"Not yet. But let's pop the hatches and get some more light down here. And fresh air, for heaven's sake."

Miles retraced his path, heading for the forward hold, noticing large drag marks in the blood, as well as numerous large footprints. The footprints looked to have been made by two different sets of work boots. They ran back and forth from the stern hold to the forward hold, all coming together, along with the drag marks, at the base of the ladder to the forward cargo hatch. The ladder itself was covered with bloody footprints.

The forward hold also contained a large, bolted-down work table across which was spread various parts of a heavy-duty diving apparatus, including a three-window copper and brass helmet, a corselet, a weighted rubber suit, and a coiled air hose. Miles wondered why a fisherman would have an industrial dive suit. As he looked it over, perplexed, something on the forward bulkhead caught his eye. The dim light of the lantern illuminated what appeared to be some sort of symbol. It looked a bit like a cursive lower-case *j* alongside a backward lowercase *t,* topped with a horizontal slash. To Miles, it looked Asian. Maybe Chinese or Japanese. As he walked toward it, it became obvious that it had been drawn in blood.

What in the hell?

He stared at the symbol, wondering what it meant, wondering why it was drawn in blood. Then he noticed something else. On a narrow workbench attached to the bulkhead to his right, there was a small, pale object. Taking a step closer and raising his lantern, Miles saw that it was a severed human finger.

"Holy Toledo," he muttered.

The finger was pointing at something that had been drawn

or written on the flat work surface. Miles bent over for a closer look. At the tip of the finger, also written in blood, were the words *Romans 1:18*.

SEVEN

Kowloon Docks, Hong Kong
Republic of China
Five Weeks Earlier

The stone-faced city man who'd spoken with my father already had two other girls with him when we set out from my village. He would not tell us where or how far we were going. He would not let us talk. He gave us very little to eat. Except for one time when we found an empty barn, we slept under the open sky close to the road. At night, I could sometimes see the seven stars of the Northern Dipper and I would silently pray to the Queen of Heaven to protect the health of my family. I did not sleep well because I was always worried that my mouse, Snow, would climb out of my tunic while I was asleep and run away.

It took us eight days—stopping in other villages and gathering five more girls as we made our way down the river valley, past many other flood-ruined farms—before we arrived at the busy docks of Kowloon, our bellies empty, our feet swollen and sore. Kowloon was a strange and frightening place. So many people. The largest buildings I had ever seen, squeezed together, so tall they blocked out much of the sky. Buildings with glass windows. Rickshaws, carts, and even loud, smokey motorcars. And everywhere, lights that burned inside of glass balls that held no candle or oil.

On the docks, stacks of crates, barrels, coal, and timber were jammed into every corner. Constant shouting and angry faces and chaos and whistles and horns and smells of cooking and coal smoke and hot tar and garbage. Even the water below the wharf smelled bad. It was nothing like the water of the river that flowed past my village. It stank of rotting fish and brine and sewage. And there were foreigners. Tall, sweating foreigners with strange clothes and deformed eyes and colorless skin. They never looked at us. It was as if we were passing through a realm of ghosts that did not recognize the living. Scared, the girls and I held hands, tight, and tried to keep our eyes on the ground.

The stone-faced city man handed us off to another man who led us to a small storage building across from the wharf. This new man had dead eyes and a loud voice. He shouted at us in some strange dialect, all but chasing us into a hot, dark storage room which he then locked. When he left us alone, one of the girls said she thought he was Hakka people, and that all Hakka want to kill all Cantonese. That made me even more afraid. I squatted in a corner and reached into my tunic to feel Snow—her warmth, her soft fur. I wondered if she was as scared as I was.

We were given no food or water all day, and had to piss and shit in a waste barrel in the corner that had not been emptied for a long time. The stench made my eyes water. It filled the whole room. I could not get away from it. I could hardly breathe.

At last, the Hakka man and two helpers came and opened the door. It was night. They had lanterns and a jug of stale water that we took turns drinking from. They took our sacks of personal belongings and piled them by the door. I hoped that meant we were leaving this terrible, stinking room. But then they had us line up against the wall and searched us all over with their dirty, groping hands, taking rings, necklaces, hair combs, and even the shoes of those of us who had them. Luckily, the man who searched me didn't find Snow or my grandmother's wooden comb hidden in the inner pocket of my tunic. For a moment, I was relieved. But then one girl asked the men what they were doing with our things, and the boss Hakka man slapped her across the face so hard that she fell to her knees, then rolled onto her side like a baby and wept.

They took our things and left.

*****

We did not see the Hakka men again until the next morning when they opened the door and rushed us outside. The sunlight was blinding after our night in the dark storage room, and I tripped and fell in the doorway. But I quickly jumped back to my feet, worried that if the men saw they might beat me for my clumsiness.

They ran us down the street to a long dock where the biggest boat I had ever seen was tied up. It was probably longer than five large river boats lined up end-to-end. Far too big to push or row. But it had no sail either. Just a tall chimney with thin black smoke coming out of it where I thought the sail should be. It had a strange flag, unreadable markings, and a sort of tall house on one end with big glass windows. And it was made of metal, not wood. Grimy, rusty metal. I could not understand why it did not sink.

The Hakka men rushed us up a ramp and onto the boat where two other men in communist tunics led us toward an open doorway on the far side of the deck. On the deck itself were stacks of lumber, rows of wood barrels, and cases of glass bottles with strange symbols on their labels. The men led us below, down many stairs, into the lower parts of the great boat. We followed them through a room full of machines and tools to a large cabinet they slid sideways to reveal a hidden hole cut through the metal wall which they pushed us through one by one. On the other side of it was a small, dark room with curving, rusty, water-stained metal walls, another waste barrel lashed to a post, an open water barrel, and a stack of threadbare blankets. Several wooden casks were lined up against one of the walls and tied down with netting. The air felt close and damp, and continuous trickles of seawater ran down the curving wall in stained and uneven lines before pooling on the floor and eventually disappearing through a small drain in the opposite corner. The men in the communist tunics spoke a dialect I did not understand, but they made angry-looking gestures that I thought meant we were not to touch the wooden casks. Then they slid the heavy cabinet back into place to cover the hole we'd crawled through, leaving us in total darkness.

EIGHT

Miles hosed the last of the blood from the soles of his boots as he stood alongside the *Lucky Lena,* now moored at the state wharf in Friday Harbor. Captains and crew were tending to the numerous fishing and workboats tied up on the adjacent docks as hungry gulls and bald eagles circled overhead, waiting for scraps of salmon and halibut to be dumped into the water from the sluice of the town's massive waterfront cannery.

Word of the bloody drifter had spread like wildfire. A large group of curious onlookers were hovering 50 feet down the wharf, where Bill had set up a police cordon, straining their necks to see over one another's heads and shouting questions at Miles who ignored them as he went about his work.

What Miles had a harder time ignoring were the flies. They'd begun to arrive as soon as the *Lucky Lena* was tied up, and now they were everywhere. Buzzing in the wheelhouse windows. Swarming above the pools of wet blood below deck. Buzzing in Miles's face as he tried to focus on gathering evidence.

Miles hated flies. They reminded him of death. Of carnage. Of the severed limbs and shattered bodies of his fellow soldiers. Invariably, the flies brought eggs. The eggs brought maggots. And maggots destroyed dead flesh damn near as efficiently as fire did. Devoured the torn vestiges of human life in a wriggling, pitiless free-for-all.

It had taken them most of the afternoon to tow the *Lucky Lena* down from Stuart Island. By the time they'd arrived, Miles was grumpy with hunger. But, after ringing the homes of Hans and Leif Jensen without success, he'd insisted on finishing his initial processing of the scene before taking a break to eat. That had ended up taking another two hours. Done at last, daydreaming of his mother's cinnamon-apple pie while his empty stomach grumbled, he was watching passengers disembark from the SS *Bangor*—a 180-foot steamer just arrived from Seattle, tied up at the far end of the wharf—when a commotion at the cordon caught his eye. A tall man in a brown suit and hat pushed his way through the crowd of onlookers, stepped over the rope barrier, and headed straight for the *Lucky Lena.*

"Hey pal," Miles said when the man drew near. "Where do you think you're going?"

"How many bodies were there aboard?" he asked as Miles stepped up to block his way.

"Come on, buddy. You saw the cordon. Police only."

"Press. *Bellingham Herald*," the man said, trying to step around Miles, who had now put up his hands to better impede the man's progress.

"This is a crime scene. It's off limits."

"This is a state wharf. I'm just walking down the public—"

"I'll tell you one more time."

The man, who was about the same size as Miles, kept pressing forward until Miles had to shift one of his feet back to brace himself.

"The public has a right—"

His statement was cut off as Miles grabbed one of the man's arms, turned his body, then bent and pinned the arm up against the man's back.

"Nobody steps aboard or gets anywhere near that vessel. It's a crime scene. Understood?"

The man remained mute, grunting against the discomfort of the hold Miles had on him. Taking his silence for acquiescence, Miles let the man go. But as soon as he did, the man turned to face him and resume his attempt to approach the boat.

"Are you kidding me?" Miles said, more to himself than the man. And as the man once again tried to slip around him, Miles stepped sideways, extended an arm and, with a hard shove, launched the man off the wharf and into the cold saltwater ten feet below. The splash brought a roar of laughter from the crowd of onlookers at the cordon.

"Listen," he said to Bill, who had come off the *Lucky Lena* to see what the hubbub was about. "I'm going to go try to telephone the Jensen homes again, just to make sure the men aren't sitting on their front porches drinking lemonade, unaware that their boat was adrift and full of blood. While I do that, would you please run over to the steamship ticket office and ask to see their passenger manifest logbooks? Copy down the names of all their passengers from this week."

"There could be hundreds of names."

"I know. I'm sorry. After that, can you find me a Bible, a nautical chart covering Haro Strait, and a tide table, and then meet me at Morgan's?" Morgan's was a rustic but consistently good wharf-side inn where Miles planned to order himself a huge bowl of local steamed clams in their buttery garlic and herb broth, as well as a quarter-round of crusty sourdough bread.

"This week's steamship passengers, the Holy Bible, a nautical chart, and a tide table. You got it."

"And actually, as you make your way through the crowd of lookie-loos, tell big Byron Willis to make sure nobody else crosses the damn cordon, alright? I see his giant head sticking out above the pack over there. Tell him there's a slice of my mother's apple pie in it for him."

"No problem."

But before either of them could leave, another tall, 20-something man appeared beside them. He carried two large leather cases—nearly the size of steamer trunks—and wore a perfectly pressed, gray wool three-piece city suit with an off-white fedora. He had what looked like a forced smile on his pale, boyish face. His sudden presence shattered Miles's renewed vision of buttery clams and warm bread.

"Hey, dammit," Miles said. "I've about had it with you

people."

"I beg your pardon?" the man said, his smile suddenly looking that much more forced.

"Get back over there and tell the rest of your lookie-loo friends that the next son of a bitch who crosses that cordon is going to get a fat lip."

The man looked confused. "No, no—I'm Ashton Floyd," the man said, setting his cases down and extending his hand.

"Who?"

"Ashton Floyd." Getting nothing but blank stares, Floyd added, "The forensics specialist."

"The *what* specialist?"

"Forensics."

"Is that for the church?"

"What? No, no. *Forensics.* The application of scientific techniques to the analysis of crime scene evidence."

"Ah, a crime scene guy."

"Well, technically speaking, I'm more of a . . ." Floyd stopped himself as he caught Miles and Bill's expressions. Then he shrugged. "Sure. A crime scene guy," he said, jerkily brushing a dandelion seed from his shoulder, then giving his immaculate suit a once-over while smoothing his lapels.

"You came from Bellingham, then?" Miles asked.

"No, Seattle. I just arrived," he said before bending over to brush every last speck of dust off the tops of his shoes.

"Seattle?" Miles asked, wondering what the hell. Whenever he'd had to call in a crime scene specialist—which had only happened twice before—he'd radioed Bellingham. It was much closer than Seattle. "Do we have an appointment?"

Floyd straightened, now looking as confused as Miles. "I was given to understand that I was sent for."

"By whom?"

"I don't know, bub. I just go where they tell me. And they told me to come here right away to help process your crime scene. I barely had time to pack before I caught the boat."

Miles tried to sort out how on earth Floyd could have gotten there so quickly from Seattle, given that they'd only towed the *Lucky Lena* into Friday Harbor three hours earlier. There were surely numerous watchers and informants—for both rumrunners and their law enforcement adversaries—on and around all of the islands near the Canadian border. Perhaps one of them had intercepted the lighthouse keeper's morning radio call to the police about the *Lucky Lena*. Or perhaps someone had spotted them towing the *Lucky Lena* down the channel. Whatever the case, someone had contacted someone else down in Seattle, and that 'someone else' had put the wheels in motion to rush this Floyd guy to the steamship bound for San Juan Island. 'Someone else' with enough power and influence to arrange for the immediate dispatch of a Seattle Police Department crime scene specialist to the outer edge of Washington State. Miles wondered who. And why.

"And you're actual police?" Miles asked, eyeballing Floyd's extraordinarily clean city slicker suit.

"Yes, of course. A detective."

"A detective?" Miles said, thinking Floyd was far too young to be a detective.

"That's right." Floyd fumbled around in his inner jacket pocket, then drew out his badge. "See?"

"Huh."

As Floyd opened his jacket to put the badge away, Miles noticed that he was wearing what had to be the biggest shoulder-holstered revolver he'd ever seen.

Floyd was nearly as tall as Miles and had equally broad shoulders. Formidable, physically speaking. But his expression and manner struck Miles as oddly unguarded for a policeman. And given the strangeness of his arrival on the scene, Miles was reluctant to trust him. Still, Miles was exhausted and needed expert help. And between himself and Bill, he figured that they could keep an eye on Floyd easily enough.

"Alright," Miles said. "My apologies for being brusque. It's been quite a day."

"Certainly."

"I'm Miles Scott," he said, at last shaking Floyd's hand. "This is Bill Shaw."

"Oh. They told me you didn't have a deputy. Part of why they sent me."

"Bill more or less came with the police station. He's unofficial but dependable. My general factotum and one-man backup. A teddy bear, despite his resemblance to Frankenstein."

"You mean Frankenstein's monster," Floyd said with a grin that disappeared as soon as he took a covert glance at Bill's towering figure and unamused face.

"Do I?" Miles asked.

"Well, I mean, strictly speaking, in the story . . ."

"What?"

Floyd swallowed. "It's just that in the actual story, Frankenstein is the scientist. Not the, uh, monster."

"Thank you for correcting me."

"I didn't mean . . ."

"You look a bit pale, Mr. Floyd. Are you well?"

Floyd gathered himself. "I'm fair. Afraid I have a bit of an irrational phobia of deep water. The boat ride up here has me a little out of sorts."

"There's nothing irrational about it. The deep waters around these islands take men's lives every year."

"A comforting thought. I look forward to the ride home that much more now."

"I'm sure you'll survive."

"Yes. Anyway, this is the boat then?"

"This is the boat. The *Lucky Lena*. Owned by a fella named Hans Jensen, from Deer Harbor over on Orcas Island. Works with his son, Leif. No sign of the men."

Miles gave Floyd a rundown of where the boat was found and what he'd already discovered aboard. The blood. The bullet holes. The heavy-duty diving suit. The radio receiver. "Looks like someone tried to sink the boat. There are remnants of a fire in the aft hold, over the top of an area that was hacked at with a hatchet. My guess is someone tried to chop through the hull, decided it was taking too long or was too much work, and then tried to set her afire instead. But that didn't work either. Seems that just as the fire began to burn through the hull, water seeped in and extinguished it. Whoever set the fire was probably gone by then, or they would have tried again. You'll notice that we tried to shore up the charred part of the hull with some tar and planking before towing her down here. Did our best not to disturb other evidence."

"I see," Floyd said, clearly dismayed.

"I know that you crime scene guys like your evidence left undisturbed. But if we hadn't shored things up, she might very well have sunk as we tried to tow her in."

"Understood."

"Now, assuming there were bodies," Miles continued, "they must have been removed through the forward cargo hatch because there isn't all that much blood in the companionway or wheelhouse. Storm last night probably washed the upper decks clean. Anyway, there's a lot to suggest that it was a rumrunner hijacking. Boat's painted gray so it can hide from patrols in the sort of lousy weather rumrunners favor—weather like we had last night. She also has two unusually big, fast engines for a boat of her type. The registration numbers were covered with creosote. All that spells rumrunner in my book. Oh—and we found a nautical chart for D'Arcy Island tacked to a table in the wheelhouse."

"D'Arcy Island?" Floyd asked.

"Tiny, almost uninhabited island just on the Canadian side of the maritime border."

"Almost uninhabited?"

"It's where the Canadian government dumps its ethnic Chinese lepers. Anyway, because of its proximity to the border, rumrunners use the island to transfer shipments. A big Canadian boat will offload cases of whiskey there. Then the American rumrunners will load them onto their small, fast boats and wait until Haro Strait is clear of revenue cutters or customs boats so they can make runs to their drop points in the U.S."

"Got it."

"There are also several 50-lb. sacks of salt in the hold, as well as markings on the floor that make it look as though objects about the size of whiskey crates were removed at some point after the blood was spilled."

"What's the relevance of the salt?"

"Rumrunner's insurance. If they they're being chased, they can toss the whiskey crates overboard, weighed down with 50-lb. sacks of salt. Then, if they get caught, there's no evidence aboard. Fifteen to twenty hours later, they motor back to the same spot where they dumped the crates overboard, by which time the salt has dissolved and they've floated back to the surface."

"Clever."

"There were also smashed bottles of whiskey below decks," Bill added.

"Yes," Miles said. "Perhaps most damning, several shattered bottles of Glenfiddich Scotch whiskey in the aft hold."

"Glenfiddich," Floyd echoed. "Only Stenersen runs whiskey of that sort of quality," he said, referring to Otto Stenersen—the high king of all Puget Sound rumrunners.

"Stenersen, eh?" Miles said. "Didn't he used to be a lieutenant with the Seattle Police Department?"

"I'm afraid so," Floyd said with the slightest hint of a smile. "Must have found booze more lucrative than brawling with Bolshevik longshoremen down at the docks."

"I'm sure. So, you think *Lucky Lena* might have been one of Stenersen's rumrunners?"

"Unless it was the captain's private stash of Glenfiddich."

"He'd have to be a pretty damned successful fisherman to afford that," Miles said.

"Tell him about the Chink symbol," Bill said.

"The what?" Floyd asked.

"Bill means that there's a symbol on the bulkhead that might be Chinese or Japanese or something."

"Peculiar."

"Not as peculiar as the fact that it was drawn in blood."

"Good lord."

"We also found a severed human finger pointing to a reference to the Bible. Book of Romans. It's written in blood too."

Floyd blinked, his mouth agape. "You're joking."

"No."

"Well, you don't see that every day." Floyd seemed, once again, to be suppressing a smile, as if it were all great fun to him. Then, all at once, he looked confused. "Why would hijackers bother with severed fingers and symbols and Bible references written in blood if they're planning to burn and sink the boat?"

"More insurance, maybe?" Miles said.

"What do you mean?"

"Something to confuse us in case the boat doesn't burn or sink? I don't know. Just speculating."

"I see," Floyd said, turning to take his first good, long look at the boat. "Anything else?"

"It might be relevant that last night's entry in the ship's log says they ran across Haro Strait to Sidney, British Columbia, then doubled back to Anacortes."

"What for?"

"Parts. Tools. Nothing interesting."

"Well, there's plenty that's interesting already," Floyd said. With that, he opened one of the cases at his feet and extracted a large black camera, as well as an instrument that looked like a pair of giant thermometers attached to either side of a steel cylinder.

"The heck is that thing?" Bill asked.

"*That* is an Assman psychrometer. Probably the only one in

the entire State of Washington."

"Ass man?" Miles said, causing Bill to smile and turn away to hide his awful teeth.

"*Ass*man. Named for its inventor, Adolph Assman, the eminent German meteorologist."

"And notorious lady killer, I'm guessing."

"It measures ambient temperature and relative humidity."

"What for?" Bill asked.

"It can help us determine how long ago all the blood was spilled."

"No kidding?"

"Speaking of which, is that blood?" Floyd asked, pointing at the large coffee stain on Miles's pants.

"No. I spilled something at breakfast this morning."

"Ah. Well. Hell of a busy day when you don't even have time to change your dirty pants," Floyd said.

Miles didn't mention that he simply hadn't bothered.

"Permission to go aboard?" Floyd asked as he removed and carefully folded his suit jacket before rolling up his shirtsleeves.

The request gave Miles pause. He certainly needed help. But he again wondered who might have sent Floyd, and why. Perhaps there was a simple, legitimate explanation.

"Be my guest," Miles said at last.

NINE

Miles asked Bill to wait on his other errands in order to keep a subtle eye on Ashton Floyd while Miles made a quick trip up to the police station to try calling Hans and Leif Jensen's wives again. As he made his way back along the wharf, Miles decided to question the group of annoying onlookers still assembled at the cordon. He knew most of them by name. Half of them looked spooked, the other half just nosy. He asked whether anyone had seen the *Lucky Lena* over the past couple of days.

"Was it a hijacking?" asked a lanky, nervous man Miles only knew as Miller—a perpetually smelly deckhand for one of the bigger salmon seiners.

"Of course it was a hijacking, you dope," said Jacob Fields, owner of a dry goods store up on Spring Street. "A rumrunner hijacking. Look at the gray paint on that boat. And the registration number is covered up. Definite rumrunner."

"Pirates hijacking local boats?" Miller said. "That's all we need. Fewer cannery jobs, fewer salmon in our nets, half the town in debt, and now this."

The conversation degenerated into a clamor of shouted questions.

"That's the Jensens' boat, ain't it?"

"The Jensens? Rumrunners? You're joking."

"If it was just rumrunners," said a guy named Sean Brennan who was a boat engine mechanic, "then why trouble yourselves? I mean, if you choose that line of work . . ." He shrugged.

"That's right," Jacob Fields added. "If they were running liquor, then they were fair game. They knew the risks they were taking. You reap what you sow."

Half inclined to agree with them, Miles nevertheless said, "We trouble ourselves because the boat is owned and crewed by our own people."

"What do you mean, *our own people*?"

"As one of you just said, the boat is owned by the Jensens," Miles said. "A father-and-son crew from Deer Harbor. From our islands." The crowd began shouting questions *en masse.*

"Was that blood you were washing off your boots?"

"Blood?" someone asked, prompting some of the faces in the crowd to grow that much more spooked.

"Did you find any bodies onboard?" asked another anxious voice.

"Did someone hurt the Jensens? Are they alive?"

"Someone said they disappeared."

"Someone said the boat is full of bullet holes."

"And full of blood. Blood everywhere."

"Whose blood?"

"Are the Jensens dead?"

"Who do you think did this, Sheriff?"

"What's to prevent it from happening again? To one of us, maybe?"

Stopping to talk had been a mistake.

*****

Miles was finally able to make contact with each of the Jensen wives when he got back to the station. Though he'd eventually want to interview them in depth and face-to-face, he ran through a short list of initial questions. Each reported last seeing her husband leaving for work, as usual, just before dawn the day before. Neither could think of any reason why anyone would want to do them harm. Neither had a clue as to who else their husbands had been seen with lately. Leif's wife, Birgit, was distraught and demanded to know what Miles had learned thus far. Miles told her of the discovery of the boat adrift—but nothing about the whiskey bottles, the bullet holes, or the blood—and assured her that he'd call as soon as they learned anything of consequence. Curiously, Hans's wife, Lena, didn't come across as at all concerned. She didn't ask Miles a single question.

After hanging up, Miles thought for a moment, then picked up the receiver once more. "Hello again, Mrs. Hampton," he said to the island's daytime switchboard operator. "I need to place another call—this one to Seattle. The number is Melrose-6123."

She connected Miles to the home of John Staggner, a high school friend who had a cousin in the Seattle Police Department. John wasn't home, but his pregnant wife answered and took a message asking that John make inquiries, through his cousin, about Detective Floyd.

"John will be thrilled to hear from you," she said. "He talks about you and Marion all the time."

"Please tell him that I'm very sorry I missed your wedding."

"Oh, don't worry yourself about that. John knows you were still overseas with the Army. Nobody could possibly blame you."

In fact, Miles had returned to the United States—indeed, to Washington State—well before the wedding. But for reasons he could never quite put a finger on, he simply hadn't gone. Even though he'd been available. Even though John Staggner had been one of his best childhood friends.

She promised Miles that she'd have John call him back as soon as he got home from work.

*****

Miles spent the better part of the next three hours aboard the *Lucky Lena*, half starved to death, keeping an eye on Floyd as he examined every inch of the boat in what struck Miles as an absurdly meticulous way. Taking photographs of the diving suit, the bullet holes, the Asian symbol, the Bible reference, the severed finger. Measuring the temperature and humidity of the air in both the wheelhouse and hold. Examining the various pools of blood. Measuring and taking a print of the severed finger. To Miles's mild surprise, Floyd was also able to pry damaged but whole bullets from three of the holes in the hull wood. They appeared, at first glance, to be .38 caliber.

"What's the point of collecting the bullets?" Miles asked as the two men slouched in the low-ceilinged forward hold where Floyd had set up a makeshift workstation.

"An excellent question. If we're ever able to recover a weapon, I may be able to tell you if it was the gun that fired these bullets."

Irritated by Floyd's patronizing manner, Miles nevertheless asked, "How on earth can you do that?"

"Believe it or not, every gun is unique. At the very least, there are always distinctive microscopic imperfections and anomalies on the inside of the barrel. When a particular gun is fired, these imperfections leave unique marks on the relatively soft metal of the bullets as they pass down the barrel. Like fingerprints, in a way. Depending on the condition of the bullets—depending on how intact they are—I can examine them under my comparison microscope and tell whether or not they were fired by any guns we manage to find."

"The wonders of modern technology."

"Indeed. And I'll tell you something else. Assuming it's human, this," he said, gesturing to the smears and puddles all around them, "is far too much blood to have come from the Jensens alone. It's definitely the blood of more than two people."

Well, obviously, Miles stopped himself from saying.

As Floyd began packing up his various instruments, Miles climbed back up to the wheelhouse, sat down at the small chart table, and took a second look at the ship's logbook they'd found among the ransacked debris. He flipped it open to the previous night's entry indicating that the *Lucky Lena* had run across the border, to Sidney, British Columbia, for a "spare prop" before doubling back to the east, to Anacortes, Washington, for "tools." Miles doubted the authenticity of the entry, thinking it was probably just fodder for an alibi in case the Jensens managed to get themselves caught. Still, if the Jensens were being clever, they very well might have entered locations near to where they were truly operating so that if they were boarded by customs or revenue agents, the log would indicate that they were in the area for legitimate purposes. In other words, the log might at least suggest *Lucky Lena's* actual, approximate locations—or intended locations—of the night before. Indeed, Sidney was quite close to D'Arcy Island—a notorious rumrunner staging area. And the town of Anacortes was near any number of popular rumrunner drop off points, being, as it was, nearly surrounded by secluded beaches and coves.

As he set the logbook aside, his eyes settled on a large hardcover text called *American Practical Navigator* lying open, but face down, on the end of the chart table. He'd noticed the book before, but hadn't touched it. Turning it over, he discovered that a square of paper had been cut out of several hundred of the pages, creating a hollow. A hiding place, maybe five inches tall by three inches wide by two inches deep. Miles stared at the hollow for a moment, then searched the table top and surrounding area for anything that might have fit inside it. But all he found were pencils, a loose button, a box of long matches, and a handheld compass. Nothing that would seem to warrant hiding.

Floyd called to Miles from the hold. As Miles met him at the companionway, Floyd handed a small, triangular paper item up through the companionway. One of its three edges was burned. "What do you make of this? I just found it in one of the pools of bloody seawater. I don't know how we could have missed it."

At first glance, Miles thought it was the corner of a dollar bill. Its unburned edges bore decorative designs that reminded him of paper currency. Taking it in hand, he realized that it was actually a small stack of eight such triangular fragments, bound together with a tiny brass fastener. He thumbed through the fragments, looking for clues as to what they were. Depending on how much of the fragment was torn away, each had the first four to five digits of a number in red type. Perhaps the first part of a serial number. The topmost read: 9749. Below the number, but in gray-green ink, was the upper half of what was clearly the capital letter T, followed by what could have been an H.

"They look official," Miles said. "Maybe bank notes of some sort. Stock certificates. I don't know."

"Looks like someone tried to burn them."

"Yes. But because they were evidence of the crime, or because they just made good kindling for someone who wanted to burn the boat?"

"Another good question. I'll take a photo. By the way, did you recover any bullet casings up there?"

"Now that you mention it, no, I didn't. Did you?"

"No," Floyd said. "The shooters must have pocketed them. Smart."

"Also, I just found a big reference book with a secret hollow in it."

Floyd again seemed to suppress a smile as he shook his head. "A secret hollow? Anything in it? Treasure map? Secret codes?"

"Nothing at all."

TEN

It was dark by the time Floyd finished processing the scene to his satisfaction. Exhausted and ready to eat his own hand, Miles locked up the *Lucky Lena,* then led Floyd up toward Morgan's Inn for a long-overdue meal.

"I can wait, if you want to go get cleaned up first," Floyd said as they approached the Inn. Despite his labors, Floyd didn't appear to have a speck of dirt on him. Miles, on the other hand, was filthy with everything from spilled coffee to engine oil to dried blood.

"I'm too hungry to bother," Miles said. "Anyway, relax. You're in Friday Harbor, not Seattle. And Morgan's isn't anyone's idea of fine dining."

Miles pulled open the inn's heavy wooden door and they were greeted by a warm gust of air that smelled of sauteed garlic and freshly baked bread. It was a largely unadorned but comfortable space of bare wood floors, exposed timbers, and twin stone fireplaces. Bill waved them over to a corner table where they could speak in relative privacy. The requested Bible, nautical chart, and tide table sat on the windowsill next to him.

The kitchen was out of clams, so Miles settled for a slab of fresh halibut pan-fried in garlic butter. Floyd ordered a roasted half chicken and a large bowl of potato and leek soup. Bill ordered nothing, but ate a quarter round of heavily buttered sourdough bread Miles gave him from his own plate.

Miles found himself cursing Prohibition, craving a glass of white wine like they always served with fish in France. Wine always seemed to make the food it was paired with taste that much better. The French had some funny notions, in Miles's opinion. But they sure as hell knew how to eat.

"I'll send my photographs down to Seattle on tomorrow's steamer," Floyd said as their plates were cleared from the table. "Hopefully our research section can tell us more about some of the evidence. Oh—and I was also able to recover two more bullets."

"For a total of five?"

"Yes. And fragments of two more. Happily, I'm equipped to examine them here."

"You mean you brought along your, uh, double—"

"My *comparison* microscope. Yes. It's in my equipment case."

"Do you have any preliminary thoughts?"

"I have. For one, marks in some of the blood smears lead me to believe that at least two people—presumably hijackers—were wearing gloves. But I also found a lot of fingerprints in the aft cargo hold, some of them preserved in dried blood. Tomorrow, I'll ship them off to the NBIC."

"To the what?" Miles asked.

"National Bureau of Criminal Identification. I doubt they'll connect the prints to anyone, unless you have a long habit of sending them your fingerprint cards from all the way out here."

"Never even heard of the place."

"Well, even so, if the prints have ever been put in the system by anyone, we might be able to match one up with an eventual suspect. Of course, it will take a few weeks for any results to get back to us. In the meantime, we'll need to get prints from the homes of the crewmen to eliminate those from our analysis."

"That shouldn't be hard to do."

"Oh, and you probably saw this for yourselves, but the dead finger was that of an adult male Caucasian. I'd guess middle-aged."

"Probably Hans Jensen's," Miles said.

"That would be my first guess."

"But why cut off his finger? To punish him? To torture him

for information?"

"Excellent questions," Floyd said. "Maybe to emphasize whatever message that Bible passage stands for."

"To emphasize," Miles muttered. "Well, it certainly grabbed my attention." He leaned back in his chair and rubbed his temples. "By the way, Floyd, I can see that you're very knowledgeable. But you don't have to keep telling me that my questions are excellent, alright?"

Floyd looked genuinely confused. "My apologies."

"It's nothing. Anyway, big picture, what do you fellas make of this mess?"

"Well," Floyd said, "like you, I think the most likely thing is that it was a rumrunner hijacking. Crew was probably murdered, chained to the anchor, and thrown overboard. It would explain why the anchor is gone. I assume hijackings are a regular thing up here?"

"They happen. But I've never seen anything like this floating slaughterhouse."

"The quantity of blood is noteworthy."

"Noteworthy? I'd call it staggering."

"Yes. And as I said before, there's far more blood aboard than could have come out of a mere two-man crew. There had to have been more people aboard."

"Word on the docks is that the Jensens always worked alone," Miles said. "They probably just drew some blood from their hijackers."

"An awful *lot* of blood."

"Maybe there were a bunch of hijackers."

"Maybe," Floyd said. "Were the Jensens armed?"

"Not according to their wives."

"They didn't carry guns? Really? In this hotspot of smuggling and piracy?"

"The San Juan Islands are peaceful, the people generally law-abiding," Miles said, sounding indignant. "The only real trouble up here is caused by outsiders."

"Strictly speaking, the crew of the *Lucky Lena* were *locals* who appear to have been running liquor."

"*Strictly speaking*, the jury is still out on that."

"Well, whatever the case, this incident could signify an abrupt end to your alleged local peacefulness. An escalation in the violence of hijackings, I mean. Let's hope it doesn't trigger a full-fledged rumrunner war."

"Amen," Miles said, profoundly troubled at the thought of such a thing.

"Getting back to my findings with respect to the blood," Floyd continued, "given the temperature and humidity, as well as the extent of gelation and rim desiccation—"

"Wait—the what?"

"How dry the blood is. Given all of that, I'd say the blood was spilled last night just after dark."

"You can be that precise?"

"To within an hour or two."

"Where'd you learn to figure that out?" Miles asked.

"I'm a bit of an acolyte of Professor R. A. Reiss. University of Lausanne, Switzerland. And I suppose you could say he's a bit of a revolutionary. The world's leading authority on criminal forensics, in my view."

"Well, well. So the blood was spilled just after dark. Okay. Bill, let's take a look at that tide table and nautical chart."

Bill took both from the windowsill and spread them out on the table.

"So," Miles said, "last night we had a sustained northwest wind of 32 to 35 knots, with gusts to 70, until around 11 p.m. After that, the wind shifted, coming out of the southwest and strengthening to 38 knots for most of the rest of the night. It finally died out somewhere around 4 a.m. Meanwhile," he said, picking up the tide table, "the tide turned at 1:37 a.m. Okay. And the *Lucky Lena* was first spotted here," he said, pointing to the waters just off Turn Point, "at 6:37 a.m." They all leaned forward over the nautical chart encompassing the American San Juan and

Canadian Gulf Island archipelagos. "So, if the blood was spilled just after dark, and assuming *Lucky Lena* was set adrift just after that . . ." Miles let his sentence hang as he used a pencil and the edge of his napkin to make several crude measurements. "I would say blood was spilled when the boat was just about here," he said, pointing to D'Arcy Island.

"Impressive," Floyd said. "And where did *you* learn to figure *that* out?"

"Pretty much everyone who grows up here works on boats at one point or another. Fishing boats, workboats, ferries, dories. You learn to read the water. I suppose you could say it's in our blood."

"I see."

"So, who hijacked the boat?" Bill said.

"Could have been some independent local pirates," Floyd said. "But I tend to think not because, given that the *Lucky Lena* appears to have been running Glenfiddich—a high-end Scotch whiskey—it was probably one of Stenersen's boats, since he's the only guy in the region whose outfit runs such high-quality stuff. And there are persistent rumors in Seattle that some new, well-informed syndicate of rumrunners is trying to horn in on Stenersen's territory. Targeting his shipments. Targeting his people. Assuming the new syndicate exists—and isn't a mere phantom conjured up by the press to explain unrelated incidents—they're supposed to be aggressive, well-armed, and possibly murderous. Whereas Stenersen doesn't even let his people carry guns."

"No guns?" Miles said.

"Nope. And although Stenersen doesn't publicly admit that he's a bootlegger, he's been repeatedly quoted as saying that the booze business isn't worth a single human life."

"Hard to take such a statement seriously, considering its source."

"He's supposed to be a very decent man."

"Said the policeman of the bootlegger," Miles said, again

wondering what Floyd's real story was.

"Anyway," Floyd said, "my point is that it's entirely possible that rival rumrunners hijacked the *Lucky Lena*."

"But rival rumrunners wouldn't have smashed a bunch of whiskey bottles," Bill said. "They'd have taken them."

"That could have been accidental," Miles said. "A few bottles hit by stray bullets maybe."

"What about the Chink symbol on the bulkhead?" Bill asked.

"That suggests another possibility," Floyd said. "It could be a tong symbol. One of the tongs sending a message. Claiming responsibility. Sending a warning to another tong, maybe."

"Another *tong*?" Bill said. "What the hell is a tong?"

"Chinese secret society. Secret brotherhood. Brotherhood being a euphemism for gang of cut-throats. Tongs run most of the vice rackets in the big West Coast cities, including Seattle. Underground gambling clubs. Whorehouses. Opium dens. Could be one of the tongs hijacked the boat."

"A Chinese gang hijacking a rumrunner?" Miles asked.

"There's plenty demand for booze in the Chinese card clubs," Floyd said. "Or maybe the *Lucky Lena* was carrying opium too."

"Meaning the hijacking was one tong stealing from another."

"It's possible," Floyd said. "There's an undeclared tong war underway in Seattle right now between three of the five main tongs. They're killing each other over turf. Over control of the rackets. Over insults. Over one tong stealing another tong's brothel slave girls. You name it. Chinatown's a bloody mess."

"Damned heathen Chinks," Bill muttered.

Miles thought for a moment, then shook his head. "It's hard to picture Chinese pulling off a boat hijacking."

"Why?"

"Because I've never seen a Chinese-crewed boat. Not ever. They all work in the cannery or the lime works. Not on the boats."

"Not at all?" Floyd asked.

"No. And frankly, I don't picture a father-son crew of fishermen from Deer Harbor smuggling opium for a Seattle tong." He thought for a moment. "Then again, it wouldn't be any stranger than a former Seattle Police lieutenant becoming the king of West Coast rum running."

"Well . . ."

"Plus, what about the charring on the inside of the hull?" Miles asked. "The scorch marks? Someone obviously tried to burn and sink the *Lucky Lena.* Tried to destroy the evidence. But if one tong was leaving the symbol to claim responsibility or send a message or whatever, they wouldn't have tried to sink her. They'd have left *Lucky Lena* and their grim message intact."

The conversation went dead for a moment as they all thought about the evidence.

"Here's another thing," Floyd said. "Why did the Jensens have that heavy, commercial-grade diving suit?"

"I don't know," Miles said. "Maybe they rented it to make underwater repairs or scrape weed off the *Lucky Lena's* hull without having to dry dock her."

"That's a deep-water suit though, isn't it? Seems like overkill for that sort of work."

"Maybe they were trying to recover something they lost overboard in deep water then. Ship's log said they ran over to Sidney for a spare propeller. Maybe the old prop sheared off the shaft and they wanted to retrieve it."

Floyd appeared lost in thought. "Well. Not my province, so I suppose I'll take your word for it. I'll tell you something else we should keep in mind though. Whoever did this was methodical."

"Methodical? There's blood everywhere."

"There's blood everywhere, but it wasn't *spilled* everywhere. Evidence suggests there was an initial amount of violence in the pilot house. But aside from that, the vast majority of the blood was spilled in the very back of the aft cargo hold, which is also where most of the bullet holes and all the blood spray patterns are. The fact that there is blood smeared and pooled all over the lower deck is probably a product of bodies being dragged about after the fact."

"So?"

"It's a reasonable assumption that, through threats or lies, the killer or killers took the time and trouble to move most if not all of their victims below decks and then corral them in one end of the cargo hold before opening fire. This suggests that there was no passion or hot blood involved. No rage. The killing was methodical. Systematic. Efficient. It suggests a certain coldness of heart on the part of the killers."

"Coldness of heart?" Miles said.

"Sounds like a lot of college-boy hocus pocus," Bill said. "What about the rest of the *real* evidence? What about the finger pointing to the Bible reference?"

"The reference was to the Book of Romans," Miles said.

"Romans 1:18," Bill said, opening the Bible he'd brought. Finding the page, he turned it so that Miles and Floyd could see.

"'For the wrath of God is revealed from heaven against all ungodliness and unrighteousness of men,'" Miles read aloud. "A warning."

"Meaning what?" Floyd asked.

"Maybe that rumrunners will pay for their evil ways," Miles said, shrugging.

"Who would leave a message like that?"

"The sort of person who would have reveled in smashing those expensive bottles of Glenfiddich. A zealot. A temperance fanatic."

Floyd pinched the bridge of his own nose as if trying to relieve a headache. But he also smiled. "Okay. So, our list of suspects has grown to include rogue hijackers, a rival rumrunning syndicate, Chinese tongs, and now temperance fanatics."

"Plus, we have a missing crew, a mysterious symbol, a bible verse, a deepwater dive suit, a severed finger, and about a million gallons of blood to make sense of," Miles added.

"There's a lot to digest here."

"You're not kidding. How about we call it a night?"

*****

On the way to his truck, after asking Bill to take Floyd up to the Tourist Hotel to get him a room for the night, Miles stopped in at the fire station to ask that, come morning, the men drag the sea floor near D'Arcy Island for bodies.

"What sort of an area are we talking about?" asked Luke Gruden, the volunteer chief, looking up from the weekly fire brigade poker game Miles had interrupted.

"Let's start with a one-mile radius."

"That's a tall order, Miles. A bit east of D'Arcy, the water is some 700 feet deep. And closer in, there are lots of rocks for our grappling hooks to get caught on."

"True."

"Plus, the tides all around there are strong and fast. I mean, our chances of actually finding anything other than clamshells and sea anemones . . ." He shrugged.

"I know," Miles said. "Just do what you can. It's the hand we've been dealt."

"Also, that's Canadian waters. We'll need the necessary permissions."

"I'll radio RCMP in Victoria to let them know what you're up to. They'll just want us to tell them if we find anything."

"Fair enough. I figure we can get hold of three boats to rig with dragging equipment. We'll start quartering the area at first light."

"Appreciate it."

ELEVEN

Arriving home that night, Miles, utterly spent, parked his truck next to the weeping willow on the edge of the orchard and shut off the engine. A chorus of frog calls echoed across the still air. Halfway to the house, he stopped in his tracks, turned, and eyeballed the family's big white barn glowing in the moonlight. It was where they stored tools and farm equipment, crates for the fall apple harvest, and a 1909 Peerless Model 25 Raceabout that he and his father had been refurbishing before the war had taken Miles away—before the Spanish Flu had taken his father.

Miles pictured the old car. It was parked by the far wall, under a canvas sheet dotted with the droppings of field mice and barn swallows. All around it, various hand tools lay, gathering dust, exactly where his father had set them down years earlier, their wooden handles probably still bearing the residue of his father's sweat.

Acting on a tip, Miles and his father had found the abandoned wreck of the Raceabout in a forested ravine off a road near Anacortes and arranged to have it hoisted out and barged to Friday Harbor. Over the next two years, and up until Miles received his draft notice, whenever they'd had spare time and spare money, they'd gathered replacement parts from junkyards in Bellingham, Everett, and Seattle and worked at restoring it to like-new condition. It was a beautiful relic of the so-called brass era of automobile production, with polished black paint, shiny brass headlamps, new button-tufted red upholstery, and the largest automobile engine Miles had ever seen. All it needed now—all it had needed since he'd left for the war—was sparkplugs, motor oil, and a new set of tire tubes. Otherwise, it was ready to gas up and go. But Miles's father had insisted on waiting until Miles returned from France before taking it for its inaugural drive. It was something they would do together, father and son.

Miles stared at the barn for another moment, imagining what it would have been like—he and his father pulling back the dust cover, firing up the big engine, then racing down a sunny country road with broad smiles on their faces and the wind in their hair.

He pictured his father's joyful face. The general look of it came to him. But then, for some ill-judged reason, Miles tried to visualize the individual parts of it—his father's mouth, his nose, his eyes. Miles struggled to remember details. Precise shapes and sizes.

Startled by this, he went to the house, removed a framed portrait of his father from its hook on the living room wall, and took it to bed intent on memorizing everything about it.

*****

Hours later, despite his exhaustion, Miles couldn't sleep. As he lay in bed, his mind spun with unanswered questions, visions of the *Lucky Lena*'s bloody cargo hold, and anxiety over what might come next. It all stoked a sense of urgency he couldn't shake.

Shortly after 2 a.m., he gave up on sleep, grabbed his binoculars, a kerosene lantern, and his saxophone, and drove out to Hanbury Point, on the far western side of the island, for a bit of night watch.

It was a warm, calm, and quiet night. After pulling to the side of the road and switching off his engine, Miles was surprised to hear none of the usual crickets or frogs singing away in the nearby pastures and ponds. He set off down the short trail to his usual lookout point atop the rocky shoreline. Once there, he turned down his lantern, leaned against a gnarled madrone tree, and scanned the entirety of Haro Strait with his binoculars. The moon had already set and a low layer of overcast obscured the stars. Spotting rumrunners or pirates out there in such conditions would be next to impossible. Indeed, all Miles could see were the distant masthead lights of a southbound ocean tug.

He sat down on a nearby boulder, took out his sax, and began working on a few bars of a new Sidney Bechet tune. The quiet that filled the gaps between notes whenever he paused for breath drove home a familiar sense of aloneness—made all the heavier by the vast surrounding darkness.

D'Arcy Island was roughly three miles due west of him, just across the Canadian maritime border. There wasn't enough light to see it. But Miles knew the little island was out there. He wondered what had happened there the night before. Wondered what cutthroat smugglers or pirates might be lurking, hidden, waiting to ambush another boat, waiting to spill more blood. And he wished, with no small measure of bitterness, that he'd chosen this spot for his night watch—instead of Cattle Point—when whatever happened aboard the *Lucky Lena* had happened. Perhaps he'd have seen something helpful. Something that would help him catch the killers. But for all his obsessive vigilance, he'd been in the wrong place and hadn't seen a damned thing.

TWELVE

Miles woke with the dawn after no more than three hours of sleep. The wind was whipping the tips of plum tree branches against his bedroom window. For what stretched into almost two hours, he tried to ignore the noise and go back to sleep. But his efforts proved fruitless, so he eventually rose, tired and frustrated.

He didn't bother to shower or shave. But in staring at his careworn face in the mirror as he brushed his teeth, he found that his mother's comments from the previous day's lunch—about his loneliness—were creeping, unwanted, into his mind. He wondered at how she always seemed able to zero in on his sensitive spots. To get under his skin. Ostensibly, she wanted to help him find happiness. But sometimes he wondered if she didn't maybe, just maybe, get some sort of sadistic pleasure out of watching him squirm.

*****

Miles parked his truck around the corner and down the street from the station. As he walked up the block, he glanced at each person he passed, watching for unfamiliar faces. For outsiders. But he did so with a growing sense of unease. Was it his imagination, or were some of the people avoiding eye contact? Acting just a hair too disinterested in his passing?

It occurred to Miles that people might actually be watching *him*. Keeping tabs. Maybe even reporting on his movements.

He told himself he was being paranoid.

He turned the corner onto Spring Street just in time to watch a frail old woman in what appeared to be a nightgown stumble out of Fields's dry goods store and fall to the sidewalk, hard, spilling her small paper bag of apricots as she hit the ground. As Miles sprinted forward to help her, he saw that it was Clarice Brennan, mother of Sean the boat engine mechanic.

"Mrs. Brennan?" Miles asked, reaching for her, helping her roll onto her back and then sit up. "Easy does it, now. Are you alright?" Her knees and palms were bleeding.

At that moment, the owner, Jacob Fields, appeared in the doorway in a dirty apron, an equally dirty towel flung over one shoulder, his hands on his hips. "I sent my clerk to fetch her son down at the docks," he said matter-of-factly.

"Mrs. Brennan, are you alright?" Miles asked again, surprised to see her at all. Last he'd heard, she was living in a home for the senile in Bellingham. She glanced all around, looking utterly bewildered as to how she came to be where she was. As she clenched her jaw through the pain, Miles saw the familiar, dark gap in her teeth where her late husband had once knocked two of them out in a drunken rage. A sharp odor told him that she'd wet and soiled herself some hours earlier. As his heart sank for her, his mind wandered to thoughts of his own mother and his nagging worries about how much longer she would be able to get around on her own. He wondered whether this was a vision of her future.

"Mother!" Miles heard someone shout, and he turned to see Sean Brennan racing up the street with Fields's clerk. "What happened?" he asked, falling to his knees at his mother's side and taking her old shriveled hands into his own. She turned and gazed at her son, looking agitated and confused. She said nothing.

"She was favoring that left hip of hers," Fields said. "Told her to be careful. But her foot caught on the door threshold when she was on her way out."

"You could have helped her," Brennan said.

"I told her to watch her feet and such. I'm not a nurse."

"Mother, you know you're not supposed to be out of the house."

"I wanted fresh fruit," she said at last, her voice meek, like that of a sad child.

"But this is the dry goods store. Where did you get these apricots?"

She didn't seem to comprehend her son's question. "I just wanted fruit."

"I'll get you fruit," Brennan said softly. "Anytime you like, you just ask me. I'll get you all the fresh fruit you like." He reached one of his big arms behind her back, the other under her knees, and gently lifted her into the air.

Miles scrambled to collect the scattered apricots and load them back into her paper bag. "How can we help?" Miles asked.

As Brennan turned, Miles saw the man's face twisted with sadness.

"I can manage," Brennan said. "If you could just put the corner of the bag between my knuckles here, I can carry it home with her."

"You're sure you don't need a hand?"

"Quite sure. Thank you."

With that he set off, cradling his mother in his arms as he carried her up the street.

"Mercy," Miles couldn't stop himself from saying as he watched them go.

"Yeah, well, time waits for no man," Fields said. "No doddering old lady, either."

Speechless, Miles watched Fields turn on his heel and disappear back into his store.

*****

Miles came through the front door of the station to find the air smelling of breakfast. Bill was already there, pouring himself coffee from a dented tin percolator and flipping a giant flapjack out of a cast iron pan he'd taken from atop the potbelly stove.

"Morning, Sheriff."

"Bill, how are you?"

"Tired after yesterday," he said, spooning a large dollop of butter onto the flapjack.

"You and me both. Where's the mysterious Detective Floyd?"

"He was here earlier, looking at the bullets under his microscope contraption. Waited for you for about an hour, then gave up and went back to the hotel. Care for a flapjack?" he asked as he poured dark molasses over the melting butter on his own.

"No, thanks." Miles poured hot coffee into his thoroughly stained porcelain mug. "Speaking of Floyd, do you have any ideas about who might have called Seattle yesterday to get him sent up here?"

"Could have been anybody. Maybe one of those meddling chumps on the county council who don't think we can do the job."

"Or one of the rumrunners' local lookouts or informants who probably keep an eye on us."

"You think Floyd's working for the rumrunners?"

"Well, he came from Seattle, didn't he? All cities breed corruption. Even in the police."

Bill smiled. "Don't start jumping at shadows just yet, Sheriff."

"Yeah, maybe not. Anyway, what do you make of him?"

"Of Floyd?"

"Yes."

"He likes to use a lot of fancy, college-boy words and expressions."

Miles smiled. "That he does. Matter of fact, if he uses the expression *strictly speaking* one more time, I think my head will pop off. Some of what he says makes sense though. And some of those new techniques he's been taught might help us."

"Book learning," Bill said, shaking his head dismissively. "Real evidence is something you can hold in your hand. Or beat out of a man when you take him to the woodshed."

"You're wise beyond your years, Bill."

"I'll say that Floyd seems like a decent enough guy, though. Genuine."

"That's my gut feeling too. Regardless, be careful what you share with him until we know more about who sent him."

"Right. So anyway, I put that list of names from the steamship office's passenger manifests on your desk there."

"Thank you," Miles said. There were several pages. "Your hand must be sore from copying down all those names."

"To be honest, they did half of it for me."

"That was unusually kind of them."

"Greetings, gents," Floyd said as he opened the front door to the station.

"Morning," Miles said, sitting down to take a look at the manifest lists.

"You want a flapjack?" Bill asked Floyd.

"Thanks, no."

"You sure? It's good sourdough batter. And I've got some fresh butter and molasses or wildflower honey to drizzle over the top of it. A man has got to eat."

"Thanks. I breakfasted two hours ago." He looked at Miles. "You feeling under the weather this morning?"

"No. Why?"

"What time do you normally get to the station?"

"I get here when I get here."

"Of course—I just, uh, for my own scheduling purposes—well, anyway, I'm glad you could join us."

Miles gave Floyd a skeptical look. "Right. How were the accommodations at the Tourist Hotel?"

"Impeccable."

"Sleep well?"

"Like a baby. It's so quiet here compared to Seattle."

"You live in the city?"

"Not downtown." Miles waited for more. "I'm on Queen Anne Hill."

"In a house then?"

"Yes."

"No kidding. I don't mean to pry, but how does someone your age afford a house on Queen Anne Hill?"

"Well . . . I—I share it with my mother."

"Ah-ha."

"Seattle has gotten really expensive. Downtown, they want five dollars a month for a room with a shared toilet down the hall."

"Five dollars a month? That's outrageous."

"It's robbery. So, you see, it just makes too much financial sense not to—"

"Hey, Floyd, you don't have to justify yourself to us. If a *grown man* wants to live with his mother, that's his prerogative."

"Yes, that's why I . . . Anyway, I discovered something noteworthy this morning."

"Do tell."

"It's about the bullets. I believe they were all fired from the same gun."

"How certain are you?"

"Ninety percent."

"So, one gunman then," Miles said.

"He still may have had accomplices. But yes, in all likelihood, one shooter—at least in the aft cargo hold. Interestingly, the bullets are .38 Long Colts. A notoriously underpowered and ineffective cartridge that the Army quit buying at least ten years ago. They're typically fired from a six-shot revolver. But I counted seven bullet holes. And mind you, there were probably more shots fired than there are bullet holes."

"Your point being?" Miles asked.

"My point being that the gunman had to reload. Had to stop what he was doing, and, mid-bloodbath, open the cylinder, extract the spent brass bullet casings from the chambers, probably shove them in his pocket so he wouldn't leave any behind as evidence, then reload each of the six chambers with new cartridges before resuming the slaughter. Like I said before, methodical, right? With all that time to reflect during the reload?"

"Cold-blooded."

"Exactly. It also suggests that our shooter didn't feel at all threatened by his prey. That he could take the time to stand there reloading."

"The victims must have been unarmed. Maybe tied up. Maybe just helpless and weak."

"Maybe all of the above. Anyway, we have our work cut out for us this morning, haven't we? Who do we start with?"

"The Jensen wives, over in Deer Harbor," Miles said, resuming his examination of the steamship passenger list. "While Floyd and I do that, Bill, can you re-canvass the docks to see if any fishermen or workboat crews saw the *Lucky Lena* anywhere on Tuesday evening, or whether they saw any other vessels in Haro Strait, especially in the vicinity of D'Arcy Island?"

"Will do."

Miles's gaze froze halfway down one of the pages of steamship passenger names.

"You find something?" Floyd asked.

"Uh . . ."

"What? What is it?"

"Nothing."

But, of course, there *was* something. The name of a single passenger who'd come in on the steamship from Seattle two days earlier. A name that conjured fond memories of fishing for sole on the beach at Mulno Cove. Of playing catch with an old grass-stained baseball. Of mud fights. Of stargazing. Of listening to jazz and swing music till all hours on a wind-up Victrola. Of dancing. Of jasmine-scented hair.

"Look, I have to step out for a bit," Miles said. "Catch up with you fellas at the top of the hour, alright?"

With that, Miles grabbed his coat and headed out the door.

*****

Miles turned his truck off the road a scant quarter mile north of his own childhood home, heading up a short drive that led to a well-maintained Craftsman bungalow. The house was fringed with beds of purple and yellow flowers that were happily soaking up the brilliant morning sunshine. He parked in the shade of a plum tree, checked his hair in the reflection of the driver's side window as he got out, ran his tongue across his front teeth to feel for bits of food, then walked to the dark wood door and gave it a feeble knock. His heart began to pound in his ears as he saw, through the panes of yellow stained glass in the upper part of the door, a blurred figure approaching. He cupped a hand to his mouth for a last-second check of his breath. Then door swung open, and there she stood—his best childhood friend.

"Hello, Marion."

"Miles!" exclaimed Marion Forde. She sprang forward to hug him and held tight for a long moment. Then she pushed him away and they gazed at one another. She wore a blouse and tie, golf knickers, and argyle socks. Her dark hair was bobbed. "As I live and breathe!" she said. "Look at you! None the worse for wear, despite the Great War."

"You cut your hair."

"That's the first thing you can think to say to me?"

"Oh, sorry. I—"

"I'm just jacking you, Miles. Heavens. How long has it been?"

"Since I left for the Army."

"Years. Too long. Far too long. I've missed you."

"Me too. My mother said you were living in New York City."

"Yes! Such an amazing place, Miles."

"But now you're back?"

"Just for two weeks. My grandfather's health is failing, so my mother asked me to come spend some time."

"I'm sorry."

"He's lived a long life. Anyway, it means I get to see you."

"I'm glad of that. But Marion, why didn't you call me?"

"Oh. It's been busy. And I wasn't entirely sure that, uh—"

"Do we have guests?" another female voice inquired from within the house. It wasn't the voice of Marion's mother. It carried a heavy Boston accent. As Miles tried to place it, another young woman appeared at Marion's side in the doorway. Her outfit was nearly identical to Marion's. But she also wore round spectacles of the sort Miles associated—perhaps narrow-mindedly—with Marxists. Her hair was cropped short, giving her an almost boyish appearance.

"Sylvia, this is Miles. My best and closest friend growing up. Like a brother to me. Closer than a brother. I've told you all about him, of course."

"So, this is Miles," she said, extending her ring-adorned hand and giving him an authoritative shake. "Sylvia Rosen. Pleased to meet you."

Still in disbelief that Marion had been on San Juan Island for two days and hadn't yet called him, Miles had to take a moment to gather his wits enough to respond. "A friend from New York?" he asked.

"And roommate," Marion said. "In New York, it's a must that you share an apartment unless you're independently wealthy. Rent there would make your eyes roll back into your head, Miles. I swear. But let's hear more about you. My mother tells me you're sheriff now."

"How very manly," Sylvia added.

"Manly?" Miles had to grin. "I wouldn't go that far. I spend most of my time chasing escaped sheep and goats, truth be told. Locking up the occasional drunk."

"You're being modest," Marion said. "I'm sure policing blows the doors off banking or lawyering when it comes to fun."

"I can't argue with that." He took a breath and his shoulders slumped just noticeably. "Look, I—I'm afraid I have to get back to the station."

"Of course. But we must catch up."

"I would like that very much. Call me later?"

"I will."

"Nice to meet you, Sylvia."

"Likewise, Miles."

THIRTEEN

The inter-island steamer wouldn't stop in Friday Harbor until just after 11 a.m., so Miles arranged for a fisherman to run him and Floyd five miles up the San Juan Channel to Deer Harbor, Orcas Island. As they were walking along the dock to the fisherman's boat, Miles heard a racket of shouting ahead and looked up to see a small cluster of men shoving one another alongside a new-looking gillnetter he didn't recognize. "Now what?" he muttered. They picked up their pace to approach the scrum before things escalated into a full-fledged brawl—or worse. "The hell is going on here?" he shouted as they met the group.

"That son of a bitch in the red cap is saying I jumped the line at the cannery," said Roy Brandt, an old local fisherman, as he did his best to be subtle about sheathing the long utility knife he clenched in his enormous, callused hand.

"Who the hell are you?" Miles asked the angry-looking young man in the red cap.

"Name's Peters," he answered.

"You aren't from around here."

"I'm from Seattle. And let me tell you something, chum. I'd been waiting at anchor just off the cannery wharf for damn near an hour, waiting to offload my catch, when this old coot motors right in and ties up just as the boat in front of me was finally pulling away and—"

"Listen," Miles said, holding up a hand.

"No, you listen, mac. I'm sick and tired of all your local bumkins always thinking they can just—"

Miles cut Peters off with a vicious backhand that split the man's upper lip. Blood immediately ran from his lip and nose.

"You son of a—"

"Be careful about what you say next," Miles said, stepping forward.

"Who the hell—who the *hell*—"

"Meet our sheriff," Brandt said, interrupting, bearing an amused smile.

That shut Peters up.

"Tell you what, city boy," Miles said. "I'm going to do you a favor. I'm going to give you sixty seconds to motor on out of here while your jaw is still unbroken."

Peters, his bloody face flushed and his fists clenched, stared hard at Miles for a long moment. Then he glanced to his right and left as if counting how many local men he and his deck mate would have to take on if they decided to fight. He spat blood onto the dock, backed away, and got aboard his boat.

"Is that how you normally handle things?" Floyd asked Miles.

Miles didn't bother to answer.

*****

The fisherman ran Miles and Floyd to Deer Harbor in a 12-foot seine skiff with a brand-new Evinrude motor clamped onto the back of it. Floyd insisted on wearing a bulky, cork-filled life vest. On the entire five-mile journey, his eyes were bugged out and his jaw locked tight while both his hands gripped the gunwales so hard that his knuckles were white.

"This boat is awfully small," Floyd said as they motored along.

"It's perfectly safe," Miles said.

"I hope you're right."

"I'm always right."

*****

They went first to Leif Jensen's home. A farmhouse very similar to Miles's family's, it sat at the end of a sunny orchard of young pear trees, a quarter mile up a dirt road that led away from the dock where they'd disembarked. Unfortunately, Birgit Jensen, who was very pregnant with twins and half frantic about her missing husband, had nothing helpful to offer aside from her observation that Leif had seemed preoccupied—"maybe even a bit anxious"—the day before he disappeared. But she figured it was because the family had been struggling over money.

"Even with salmon season in full swing?" Miles had asked.

She explained that there'd been so much competition from other boats the last couple of years, with fewer salmon to catch in the immediate area and salmon prices still low, that her father-in-law had considered moving the whole family out to Sekiu or Westport to be closer to richer fishing grounds where fewer boats operated. "But Lena, my mother-in-law, quashed that idea without giving it a second thought," Birgit said, shaking her head. "She wouldn't hear of it. Said Deer Harbor was her home."

"Are you not on good terms with Lena?"

"Are *you* on good terms with *your* mother-in-law?"

"I'm not married."

"Oh—oh, I'm sorry. I tend to assume that men of your age . . . Anyway, I suppose I get along with Lena as well as I have to."

"Most of the fishermen around here still seem to be doing alright," Miles continued. "They may not be making the same money they did a few years ago, but they don't seem alarmed just yet."

"Well, yes, but Leif and his father had also just put a lot of their money into upgrading the boat. I know it made Leif anxious."

"What did they upgrade? The engines?"

"I think so. But Leif doesn't really talk about his work with me."

"Did he have any run-ins with anyone recently?" Miles asked.

"Any confrontations?"

"Leif? Heavens, no."

"What about Hans?"

"I wouldn't know. But I doubt it. He's a very gentle soul."

"Who do Hans and Leif associate with?"

She shrugged. "With themselves. With each other. They're not sociable."

"Have you known of either of them to be interacting with any other men at all recently?"

"Just the man at the Friday Harbor fuel dock, and then those little Oriental unloaders over at the cannery wharf."

Birgit appeared genuinely mystified by Leif's disappearance. She said the men probably just fell overboard while trying to pull in a net and were now marooned on some little islet, waiting to be spotted by a passing boat. But there was doubt and fear in her voice. She begged Miles to call her the minute he learned anything. They asked her for a household item that would have Leif's fingerprints on it.

"Why do you need Leif's fingerprints?"

"It helps us identify any prints that aren't his," Floyd said. "It may help us figure out if anyone else was aboard the boat."

"Who else would have been aboard the boat?"

"Well, Mrs. Jensen," Miles said. "That's what we intend to figure out."

She gave them Leif's Lillehammer tobacco pipe on the condition that it be returned when they were done with it. "He will definitely want this back."

Miles again refrained from mentioning the vast quantities of blood or any of the other evidence of mortal violence aboard the *Lucky Lena*.

*****

Hans Jensen's home was much closer to the Deer Harbor dock, on a tree-shaded lane running parallel to the harbor. Both the front yard and the simple, white house were neat and well-maintained. The paint was bright, and the beds of sweetbriar roses and pink zinnias lining the walk were weedless and abuzz with honeybees. But what Miles could see of the backyard encompassed a ramshackle chicken coop and the disorganized claptrap of commercial fishing: buoys, folded purse nets, a rack of gaffs and wooden booms, a damaged prop laying in the weeds, and, under a tin roof extending out from a tool shed, some sort of machine. Miles shielded his eyes from the sun to get a better look at it. It had a metal framework housing what looked like several brass piston cylinders and gauges, along with large metal flywheels to either side. Flywheels with long handles. Two of the pistons had been removed, and their various parts—large and small—sat on a small workbench next to an assortment of hand tools.

Floyd noticed Miles's stare. "You looking at that metal contraption?" Floyd asked.

"I am."

"What is it?"

"Might be an air pump of some sort. Maybe for that diving suit we found aboard the *Lucky Lena.* Piston cylinders are all taken apart. Must need new gaskets or valve work or something."

"That shoots holes in your theory, doesn't it?"

"My theory?"

"That the Jensens rented the diving apparatus to scrape seaweed off the hull of their boat. What I mean is, would Hans go to all the trouble of disassembling piston cylinders to make repairs like that if he'd rented the apparatus from someone else?"

"Seems unlikely."

"Ergo, Hans probably owns it," Floyd said as they neared the front door of the house.

"Big investment for a fisherman. Those things cost a small fortune."

"Exactly my point. So why did he buy one?"

Before Miles could give the glossy, pale-yellow front door a knock, it opened to reveal a stern-faced, gray-haired woman in a kitchen apron.

"Mrs. Lena Jensen?"

"Sheriff?"

"Yes, ma'am. And this is officer Ashton Floyd, who is visiting us from Seattle."

"*Detective* Ashton Floyd, actually," Floyd said, drawing a glare from Miles.

"Have you found Hans?"

"Not yet, ma'am."

"Have you spoken with Leif's wife, Birgit, yet?"

"Yes, ma'am, we have."

"What did she tell you?"

"May we come in?"

She appeared to deliberate for a moment, then, without a word, turned and led them to an austere but spotless parlor where she had them squeeze, side-by-side, into a small and surprisingly rigid loveseat to wait as she went to retrieve a pot of tea.

"Comfortable?" Miles muttered as they sat, crammed together, staring at the same wall.

Floyd grinned. "Feels like this thing is full of gravel."

"I gather she doesn't want us to stay here long."

The room was adorned with little more than lace curtains, a scattering of ceramic cow figurines, and decorative plates depicting Norwegian folk dancers. Yet something told Miles that Lena Jensen wasn't someone who much liked dancing.

Returning, Mrs. Jensen served the tea in her finest bone China, added a small cookie to each saucer, then sat down in a simple wooden chair facing the men.

"Mrs. Jensen," Miles said. "Let me begin by confirming that you still haven't heard from your husband or son."

"Don't you think I would have already told you?"

"Do you have any idea what your husband and son were up to the night before last?"

"Up to?"

"What they were doing."

She sat stone-faced and quiet for several moments, before at last replying, "Fishing."

"At night?"

"Coming back from fishing."

"Do you know where from?" She remained quiet. "Around Salmon Bank or Smith Island, maybe?" he asked, naming major salmon fishing areas in the region. "Haro Strait? Any idea?"

"No."

"Can you think of anyone who might have wished them harm for any reason?"

"No."

She gave the same unexpanded answer to most of the same questions they'd asked Leif's wife, Birgit—concerning whether Hans or Leif had been acting or doing anything at all out of the ordinary recently, whether they were in any sort of financial trouble, whether either of them were gamblers, drinkers, or brawlers, or whether she could think of anything at all that might help in their investigation—even a mere vague suspicion of something. Her replies were uniformly curt, her manner stern. Miles had always thought of Scandinavians as a reticent ethnic group, by and large. But Lena Jensen took it to a new extreme. He might as well have been talking to a brick wall. Until he asked his most direct question yet.

"Mrs. Jensen, do you have any reason to believe that Hans and Leif might have been transporting contraband? Liquor, for example? Or black-market opium?"

For a split second, Lena's face changed ever so slightly. She blinked a few times and pursed her lips. Then her expression quickly returned to normal. "Of course not. And I take the greatest possible exception to your suggestion."

"Question, not suggestion, Mrs. Jensen. And to be perfectly honest, rum running doesn't interest me in the least. Not my jurisdiction. Not my concern. But I do want to figure out what happened so that we can hopefully find your husband and son."

"I don't know anything about what you speak of."

"The potential paydays of rum running would be tempting to anyone. Understandably tempting. Especially to someone who feels responsible for a growing family. Someone who is perhaps under financial strain."

She flared. "Who said anything about financial strain? Birgit? Did she say that?"

"I also ask because we found evidence of Scotch whiskey bottles aboard the *Lucky Lena,* as well as large bags of salt of the sort rumrunners sometimes use to temporarily sink liquor crates."

Though her face remained colored, after a mute moment, she remastered her emotionless stare. "No. As I said, I don't know anything."

"The boat also has two very new, very costly, very powerful gasoline engines. Fishing boats don't typically have engines like that. They have chug-chugging diesels. It is also equipped with a modern and very expensive radio receiver—another thing you don't often see on fishing boats."

She sniffed. "Hans wanted to convert his fishing boat to a combination workboat so that he could run cargo."

"Very quickly, it seems."

She shrugged.

"What about the fancy radio?"

"I keep house, sheriff."

"I see. Then you probably wouldn't be able to tell us anything about the dive suit and air pump either."

"Dive suit?"

"We found a heavy-duty dive suit on board. There's also what appears to be an air compressor sitting in plain view under your shed roof out back. What was he using those for?"

"I have absolutely no idea. Probably the paraphernalia of yet another one of his crazy . . ." She stopped herself.

The men waited for more. Miles picked up and pretended to

examine one of the small cow figurines from the coffee table. Floyd pretended to take notes. They let the silence hang. Let it do its work on Lena.

"Sheriff, my husband is a simple, hard-working man. You're mistaken if you think he's some clever schemer or rumrunner."

Does she mean 'simple' as in uncomplicated, or 'simple' as in dumb? Miles wondered.

The interview was going nowhere. Miles decided to drop a bomb. "There was also quite a lot of blood on board."

Lena's lips tightened and the corners of her mouth turned downward just perceptibly. "Probably just from an accident. It's not unusual for—"

"A *lot* of blood, Mrs. Jensen."

"I don't . . ." She sat perfectly still. But her eyes had popped wide. Twenty silent seconds ticked by. "If that's all, gentlemen, I have things that must be tended to," she said at last.

"Actually, would you mind if we took a look around?" Miles asked.

"Yes, I would mind."

"May I ask why?"

"This is my home."

"Certainly. But you understand that we're trying to figure out where your husband is, and that we might very well find something here that could aid us?"

"I value my privacy. And I'm certain there is nothing in my home that will tell you where my husband is."

As with Birgit, they asked Lena for an object that would have Hans's fingerprints on it. Floyd suggested a coffee mug. But in Miles's experience, Norwegian housewives of Lena Jensen's sort washed and hand-dried used dishware before it could even so much as be set down in a sink, so he asked for something else. Without any apparent hint of emotion or reluctance, she handed over Hans's expensive looking wooden Hnefatafl game board that she said would have both Hans and Leif's prints because they'd played each other after church every Sunday for many years. She didn't ask that it be returned.

*****

"There was black pepper in those cookies," Floyd said, pulling a face as they left the house.

"It's some traditional Norwegian thing," Miles said. "Not my favorite." He shook his head. "I feel sorry for Hans."

"Maybe he liked pepper cookies."

"No, not because of the awful cookies. Could you imagine being married to that old harpy? I mean, there we are, two complete strangers sitting in her parlor, and without even knowing whether her husband is alive or dead, she's implying that he's a chump who has a habit of blowing the family's money on hair-brained schemes. Poor guy was caught between a rock and a hard place, wasn't he? With that harridan pressing him to make more money, but then flat-out refusing to even consider moving to a town where he might actually be able to make more money at his trade."

"She was being evasive, too," Floyd said. "She knows something."

"Or at least suspects something. Maybe Hans kept her in the dark. But her female intuition tells her that he was definitely up to no good. Let's turn up this alley," Miles said, steering Floyd onto a rutted dirt path that led around the back side of the Jensen's property.

"Where are we going?"

"Hans's tool shed."

"The shed next to that air pump contraption?"

"It's the only shed I saw. I want to get a look inside."

"Why?"

"If I wanted to keep something hidden from my belittling, harridan wife, I'd keep it out back in my tool shed. The man's domain."

"Ah. But wait—you can't just break into his shed."

"I'm sure it won't be that difficult."

"No, I mean you need a warrant."

"A warrant?"

"Under the Fourth Amendment, for a lawful search—"

"I know what a warrant is, Floyd. My question wasn't literal."

"So, then—"

"Floyd, we're on Orcas Island. It's the edge of the world. 50 miles from nowhere. Let's not be anal," he said as they reached the back of the Jensens' property. He walked to where Hans's shed blocked him from direct view from the house, in case Lena happened to look out her back windows. Then he hopped the short picket fence and made his way to the shed's side door. To his relief, it wasn't locked. He turned the knob, gave a gentle shove, and he was in.

The dim interior smelled of dust, burlap, chicken feed, and turpentine, and the only light came from the narrow slit where Miles left the door open a crack. There were well-used garden tools, sacks of feed, jars of nails, hand planes, hammers, various cans of paint and solvent, and one small wooden chest of drawers. Miles went straight to the drawers and began opening them. The first held carving knives and carpenter's pencils. The next, documents. An invoice for 400 fir saplings clipped to a county plat map of a parcel of land just inland from Deer Harbor—perhaps for a Christmas tree farm. Another plat map with arrows and handwriting marking a 'bat cave' up on Mount Woolard, attached to clippings from an outdated U.S. Army index of guano acquisition prices—guano being something the Army once used as a source of saltpeter for its gunpowder. Finally, there were sketches of some sort of rope and pulley mechanism—possibly a hoist Hans intended to install on his boat.

The third drawer contained another sheaf of papers. A nautical chart, an outdated tide chart, and at least a dozen old newspaper clippings. The nautical chart, which covered Haro Strait and D'Arcy Island, was covered with pencil marks. Areas circled, then crossed out and marked with specific dates. Scribbled mathematical calculations. Times and tides. Wind speeds. Depths. As for the newspaper clippings, they all dealt with a single topic.

*****

"What topic?" Floyd asked, eyeballing the nautical chart Miles had burgled as they neared the Deer Harbor dock.

"The wreck of the RMS *Empress of Burma.* A steamship that was headed from Vladivostok, Russia to Vancouver in 1918. It wandered out of the Haro Strait shipping lanes in the late-night darkness, then tore its hull open on the kelp reefs off D'Arcy Island and sank. Somewhere around here," he said, pointing to an area on the chart east of D'Arcy Island.

"I remember reading about that in the *Seattle Times.*"

"This tide chart covers the week of the sinking," Miles added. "It happened when I was over in France. Missed the whole circus. Fortunately, several other vessels were near enough to answer the distress signal, and all but two of the 380-odd passengers and crew were rescued."

"You figure Hans had some kind of salvage scheme in mind?"

"It would explain why he has a deep diving suit and air pump. But to my knowledge, nobody knows exactly where the wreck went down. The ship's forward momentum and a fast-running tide took it into a fog bank as it was sinking. By dawn, there was no trace of her. She's probably in relatively deep water."

"This chart says the area east of D'Arcy is only 115 feet deep."

"115 *fathoms* deep. That's almost 700 feet."

"Oh. Then why on earth would Hans go to the trouble? A lost wreck, possibly in water so deep nobody could dive to it. What's the point? What's his angle?"

"I don't know. But nobody really knows how deep the wreck

is. Maybe it's in shallower waters after all."

"So, let's say Hans located it and it's at an accessible depth. Then what?"

"Beats me. He obviously wasn't equipped to salvage the scrap metal. Maybe the propellers are worth something. Not my province, I'm afraid."

FOURTEEN

Miles got back to the station in the early afternoon to find Bill waxing his boots.

"Any updates, Bill?"

"Luke Gruden radioed to say that they've dragged about an eighth of a square mile of the bottom over near D'Arcy Island, but haven't found anything yet. Oh, and they've already lost two drag rigs by snagging them on reefs. They want to know if you're going to reimburse them. Gruden said he told you so."

"Wonderful. Any calls for me?" he asked, his mind on Marion.

"Yes. But, uh, where's Floyd?" Bill asked, his voice suddenly hushed.

"Ran to his hotel to change out of his salt-sprayed clothes. Why?"

"A fella named John Staggner called. Said he was an old friend of yours. Said he had his cousin in the Seattle Police Department ask around about Floyd."

"And?"

"Said Floyd is supposed to be a straight shooter. A Boy Scout."

"Huh. Well. They always look like that on the outside, right?"

"Some of the cops think he's some sort of a protee, uh, proto . . ."

"Prodigy?"

"That's the word. But Mr. Staggner also said some of the cops don't like Floyd. Call him a know-it-all."

"Ah! He's a pedant." *And probably a lonely man because of it,*

Miles thought.

"He's a what?" Bill asked.

"A pedant. He makes an ostentatious display of his academic . . . He likes to look smart."

"Ah. Well anyway, Mr. Staggner also said you're a rat bastard if you don't call him back to catch up, or better yet come meet his new wife."

"A *rat bastard*?"

"His words."

"Any other calls?"

"No, sir," Bill said. "But I talked to every man on the docks this morning. Not a one of them saw *Lucky Lena* on Tuesday. And the only vessels anyone remembered seeing in Haro Strait or anywhere near D'Arcy Island that evening were two big steamships and one salvager."

"A salvager," Miles echoed, thinking about the dive suit again.

"The *Deepwater Doubloon*, out of Seattle."

"Salvaging what? A wrecked fishing boat?"

"Nobody said. And nobody has seen hide nor hair of *Lucky Lena's* crew. Seems they vanished into thin air."

"Well, shoot," Miles said.

"Also, your mother was just here. Said you forgot your lunch again. Left a basket on your desk."

"Did you look in it?"

"Of course."

"Any cookies?" Miles asked.

"No, sir. No cookies. In fact, she told me to mention that to you."

"She told you to mention to me that she didn't include any cookies?"

"She did."

"For heaven's sake."

"Your mother still makes your lunch?" Floyd asked, appearing in the open front doorway. "Well, well."

"She lives close, and makes herself lunch anyway," Miles said. "It saves money over eating at restaurants."

"Hey, you don't have to justify yourself to us, Miles," Floyd said. "How did you phrase it? If a *grown man* wants his mother to make his lunch every day, that's his prerogative."

That got a laugh from Bill. "He got you there, Sheriff."

"Alright, alright," Miles muttered, grinning. "Where's that giant revolver of yours, funny man?" he asked Floyd.

"At the hotel."

"Bring it to this next interview."

"Really? On this island of sheep and goats and septuagenarians?"

"Yes, really."

"Want me to come along too?" Bill asked.

"I appreciate it, Bill. But if two armed police can't handle one local looney, we need to look for other jobs. Plus, I need you here in case anyone calls in with something important."

Miles grabbed his gun belt from a hook behind his desk, strapped it on, and holstered a fully loaded Model 1911 pistol that he took from a locking desk drawer. Then he and Floyd drove over to the hotel so that Floyd could retrieve his own gun.

"What on earth is that cannon you carry?" Miles asked, eyeballing the large-frame, long-barrel revolver in Floyd's shoulder holster as he got back in the truck.

"Colt New Service. .45 caliber."

"Looks heavy."

"It's no feather. But it always shoots when I pull the trigger. Straight as an arrow."

"Good to know."

"You going to tell me why we need our guns?"

"This next fella, he's big. And volatile."

"Volatile? What is he, a drunk?"

"A preacher."

"Preacher?"

"Lay preacher. Zealot. Temperance fanatic."

"Temperance fanatic! A suspect at last."

"Yes. The good Reverend Gabriel Leviticus McCaskill."

"Middle name Leviticus? And a Highland Scot name? I think I get the picture."

"He moved here from some dead mining town out in the desert wastes of northern Nevada."

"To the deserts go the prophets, as they say."

"And *from* the deserts come the lunatic zealots. McCaskill's a mossy, hotheaded Puget Sound version of Billy Sunday."

"Who?"

"You're not a baseball fan? Billy Sunday was a so-so hitter for the White Sox and Phillies before retiring to become a crazy evangelical prohibitionist who traveled the country preaching fire and brimstone sermons about booze being an instrument of Satan. He even came and spoke at the Odd Fellows Hall here when I was a kid. McCaskill just plagiarized about half his sermon."

"Plenty of regular folks say booze is the Devil. What makes you call McCaskill a lunatic zealot?" Floyd asked.

Miles considered the question. "I'll tell you a little story, Floyd. When I was a kid, I watched McCaskill lash a man with a horsewhip. I mean to within an inch of his life. The man was a drunk, and his now ex-wife was a member of the good reverend's small congregation of sadistic, half-rabid temperance loonies. She asked the reverend to help straighten her husband out. Get him sober. So McCaskill literally dragged the man out of a saloon by his hair, out onto Front Street, where he whipped the living hell out of him right there in broad daylight, shouting scripture between blows, while half the town stood watching like a bunch of damned pigeons."

Miles lost himself in the memory for a moment. McCaskill shouting at poor, stumbling, whimpering Rupert Hawkins, calling him a drunken worm. Beating him savagely. Beating him to the ground, then hollering that he stand back up and face the Lord's punishment. That he drink the wine of God's wrath, poured full strength into the cup of his anger—or some such thing. Telling Hawkins that he'd be tormented with fire and sulfur, and that the smoke of his torment would go up for all eternity. Miles remembered blood flowing from lash cuts on Hawkins's arms, back, neck, and face. Remembered the man at last falling unconscious, his face coming to rest among a scattering of horse droppings in the middle of the muddy street. For his grand finale, McCaskill had thundered to the audience gathered round, "The saloon is the church of the anti-Christ. Liquor steals the soul. Close the saloons, I say. Take the temptation of the Devil's drink away to spare our weaker brothers and sisters."

"Where was the sheriff during all of this?" Floyd asked, bringing Miles back to the present.

"Watching, like everybody else."

"Sounds like the Wild West."

"There's more. A week later, on a hot, dry, moonless July night, the back porch of that same saloon mysteriously caught fire. Building burned to the ground, causing severe burns to the live-in owner and a member of the volunteer fire brigade. No witnesses. No arrests. But probable arson."

"And you suspect McCaskill."

"Damn right I do."

*****

They took Miles's truck out Beaverton Valley Road, into the heavily forested interior of the island, to where Reverend McCaskill had his homestead and self-styled chapel. As they turned off the main road, a dense canopy of tree branches blocked out the sky above the long, winding, fern-lined dirt drive.

"Now *this* is the forest primeval," Floyd said. "Did you ever read Longfellow?"

"My mother made me."

"How cruel."

"She's a retired English teacher."

"Ah."

"I hate poetry."

"So do I."

They emerged into a clearing, maybe an acre in size. Much of it was dotted with large tree stumps—the dead ruins of a once pristine and ancient forest. A cabin with a mossy roof stood alongside a small, unadorned clapboard chapel. McCaskill stood next to it with his back to them, wearing nothing but heavy boots and a homespun loincloth, splitting rounds of maple firewood with a heavy axe. Miles parked the truck and double-checked the chamber of his gun to ensure it had a bullet in it. "This should be nothing if not interesting," he said. "Stay alert."

They got out and approached McCaskill from different angles. Floyd had to go around a large tree stump with a hatchet lodged in the top of it. It stood a few feet from a filthy, overcrowded chickencoop in which several pitiful fowl were missing large patches of feathers and had inflamed peck wounds on their hind quarters. Distracted by the spectacle of the coop, Floyd stepped into a scattering of severed chicken heads alongside the stump.

"Oh!" Floyd said, drawing Miles's attention.

The heads were in various states of decay—some of them relatively fresh, some already hollowed out by wriggling maggots. Flies buzzed overhead. Vertebrae protruded from under bloody neck feathers, and any chicken eyes that were open were glazed with a milky, gummy film. Miles watched as Floyd, looking revolted enough to vomit, tiptoed out of the patch of heads and wiped the soles of his shoes on a clump of dandelions.

McCaskill still held his big axe but had stopped chopping wood and was now turned to face them.

"Reverend," Miles said, coming to a stop a good twelve feet away.

McCaskill—all six-foot-four of him—stood mute, staring at

Miles. He had a long red beard to match his long red hair. His muscular body glistened with the sweat of his labors as his eyes scrutinized the officers with a penetrating, hostile intensity.

"We need to ask you some questions," Miles said. "Put the axe down on the ground and step back away from it."

McCaskill continued to stare. At last, he set the axe down at his feet and in a deep, husky voice said, "You're Nellie Scott's boy."

"And sheriff. We need to know where you were the evening before last."

"Where's Sheriff James?"

"I'm filling in until he comes back."

"You didn't answer my question."

"Sheriff James is convalescing."

"What's wrong with the old bastard?"

"Back trouble."

McCaskill shook his head. "No. Not back trouble. I don't think so."

"Reverend, where were you the evening before last?"

"So, you're just the *acting* sheriff then. Temporary."

"Call it what you will."

"I don't have to call it anything. That's what you are. Acting."

"And sworn in by the county government to enforce the law. So, I'll ask again. Where were you the evening before last?"

"Why do you need to know that?"

"It pertains to an investigation."

"Into what?"

"A murder."

At this, McCaskill's eyes grew dark.

"'Whoever sheds human blood by humans shall their blood be shed, for in the image of God has God made mankind.'"

"Rev—"

"'You shall not murder. Love your neighbor as yourself.'"

Miles took a breath. "Right. I saw your deep love for your neighbor at work when you horsewhipped Mr. Hawkins in the street a few years back. He shed a fair bit of blood too, didn't he?"

The hint of a sinister smile appeared McCaskill's face. "I was trying to save him."

"Kind of you."

"Hawkins was in a saloon partaking of alcohol. I had as much moral right to beat him as I do to beat my own wife when it's called for."

"Of course."

"I trust you know your Book of Ezekiel, Sheriff. If I do not speak out to dissuade a wicked man from his ways, that wicked man will die for his sin, and the Lord will hold me accountable for his blood. But if I do warn the wicked man to turn from his ways and he does not do so, he will die for his sin, yet I will be saved."

"Look, I'm going to ask you one more time—"

"I was here Tuesday evening."

"Here?"

"Right here."

"All evening?"

"All day and all night."

"Doing what?"

"Praying. Threshing barley. Praying again. Greasing a pivot joint on the well pump. Praying, eating, praying, sleeping."

"Can anyone else confirm your presence here?"

"God."

"Right. Anyone else?"

"No."

"Not even your wife?" Miles asked, already knowing she'd left McCaskill the year before and moved back to Nevada. McCaskill didn't answer.

"Reverend, are you familiar with Romans 1:18?”

McCaskill squared his shoulders and looked Miles right in the eye as he spoke. "For the wrath of God is revealed from heaven against all ungodliness and unrighteousness of men."

"I'm obliged to ask you—"

McCaskill raised his hand. "Are you arresting me?"

Miles exchanged glances with Floyd before muttering, "No."

"Then go with God."

"Do you own a boat, reverend?"

Not bothering to answer, McCaskill bent his powerful back to pick up his axe, prompting Miles and Floyd to move their hands toward their guns. But then he turned and went back to his woodpile as if the men had already left.

Miles gave serious thought to cracking McCaskill over the back of the head with the butt of his pistol. But insolent or not, the man was a so-called preacher. The public, and the county council, wouldn't be impressed by an attack on an alleged holy man. Still, Miles was tempted.

As they walked back to the truck, Floyd spotted a small chisel sitting on the top of another tree stump McCaskill seemed to be using as a rough work table. Floyd sidestepped over to the stump and, with just the tips of his thumb and foreigner, carefully picked up the chisel by its blade. "For fingerprints," he said in response to Miles's questioning glance.

*****

"Took it kind of easy on him, didn't you?" Floyd asked as they drove off McCaskill's property, back out onto the main road to Friday Harbor.

"Two of the more screwball county councilmen are members of his congregation."

"And the sheriff answers to the county council."

"Correct."

Floyd nodded. "Then I'm glad I didn't pipe up."

"What do you mean?"

"It would have needlessly enraged him. But I was dying to point out that Jesus turned water into wine for his apostles."

Miles smiled. "I suppose, like most religious people,

McCaskill interprets scripture to say whatever he wants it to say."

"I'm guessing you aren't religious."

"Good guess."

"Not at all?"

Mile shrugged. "Let's say I'm agnostic." He considered asking Floyd whether he was religious, but he didn't see much of a point.

"Unfortunately," Floyd said, "all we learned is that McCaskill has no verifiable alibi. Though I will say his responses and demeanor were extraordinarily odd. It seemed as if he were angry and amused at the same time. What do you suppose that was about?"

"Who knows?" Miles said. "You ask me, lay preachers are all lunatics. I mean, really, you can't find *one* mad hatter denomination that'll stoop to take your application money and ordain you? That's saying something."

"Amen."

"What did you make of him?"

"You mean do I think he's a killer?" Floyd asked.

"Yes."

"With all that smoldering anger? Bearing in mind that he's perfectly willing to horsewhip a man unconscious as half the town looks on? Sure. I could see him snapping. Smiling as he cut someone's throat open with a straight razor."

"And again," Miles said, "he'd probably find some way to twist scripture to justify it."

"They always do."

They passed a car headed in the opposite direction, trailing a thick plume of blue oil smoke that got them both coughing.

"Then again," Miles said once they cleared the smoke, "McCaskill's hot-blooded. And you said the murder scene implicated a methodical, cold-blooded killer."

"Well, I'm no doctor of psychology. But yes, I would guess that whoever hijacked the *Lucky Lena* may be afflicted with *mania sans délire*."

"Sounds like a French cheese."

"It's something Doctor Julius Koch would call *psychopastiche.*"

"For heaven's sake, speak English, man."

"Psychopathy. Moral insanity. A lack of empathy or remorse."

"Your point being that a raging hothead like McCaskill would have left behind a very different-looking crime scene—especially if he were dealing with rumrunners."

"I think the crime scene would have been more indicative of a furious anger."

"Like how?"

"I don't know. Maybe he would have nailed his victims to crosses."

FIFTEEN

"Any calls for me?" Miles asked once again as soon as he and Floyd walked through the front door of the station.

"No, sir," Bill said. "Are you expecting a particularly important call or something?"

"I—no."

"Well, anyhow, did you get to look over the steamship passenger lists yet?"

"Only the first page."

"Take a look at this," Bill said, handing one of the pages to Miles. "About halfway down."

"What is it?"

"Two Chinks came in on the *Bangor*," Bill said.

"Two Chinese arrived from Seattle on the SS *Bangor*?"

"Last Saturday. Three days before the bloodbath on the *Lucky Lena*."

"Is it unusual for Chinese to come in on the *Bangor*?" Floyd asked.

"Very," Miles said. "Especially in September. Most Chinese here are seasonal cannery workers. They come up in early summer, usually by hitching a free ride from Seattle or Port Townsend on one of the cannery's tenders or cargo boats—not on the regular passenger steamer."

Halfway down the page, Miles saw the names Wong Chun Ting and Kwan Ping.

"May I?" Floyd asked, looking over Miles's shoulder. "Those are Cantonese names."

"Pardon?"

"Those names. They're Cantonese people. The surnames, Wong and Kwan, are Romanized in the Cantonese manner."

"Romanized?"

"Changed from traditional Chinese to our alphabet."

"Ah."

"There are dozens of dialects and individual languages in China," Floyd said. "Mandarin and Cantonese, for example, are different languages. They share some vocabulary, but are considered mutually unintelligible."

"As if this case couldn't get any more complicated," Miles said.

"In each language, they tend to convert words to Roman script in differing ways. Like if you speak Mandarin, Wong and Kwan are spelled h-u-a-n-g and g-u-a-n, respectively."

"All sounds like barbarian gibberish to me," Bill mumbled.

"My point being," Floyd continued as he handed the manifest back to Miles, "that a lot of the Seattle tongs are made up of Cantonese people."

"And the two Chinks are still here," Bill said.

"Is that right?" Miles asked.

"Their names aren't on any departure manifests. So, unless they hired a private boat to take them off the island—which I doubt a couple of dirty coolies could afford—they haven't gone nowhere."

"Then first thing tomorrow, let's try to find masters Wong and Kwan."

"Here's something else," Floyd said, still looking at the list, sounding surprised. "Edward Callahan arrived on the same boat as Wong and Kwan."

"Who's Edward Callahan?" Miles asked.

"A bigwig in the Knights of Labor."

"Isn't that some sort of guild?"

"No, it's a scattered, dying labor union."

"Oh—right, right."

"Matter of fact," Floyd went on, "Callahan was one of the

ringleaders of the Seattle General Strike of 1919. And he's big on anti-Oriental rhetoric. Former Mayor Hanson had the police knock him over the head and throw him in jail for promoting Bolshevism amongst the longshoremen. I guess he's finally out on parole."

"A red who doesn't like the yellows, huh?" Miles said. "And here I thought the Bolsheviks were promoting one big, happy, hand-holding family of workers."

"Right," Floyd said. "Big, happy, and family. Isn't there a contradiction in terms in there somewhere?"

"You think Callahan's being here might have something to do with our investigation?" Miles said.

Floyd took a swallow of stale, bitter coffee and pulled a face. "I doubt it. It's just interesting."

*****

Back home, over a supper of hot Irish stew and soda bread, Miles gave his mother an overview of the case and what they'd learned so far.

"Needless to say, I doubt the hijackers were local," he told her at the end of his summary.

"Don't be naïve," Nellie said.

"I'm—" *Don't respond. Just breathe.* "Is there dessert?"

"Not for you."

He shook his head and sopped up the last of his stew with a piece of soda bread. "This stew is delicious."

"Thank you. Have you given any more thought to taking Sophie Gunderson to the Odd Fellows Dance?"

"For the last time, I am not taking Sophie Gunderson to the dance. Not for all the dessert in this house."

His mother stared at him. It seemed to Miles that she didn't blink. "I've been giving further thought to our conversation during yesterday's breakfast, Miles."

Here we go again.

"I know that you haven't been sleeping well," she said. "That you've been venturing out in the middle of the night."

"So?"

"What do you do out there night after night?"

"Keep an eye on things. It *is* my job."

"Do you set your alarm clock to wake you?"

"Why is that relevant?"

"Do you?"

"No."

"Then what is it that wakes you?"

"I don't know." He shrugged. "Noises. The call of nature, maybe."

"No."

"No? Wait, is this another one of those questions you ask where you already know the answer but just want to toy with me?"

Nellie reached out and whacked his knuckles with her serving spoon again.

"Hey!" He drew his hand away and rubbed his throbbing knuckles.

"I don't care for your tone." As she said this, presumably not wanting to miss out, Monsieur Rousseau dug his claws into Miles's leg under the table.

"Ow! Devil cat!"

Nellie gave him a moment to gather himself. "What is your mind dwelling on when you wake up in the middle of the night, Miles? Don't lie, or I'll know and I'll whack you again."

He turned to stare out the kitchen window that looked over their orchard. "What's my mind dwelling on as I wake?" He took a breath. "I don't know. Usually nothing, I guess."

"Do you wake feeling anxious?"

Now he met his mother's gaze. "I have an easy life, mother. An easy job, a roof over my head, plenty to eat. What would I be anxious about?"

"That doesn't answer my question."

"Anxious?" he said again. "It's hard to say whether—"

"We all need love, Miles."

"Huh?"

"It's human nature to need it. Without love, our lives are empty and lonely and dark and we grow anxious."

"And taking Sophie Gunderson to the Odd Fellows Dance will fix it?"

"Don't be fatuous. I'm telling you that love is the remedy for your anxiety."

"If you say so."

"You know I'm right."

"You always say that."

"I'm always right," she said as Monsieur Rousseau hopped up onto her lap and turned to stare at Miles with his unblinking demon eyes.

Forgoing a rebuttal despite the temptation, Miles took another deep breath and rubbed his whacked knuckles. "Anyway, I have another interesting bit of news."

"Tell me."

"Marion Forde is back in town."

Nellie stared, expressionless.

"You have no response?" Miles asked. "Wait—did you know already?"

Silence.

"You did. You knew she was here. And you weren't going to tell me?"

"I know how you feel about her."

Miles shrugged. "She's my best and oldest friend."

"Friendship is fine. Courtship is something else entirely."

"Who said anything about courtship?"

"I'm not a fool."

For the sake of his knuckles, Miles again held his tongue despite all of the biting responses that came to mind. "I'm at a bit of a loss, then. Ten seconds ago, you were telling me I needed to find love. What are you telling me now? You don't approve of

Marion?"

"I like her very much. But she is not for you."

Miles's jaw froze open. "Why on earth would you say that, Mother?"

"She—San Juan Island is not the place for Marion Forde."

"Who is it the place for?"

"Not her."

"Mother, we grew up together. We already know each other like family. We share a million common interests. We're like two versions of the same person."

"But you're a man."

"Correct."

"Marion is not for you, Miles. She's never been interested in you in a remotely romantic way. And whatever she experienced living in New York for two years has made her even more unattainable. Trust me."

"I don't know what you're talking about."

"Miles, for your own good, and if you genuinely care one bit about Marion's happiness, you mustn't pursue her."

As he washed the dishes, Miles dwelt on his mother's once again confusing and acutely irritating comments. He couldn't fathom why she would describe Marion as unattainable. Was he somehow beneath Marion now that she'd lived out east? That was ridiculous. He was intelligent, more or less. He was cultured, wasn't he? He'd been to Europe. He played Sidney Bechet, for heaven's sake.

You play the saxophone like a bull moose, his mother repeated in his mind.

Halfway through scrubbing the stew pot, he realized he was grinding his teeth.

*****

Miles rang Marion as soon as his mother went to bed. "You were supposed to call me," he said, barely speaking above a whisper so that his mother wouldn't hear.

"I know. I meant to. My mother has been very needy today. She's worrying about my grandfather."

"Of course, of course. I'm chiding you. What are you doing right now?"

"Right now?"

"Let's sneak down to Mulno Cove and have a bonfire," he suggested, referring to their favorite childhood stomping ground.

"Bonfire?"

"And catch up."

"Well, Miles, I couldn't just leave Sylvia here, you know, at the mercy of my crazy mother," Marion said with a laugh.

"So bring her."

"She's already preparing for bed."

"I see. Well, I know I'll see you tomorrow night."

"Tomorrow night?"

"The Odd Fellows Hall Dance. You wouldn't miss that."

"Oh! No, I wouldn't! How fabulous!"

"I'll pick you up at seven."

"That sounds just great, Miles, except that your truck only has two seats."

"So?"

"I'll have to bring Sylvia."

"Ah."

"She *is* my guest here."

"Of course. Yes, of course. Well, I'm sure we can all squeeze into the truck."

"Squeeze into your truck in our finest dresses? Ha. I think we'll just meet you at the Odd Fellows Hall."

Damn.

"Okay, then. Sounds good."

He hung up, frustrated that he wouldn't have Marion all to himself. But picturing her dancing across the floor of the Odd Fellows Hall in some fancy New York dress brought a smile to his face. Made him feel warm all over.

He turned off the main floor lamps, brushed his teeth, and got into bed, where he had an utterly tranquil night of deep and uninterrupted sleep.

SIXTEEN

One Month Earlier

The first stretch of time on the boat was like a bad dream. The room we were in was cramped and cold and loud, with a noise like never-ending thunder. We were given no food. The boat rolled and pitched, throwing us against the walls or into one another even if we sat on the wet floor. During a very rough period, one of the heavy wooden casks broke loose and rolled around, smashing into us and crashing against the walls until we could tip it on end in a corner and wedge blankets against it. There were twisted ankles and jammed fingers and bloody noses. And since we couldn't see in the darkness, we had to grope around to find anything, including the waste barrel that we each visited over and over again to vomit because of a strange nausea we all seemed to get at once. At least, since we hadn't been fed, there was little to throw up.

I had no idea when it was day or night. But now, at least, there was nobody to keep us from talking. Sitting against the cold metal walls, holding hands in the darkness, clumping together for warmth, a few of us whispered to each other. We learned that we were all from small, poor villages like mine, from up and down the great river valley. The young daughters of farmers and craftsmen, our homes and villages ruined by the flood, our families hungry. All with the same story of hushed conversations between our fathers and the man from the city. Of being sent away from our families without explanation. Of tearful but obedient departures. Some of us shared our names. Some of us were afraid to. There was a girl named Liu and a girl named Cai. Also, Zhong and Chen. All of us ached with hunger.

Feeling as if my belly might collapse in on itself, I started to daydream about food. Special dishes for holidays in those few years when the harvest was bountiful. When times were good. Boiled eggs with a little bit of salt sprinkled on top. Steamed dumplings filled with pork and ginger and dipped in black vinegar. Moon cakes filled with sweet lotus seed paste. Cups of hot, strong tea. I could picture these treats sitting on the little round table in our house, the hot dishes still steaming, the moon cakes stacked two and three high. The family gathered around. My grandmother still alive. My older brothers still with us. My father smiling. All of us grateful for our good fortune.

The boat leaned way over and one of the girls fell against me, shattering my vision of delicious food, returning me to the present. I licked my arm because the salt on my skin tasted good. But it didn't fill my belly. At least there was water. Sometimes I would take the cup lashed to the water barrel and spill some on the floor and let Snow drink from the little puddle while I held her.

SEVENTEEN

Miles sprang from bed in the violet predawn light and made himself a breakfast of fried eggs, buttered toast, and strong coffee. He cut his mother a bouquet of fresh dahlias, left it in a mason jar of water on her sewing table, then hummed "Cuban Moon" as he drove to work thinking that someone should invent a radio that could be installed in a car.

Entering the station, he smiled upon seeing Floyd carving up one of Bill's giant flapjacks. It was drizzled with honey and a large scoop of fresh butter was slowly sliding toward the edge, leaving a track of melted goodness as it went. "Bill makes a damned good flapjack, doesn't he?" Miles asked.

"The best," Floyd answered through a big mouthful.

"You'll need a 10-hour nap after you're done though. I suspect that he makes them out of buttered concrete. But he'll neither confirm nor deny."

That got a smile from Bill. "It's a secret recipe."

Miles told the men of his suggested first stops for finding Wong Chun Ting and Kwan Ping, the Cantonese men who'd arrived on the *Bangor* shortly before the *Lucky Lena* killings. Bill balked at Miles's idea of visiting what Bill liked to call Chink House—the rooming house, known to most islanders as China House, that housed a substantial number of the Chinese seasonal workers who came for jobs at Friday Harbor's cannery during salmon season. So Miles and Floyd set off on their own. It was a simple, white-painted wooden building that reminded Miles of common army barracks.

China House was situated on a small hillside a few blocks up from the southernmost end of the town waterfront, its surrounding grounds planted with various leafy green vegetables sown in neat, weed-free squares of rich tilled earth. Three slouching Chinese men in worn out homespun work shirts and trousers eyeballed Miles and Floyd from a narrow deck that ran along one side of the building, watching them right to the door as they smoked what looked like hand-rolled cigarettes. Entering, Miles and Floyd were greeted by the smell of frying onions wafting into the tiny front office from a doorway leading to the kitchen. The office, with its curiously low ceiling, had a simple wood desk and was decorated with nothing more than a Chinese calendar and a small brass chime that hung from a derelict ceiling fan. An aged Chinese man in an oversized work shirt was reading a Chinese language newspaper. He rose from a creaking desk chair as the men walked in.

"Oh, Mister Miles," the man said, smiling as he gave a short bow.

"Henry. How are you, sir?" He'd only ever known the man as Henry and had no clue as to his surname. Nor his real given name, for that matter.

"Business slow. But good health. No back pain now."

"I'm glad to hear it."

"Yes. How I can help you, Mister Miles?"

"We're looking for a couple of Chinese fellows who came into town this week. I figured they might be staying here. We just need to talk to them for a minute or two."

"This week?" Henry asked, just as another Chinese man—a cook by the look of him—appeared in the entrance to the hallway and gave Henry a hard stare. "Oh, ah, no. Nobody new in house this week. No new men in house since June."

"Are you sure? Their names are Wong Chun Ting and Kwan Ping. Floyd here says they're Cantonese."

Hearing this, Henry met his cook's stare for a brief moment, then said, "Cantonese?" Miles had always thought of Henry as a cool customer. Stoic. But now he looked spooked. The cook did too.

"Came up from Seattle on the *Bangor* last Saturday," Miles said. "The steamship office has no record of them departing, so I assume they're still on the island."

"Ha. I," Henry managed before going mute.

"You know these men, I take it?"

"Oh, ah, no."

"No?"

"No men like that here. No Cantonese here. No."

"But you've seen them? Or at least heard about them?"

"I—no. No."

"You look troubled, Henry."

"Oh, Cantonese, you know, not good people." He put on a toothy smile. "Cantonese eat anything!" he said with sudden volume before belting out a laugh that lasted a moment too long.

"You aren't Cantonese?"

"Me? No! No, I am from Sichuan Province."

"I see. Well, we'd like to speak with your boarders, regardless."

"All at cannery."

"Except the three sitting out on the deck?"

"Right. Right. No work for them today. New machine take their jobs."

"New machine?"

"For fish. Yes. New machine take many jobs."

"I'm sorry to hear that. But since they're here, we might as well start with the three men outside."

"Yes, yes. Okay. You want I interpret?"

"Please."

"Yes. No problem," Henry said, coming out from behind the desk and leading the officers out the front door. But when they turned the corner onto the deck, the three men were gone.

EIGHTEEN

Friday Harbor's fish cannery sat on a broad pier held up by dozens of creosoted pilings, most of which were leaning to some extent, making the whole structure look as if it might collapse and fall into the water at any moment. The building itself was a giant windowless block of weathered tin and wood siding, featuring numerous gaping service entrances for taking in netloads of whole salmon and halibut and turning out crates of canned fish. As Miles and Floyd approached, a handful of Chinese men in filthy work clothes who were smoking out front made themselves scarce.

"What a smell," Floyd said as they got close.

"At least the cannery is usually downwind of town. When we get a rare east wind, the restaurants all close down because nobody can eat with that stench hanging in the air."

The smell was twice as bad once they stepped through the front door, the fishy air thick and damp. The building was filled with men, machinery, and equipment—chutes, conveyer belts, can fabricators, vats, and steam kettles—humming, squeaking, clanking, and hissing in a symphony of industrial noise. At a steel table running the length of the far wall, a dozen Chinese laborers wearing bloody, slime-smeared aprons and holding long steel knives were gutting hundreds of salmon that had just been offloaded from a fishing boat tied up on the harbor side of the building. Many of the fish were still alive, their mouths opening and closing as they seemed to gasp for air even as the laborers sliced their bellies open from anus to gills, ripped out their living guts, and tossed them into a waste sluice that ran under the table and out of the building. The sluice, in turn, led to a crusty pipe that discharged a steady stream of guts, fins, heads, and bloody water out the back of the cannery and into the harbor below where half a dozen bald eagles perched on pilings waiting to scavenge the best bits.

"You alright?" Miles shouted at Floyd over the noise. "You look a bit pale."

"It's an ugly business."

"Just thank your lucky stars you're at the top of the food chain."

"Amen."

In the middle of the cannery floor, halfway down a conveyor belt-fed processing line, stood a monstrous, new-looking machine of moving gears, levers, and pistons. Whole salmon were going in one end of the machine and coming out the other end gutted with heads and fins removed.

"Impressive, isn't it?" a white man shouted over the noise from just behind them. It was the foreman, Clyde Crieff, one of only two non-Chinese in the building. "It's the Smith Butchering Machine, better known as the Iron Chink. Guts salmon as fast as my ten best Chinese put together. You're looking at the future, boys."

"Can we talk somewhere?" Miles shouted back.

"Office," Crieff said, pointing at a door in the south wall of the cannery. He led them across the busy floor. As they made their way, it struck Miles as odd that none of the Chinese men in the building made eye contact with him. But it was clear they were keeping tabs on the officers with their peripheral vision, because they invariably drew away whenever the white men approached.

"What can I do for you, Miles?" Crieff asked once the door was shut, cutting off most of the noise. Crieff had employed Miles as a part-time truck driver for a couple of seasons shortly before the war. They liked each other.

"Looking for a couple of Chinese," Miles said.

"You came to the right place."

"Cantonese men. Names of Wong Chun Ting and Kwan Ping. Arrived last weekend."

"Oh. I haven't brought on any new guys since June. In fact, with the Iron Chink up and running, I'm having to lay men off. They keep coming back each morning, asking, *More work? More work*? I've been telling them no more work. They just keep coming back. Probably hoping the machine breaks down. Feel kind of bad for them, truth be told. They're good workers."

"Can we ask your men if they've seen or heard of these guys?"

"Be my guest. Incidentally, have you fellas seen Angus Cooper around?"

"Cooper," Miles repeated. "Captain of a workboat, right? The *Dahlia* or the *Daisy* or whatever?"

"The *Daisy*. Yes. That's the fella. Widower. Lives out Bailer Hill Road. Has a young daughter who's a lunatic. He was supposed to bring me a shipment of tin blanks for the canning machine day before yesterday. I paid him in advance, and off he went to Bellingham. Now I can't find him anywhere. And I'm about to run out of tin."

"We'll ask around. In the meantime . . ."

"Of course, of course. Wu?" he shouted. A Chinese man in clean clothes appeared in the doorway to an adjoining room. "Mr. Wu here is my bookkeeper and liaison with the other Chinese employees. He can interpret for you if you like."

After explaining, in halting English, that he and all the cannery workers were Mandarin speakers, Wu led the officers through the cannery, going from man to man, asking the same series of questions. Did anyone know the mysterious Cantonese men? Had they seen them? Heard anything about them? Did they have any idea as to their whereabouts? Once again avoiding eye contact with Miles, even as they answered his questions, they all pled utter ignorance. But they also looked scared. Every last one of them.

*****

"So, what was going on there?" Floyd asked as they walked back to the station.

"You mean with the reticence over speaking with us?" Miles said.

"With the *terror* over speaking with us, I'd call it. Are they that afraid of the law? Of white men?"

"They shouldn't be. I don't think anyone messes with them up here. And they basically keep to themselves. Never cause any trouble. And come to think of it, they never seemed particularly fearful back when I drove a truck for the cannery."

"Maybe they fear retribution."

"Nobody likes a rat," Miles said.

"But retribution from their fellow laborers, or from someone else?"

"You mean our recent Cantonese arrivals?"

"Well, as I mentioned, the tongs are largely made up of Cantonese. And the tongs each have contingents of hard men they call *boo how doy*, or highbinders. They're the soldiers. The dreaded enforcers."

"Hatchet men."

"If you like. They've certainly been known to plant hatchets in their enemies' skulls now and then. Hatchets, ice axes, meat cleavers. You name it."

"Are you suggesting that the Cantonese men who arrived on the *Bangor* may be two of these tong highbinders, as you call them?" Miles asked.

"It would explain the uncharacteristic fear on the faces of the cannery workers."

"And it might substantiate the theory that a tong was involved in the hijacking of the *Lucky Lena*. Like maybe the highbinders were the perpetrators."

"Or maybe it was their tong's shipment that was hijacked, so they're here trying to figure out what happened. Trying to figure out who to exact their revenge on."

The men froze in their tracks as a black-tailed doe and her two downy, speckled fawns emerged from an alleyway and crossed the street a few dozen yards ahead of them before disappearing into a thicket of blackberry bushes.

"So, Floyd."

"So, Miles."

"There's a social event this evening."

"Social event?"

"A dance, *strictly speaking*," Miles said with a smirk. "At the Odd Fellows Hall. The annual summer knees-up."

"Sounds like the event of the season."

"It's a big thing for the islands. A lot of young people come in on the inter-island steamer."

"Like young people from Deer Harbor? Friends of Leif Jensen, maybe?"

"Exactly. Might be a good chance to find out if anyone has heard anything. It's a small county, in some ways. Insular and gossipy. Word travels quickly. Anyway, it's after work hours. But if you're interested, you're welcome to come along. We'll get you back to your hotel before bedtime. Your mother will never be the wiser."

"Ha-ha. What are you going to wear?"

"What am I going to *wear*? I'm pretty sure you're the first man to ever ask me a question like that."

"I mean what's the dress code?"

"Have you never been to a dance hall?"

"Sheriff," Bill shouted, trotting down the street from the opposite direction.

"What is it?" Miles asked as they converged.

"Jake Wolfram said he saw the two Chinks."

"Jake Wolfram?"

"Driver for the Roche Harbor lime works."

"Oh, right."

"Jake was waiting for a scheduled pickup down by the docks last Tuesday when he saw two unusually well-dressed Chinks come out of the terminal as the *Bangor* was unloading. Saw them hop into Rupert Hawkins's car, quick, and drive away."

"Rupert Hawkins, huh?"

"Yes, sir."

"*Quick,* like the Chinese wanted to keep a low profile? Like they didn't want to be seen?"

"That's how it sounded."

"Who's Rupert Hawkins?" Floyd asked.

"Remember my story of Reverend McCaskill horsewhipping a drunk in the street?"

"How could I forget?"

"Hawkins was the drunk. He's an on-again, off-again deckhand for any captain desperate or fool enough to hire him on for a day or two. And sometimes he makes a little extra hooch money by working as an unofficial taxi, picking people up from arriving steamships in his rusty old Crow-Elkhart."

"Let's go talk to him."

"Tomorrow. He'll be three sheets to the wind by this hour. Won't remember his own name."

*****

Miles and Floyd spent a tedious couple of hours examining duplicate sets of the fingerprints Floyd had lifted off the *Lucky Lena*, comparing them to samples they'd obtained from the various objects they'd seized. To Miles's disappointment, none of the prints taken off the boat matched any taken from Reverend McCaskill's chisel—though McCaskill would likely have been wearing gloves if he were the hijacker. And aside from the expected matches to the objects taken from the Jensens' homes, the one notable discovery was that a print Floyd took off of the severed finger matched the print of Hans Jensen's index finger taken off his wooden game board.

"Well," Miles said, sounding down, "if Hans Jensen is still alive, which I tend to doubt, then he's probably very unhappy."

Yearning to stretch their stiff legs, Miles and Floyd walked down to the docks to ask if anyone had seen Angus Cooper, his boat the *Daisy*, or two unusually well-dressed Chinese men. No one had. All Miles and Floyd got for their trouble were frantic questions from wide-eyed fishermen and deckhands. Had the police caught the killers yet? Had they at least found the Jensens' bodies? Did they have any promising leads? Did the sheriff think any of them were in danger? Nobody had anything helpful to say.

NINETEEN

The calm, warm air smelled of dry grass, and the sky was lit the deep blue-purple of dusk as Miles and Floyd made their way across town toward the Odd Fellows Hall. The *de facto* hub of island social life, it sat on a bluff a block up from the waterfront, commanding a stellar view of the expanse of Friday Harbor. Boats of all sorts bobbed in its sheltered waters, the reflection of their anchor lights seeming to create a second universe of stars below the town.

The façade of the hall itself was adorned with large amber lightbulbs that hung from strings of sagging wire. Groups of well-dressed young people were converging on the hall from all directions, including at least two dozen who were hiking up the hill from the just-arrived inter-island steamer. Even from nearly two blocks away, Miles could hear live music from within.

As they walked through the front door, Miles and Floyd were greeted with the cacophony of loud music and innumerable conversations, along with stuffy air that smelled of perfume, tobacco smoke, and sweat. Strings of multicolored lights spread outward across the ceiling from a point directly over the stage where a tuxedoed, fourteen-piece band from Seattle played away under red, white and blue bunting that had been left up since the 4th of July. There were rows of small tables flanking the walls—one of which held plates of tea cakes, a large punchbowl, and glasses. But most of the partygoers were either standing in groups toward the back of the hall or dancing up near the stage.

"You're a jazz aficionado, right?" Floyd half shouted. "This song. It's Paul Whiteman, isn't it?"

"The so-called King of Jazz. Yes."

"You sound dubious."

"Paul Whiteman is a white man."

"So?"

"If any man can be called the king of jazz, that man would have to be a negro."

"That right?"

"Hey—see her, over there," he said, pointing to a young woman in a yellow silk chiffon dress. "I'm pretty sure she's from Deer Harbor. Let's go see if she knows Leif Jensen."

She did know Leif Jensen. But not well enough to know anything useful to the investigation. It was the same story with two other Deer Harbor residents the young woman directed them to.

"Now what?" Floyd asked as they went out the back door to get some fresh air on the lawn.

"Let's linger for a bit. More folks may arrive yet."

"From Deer Harbor? Any who were going to come would have arrived on that last inter-island steamer, don't you think."

"Got somewhere else to be?"

"Well . . ."

"The music's good, isn't it?"

"I suppose."

"Alright then."

"Can I ask you something?" Floyd said as they leaned against the outside of the building. "How does a 24-year-old end up as sheriff of an entire county?"

"I was only a deputy until around six months ago. As McCaskill was so happy to point out, I'm only acting sheriff. Because Sheriff James isn't well."

"Back trouble, right?"

"Officially, yes. Unofficially, between you and me, he's going senile. The family doesn't want people to know."

"I see. Still, there must be other deputies with more experience. No offense."

"I was the only deputy on San Juan Island. The other two live on Orcas and Lopez islands. But Friday Harbor is the county seat, so it needs somebody, and nobody wanted to move here. So lucky me, I got to be acting sheriff."

"You don't sound terribly enthusiastic."

"I didn't even want to be a deputy. It was my mother's idea. Said I needed a respectable, steady job before any of the domesticated local hens would deign to marry me. Heaven forbid."

"So why not fish or farm or something?" Floyd asked. "Why be a copper if you don't like the work? Being a lawman isn't anyone's idea of lucrative, obviously."

"It's what I know. Because I'm big, they made me a military policeman when I was with the AEF," he said, referring to the American Expeditionary Forces.

"You were in the Great War?"

"Spent three months guarding supply yards and busting drunk doughboy heads in Neufchâteau, then had another few months in Verdun."

"See any combat?"

"Sure. In the bars."

"Well, what does your father do?"

"He died when I was overseas. 1918."

"I'm sorry. Spanish flu?"

"Yup," Miles said, his mind randomly flashing back to a happy memory of his father teaching him how to operate a Bull tractor they'd borrowed to plow one of their fields, then laughing himself to tears when Miles fell face-down in the mud while trying to hand-crank the engine.

"Since we're on the subject," Miles said, "how did *you* get to be a detective at such a young age?"

"Part ability, part luck."

"How's that?"

"As for ability, when I was a rookie, I latched onto a detective who was looking into a stabbing on my beat off Yesler Way in

Downtown Seattle. He taught me the basics of crime scene analysis. I was hooked, so I took a couple of semi-related classes at the University of Washington. Turned out there was a need in the department for some of the new scientific techniques I'd learned about at UW."

"And the luck?"

"My father knew the chief of police through his Masonic Lodge. Chief did him a favor."

The allegedly crooked chief of police, William Severyns, Miles thought. *Well, well.* "And what does *your* father do?"

"Feeds daffodils."

"A gardener?"

"No, he's dead too."

"Oh. I'm sorry. Spanish flu?"

"Got hit by a truck after stepping off the trolley on 1st Avenue. Ironic, given that he ran a trucking company."

A trucking company, Miles thought, wondering whether it ran booze for the crooked chief of police. He eyeballed Floyd with resurgent suspicion. The guy seemed so sincere. But it just didn't add up—how he was already a detective at age 24, and, more importantly, how he suddenly appeared in Friday Harbor to help investigate a probable rumrunner hijacking.

As they stepped back inside, Miles noticed that a crowd had formed around two women who were stomping and twirling through dance moves as the band blasted out a fast-paced tune Miles hadn't heard before. As he maneuvered for a better look, he saw that one of the dancers was Marion. His face broke out in a smile.

She was stealing the show in a low-waisted, knee-length dress adorned with countless strings of tiny, jade-green glass beads, a cream-colored feather headband around her dark bobbed hair, and a pair of pearl necklaces that flew about as she danced. Her face was flushed with effort, but she smiled. Next to her, her friend Sylvia—striking in her own right with her short hair pomaded back and dressed in an understated blouse and tie, trousers with suspenders, and what looked like a men's hat. The women mirrored one another's dance moves in almost perfect synchronicity. But all eyes in the hall, male and female, were locked on Marion.

"Recognize anyone else from Deer Harbor?" Floyd shouted over the music. "Or can we finally get out of here?"

"Hold on. I need to talk to somebody."

As he said this, the band wound up the song and shared the crowd's uproarious applause with Marion and Sylvia. Shifting gears, the bandleader got his players started on a slower song. As the circle of spectators dispersed, Marion spotted Miles, grabbed Sylvia's hand, and led her right toward him.

TWENTY

"There you are," Marion said to Miles with a beaming smile and a long hug as they came together in the middle of the dance floor. "I was worried you weren't going to come."

"Here I am," he said with a huge smile of his own.

Marion gave him an expectant look, then gestured toward Floyd.

"Ah, oh," Miles said. "Mr. Ashton Floyd, may I introduce my very good friend, Miss Marion Forde, and her friend, Miss Sylvia, ah . . ."

"Rosen," Sylvia said, shaking Floyd's hand.

"Rosen. Yes. Forgive me."

Floyd stood ramrod straight, as if at attention in front of an Army drill sergeant. He didn't so much as mutter a greeting.

"Floyd?" Miles said. "You doing alright?"

"Yes. Fine. Thanks."

"Okay, then," Miles said before turning back to Marion. "Tell us, what was that dance you two were just burning up the floor with?"

"It's a new one they call the Black Bottom," Sylvia said. "We just learned it at a negro joint called Leroy's Harlem Cabaret."

"In New York?"

"Yes, sir. New York City."

"Which means it'll be popular out here on the West Coast in about thirty years," Marion said with a wink.

"You two had the hall transfixed," Miles said. "Of course, Marion has always been a hell of a dancer."

"So have you," she said. "Promise you'll dance the Texas

Tommy with me later."

"If the band will play it."

"I'll make them. Let's go outside for a cigarette."

From the back of a nearby chair, she grabbed a small, green, beaded purse that matched her dress, then led them out the back door to where Miles and Floyd had stood barely five minutes earlier. Extracting a tiny, silver cigarette case, she got herself and Sylvia cigarettes, both of which Sylvia lit with a smooth flip of her lighter.

"Either of you care for a Lucky Strike?" Sylvia asked. "A little puff-puff to take the edge off? Mr. Floyd? You certainly look like you could use it. No offense."

"No thanks," the men said in unison.

"A relaxing evening stroll then?"

"Maybe in a bit," Miles said. "We're kind of still on the job."

"At this hour?" Marion said. "Moonlighting as bouncers?"

"We're hoping to see someone from Deer Harbor who can answer some questions for us."

"We won't pry, then."

"We won't?" Sylvia said.

"Why don't you tell us about New York," Miles said.

"Oh, Miles," Marion crooned. "It's glorious. Absolutely divine. The music, the dancing, the art, the food. All the different sorts of people. The frenetic pace. The architecture—holy cats! They have skyscrapers there that make the Smith Tower look like a child's toy. Lots of them."

"I passed it on my way back from Europe," Miles said. "We docked in New Jersey and I had to get straight on the train, so I didn't get to visit Manhattan Island. But the skyline alone was something to behold."

"Once you visit," Marion said, "once you feel the city's surging energy, you just know this is going to be America's century. But blah, blah, blah. Enough about New York. What about you? How was the war? You don't look any the worse for wear."

"Not on the outside."

"What do you mean?"

"I'm pulling your leg. Ah—what can I tell you? France taught me to love good food. To love wine. Of course, now I can't get any thanks to Prohibition."

They all waited for him to say more. He didn't.

"Well, that was an exhaustive report," Sylvia said. "Thanks for enlightening us."

Miles smiled. "Ah, you know. It's sort of hard to describe."

"Were you in many battles?" Marion asked.

"Marion!" Sylvia said, shaking her head in disapproval of the question.

"No battles, as a matter of fact. I was always in the rear areas. A military policeman. Still, I saw a lot of truly horrible, uh . . ." His voice trailed off as he turned his head away, staring out into the darkness. "Sorry."

"Well, you're back, safe and sound, thanks be to God, his archangels, and the Great Northern Railway," Marion said. "And now you're sheriff. How about that?"

"It's a living."

"Do you have any good crime stories?"

"Oddly enough," he said, "we just started working a probable multiple murder aboard a fishing boat out of Deer Harbor."

"I heard. What's the scoop?"

"Well, it all started Tuesday morning when the lightkeeper at Turn Point spotted—"

"Miles, it's an active investigation," Floyd said. "We really shouldn't discuss it."

"He speaks!" Sylvia said with exaggerated shock. "I was beginning to wonder if you were mute, Detective Floyd."

"Oh, I . . ." Floyd stammered.

"Marion is family, Floyd. And who is Sylvia going to spill the beans to? She's from New York."

"Yes, ah, be that as it may, I don't think—"

"Floyd, let's not lose our sense of perspective," Miles said.

Hearing no further protest, he went on to tell the women all about the *Lucky Lena* investigation.

"So where do things stand now?" Sylvia asked once he'd finished.

"The father and son crew has dropped off the face of the earth without a trace. And, in a nutshell, the perpetrators could have been temperance fanatics, a competing gang of rumrunners, a local pirate, a Chinese tong, maybe a competing salvager, or maybe someone we haven't even thought of yet. We're considering a bunch of different theories, trying to figure out what to do next."

"Probably rumrunners," Marion said. "It's the only thing around here that pays these days."

"What do you mean?" Floyd asked.

"He speaks again!" Sylvia said.

"Marion means that the local economy is in the doldrums," Miles said. "Prohibition obviously closed the saloons. The lumber mill shut down last year when the company relocated to Port Angeles. The creamery burned to the ground. And the overall salmon catch isn't nearly as big as it was in the past. Not to mention that apparently that fish cleaning machine you saw just displaced half the cannery workers. So we're seeing a lot of ripple effects. Folks moving away. Bank foreclosures and evictions. The island's only haberdashery closed three months ago. Bailey's tack shop closed a month after that. And now Jacob Fields is even talking about closing his dry goods store and moving to Bellingham."

"I guess law enforcement is the line of work to be in," Floyd said.

"Unless there's nobody left to pay taxes."

"Wait—why would a competing rumrunner or temperance fanatic paint a Chinese character on the wall?" Marion asked. "And how would they know the symbol in the first place?"

"Why would a Chinese tong highbinder make reference to the Bible?" Miles asked in response. "For that matter, how likely is it that a Chinese would even know anything about the Bible?"

"There are millions of Chinese Christians," Sylvia said.

"There are?"

"Remember learning about the Taiping Rebellion in high school history class? The Christian-led uprising against the Qing Dynasty in 1850? The biggest civil war in all of human history?"

"Missed that one."

"You know who you should talk to?" Marion said. "That unfortunate soul, Akroyd."

"Akroyd?" Miles asked.

"The old hermit who lives in a shack out near Sunset Point."

"Oh, yeah. That really hairy guy. Oddball. Why would we want to talk to him?"

"My mother is certain he's a lookout. An informant for the rumrunners. Or maybe for the revenue agents, though I doubt they pay as well."

"Your mother?"

"You know my mother, Miles."

He did. She knew everyone and everything that went on on San Juan Island. A kind person would call her extraordinarily sociable. A blunt person would call her an obsessive gossip.

"What makes her think Akroyd's a lookout?"

"First of all, more than once, fishermen scanning the shore with their binoculars have caught him watching Haro Strait with an enormous, high-powered telescope he keeps in his shack."

"Is that right?"

"Yeah. Now how on earth did he afford a big, fancy telescope?"

"From all the money he saved by not getting shaves or haircuts?"

"And think about this: he has his own phone line. A squatter. An unemployed hermit. Not a party line, mind you, but his own dedicated, private phone line. Imagine!"

"Huh," Miles muttered, his mind spinning with thoughts of what information the hermit Akroyd might have for them.

"Anyway, how is everything on the home front?" Marion asked. "And how is our third musketeer, the Stag?" she asked, referring to their good mutual friend, John Staggner.

"He's living in Seattle. Actually, I spoke to his wife just yesterday," Miles said, abruptly stopping himself, realizing that he couldn't elaborate since he'd called Staggner to check up on Floyd.

"How was the wedding?"

"Oh, I'm afraid I didn't make it."

"Holy cow. You still hadn't gotten home by then? That's the Army for you."

"Well, I was. It's just that I . . ."

Marion looked at him expectantly, uncomprehendingly.

"I had some things I had to deal with. A conflict."

"When's the last time you guys got together?"

Miles took in a breath. "Before I went to boot camp. But I haven't seen you since before then either."

"Huh. So, who are your friends up here now? Who do you fish with?"

"I don't do much fishing these days." He shrugged.

A quiet moment passed. Marion shot Sylvia a worried look. But then the band struck up another song that made Marion smile with delight. "Sylvia! The Shimmy!" She grabbed Sylvia by the hand, told the men they'd be back, and ran indoors.

"I think I now understand why we waited here," Floyd said.

"Hey, now. I was truly hoping for more attendees from Deer Harbor."

"Don't worry about it. I take it Marion was your high school sweetheart."

"Sweetheart? No, no. She was too classy for any of that nonsense."

"Too classy to be your sweetheart?"

"I mean, too classy for dalliances. Always kept the boys at arm's length."

"How admirable. So you were just friends."

"Best friends. We grew up together. We've known each other since before starting school. But yes, just friends."

It wasn't quite that simple, of course. But Miles didn't want to explain. Instead, he drifted into a vivid memory of throwing rocks with Marion down at Mulno Cove, seeing who could skip them the farthest out across the water. It was late spring, the year they'd each turned twelve. The weather had finally gotten warm enough that they could wear swimsuits. And in watching Marion's body strain, watching her long arms and legs flail as she threw rocks, it occurred to Miles, for the very first time, that there was something different about her now—something that gave him an odd, unfamiliar tingle in the core of his abdomen. She'd always been a great friend. He loved her as a friend. But now, on the first warm day of the year, the first time since the previous autumn that he'd seen her bare arms and legs—the graceful lines of her smooth, fit, fair-skinned arms and legs—it was clear that something had changed in her. And in the way he felt about her.

In hindsight, of course, Miles saw that day at the beach as the clear beginning of his attraction to her. But it wasn't until a balmy summer night four years later that, at the county fair—as they sat on a bench under the glow of carousel lights, with the scent of popcorn and caramel apples and dry grass in the air, in a whirlwind of carnival bliss, surging hormones, and juvenile carelessness—he'd leaned over and tried to kiss her on the lips. Oblivious to his move, she'd shifted as he came close so that his nose ended up colliding with her cheek bone. Then, somehow, their cheeks had touched, and he felt the softness of her skin, caught the delicate jasmine scent of her hair. It was a glancing, fleeting contact. A delirious, blink-of-an-eye moment. Yet enough to send a shudder of joy through Miles's teenage body. To entrance him.

But then, with a suddenness that startled him, she'd given a yelp, ducked, and run off into the night.

He didn't see her again until school the following week. They never talked about it. And things seemed, at least initially, back to normal, as if it had never happened. But Miles—who was just self-aware enough to know that his adolescent male brain wasn't particularly good at processing emotional signals—knew he'd crossed some sort of invisible line in their relationship. And sure enough, over time, he came to realize that something had broken that day. From then on, Marion was always a bit more restrained around him. A bit more distant.

Moving forward, through a combination of self-delusion and sheer force of will, he'd convinced himself to regard her more as a sister or cousin. Desperate to maintain what relationship he had with her—desperate to not lose any more of the closeness—he banished, as best he could, all thoughts of his attraction to her. Yet it was always there, just below the surface. A yearning. An ache. And when, on occasion, he allowed himself to dwell on it, it triggered a profound and disorienting sadness.

"So your romantic interest in Marion is a recent development?" Floyd asked, jolting him back to the present.

"What do you mean?"

"It's written all over your face."

"Is it really? Damnation. Well, I won't argue the point." He paused. "It's funny. Growing up, she was like family to me. A sister. But now, seeing her as an adult . . ." He shook his head. "What about you, then?"

"What about me?"

"You tensed up as soon as they met us."

"I did?"

"Are you uncomfortable talking to women?"

"No. Well, yes. I suppose I am, to some extent. Beautiful young women, anyway."

"So, you don't have a girlfriend?"

"I'm too busy with work."

"Right. Have you ever, though?"

"One time, I sort of . . . Well, no, not really. You?"

"I've never been in a formal relationship, per se. Of course, in France, during the war, when men found themselves in Paris while on leave—a city full of beautiful, flower-scented women and nearly emptied of Frenchmen of fighting age—there were opportunities for, shall we say, informal sorts of—"

"Spare me."

Miles smiled. "What do you say we go back inside and watch those two live wires dance the Shimmy?"

They reentered the hall just in time to see Marion haul off and punch a young man square in the jaw, sending him stumbling backward into a stack of chairs while Sylvia looked on with a grin. Miles ran up to find out what the problem was as the band kept on playing.

"Little creep wouldn't keep his hands to himself," was Marion's entire explanation, shouted over the music. The man got to his feet, held a hand to his bleeding mouth, and departed, looking dejected.

"Technically, I should arrest you for battery," Miles said with a smile.

"Ha. Come dance with me." Marion grabbed his hand and led him to the dance floor.

"What about you then?" Sylvia asked Floyd.

"Me? Dance? Oh, no. I don't generally—"

Sylvia grabbed his hand and cut off his explanations with a yank of his arm, dragging him forward as his face turned beet red.

To the envy of every man there, Miles and Floyd did their best to dance with Marion and Sylvia through three consecutive songs. Miles did remarkably well for not knowing the latest steps. Floyd, blushing and looking hugely awkward the whole time, was a disaster. They took a break for glasses of punch, switched partners and danced again until their faces glistened with sweat, then had another round of punch, each of them drinking so much of it that their upper lips were stained an unnatural red.

When it came time to go, Miles suggested they all take a beach walk under the full moon.

"No," Marion said as they stood together under the awning out front, the women once again smoking. "We're whipped. Still adjusting from Eastern Time."

"Still?"

"Well, maybe not. But we didn't do a whole lot of sleeping last night," she said, giving Sylvia a covert wink.

"I'm sure you'll sleep better tonight," Miles said. "Drive you home, at least?"

"Sylvia drove my mother's Ford. See you soon, though?"

"Of course."

"Good night, then."

"Good night," Miles said, worried that he detected the return of that same old distance in her voice as he watched her walk off into the night, hand-in-hand with Sylvia.

"Are we going to interview this Akroyd fellow tomorrow?" Floyd asked.

"Akroyd," Miles said, happy to have something to displace his worry. "Yes. First thing in the morning."

"Solely on the basis of Marion's mother's suspicion?"

Miles smiled. "In all my life, Floyd, I've never known her mother to be wrong about anything. Not once. Should be interesting."

TWENTY-ONE

Three Weeks Earlier

Finally, someone moved the cabinet aside and opened the hole, letting in light. It was a fat Cantonese man in a greasy brown work shirt and trousers. He had a large bowl of rice and jugs of water to refill our barrel. Except for a girl who'd hit her head quite hard in a fall the day before, we all ate the rice with our dirty hands until we could stuff no more down our throats—until we felt ill. I even snuck a tiny ball of rice into my tunic for Snow to eat. The girl who'd hit her head ate nothing. She just sat, quiet, as if unaware of the present, her eyes looking like they were focused on something beyond the walls of our little secret room.

In the light, we saw that the wooden cask that had previously broken loose had a big crack in it. We could see inside. It was full of something dark brown that looked like tar and smelled like damp earth and roasted nuts. I wondered if it was something I could eat.

Seeing the cracked cask, the fat man cursed, then went and got a tarp and rope to wrap the cask and lash it back down with the others. In a dialect I barely understood, he told us not to touch the casks. That anyone who touched the casks would be punished.

As we ate, he stared at us like a hungry dog, looking each of us over one at a time. When we were done eating, he pointed to one of the girls and gestured for her to come with him. She asked why. He became angry and shouted, so she did as the fat man wanted and climbed out the hole. Following her, he slid the cabinet back into place, closing the hole and leaving us in darkness once again.

As I sat back down against the cold, damp wall, unable to see anything, a vision came into my mind of my father weeping as I left our house. I began to wonder if I would ever see him again. I missed him terribly. I missed sharing tea with him in front of the house while watching the sun rise over the distant hills. I missed his crafty look like when, every year, he snuck me a bigger piece of sweet nian gao than he gave to my older brothers on Lunar New Year's Eve. I missed his laugh. His kindness.

Some hours later, the fat man brought back the girl he'd taken away. Before he closed the hole, while light came through from the next room, I could see that she looked terrified. Terrified and sad. Whispering, I asked her what was wrong. She would not speak. Not at all. I asked if she was hurt—if the fat man had hurt her. She said nothing.

TWENTY-TWO

The next morning—an overcast and blustery one—Miles, Floyd, and Bill crammed into the cab of Miles's truck and took a forested road that cut across the island to Sunset Point, on the western shore, hoping to have a word with the mysterious Akroyd.

Miles wanted Bill to bring his heavy prybar in case they had to break into Akroyd's shack. So just outside of town, they stopped at the two-room cottage Bill had shared with his father since November 1918, when his father suffered a stroke that left one side of his body paralyzed. Bill's father was napping in their shared bedroom, so Miles and Floyd waited in the small sitting room as Bill tiptoed through to the wardrobe where he kept his prybar.

The sitting room was simple and austere, with a couple of homemade maple chairs, a well-used fireplace, and nothing by way of décor except for a collection of empty liquor bottles of various shapes and colors lined up on the windowsill. Miles took a peek through the doorway to the very small kitchen and pantry. Homemade salamis hung from strings tacked to exposed joists in the unfinished ceiling. Several of them were caked with something yellow. A basket of giant, ripe tomatoes sat on the counter next to the sink. There was no other produce.

"You still haven't washed your pants," Floyd said to Miles as they waited, gesturing to the old coffee stain.

"Thanks for pointing that out. I see you're as fancy as ever, wearing a pressed city suit even though we're going bushwacking."

"My mother says dress for the job you want, not the job you have."

"You aiming to be the next Douglas Fairbanks?"

"I have to ask," Floyd said as Bill reappeared holding his huge metal prybar. "Why do you keep that thing in your bedroom?"

"For rats."

They returned to the truck and got back on the road.

"You have some beautiful tomatoes in your kitchen, Bill," Miles said.

"Thanks. Grew them myself, in the back yard. My father loves tomatoes."

"And what was that yellow stuff covering the salamis in your pantry?" Miles asked

"Polenta."

"Polenta?"

"Cornmeal. My mother was Italian."

"Why is it on the salamis?"

"Is draws out some flavor. Makes the cornmeal taste better."

Bill's explanation made Miles wonder just how bad off Bill and his father really were. Then he remembered that Bill hadn't even ordered dinner at the inn the other night. It hadn't crossed Miles's mind that Bill couldn't afford it.

"Looks like you've added some bottles to your collection," Miles said to change the subject.

"Yessir," Bill said. "Found a very old-looking rum bottle in the woods by English Camp." English Camp was an abandoned British Royal Marines base on Garrison Bay. It had been built during the so-called Pig War of 1859, when Great Britain and the United States faced off over competing claims to San Juan Island—a confrontation that nearly turned bloody when an American farmer shot a trespassing pig owned by an employee of Britain's Hudson's Bay Company.

"Rum, eh?" Miles said. "Could be a discard from the Royal Navy. That would make it very old, indeed."

"It sure looks old to me."

"A collector's item. Valuable, maybe."

"That would be nice."

"Find any Glenfiddich bottles?" Floyd asked, joking.

"No," Bill said so quickly and so loudly that Miles turned and looked at him. In truth, Miles couldn't have cared less if Bill found an intact bottle of whiskey—as long as it wasn't, by some miracle, from the *Lucky Lena* and still useful as evidence despite floating around in salt water and washing up on a beach. Whatever the cause of Bill's tension, Miles found it a little amusing.

"You collect old bottles?" Floyd asked.

"Yessir. It's a hobby of mine."

"Where do you find them?"

"All over. I walk the roads and trails a lot. Sometimes the beaches."

"What do you do with them?"

"If they're valuable, I sell them. Usually, I just like to look at them."

My mother would say you need a girlfriend, Miles thought. *She'd say that you're lonely.*

*****

Barely half a mile from town, Bill, looking thoroughly uncomfortable straddling the gearshift, asked if he could ride in the back of the truck, so Miles pulled over to accommodate him.

"You think this Akroyd fella is actually going to talk to us?" Floyd asked and they got back underway.

"He's a squatter," Miles said. "Which means we can evict him from his home."

"That would be rather un-Christian."

"For heaven's sake, Floyd. We're not really going to evict him. But he won't know that. It's just leverage to make him talk."

"Ah."

"Of course, he still may not talk. He's rarely seen anywhere, let alone in town. And when he is seen, he never speaks. I don't know that he *can* speak. Nobody really knows anything about him. To be honest, I forgot he was out there. I'm sure I haven't seen him since before the war."

*****

Though Akroyd's shack was in dense forest well off the road, they found it with relative ease by parking under and following the only telephone branch line in the vicinity of Sunset Point that diverted from the main roadside line into seemingly trackless woods. Their progress slowed by dense underbrush, they followed the line, from pole to pole, through thorned blackberry vines, stinging nettles, ferns, and trees of all kinds until they at last began to catch glimpses of the waters of Haro Strait thorough the gaps. At the same time, they began to smell coffee and smoked bacon.

After a few more minutes of bushwacking, a shack came into view. Constructed of raw logs and scrap lumber, the leaning, makeshift structure stood in a small clearing on a high, rocky and wind-whipped bluff protruding from a small cove. Smoke blew sideways from a short tin chimney. Behind it, just offshore, a small pod of minke whales was passing to the south.

"Akroyd," Miles shouted, stopping about twenty feet from the door. "Police. We need to talk to you."

They waited a moment. The door didn't open. Nobody answered. All they heard was the wind blowing through the trees.

"Akroyd, are you in there?"

Still nothing.

"There's an outhouse," Bill said, pointing to the far corner of a clearing on the opposite side of the shack.

"He would have heard us from there," Miles said.

"Maybe, maybe not. He's pretty old."

"If you want to check the outhouse, Bill, be my guest," Miles said as he walked up to the warped, rickety door of the shack. Trying the thoroughly corroded knob, he found it locked.

"What do we do now?" Floyd asked.

"We use the prybar."

"Wait—what?"

"What did you think we brought it along for? Actually, maybe I can just kick this thing in."

"Miles, we talked about this. We don't have a warrant."

"You and your warrants," Miles said as he raised a leg and knocked the door in with one powerful kick. "After you, sir."

Floyd gave him a dubious look, then went through the dark doorway. It was surprisingly warm and quiet inside. The close air smelled of bacon, coffee, and exceptionally sour body odor. The one-room interior was Spartan, the walls, floors, and ceiling constructed of bare, rough-hewn wood. Rudimentary shelves held a few books and trinkets. For furniture, Akroyd had a cot, a filthy, threadbare wingback chair, a scratched-up chest of drawers, and a small table with a crude wooden stool. Everything looked to have been either inexpertly homemade or salvaged from the town dump. An unlit lantern hung from an exposed rafter, and a small cast iron stove was set in a dark corner, embers glowing red from within. But the things that held Miles and Floyd's attention were a new-looking telephone mounted to the wall next to the cot, a four-foot brass telescope on a tripod, and a giant window that looked out over the water. The window had a commanding view of a wide swath of Haro Strait, including the dark shape of D'Arcy Island a few miles due west of where they now stood.

Miles wondered how a man could live such an isolated existence, largely cut off from any sort of community. A natural introvert, solitude often appealed to a part of him. But sooner or later, it always got old, and he'd find himself yearning for human contact. In any form, with damn near anyone. It made him wonder whether something had happened to Akroyd—some trauma, perhaps—to drive him to this extreme, lonely lifestyle.

"He was just here," Floyd said as he examined the stove. "This pan of bacon is still warm."

"So is this coffee, barely," Miles said, touching a half-finished mug that sat on the table.

"Think he heard us and ran for it?"

"With all the wind noise outside? I doubt it," Miles said.

"Maybe he's just down at the cove, doing his dishes or what have you."

"Or maybe he was warned."

"Warned?" Floyd asked.

"Well, it would be odd, wouldn't it, that the man—a poor man—would take the time to fry up good bacon and brew a big mug of good coffee, then up and leave it to get cold?"

"Warned how?"

Miles gestured toward the telephone.

"Oh, of course. But by whom?"

Maybe you, Miles thought, as it occurred to him that Floyd could have rung Akroyd from his hotel just before they left town.

"You sure he's poor?" Floyd asked.

"Look at this dump."

"Look at that expensive telescope. Look at that modern telephone with its dedicated private line. And, hey—look at this," Floyd said, lifting a fine gold pocket watch from a corner of the table. He opened it and looked at its face. It was running and accurate.

"Let me see that," Miles said, taking it from Floyd and studying it for a moment. "I'll be damned."

"What?"

"There was this guy who graduated from high school here a couple of classes ahead of me. He ended up moving away to Tacoma. Name of Baxter. Anyway, one day late last year, he shows up at the police station with a big smile on his face, a manner that was excessively familiar given that we'd hardly known each other. He had a pocket watch just like that one. I mean the exact same watch. He tried to give it to me as a token of appreciation for my fine work in keeping the peace in his hometown, or some such nonsense."

"A kind enough gesture."

"Sure. He also had a bolt of fine blue Chinese silk from a notoriously pricey Tacoma department store. The silk, he'd said, was a gift for my mother. A so-called 'long overdue thank-you gift' for her tutoring him in mathematics years before."

You're welcome to deliver it to her yourself, Miles had told Baxter. *I'm sure she'd be delighted to have a visitor.*

Oh, no. I'm sure she's busy.

She isn't.

Still, I wouldn't dream of intruding—of calling unannounced. It would be unmannerly.

Miles had stood looking at the man, perplexed. But the next thing his surprise visitor had said cleared everything right up.

Say, Miles. Since I have you, it just so happens that my employers are looking for someone of just your position and reliability for some very easy side work.

Oh?

In a nutshell, they need someone they can turn to for market research up here in the islands.

Market research?

Simple information that would take no time at all to gather. They'd pay handsomely for it. And they have all sorts of fine things, like that silk for example, that they'd be happy to pass along as frequent tokens of gratitude.

Uh—huh. And what is your employers' line of business?

Shipping.

Of course. The shipping of certain libations, I would guess. So, I imagine your employers are interested to know when revenue boats, like the USRC *Arcata, are seen in the area. They're probably also hoping that I might be willing to look the other way when some of their own shipping activities are suspected or observed.*

Baxter stood silent, expectant.

Look, pal, Miles had said to him. *Tell your employers they can keep their pocket watch and their silk and their money. There's a line I just don't cross. That being said, you can tell them that I'm a bit of a libertarian, and that I give less than half a damn about rum running. People are going to get their booze one way or another, no matter what the law says. And if a man wants to have a glass of wine with his dinner or wants to drown himself in gin, that's his business and his responsibility. It isn't something I ever intend to go after. So they needn't worry themselves.*

Back in the present, Miles gazed at the gold pocket watch and wondered what the rumrunners would have paid him. Wondered if he could have bought himself a phonograph player or a new truck, or could even have afforded to move out of his mother's house. Then he wondered whether Floyd had accepted such a watch—or whatever cash it took to afford those fancy suits.

Stop being so paranoid.

They performed a cursory search of the shack. There wasn't much to see. Bent utensils, dented cookware, candle ends, numerous pencil sketches of birds, and a few books—each of which Miles checked, to no avail, for hollowed hiding spaces like the one he found in the navigation book aboard the *Lucky Lena.* However, opening one of the larger books—titled *Guterson's Pacific Coast Ornithology*—Miles found that its content had nothing to do with birds. "What have we here?" he said, flipping through pages that appeared to be those of a standard ledger book. "A false cover. Is our friend Akroyd a hobbyist accountant?" He set the book on the table and opened it to a random page. "Jackpot."

"What is it?"

"A logbook of vessel sightings."

The entries were made in neat and exceptionally refined penmanship. They included dates, times, locations, courses, descriptions, and, in many cases, registration numbers or names. *March 20, 4:22 p.m., white Keesling-made workboat, registration number M-298, two miles southeast of D'Arcy Island, headed due south until disappearing in fog near Vancouver Island,* read one entry. *March 21, 9:55 a.m., longline fishing boat "Wild Rose," Canadian flag, registration number V025M, mid-channel, prob. inbound course for Port of Sidney,* read another. Other entries on the page were similar. There was even one for the revenue cutter USRC *Arcata*, reported as steaming north, near the shore of San Juan Island, no doubt patrolling for rumrunners. Another that struck Miles as particularly interesting, even a little bit funny, mentioned the notorious 250-foot, five-masted Canadian schooner *Malahat*—which was well known to be a major supply ship to U.S. rumrunners—mysteriously disappearing behind D'Arcy Island, only to emerge more than three hours later and sail on toward the open Pacific. It had surely dropped a load of booze on the island, or had simply rendezvoused with one or more small, fast American rumrunning boats behind the island and out of sight of American revenue agents.

"Perfect," Miles said. "This is just what we need. Looks like Akroyd marks down everything—rumrunners, supply ships, and revenue cutters alike."

"Why would he watch both revenue cutters *and* rumrunners?" Floyd asked.

"Maybe he's obsessed."

"Or maybe he works for both sides."

"As an informant for the rumrunners *and* for the revenue agents? You have a dirty mind, Floyd. But it's an interesting theory. And if he is playing for both sides, he'd better hope they don't find out."

Miles flipped through dozens of pages to find those covering the past week. "Oh, no. No, no, no—you're kidding me."

"What?" Floyd asked.

"The log entries stop a week before the *Lucky Lena* was spotted adrift."

"You're joking."

"See for yourself," Miles said, sliding the ledger book across the table.

Floyd took a look. Indeed, the last entries covered the week previous. After that, the ledger pages were blank.

"Hold on. Look at this," Floyd said, pointing to the

innermost side of the open ledger page. Barely protruding from the stich and glue binding of the book, Miles saw the thin, clean-cut edge of a missing page. "Someone cut it out."

The men stared at each other, pondering the same troubling implications. Then Miles went back out the door and scanned the surrounding woods, hoping to catch a glimpse of Akroyd spying on them from behind a tree.

"Akroyd!" he shouted. Hearing no response, out of sheer curiosity, Miles strode to the edge of the bluff and looked over. It was a good thirty-foot drop to where short, dark blue waves broke against jagged gray rock. The water grew deep and dark just a few feet from shore. The tops of a small kelp forest floated a little further out. A loud double screech drew Miles's attention to a high snag in a knotty, rugged old fir tree that stood apart from the rest of the forest and close to the edge of the bluff. There, an adult bald eagle stared down at him with its permanently aggressive hunter's eyes. It watched him for a long moment before turning its gaze out to sea. In its talons, Miles could see a flatfish—probably a sanddab or a small rock sole—in the process of being torn up and eaten alive.

Miles did a slow turn, scrutinizing the area for anything notable. "Akroyd!" he shouted into the forest once again. "If you can hear me, you aren't in any trouble. We just want to talk about the boats you've seen. If you're around, please come out."

He waited. But no one answered. And no one came.

TWENTY-THREE

Back in town, Miles slowed as if to park in front of the station, then sped back up and passed it by.

"Where are we going now?" Floyd asked. "I need to use the toilet. And I imagine Bill is getting cold riding in the back."

"Making a quick detour to the telephone switchboard office. I have an idea."

They passed a small upright fountain of chiseled granite flanked by two scrawny, juvenile Dutch elms in a circle of land at the base of Spring Street, just up from the wharf.

"What's the story with the pathetic little trees and fountain back there?" Floyd asked with a smirk. "Is that the best Friday Harbor can do for a public park?"

"It's a memorial to our soldiers lost in the Great War. Thanks for noticing."

"Oh, I—"

"Folks wanted a memorial because some of the boys' bodies never came home for proper burial. One tree represents the Army, the other the Navy. They're pathetic, to use your happy adjective, because the Women's Study Club, at their own expense and by their own efforts, planted them just this year."

"I apologize."

*****

The switchboard office, which connected every single phone call between San Juan Island and anywhere else in the world, was in a small stand-alone building of red brick on the edge of downtown. Peering through the window of the front door, the men saw Eustace Hampton, the operator, asleep in a tall chair next to the switchboard. She wore an uncomfortable-looking headset with large black ear pads, and her mouth hung open so wide they could see that she was missing several of her molars. On the switchboard itself, several tiny yellow lights glowed above sockets linked to one another via a tangle of red, black, and gray cables. Miles gave the window a gentle tap. But it was still enough to make Eustace half jump out of her chair and knock over a cup of tea that stood on the console. She scowled, covered the tea with a cloth napkin, slipped her feet into a pair of bedroom slippers, and came to the door.

"Good day, Mrs. Hampton," Miles said.

"I don't appreciate being startled."

"I knocked as gently as I could."

"It's impolite, nonetheless. You could have come back later."

"I'm afraid time is of the essence, Mrs. Hampton. May we have a look at your logbook?"

"I beg your pardon?"

"I need to know who has been on the other end of calls to and from Akroyd's place this past week or two. And, for that matter, what they've been discussing."

She put her hands on her hips. "You wish to know who Mr. Akroyd has been talking to and what they've been talking about on Mr. Akroyd's *private* line?"

"Correct."

"And I assume you have a warrant or court order to show me."

Miles glanced at Floyd, who was already smiling at him.

"I don't. But this is an urgent matter, Mrs. Hampton."

"Why don't you ask Mr. Akroyd?"

"We tried to. He's nowhere to be found."

"Your request is most improper."

And you're welcome for chasing down your stinking sheep when they got loose last week, you old bat, Miles thought.

"You are aware, Mrs. Hampton, of the situation with the *Lucky Lena*," Miles said.

"Of course."

"Between you and me, Akroyd's telephone conversations may prove vital to our investigation."

"You need a court order, Miles."

Not *sheriff*. Not even *acting sheriff*. Just *Miles*. "The county judge won't be on San Juan Island until Monday. We're trying to bring the killers to justice, Mrs. Hampton. Trying to prevent another murder, even. There are exigent circumstances to consider."

"Rules are rules. If you want to pry into that poor, mad bird watcher Mr. Akroyd's private conversations, you'll have to get a court order."

*****

"Don't say it," Miles said as they all squeezed back into the truck, a thoroughly chilled Bill having elected to ride up front again.

"Don't say what?" Floyd said.

"That I should have had a warrant."

"Ha, ha. Well. That Eustace Hampton is a tough cookie, isn't she?"

"She's Lutheran. An entire denomination of humorless hard-asses, my view. Everything by the book. It grows tiresome."

*****

Back at the station a few minutes later, Miles was brewing a fresh batch of coffee while Bill held his cold pink hands close to the stove and Floyd looked through the logbook they'd taken from Akroyd's shack.

"This guy was meticulous," Floyd said. "He even has entries for big, blue water steam ships, like the SS *Marglen*, which I believe is a Canadian Pacific ocean liner. That couldn't possibly have any relevance to rum running."

"Maybe he was just obsessed with ships in general," Miles said.

"Old guy was a loon," Bill added.

"You speak as if he's dead," Miles said.

"Here's an interesting thing," Floyd said. "There are several days, each falling within the last three weeks for which we have log pages, on which Akroyd observed the *Lucky Lena* loitering near D'Arcy Island for more than an hour."

"Akroyd positively identified it?" Miles asked. "Then its registration number must not have been covered up with creosote yet. Does it say what they were doing? Maybe fishing? Diving? Going ashore for stashed crates of Glenfiddich whiskey?"

"It just says loitering. The thing is, on two of those occasions," Floyd continued, "there was another boat observed loitering in the same general area."

"Don't leave it as a cliffhanger, Floyd. What other boat?"

"Akroyd couldn't tell. The entry describes a Trafton-built workboat, registration obscured. Looks like the Trafton was there at the same time as the *Lucky Lena* on the last day for which there are any entries. Saturday before last."

Miles turned around. "Angus Cooper!"

"What?" Floyd asked.

"Remember, at the cannery, Clyde Crieff said Angus Cooper hadn't turned up with a shipment of tin can blanks Crieff had prepaid him for?"

"Yes."

"Cooper's boat's a Trafton. The *Daisy*. I'm certain of it." He picked up the phone. "Hello again, Mrs. Hampton. No—excuse me, no, Mrs. Hampton. I'm not calling about Mr. Akroyd's private phone conversations. Heaven forbid. No, I need to place a call to Clyde Crieff at the cannery, please. Yes, I'll stand by."

After an inordinately long wait, causing Miles to suspect that

Mrs. Hampton was taking her sweet time to spite him, he was connected with Clyde Crieff. Miles asked him about the tin delivery.

"Well?" Floyd asked as Miles rang off.

"Angus Cooper still hasn't shown up."

TWENTY-FOUR

Miles and Floyd spent the next hour searching for Angus Cooper, captain-owner of the Trafton-built workboat, the *Daisy*. There was no sign of the man at his small, simple house out on Bailer Hill Road, so, despite Floyd's usual protest about not having a warrant, Miles kicked the door in. It was a poor man's house, everything cheap and threadbare. A pantry stocked with poor man's food—lard instead of butter, grits instead of oats, potatoes instead of meat.

It looked as if someone had left in a hurry. Men's and young girl's clothes were scattered about the creaking wood floors of the two bedrooms. Drawers were left open, including one in a dusty China cabinet that held a silverware divider but no silverware.

"As you may recall Crieff telling us, Cooper's a widower," Miles said as they looked around. "I believe his wife died at least five years ago."

"That would explain the lack of décor."

"And he has a young daughter, Milly, maybe seven or eight, who should probably be in a lunatic asylum. She's helplessly mad. Of course, Cooper can't afford to get her the care she needs. So he keeps her here, locked up, while he's at work."

"Then I hope you'll pay for the repair to his front door."

"I will."

"So, what's your theory here?" Floyd asked. "Desperate for money to get proper care for his daughter, he hijacked the *Lucky Lena*, murdered the crew, panicked, took the family silver, and ran for it?"

"I don't know. Hijacking and murder? He doesn't seem the type."

"Is there a type?"

"If there *is,* Cooper isn't it."

"Desperation can do strange things to people."

*****

They found one of Cooper's immediate neighbors at home—an old woman who said she would sometimes help keep an eye on Milly when Cooper was in a pinch. According to her, Cooper said that he was taking Milly down to Seattle to visit a cousin this week, and that he'd be back this coming Saturday. Cooper had asked her to keep an eye on the place.

*****

By the time they got back to the station, Bill had returned from asking the men on the docks if anyone had seen Cooper or the *Daisy* since the morning the *Lucky Lena* was spotted adrift. None had. Both man and vessel had been gone for days. But two different fishermen told Bill that Cooper had been seen with Rupert Hawkins a fair bit the week before Cooper disappeared, and that Cooper had maybe even hired Hawkins on as a temporary deckhand.

"The same Rupert Hawkins who Reverend McCaskill once horsewhipped?" Floyd asked.

Miles nodded. "And the same Hawkins who was seen picking up two well-dressed Chinese from the steamship pier on Tuesday."

"Hawkins a worthless drunk," Bill said.

"Well, drunk or sober, I think we need to have a word with him sooner rather than later," Miles said.

TWENTY-FIVE

Taking a first stab at finding Rupert Hawkins, Miles and Floyd returned to the waterfront and began walking the docks.

"Look at that," Floyd said in a tone of boyish wonder as he stopped and pointed at a floating dock below one of the piers. There were two sea lion pups with big brown eyes that reminded Floyd of his first dog, Birdie—a kindhearted Labrador. The chubby pups were clumped together for warmth, butting noses and squawking at each other. "That's unbelievably precious."

A loud bang caused both men to flinch and crouch for cover. One of the pups let out an ear-piercing cry that was followed by two more loud bangs. From his crouch, Floyd scanned the area until he saw the mechanic, Sean Brennan, standing on the aft deck of a moored 50-foot fishing boat, pointing a smoking pistol at the pups. One of the pups lay bloody and dead on the dock. Though shot, the other managed to drag itself to the edge and drop into the water just as Brennan was jumping up onto the dock and aiming his pistol to finish it off. It swam, erratically, down into the dark depths, blood trailing behind it. Brennan kicked the dead one in after it, then hopped back into the stern end of the fishing boat as if nothing had happened.

"Mary and Joseph!" Floyd shouted when the shooting and crying abated.

"Easy, Floyd," Miles said, placing a hand on Floyd's shoulder. "All is well."

"All is well? Damnation!" Floyd said, his eyes wide.

"What I mean is that was normal."

"Hell's bells! I'll tell you what—you people are really hard on animals up here. You know that?"

"Adult sea lions decimate the salmon population."

"Those were pups."

"For now, they're pups. Before you know it, they'll be fully grown, each of them eating 20 pounds of salmon a day. It's them or us," Miles said, walking toward the aft end of the boat Brennan had boarded. There they found him carrying on as if nothing had happened, wearing frayed but clean coveralls, and filing one end of an unrecognizable, greasy metal engine part on a worktable set up on the deck.

"Hey there, Brennan," Miles said.

Brennan set his filing tool down and looked up as he wiped his hands with a dirty rag. "Afternoon, Sheriff."

"What kind of engine part are you're working on there?"

"That's a valve actuating rocker off this old girl's Liberty L-12 gasoline engine."

"Are you a mechanic?" Floyd asked.

"No, I'm a ballet dancer," he said, bursting into what struck Miles as the forced laughter of someone who isn't sure they're actually funny.

"Detective Floyd is a city boy," Miles said.

"No kidding?"

"How's your mother?" Miles asked. "That was quite a spill she took up on Spring Street the other day. She doing okay?"

Brennan went somber. "She's alright. A little scratched up is all."

"Glad to hear it. Is she here for a visit? I heard she was living in Bellingham now." *At an old senile folks' home,* he barely stopped himself from saying.

"She was. But she belongs here with me."

"I see. Well, we're trying to find Angus Cooper. Seen him around, by chance?"

"No, sir. Haven't seen him or his boat. But the guy owes me a good sum of money, so I'd be grateful if you'd let me know when you find him. Or at least let him know that we can work something out and that he doesn't have to hide from me. It isn't like him to be late paying his invoice. But he is late. Very late, in fact."

"You did some work for him?"

"Early last week, and also the week before that. He got a new L-12 too. Needed help installing it."

"He got an L-12 for the *Daisy*? That's a lot of engine for a boat of that size."

"It is. But everybody seems to want the L-12s these days."

"I guess everybody's in a big hurry," Miles said.

"A sign of these modern times, I suppose," Brennan said. "Needless to say, I don't ask too many questions."

"I should think not. Where are folks getting all of them?"

"The L-12s? They're stripping them off surplus airplanes back from the war, down at Boeing's airfield in Seattle."

"Clever. And then they bring them to you, our local Liberty engine authority."

"I wouldn't presume to call myself an authority. But I've installed a few. And I'm the only fella north of Everett who knows how to do it right."

"How about Rupert Hawkins? Heard he maybe did some work for Cooper recently too."

"That he did. Angus hired him to come along a couple of times when we were trying out the L-12 in the *Daisy* earlier this week, just to have an extra set of eyes and hands if Angus and I had to both be below working on the engine while underway. But Angus only used him for two days."

"Only two?"

"Rupert was drunk by the end of the second day. Man can't keep off the hooch. He must have been sneaking sips from a flask while Angus and I were below working on the engine. By the time we got back to Friday Harbor, he could barely stand up straight to rope a deck cleat."

"What day was that?"

"Let's see—Monday, I believe."

"What about Tuesday?"

"No. Angus sailed without him on Tuesday."

"You're sure?"

"I saw him moping around here Tuesday afternoon, when I'm positive Angus was out on the water. I'd been aboard the *Daisy* while Angus warmed up the engine, keeping an eye on her oil temperature. Then I cast off the *Daisy's* lines and watched him motor away."

"By himself?"

"Yes, sir."

"Seen Rupert today?"

"He was walking the docks about an hour ago. Looking for work. Nobody will hire the poor bastard because he's so unreliable. But you might try the, uh . . ."

"The what?"

"Well, you know." He shrugged. "The Smokehouse."

"The Smokehouse?" Floyd asked.

Brennan smiled. "I'm sure they have much fancier names for them in the big city."

"The Smokehouse is a speakeasy up at Roche Harbor," Miles explained. "Worst kept secret on the island."

"And I'm afraid that it's well into Rupert's drinking day by now," Brennan said. "You'd be better off waiting until morning before trying to talk to him. It'll be a lot easier then."

*****

It started to rain as Miles and Floyd left the harbor and began making their way back up toward the station. It was a cold, hard rain that fell from a low, cast-iron sky. They were both soaked to the skin in moments, both cursing themselves for not wearing their raincoats to the docks.

"So what about that guy?" Floyd said, wiping raindrops from his face and gesturing back down toward the docks.

"Sean Brennan? What about him?"

"Do we consider him a suspect? He was working on the *Daisy*, after all. Working with Angus Cooper."

"No. He's straight, if a bit awkward."

"Awkward? I'd call him impertinent, smarting off to a police officer he's never met before."

"You were in plain clothes. How could he have known you're police? Anyway, don't take it personally. He tries to be funny. It doesn't always come off quite right."

Floyd shook his head. "He has a cold heart."

"Because he shot those pups? Floyd, I told you. That's normal up here. It doesn't mean he suffers from psych, uh, psycho . . ."

"Psychopathy. Moral insanity."

"Anyway, you have to give Sean a little bit of a break if his social skills are off," Miles said. "His father was a mean old drunk who disappeared off the inter-island steamer when Sean was a teenager. Probably had one too many whiskeys and fell overboard. And before she went senile, his mother was a genuine recluse. Point being, he didn't have much in the way of social role models."

"A background of family instability?" Floyd asked. "A childhood characterized by emotional neglect and abuse?"

"You should have seen how compassionate and gentle he was with his mother when she took a spill up on Spring Street the other day."

"I'm sure Jesse James loved his mother too. Didn't make him any less morally insane."

Miles snorted. "Personally, I respect him for adapting to challenging times up here—what with the downturn in fishing jobs and all—making himself the go-to guy for Liberty engine installations," he said as they walked through the door of the station.

"You talking about Sean Brennan?" Bill said, handing them each a hot mug of coffee as they shucked their wet shoes and dragged chairs over to the warmth of the wood stove.

"Yes, Brennan," Miles said. "Sounds like he's setting himself up as the main L-12 installer in the northern half of Puget Sound."

"Well, he meant to, anyway," Bill said.

"You mean it isn't working out? I'd think there's plenty of demand for his services."

"There is. But he got ripped off. Took out a big loan at Dexter Horton Bank, putting his shop up for collateral. Then some shady broker in Seattle took Brennan's down payment for ten Liberty engines, but turned around and sold them to some other guy in Tacoma who agreed to pay more. The guy pocketed Brennan's down payment and disappeared."

"How do you know so much about his private business?" Miles asked.

"We play cards now and then."

"Did Brennan report the theft to Seattle PD?" Floyd asked.

"He says it wouldn't matter. Says the broker's long gone to the Alaska Territory. Nobody will ever find him. Anyway, now he's broke. Had to bring his mother home from the Bellingham senile home because he couldn't pay the fee anymore. Bank will probably take his shop."

"You'd have never known he was in such dire straits the way he carries himself," Floyd said. "All jocular and cracking wise." He took a big sip of the coffee Bill had given him. "Holy cow, you gents brew some strong coffee up here. If I drink much more of it, I'll never sleep again."

"It's good to drink something warm," Miles said. "We can't be letting you catch pneumonia."

Marion came charging through the front door, collapsing her umbrella and shedding rainwater all over the floor.

"Oh, sorry about that," she said.

"Not to worry," Miles said. "It's nothing."

"Could one of you possibly give me a ride home? Now that I have a big box of perishable groceries, my mother's car of course refuses to start."

"I'd be happy to," Miles said, putting his wet shoes back on and hopping to his feet. "Want me to look under the hood too?"

"I already had Stieg Albertson come down from his garage. He says the magneto is rusted. But he doesn't have any in stock, so he'll have to order it from Seattle."

"Well, I'm happy to drive you. Shall we?"

Miles led her to his truck, parked half a block up the street, as she held her umbrella above the both of them. "What's in the box?" he asked.

"Two chickens, a dozen eggs, celery, onions, and a box of salt crackers. Sylvia is going to make my grandfather a pot of soup she says they call 'Jewish medicine' back east. Some sort of chicken soup with cracker crumb dumpling balls. She claims it will cure anything."

"Sylvia is Jewish?"

"With a name like Rosen? Of course."

"I wouldn't know. I've only ever known one Jewish person. In the Army."

"Sorry. Living out east, you hear a lot more variety in names. Not everybody is named Andersen or Olsen or Larsen like they are around here."

"Can I talk you into a drive out by Pear Point?" he asked as he started the engine.

"In the pouring rain? Sounds lovely, Miles. But I need to get this raw chicken into my mother's ice box."

"Oh, of course."

Miles racked his brain for something interesting to talk about. Nothing came to his oddly agitated mind. Then Marion beat him to it.

"I hear you like jazz," she said.

"Jazz. Yes, jazz."

"Jazz, yes, jazz? Illuminating, Miles."

"Well, I mean—"

"What jazz do you like?"

"Do you know jazz?"

"I live in New York."

"Ha. Yes. Well, my all-time favorite is a saxophone player named Bechet. I saw him at this little hole in the wall in London after the war."

"Sidney Bechet."

"You've heard of Sidney Bechet?"

"I've seen him play."

"You're joking."

"No. He plays with Will Marion Cook's Orchestra. Saw him play an improvised solo at this incredible Harlem joint, Club Deluxe. That was when he still played the clarinet. He's wonderful."

By now Miles was smiling from ear to ear. "You amaze me, Marion."

"I am amazing."

Miles gazed at her until he almost missed a turn. "Oh, hell," he said as he hit the brakes and swerved, his face flushing red. "Sorry about that."

*****

Miles parked in Marion's driveway. "Take a look at this," he said, taking his Buescher from behind the seat.

"Miles Scott," Marion said. "Don't tell me you play the saxophone."

"After a fashion."

"I must say, you amaze me too."

"See if you recognize this one." He played her a couple of minutes of a tune, then paused. "Well?"

"It's a beautiful song," she said.

Miles wondered whether by calling the song beautiful she was trying to avoid commenting on his playing of it. The bottom fell out of his self-confidence.

"Sad, but beautiful," she added. "Is it Sidney Bechet?"

"He plays it. But it was written by the late, great Charles

McCarron. 'Blues My Naughty Sweetie Gives to Me.

"I'm going to have to buy the record. Or I'll just take you back to New York so you can play it for me."

His confidence came charging back.

"Why don't you just stay here?" he said.

"Ha."

"Really, though."

"I'm a city mouse, Miles."

"Since when?"

She gave him a sad smile and shrugged.

"I'll play Bechet for you every day. Every night. I'll practice and get better."

It seemed to Miles that, for a split second, a look of not quite entirely concealed apprehension flashed across her face. It confused him. Was it just his imagination? Or was she just trying to be nice when, in fact, she disliked his playing?

"And I'd take you fishing anytime you want," he went on, trying another tack, his speech quickening. "Just like before the war. We could throw the baseball until our arms fall off, then listen to Red Sox games on your mom's radio. Have bonfires. Everything you love."

"It's certainly a lovely vision."

A quiet moment passed between them.

"Are you free for dinner this evening?" Miles asked.

"Dinner. Well, I have Sylvia."

"Sylvia. Yes, of course. I meant are you both free for dinner?"

"Tonight. I . . ."

"You have plans already?"

"Ah, no. Nothing that can't wait, I suppose. We'd be delighted."

"Excellent. Morgan's? Say seven o'clock?"

"Yessir."

"Pick you up just before."

She got out, and he sat there a moment wondering at

Marion's odd tone of voice.

*****

The phone was ringing as Miles got back to the station.

"County sheriff," Bill said, answering. "It's for you," he told Floyd. "A Sergeant Clark from Seattle."

"Ah!" Floyd said, grabbing a notepad and pen. "Our research section. Hopefully, they'll have some answers for us." He took the phone. "Hello, sir. Yes. Yes, I see."

The conversation ran barely a minute before Floyd rang off.

"Anything interesting?" Miles asked him.

"Oh, yes," he said, smiling. "Hugely interesting, in fact. For starters, the symbol on the bulkhead of the *Lucky Lena* is indeed Chinese. Cantonese, in fact."

"Cantonese, like the tongs."

"Exactly."

"What does the symbol mean?"

"It means *death*."

"Death? How appropriate."

"There's more. The diving suit we found aboard is a Kretchmar Model VI, manufactured in Hamburg for the Imperial German Navy. Probably sold off as surplus after the war."

Miles stared at Floyd for a moment, then took a sip of hot coffee. "A Chinese symbol for death and a German deep-water diving suit. Damnation, Floyd. Instead of bringing clarity, the information we gather just seems to make things that much more confusing." He gulped down the rest of his coffee. "Well, maybe rummy Rupert Hawkins can tell us something useful. Bill, we're going to run out to Roche Harbor to see if we can find him at the Smokehouse, drunk or not. If you have time, I'd be grateful if you stayed to cover the phone."

"You bet."

TWENTY-SIX

"I can't believe you allow a speakeasy to operate on the island," Floyd said as Miles drove them northeast, toward Roche Harbor, after swinging by the hotel so Floyd could retrieve his raincoat. "You're the sheriff, for heaven's sake."

"Seattle has speakeasies up the kazoo."

"Yeah, but . . . Never mind."

The windshield of his truck began to fog, so Miles cracked his window open despite the rain. "You know something that's strange about the United States?" he said. "You can get opium from your doctor and take it until your brains melt out of your ears. Yet you can't have a glass of Bordeaux with your steak. Where's the sense in that?"

"The law is the law."

"That it is. But it makes you wonder about the politicians who make it."

Miles swerved to miss a possum that had wandered, half blind, out of the tall grass and onto the pavement. The road led through gently rolling, largely forested terrain, sometimes passing a pasture or small farm where animals of all sorts—sheep, goats, pigs, cows—crowded under the inadequate tin roofs of their various pens and corrals, looking uniformly miserable, trying to find a bit of shelter from the rain.

Eventually the road emerged into a vast area of enormous stumps, the land on both sides clear-cut of all trees, harvested for fuel in lime kilns. They soon began curving down toward Roche Harbor—a company town of limestone quarries, kilns, warehouses, docks, rooming houses, a hotel, a Methodist church, and, a bit separated from the rest of it, the speakeasy folks referred to as the Smokehouse.

"That's Jap Town, over there," Miles said, pointing to a detached cluster of cottages at the north end of the harbor where colorful textiles hung wet and heavy from laundry lines strung in the adjacent trees. "I'm going to park up the road a bit in hopes that we aren't noticed."

"By whom?"

"Don't worry about it. The Smokehouse is on an old pier on the far side of the lime works. We'll just tiptoe through the edge of town, take a look in the speakeasy, then sneak back out."

"Why sneak? You're the sheriff."

"That's the second time you've reminded me of that in the past half hour."

"My point is, you can go where you please."

Miles took a breath. "Floyd, right or wrong, this place is sort of a town apart. The lime works brings a lot of money into the county. It employs hundreds. In general, the company doesn't cause us any trouble. But the owner is rather territorial. Man by the name of Errol Buchannan. You've probably heard of him."

"I don't think so."

"He's another hotheaded highland Scot, and a robber baron if ever there was one. Has legislators down in Olympia in his pocket. Fires any of his employees who don't vote for the senators and congressmen he approves of. Entertains Seattle power brokers on his lavish private yacht. And he rides the property on horseback with a shotgun slung over his shoulder like Pancho Villa, usually with a couple of goliath security henchmen in tow, all to keep a tight leash over his workforce."

"Again, so what? You're the sheriff."

"*Acting* sheriff. Put it this way: maybe it's beneath him, but for whatever reason, Buchannan has, so far, not involved himself—or his vast sums of money—in local island politics. And the county councilmen, who are my bosses, have made it abundantly clear since I took over as acting sheriff that they do *not* want me to rock that boat."

"Money and politics," Floyd said, shaking his head. "Same old story. Even way up here in the middle of nowhere."

"Anyway, with any luck, we don't run into the son of a bitch."

"I take it you have a history with this guy."

"A history of not recognizing him as God, which does seem to stick in his craw."

They parked against a dense, roadside thicket of second-growth maples and hoofed their way down to the harbor. A three-masted schooner was moored at the end of a long service pier, and thick-necked men in work clothes were rolling large barrels out to it from a warehouse on shore. Miles and Floyd walked at a deliberately casual pace, keeping close to the various waterfront buildings, hardly seeming to draw a glance. They heard harsh laughter coming from within the elegant Hotel de Haro. Miles pictured fat, drunk, besuited tycoons sitting on red velvet chairs and puffing on huge cigars as they swapped stories about robbing their employees of their dignity.

Further on, they passed the great lime kilns—at least half of which were running, billowing smoke from their chimneys, putting off a tremendous heat that could be felt from many feet away. Miles found their bone-penetrating warmth comforting on the otherwise cold, wet day. It helped cut the tension between his shoulder blades. By the time they passed the last kiln, he was as relaxed as he'd felt in days.

The pier—which was once a service dock and auxiliary tie-up for cargo ships—was a high, narrow, and crumbling affair with warped, partially rotted planks, popped nails, and patches of slippery green algae. Someone had sprinkled its surface with gravel to help with traction. Still, it had no railings. A misstep or a good slip, and a person would drop 20 feet to the bone-chilling water. Watching where they put their feet, the men slowly made their way out toward a rickety cedar shanty that stood on the much wider far end of the pier, well over 200 feet out from the shore. A curl of white wood smoke leaked from its tin chimney, then dissipated without rising in the still, heavy air over the rain-rippled surface of Roche Harbor.

"Welcome to the Smokehouse," Miles said.

It wasn't the type of place to ever be bothered with by federal officials, and local officials had always looked the other way, so there was no security or even so much as a lookout. Miles and Floyd simply walked up and opened the front door. A thin but aromatic haze of warm smoke enveloped them as they entered. Inside, dozens upon dozens of bright red salmon filets hung from dowel racks like drying laundry while a fresh handful of green alder branches smoldered over a small brazier of hot coals in the corner.

"Needless to say, the front half still functions as a legitimate smokehouse this time of year," Miles said. "You can always tell who's been out here sipping hooch by the smoked salmon smell on their clothes. It's a dead giveaway."

Floyd glanced around, his mouth watering. He loved smoked salmon. Then he took a peek into a big garbage barrel that stood next to another door. "Take a look at this," he said, pointing down into it. Bending over for a look, Miles saw that it was full of empty liquor bottles, three of which were for Glenfiddich Scotch whiskey. The men gave each other puzzled looks. Then they opened the second door and stepped into a somewhat larger back room with a short bar, four empty barstools, and eight small tables jammed in so tight that they touched. As they entered, the half dozen customers and solo barkeep looked up with faces frozen in utter surprise. Nobody said a word. Miles scanned the room for Rupert Hawkins. If he'd been there, he was gone now.

"Looking for Rupert Hawkins," Miles said to no one in particular.

Silence.

"Hawkins, I said. Anyone seen him?" Miles turned to the barkeep. "Who are you?"

"Nobody," the shiny bald-headed man said as he gripped a bar towel in one white-knuckled hand and continued to rub a highball glass that was already dry.

"Your name, fella. Or I'll frog march you right out of here and take you to the woodshed."

"Davis."

"Are you the owner, Davis?"

"No. Mr. Chiu is the owner."

"Who's Mr. Chiu?"

"A Chinese."

"No kidding?"

"He's not here."

"I can see that. You serve Glenfiddich Scotch whiskey. Where did it come from?"

Davis's eyes began to blink with an odd frequency. "Look, I just tend bar. Hawkins, you said? Right? Rupert Hawkins? He was just here."

"How long ago?"

"Maybe fifteen minutes. He got a phone call, then left."

"You have a phone out here?" Miles asked, his tone betraying his surprise.

The barkeep pulled an ancient Kellogg candlestick phone from under the bar. "Party line we share with the Hotel de Haro," he said. "Comes in handy when people need help getting home."

"It was you who answered the call for Hawkins, I assume."

"Yessir."

"Recognize the voice?"

"No, sir."

"Describe it."

"A man. Regular sort of voice. Just asked for Hawkins, so I handed it over."

"What did Hawkins say while he was on the phone?"

"Nothing really. Just hello, and a couple of okays. Then he hung up and left."

"Where did he go?"

"I don't know, sir. That's the God's honest truth."

Miles took the phone, picked up the handset, and tapped the

cradle. It took a moment for the operator to answer.

"Switchboard. How may I direct your call?"

"Hello again, Mrs. Hampton."

"Sheriff. I didn't expect to hear your voice on this line."

"I'm sure you didn't. I need you to tell me who you last connected to this number."

"Now, Sheriff. We've been over this."

She reiterated her demand for a court order. Miles hung up, ground his teeth, and glared at the barkeep with a look that made it clear he was looking for someone to take out his frustration on.

"I can tell you that he owes Mr. Chiu money," the barkeep offered.

"Hawkins does? Why?"

"Mr. Chiu extended him credit."

"How much credit?"

"It's up over $52 now."

"$52? For whiskey? You're feeding me a line."

"No, not for whiskey. For cards."

"Gambling?"

"Well, yes. The regular Friday stud game."

"Hawkins is $52 in the hole from a poker game? That's a serious debt. Is he overdue on making payments?"

"Yes."

"And I imagine Mr. Chiu is extremely eager to get such a large sum of money back."

The barkeep just stared.

"If you're looking for Rupert, why not just ask his old lady," an obese, bearded man slurred from the shadows of a far corner of the room.

"Who's his old lady?"

"That's her right there," he said, pointing to a slouching, filthy creature Miles had mistaken for a man. Her hair was in tangles and the skin of her face was terribly weathered.

"Mannix, you bastard," she said to the obese man. "Why

can't you mind your business?" Her hands gripped a half-empty tumbler of a clear, colorless spirit. She stared down at her table, refusing to make eye contact with Miles or Floyd.

"What's your name?" Miles asked her.

"I ain't his old lady. Jane."

"Jane what?"

"Hill."

"You aren't his wife?"

"His wife left him years ago."

"You work for the company?"

"I wash dishes at the hotel, don't I?"

"Where did Rupert go?"

"Like I said, I ain't his old lady."

"Look at me, Miss Hill." She did. "Give me something, or I'll haul you right to jail, and you can drink nothing but water for the rest of the week. How does that sound?"

"What can I give you when I don't know nothing?"

Miles gave her a hard stare. "Have you ever seen what happens to a boozer when they're cut off from booze, Miss Hill? It's ugly. Usually kicks in on the second or third day."

"But Sheriff, like I told you—"

"First come the sweats, the fever, the confusion—ten times worse than any flu you've ever had. Then come the shakes and hallucinations. Then holy terror. Madness. I've heard men say they saw the devil himself appear at the foot of their bed—those who survived to tell the tale, that is."

"Sheriff, please."

"Rupert's been drinking a lot," said the obese man in the corner.

"Mannix, I told you to mind your business," Jane Hill growled.

"I'm giving them something so they don't take you away, you stupid hag."

"Rupert's been drinking a lot?" Miles asked her. "More than usual?"

She shrugged. "Maybe. Probably."

"Has Rupert been up to anything funny lately?"

"He's always up to something funny."

"And?"

She looked back down at the table. "Just, I don't know—last week he was bragging on another one of his schemes. How it was going to make him rich."

"What scheme?"

"He didn't say. I told him he was feeding us all a line, trying to convince us he's something he ain't. But he said just watch him. Said he had something big in the works. Said he'd be in the catbird seat soon, with more gold than anyone could ever spend."

"Gold?"

"Money."

"Did he say money, or did he say gold?"

"Well, I—money, I think. I don't rightly remember. Maybe he said gold. If he did, he probably meant it, you know, uh . . ."

"Symbolically?"

"Yeah. Sym, uh—you know, gold, as in money. But that was last week. This week he ain't talking about any gold. This week he's just drinking himself silly and looking like he saw the ghost of Indian Chief Leschi."

TWENTY-SEVEN

"Rupert got a phone call and abruptly left fifteen minutes before we arrived," Miles said as the door of the speakeasy closed behind them and they walked back up the pier toward shore. "Of course he did. I'll tell you, Floyd. It's starting to feel like we're always just a few minutes late. Always one step behind."

"The owner's name, Chiu," Floyd said. "It's another Cantonese name. The Mandarin equivalent is Zhao."

"So," Miles said, "the tongs are Cantonese. And now we have a Cantonese speakeasy owner whose barkeep is serving high-end Glenfiddich in his low-end rat hole of an establishment—this just after a probable rumrunner was very possibly relieved of a shipment of Glenfiddich."

"Plus, we have Rupert Hawkins," Floyd said, holding up a finger as he made each point, "who was recently seen giving two unusually well-dressed Chinese men a ride from the steamship terminal, who we already know was working with Angus Cooper aboard the *Daisy* this past week, who owes Chiu an awful lot of money in gambling debts, and who has been drinking even more than usual, looking like he saw a ghost, and recently bragging about something big being in the works. Something maybe involving gold. That's too many things lining up for it all to be a coincidence."

"I wouldn't put too much weight on what that poor drunk woman thinks she may or may not remember."

"Sure. But saying *money* is one thing. Saying *gold* is quite something else. They aren't words you tend to confuse."

"Still."

"You know, it's common for wealthy families to bring their gold with them when they emigrate via steamship," Floyd said.

"What does that have to do with anything?"

"I'm thinking back on all the stuff you found in Hans Jensen's tool shed. The Haro Strait nautical charts, the tide charts, the old newspaper clippings."

"About the wreck of the *Empress of Burma*?"

"Yes. Consider this—we know the *Lucky Lena* and the *Daisy* were observed, on more than one occasion, loitering in the general vicinity of where the *Empress of Burma* sank, out off D'Arcy Island, right? And didn't you say someone spotted an actual salvage ship in that area the evening before the *Lucky Lena* was spotted adrift?"

"The *Deepwater Doubloon* out of Seattle. Yes. A professional salvager. You think they were diving the wreck for lost gold?"

"It would explain why the Jensens had an expensive German deep-water diving apparatus," Floyd said. "Maybe word got around that the wreck of the *Empress of Burma* has been found. Maybe there was known to be gold aboard. Maybe there was a race on to recover it. Or maybe the Jensens were already in the process of bringing it up, someone found out, and then robbed them of it."

"That's a lot of maybes," Miles said, wondering at Floyd's sudden focus on a theory he was sure was nothing but a potential distraction. His suspicions of Floyd stormed back to the forefront of his mind. "Do you think somebody warned Rupert Hawkins that we were coming?" he asked, watching Floyd's face carefully.

"Warned? I suppose anything is possible," he said, looking genuinely thoughtful. "But who would have warned him?"

For a brief moment, Miles wondered whether Floyd had been in his hotel long enough to make a phone call when they'd stopped by for his raincoat. He'd have had to be very quick in making one, as he'd only been inside for a couple of minutes. But it wasn't beyond the realm of possibility.

With a splash, a California sea lion surfaced just below them, peered up with giant brown eyes, and gave them a deep, loud moan, probably begging for the food it was accustomed to getting from company workers who dumped their lunch leftovers off the dock. Distracted by it, Miles stepped on a long rusty joist nail nestled in a gap where one of the old pier planks had rotted away.

"Son of a whore!"

"What is it?" Floyd looked down to see a good inch of nail sticking, dead center, out of the top of Miles's shoe. "Oh, damn, Miles."

Gritting his teeth as beads of sweat broke out along his hairline, Miles slowly, gingerly raised his foot until it slid free of the nail.

"I knew I should have worn my damned boots," he said, wincing.

"We'd better get you back to the station," Floyd said.

But Miles hardly heard him. His mind was preoccupied with the fact that he'd have to catch the last steamer to Bellingham that evening so he could go to the hospital for tetanus antitoxin serum. That he would miss his dinner with Marion.

*****

As they were about to pass the Hotel de Haro, Miles and Floyd spotted the lime works owner, Errol Buchannan, and two broad-shouldered members of his security detail—each of them carrying 12-gauge shotguns—coming straight at them from up the wharf.

"This should be interesting," Miles muttered while they were still out of earshot.

Buchannan wore a bowler hat, a close-cropped red beard, and a dark three-piece suit. His men were similarly attired. None of them were smiling.

"Errol," Miles said. "What a wonderful surprise."

"You know you've let a Bolshevik onto your little island?"

"The hell are you talking about?"

"Edward Callahan of the Knights of Labor. Here to stir up trouble. Man should be shot for treason."

"I'll bear it in mind."

"I bet you will," Buchannan said, his cold, pale blue eyes measuring, assessing. "What are you doing here?"

"Looking for someone at the Smokehouse."

"Why?"

"A matter of police business."

"You're limping."

"I stepped on a nail on your pier. Went clean through my foot. Consequently, I'm not in much of a mood to deal with your territorial pissings right now, Errol.

"You have no cause to interfere with goings-on at the Smokehouse."

"You mean aside from the naked disregard of state and federal law?"

"Nobody sought my permission to enter my property."

"Yeah, well, I don't know that you're aware of this, Errol. But my jurisdiction actually includes your little company town here."

Buchannan's expression remained impassive, so much so that it was menacing.

"Remember, Sheriff. If it weren't for my company town, the rest of you hayseeds wouldn't have phone lines or electricity yet."

Miles turned to Floyd, then said, "And on the seventh day, he rested."

"You're the second trespasser at the Smokehouse that I've had to deal with today," Buchannan added. "I have better things to do with my time."

"I thought the Smokehouse was open to the public."

"Not if a person is only there to interfere."

"Who was interfering?"

"Aside from you? That crazy lay preacher, McCaskill."

"McCaskill was at the Smokehouse?"

"He was huddling in the trees just off the end of the pier, watching who came and went, mumbling fire and brimstone quotes from the Good Book."

Miles and Floyd exchanged looks.

"Look, Sheriff. I'm asking you, as a gentleman, to not interfere with what goes on at the Smokehouse. There'd be general mutiny among my workers."

"Maybe you should pay them more, and in something other than company scrip. Like dollars, say."

"Working-class men like you need their petty distractions. It gives them something to live for. Otherwise, why get out of bed? Why go to work?"

"Don't worry, Errol. Nobody is going to pull the plug on the Smokehouse. Incidentally, did you know they're serving Glenfiddich in that rat hole?"

"No."

"Know where it came from?"

"No. Anything else?"

"The card room is run by a Chinese, is it not?"

"What of it?"

"Is he a member of one of the Seattle tongs?"

The robber baron gave Miles a hard look. "You read too many dime novels, Sheriff."

"Are you refusing to answer my question?"

"Whether the owner of the Smokehouse is a member of a tong? I'm not in the habit of asking questions like that. And frankly, I don't care."

"As long as the money comes in, right?"

"What is that supposed to mean?"

"I mean the establishment is on your company's property. You get a cut of the action, don't you? Or would you rather I call it above-market rent?"

Buchannan's eyes narrowed. "Sheriff, I'll tell you what—you take care of your fiefdom, and I'll take care of mine." The men stared each other down until Buchannan said, "Anyway, you'd better scamper back to your little fish camp of a town or you're going to be late."

"Late for what?"

"For supper, boy. Doesn't your mother still cook your supper every evening? Don't you still live in your mother's house?"

Miles's right hand rose until his fingertips just touched the cold steel butt of his holstered pistol. He gave serious thought to stepping forward and pistol-whipping Buchannan across the face—a feat he could manage without compunction. But he knew that Buchannan's escorts would gleefully crack his ribs—or his skull—with the butts of their shotguns before he could disengage. Buchannan knew it too.

It was Buchannan's way of reminding Miles of who was really in charge—and that money always trumped the law.

Miles took a couple of deep breaths through flared nostrils before he and Floyd turned and walked away.

"That was enlightening," Floyd muttered once they were out of earshot.

"Was it?"

"I learned that not only does your mother still make your lunches for you, but you still *live with her* as well. Surprise, surprise."

*****

The moment he got back to the station, Miles rang Marion and told her about the rusty nail.

"So," he said, "unfortunately, I'm going to have to catch tonight's boat to Bellingham so that I can get the tetanus antitoxin serum at the hospital first thing in the morning. Which also means that I can't meet for dinner."

"You don't have to trouble yourself with all that," Marion said.

"Only if I want to live."

"Nonsense. We'll just call Swedish Hospital in Seattle and have them send the serum up on the *Bangor* tomorrow morning."

"They'll insist that it be prescribed to a medical professional to administer the injection."

"Right. We'll have Sylvia make the call."

"Sylvia?"

"She's a nurse. She was in the War."

"Sylvia was in the War? You're kidding."

"I'm not. So we can have dinner after all. See you in an hour."

Miles was elated. He hung up the phone with a huge smile on his face. At that moment, Bill came flying through the door. "Sheriff, I've been looking all over for you."

"I was out at Roche Harbor, like I told you. What's up?"

"Akroyd's body washed up at Smallpox Bay."

After a stupefied moment, Miles almost chuckled. "Of course," he muttered, reaching for the phone to re-cancel dinner with Marion.

TWENTY-EIGHT

It took Miles, Floyd, and Bill the better part of an hour to get back out to the far side of the island and make their way down a short trail to Smallpox Bay—a small indentation in the western shore, barely 200 feet wide at its mouth and flanked by rocky outcroppings. It was less than a mile south of Akroyd's shack near Sunset Point. At the head of the bay, there was a small gravel beach just big enough to accumulate a few driftwood logs—and, today, a body discovered by a dairyman who'd walked down from his nearby farm to exercise his Labrador retrievers.

The men stood around Akroyd's scrawny corpse. It was beached, face up, along a line of seaweed and other debris near the high tide line. His stringy hair and beard were a sandy, disarrayed mess. He was shirtless and shoeless, his skin a shriveled and lifeless white. His vacant eyes were partially open and his mouth agape as if he'd died wanting to speak. But something—probably related to the large gash on the left side of his head—had stopped him.

Floyd knelt down for a closer look. "This injury to his head is at least six inches long. It's ragged. Irregular. I can't think of the right word. Maybe an indentation from the edge of a big, jagged rock."

"I wonder why he's half naked," Bill said.

"His shirt and shoes could have come off in the water as the surf and tide pulled and tumbled him," Miles said.

"Or, if he was fleeing, he might not have had time to dress," Floyd said.

"Fleeing from what?" Bill asked.

"Or who?" Miles said. "Alright. Let's take stock. He was probably alive this morning, given that we found warm coffee and bacon and a hot stove at his shack. It's a possibility that he heard us coming, ran for it, and, say, lost his footing and fell off the bluff, cracking his head and falling into the water in the process."

"That strikes me as unlikely," Floyd said, "because I doubt he could have heard us coming with all the noise of the wind whistling through the trees this morning."

"Good point," Miles said. "For that matter, if he'd caught sight of us coming down the trail, then we probably would have been close enough to see him run for it. Of course, it's also possible that someone called and warned him that we were coming, and that it led to the same result."

"Another possibility," Floyd said, "is that someone else got to the shack just before we did, and, for whatever reason, prompted Akroyd's flight and consequent fall. Or even that that someone cracked Akroyd's skull with a big rock, then tossed him into the water."

Miles shook his head. "Someone who always seems to be one step ahead of us."

"Let's not start hatching conspiracy theories just yet," Floyd said. "Still, assuming it's a viable possibility, why would someone kill Akroyd?"

"You might also ask why someone would cut pages out of Akroyd's vessel observation logbook covering the very day the *Lucky Lena* was hijacked, assuming it wasn't Akroyd himself who did it. Maybe he really was working for both sides, like you theorized."

"And maybe somebody figured out he was a double-dealer," Floyd said, "and terminated his employment with extreme prejudice."

"Whatever the case, I sure would like to have a word with Rupert Hawkins and Angus Cooper." Miles exhaled and looked out to sea. "What a day. I suppose we'd better wrap him up and get back to town. It'll be getting dark soon."

"Shouldn't we go try to find Hawkins at his house?"

In futile hope of still getting to see Marion, even for a short time, Miles had been trying to ignore the little voice in his head that had been asking the same question. "Well, there's, uh . . ."

"There's what?"

"Nothing. You're right. We should." Miles straightened his back. "This day is just never going to end, is it?"

*****

They arrived at Hawkins's shotgun house on the edge of town just as it was growing dark. Though it stood on a quiet street of well-maintained homes, Hawkins's place was a dump—its roofline sagging, its paint flaking, its yard overgrown with weeds. There was no light within.

The men marched up to the door and gave it a loud knock.

"Hawkins!" Miles shouted. "It's the sheriff! Open the door!"

Nothing.

"He's probably passed out in there," Bill said.

Miles gave the door another pounding. It made no difference.

"I've come to assume that you'll kick the door in whether you have a warrant or not," Floyd said.

"Safe assumption," Miles said. But just as he lifted his leg and took aim with the flat of his foot, he thought twice and tried the knob. It was unlocked. He threw the door wide open. "Hey, what do you know?"

Entering, they were greeted by stagnant air carrying the combined odors of spilled whiskey, bile, and old urine. Odors of such pungency that they made Miles's eyes water. "Holy cow," he muttered.

"Holy drunk cow," Floyd said. "Make that an entire dairy of sick, drunk cows wallowing in their own piss."

"Nice turn of phrase, Floyd," Miles said, pulling his shirt up over his mouth and nose.

"Does Hawkins smell as bad as his house?" Floyd asked.

"He's no gardenia."

"How do people ride in his car when he's working as a taxi driver?"

"I imagine they hold their breath."

Miles tried the light switch, but nothing came on, so Bill retrieved a small lantern from the truck, and they took a look around as a trio bound to the light.

Though technically a house, the inside made Akroyd's shack seem clean and well maintained by comparison. The wood floor was soft in multiple spots. The walls and interior doors were damaged and stained by the scratching of long-departed dogs. There was a filthy, bare mattress in the far corner of the front room. Mouse droppings all over the kitchen floor. No food in the pantry, save for one dented can of scrapple that looked as if someone had tried to open it by bashing it with a sharp rock. Broken glass on the floor appeared to be that of a liquor bottle.

"Glenfiddich?" Floyd asked.

"Impossible to say," Miles said. "There's no sign of a label. But I doubt it. The glass is dusty. Looks like it's been here for a while. And old Hawkins usually goes for the cheapest hooch he can find. Stretch his dollar."

The back room, which had a bad leak in its crumbling ceiling, had no furniture at all. There was, however, a brand-new pair of high-quality black and white wingtip shoes standing just inside the door.

"Look at those," Miles said.

"A fella lives in a house that stinks of urine, has next to nothing in his pantry, is known to spend every red cent he has on cheap hooch, but has a brand-new pair of expensive wingtips? Not worn hand-me-downs from one of the church groups?" Floyd said.

"Perhaps he's something of a dancer."

That drew a snort from Bill.

"A dancer who just came into some money," Floyd said. "More money than he needs to keep himself soused."

They searched the house for as long as they could stomach the smell, found nothing else of interest, and finally called it quits as their lantern began to run out of fuel.

"Maybe we'll have better luck tomorrow," Floyd said.

TWENTY-NINE

Miles, Floyd, and Bill stood around Miles's desk, polishing off the second pot of coffee of the morning, examining a nautical chart, tide table, and wind direction log to make sure their theory that Akroyd had died near his shack by Sunset Point before drifting to Smallpox Bay was viable. Sylvia came through the front door of the station wearing what looked like men's wool army pants and bearing a small wooden box.

"Ta-da!" she said. "Your tetanus antitoxin just arrived on the steamer from Seattle."

"Lucky me," Miles said.

"Don't like needles?"

"Hate them."

"Be a man," she said.

"How long will this take?"

"Fifteen minutes."

"Fellas, why don't you head up to the restaurant, and I'll come meet you after the fun here. Order me some biscuits with butter and raspberry jam, will you?" He turned to Sylvia as the men departed. "Where's Marion?"

"At her grandfather's bedside. Roll up your sleeve or take off your shirt."

"Oh. Hey, I apologize for having to cancel dinner last night."

"Having to deal with a dead body is a reasonable excuse, Miles. I'll let you off the hook this one time."

He rolled up a sleeve as Sylvia took a large ampoule of amber liquid from the box. To Miles, it looked like a miniature bottle of bourbon. Then she began assembling a very large hypodermic needle.

"That's a big needle," Miles said.

"I'll say it again. Be a man." She snapped the top off the ampoule and began filling the needle. "Would you believe that they extract this antibody serum from the blood of horses?"

"You're joking."

"Nope. It's a wonder of modern medicine. We used a lot of it in France, to treat soldiers with deep shrapnel wounds."

"Marion mentioned that you were over there."

"Yes, indeed. A volunteer with the Army Nurse Corps, attached to the 26th Infantry Division."

"Near the front?"

"I worked in a surgical field hospital outside of Château-Thierry during the Second Battle of the Marne, so yes."

"Holy hell."

"That sums it up."

"You must have seen . . ."

"Things that are fortunately beyond most people's imagination. Yes. I imagine you did too."

"Well, like I said, I wasn't in the trenches."

"I'm sure you saw plenty."

"It isn't really something I'd normally discuss in the presence of a lady."

That got a laugh from Sylvia. "A *lady*?"

"I mean, I suppose that I . . ."

"You don't like to talk about it, period. Lady or not."

"Right."

"And how are you doing now?" Sylvia asked.

"What do you mean?"

"I mean that the experience of war changes people. Changes how they look at life. I'll certainly never be the same. So naturally, I was wondering about you. Are you happy?"

"Am I happy?"

"Your mother said you're struggling."

"What? When did you talk to my mother?"

"She came for tea with Marion's mother. She's worried about you. Said you haven't been the same since you got back. Said you're disengaged. Sad, even."

"Is that right?"

"For me, coming home was tough. All the troubles and routines of everyday life seemed so petty. So meaningless. Not worth bothering with."

Miles sat stupefied. Sylvia had just described his state of mind as if she'd read it.

"And, of course, nobody understood how I felt," she added, "which made me feel so utterly alone. So isolated."

He tried to say *yes*, but the word refused to come out.

"Do you talk to anyone?" she asked.

He took a breath. "About the war? No."

"Not your mother? Not your buddies?"

"Nobody."

"Talking about it is part of the healing process, Miles."

"I'll take your word for it. Anyway, you can't describe it to people who weren't there."

"I was there. Try me."

"You mean right now?"

She nodded. "I promise I won't go weak at the knees, Miles. What haunts you?"

"I don't think I—"

"Oh, go on!"

Miles gave her an apprehensive look. Then he winced as, against his will, a terrible image came back to him.

"You're remembering something," she said. "I can see it in your eyes."

"Yes."

"What is it?"

"I would really rather not revisit—"

"Miles," she said, her voice gentle and reassuring. "Trust me."

He took a series of breaths, looked at Sylvia, looked away,

looked at her again. At last, he said, "Sometimes we'd escort supply convoys to the advance base hospitals."

"Go on."

He took another breath. "One time, during a big battle, the hospital was short-handed and needed help unloading, so I took boxes off the trucks and carried them inside a triage area." He paused.

"And?"

"It was just . . . there were odors. Formaldehyde. Rotting flesh."

Miles went quiet, losing himself in memory. His jaw grew tight. Inside the hospital, there were mortally wounded men everywhere. Wounded men and corpses. So many corpses. Some under blood-soaked sheets. Some out in the open. Burned, blistered. Faces that were missing eyeballs. Missing jaw bones, cheeks, noses. Whole limbs torn off of mangled bodies. And they just kept coming. Like a river. Endless truckloads of shattered men and corpses coming back from the front, being offloaded onto muddy, bloody litters and brought into the hospital.

She reached out and squeezed his hand.

He continued. "What happened was," a breath, "I had to take this one box through to an enclosure out behind the hospital. Near the incinerator and the garbage bins." He stopped. He shook his head. "There was this . . ."

"This what?"

"There was a crate—Ow!" he said as she jabbed him with the needle.

"Sorry. I thought it would be better if I didn't warn you."

"Better than what?"

"Count yourself lucky, Miles. In our grandparent's generation, they didn't have this stuff. You'd stand a good chance of dying a horrible death. Lockjaw is nobody's idea of pretty."

Miles rubbed his shoulder. "Are we done?"

"You were about to tell me something. About something you saw in the war. A crate."

"Forget it."

"Hey, I wouldn't have jabbed you if I thought it would put your off your story. Now tell me."

"Another time. Can I go?"

"No, sir. I'm going to keep an eye on you here for a few minutes to make sure you don't have a reaction to the serum."

"Reaction?"

"Like anaphylaxis. Do you have any coffee in this place?" Miles started to get up. "No, no. You stay put," she said, so he pointed to the coffee cabinet and percolator.

"Want a cup?" she asked.

"Why not?" With a newborn sense of connection—of affection—he watched her prepare the coffee. But then a troubling thought crossed his mind, clipping the wings of his high spirits. "Can I ask you something, Sylvia?"

"Of course."

"Is there another man?"

"Pardon?"

"Another man courting Marion?"

"No."

"You're sure?"

"Positive."

"Huh."

"You sound perplexed, Miles."

"It's just that we used to be very close. Inseparable, really."

"I know. She's told me all about it. About you."

"She has? The thing is, she didn't even let me know she'd come home. I had to discover it for myself."

"I know for a fact that she intended to call you."

"But not right away?"

Sylvia gave him a sympathetic look. "I'm not sure what to tell you, Miles. I mean, a rose is a rose is a rose is a rose."

"What?"

"It's a quote from Gertrude Stein."

"Gertrude Stein?" Miles repeated, a bewildered look on his

face as he watched Sylvia scoop coffee grounds into the percolator from a big red Hills Brothers can. "I mean, I get that life can change people," he said after a moment. "But friendship should endure."

"I'm certain that it does."

"Well, you've been her roommate for a year or so, right? What do you think she's looking for in a man?"

Sylvia set the percolator on the hot stovetop, then wiped her hands on her trousers before answering. "I really couldn't say, Miles."

THIRTY

Miles stuck his head into the office of Dr. Jon Boren—Friday Harbor's lone physician and de facto medical examiner—as he was headed to meet Floyd and Bill for breakfast. "Good morning, Doc. Got any more information for us?"

"Yes, indeed, Miles. Yes, indeed. First and foremost, Mr. Akroyd didn't drown. His lungs had ceased to draw breath before he was in the water. But his skull was crushed with a rough object of some sort. Like a rock. No doubt the cause of death."

"Did someone hit him over the head, or did he fall head-first onto the rocks near Sunset Point?"

"Impossible to say. Especially after the body was adrift on the tide for several hours. All I can tell you for certain is that his skull was crushed in and that it was the head injury that killed him."

"You're absolutely sure he didn't drown?"

"Positive."

"Alright. Thanks, Doc. Oh, wait—I don't suppose you've seen Angus Cooper or Rupert Hawkins in town this morning?"

"Not this morning. But Rupert was at church last night."

"Church? Rupert Hawkins?"

"Yes, Rupert Hawkins. I have a bridge game in the basement on Saturday nights—me, Giles from the bank, and the Anders brothers. Anyway, we're coming upstairs to leave at the end of the night, and there's rummy Rupert kneeling in the front pew, white-knuckled hands clasped in prayer. A sight I never thought I'd see in my lifetime. I didn't even know he was Methodist."

"He probably didn't know that either. Did you speak with him?"

"No. It clearly wasn't the proper time."

*****

Miles met Floyd and Bill at the restaurant, gorged himself on buttermilk biscuits, and filled them in on Dr. Boren's findings, as well as the doctor's rather surprising report of witnessing Rupert Hawkins praying in church.

"Rupert Hawkins again," Floyd said. "Praying for what? Forgiveness?"

"God knows."

"We really need to have a word with that guy."

"We'll stop by his house in a bit. But first I'd like to know exactly what McCaskill was doing out by the Smokehouse pier yesterday."

*****

With Bill again opting to ride in the bed, they drove Miles's truck back out to Reverend McCaskill's property, back down the long dirt drive that wound through the dark forest to the clearing where the lay preacher's cabin and clapboard chapel stood. The preacher was nowhere in sight. The men got out and strode to the front door of the cabin. At least four cords of freshly split maple firewood sat in a tall pile just to right of the door, but no smoke rose from the chimney. As Floyd and Bill hung back a few feet, Miles gave the door a loud knock.

"McCaskill. Open up if you're in there."

He waited half a minute.

"McCaskill," he shouted, banging on the door again.

"Should we take a peek?" Floyd asked, pointing to the cabin's one window, set a few feet off the ground on the side of the house facing the chapel.

"No. Crazy bastard might pretend to startle and use it as an excuse to shoot us out of our boots. Let's go check the chapel."

They made their way to the front steps of the chapel. Miles was about to turn the handle of the door when someone gave a loud whistle from behind them. Turning, they saw McCaskill, stark naked, standing in the frame of his cabin's back door, all six-foot-freckled-four of him, with his long, stringy red hair and beard hanging damp and clinging to his body as if he'd just stepped from a bathtub. He held a shotgun with one hand, its barrel pointed at the ground. It was a single-barrel break-action gun, which meant he could only take one shot before having to reload. But it looked to be an old Champion 10-gauge. A very powerful gun.

"You're trespassing," he thundered.

"We're looking for you," Miles said, thinking that if McCaskill made so much as a twitch toward raising his shotgun barrel, he'd draw his own .45 and fill him full of lead.

"The hell do you want?"

"Put the gun down and come out here where we can see you."

"Why?"

"We want to talk to you."

"Talk right here."

"What were you doing up at Roche Harbor yesterday?"

McCaskill shrugged.

"You were witnessed loitering near the Smokehouse pier, as if keeping watch. Errol Buchannan said he had to run you off."

"So you're aware of the Smokehouse, Sheriff?"

"Everyone knows about the Smokehouse."

"Then you're fully aware that you have an operating speakeasy on the very island for which you are responsible for enforcing the law. For enforcing Prohibition."

"I'm not here to debate with you, McCaskill. And I'm sure you'd like to get back to packing your bags for the Rapture. So I'll ask you again. What were you doing at the Smokehouse?"

"What is a citizen to do when the sheriff won't enforce the law?"

"Are you enforcing it, Reverend? Without authority? Going vigilante?"

Again, McCaskill shrugged. "Do your job, Sheriff, or someone else will do it for you."

"If you try to do it, I'll lock you up."

"'First cast the beam out of thine own eye, and then shalt thou see clearly to cast the speck out of thy brother's eye.'"

"The hell is that supposed to mean?"

"'Thinkest thou this, O man—you who judge those who practice such things and yet do them yourself—that thou shalt escape the judgment of God?'"

"Were you at the Smokehouse looking for Rupert Hawkins?"

At this, McCaskill grinned a dark and menacing grin, revealing two large gaps where teeth had once been. "Are you arresting me?"

"That depends."

"No, it doesn't. Good day. And may God have mercy on your soul," he said, slamming his thick wood door shut. The men could hear him barring it from within.

"That man is starting to get under my skin," Miles said.

"Does he ever wear clothes?" Floyd asked. "Or does he think he's Tarzan of the Apes?"

THIRTY-ONE

For once, something went their way. Heading back to the station, Miles spotted Rupert Hawkins's old Crow-Elkhart sedan coming up Second Street. "Son of a bitch," he muttered.

"What is it?" Floyd asked.

Miles positioned the truck in the middle of Second Street to block both lanes. "Hawkins," he said, nodding toward the dirty and thoroughly dented car coming to a stop in front of them. Hawkins kept both hands on his steering wheel and averted his eyes as if looking at the police would cause his body to burst into flames. Miles could see the silhouette of a passenger in Hawkins's back seat. Bill hopped out of the back and went to stand behind Hawkins's car. Miles and Floyd followed suit—Floyd taking the passenger side and Miles the driver side. The windows were already down, probably because of the smell.

"Hello, Rupert," Miles said. "You're a hard man to find."

Hawkins took a furtive glance at him. He had puffy, red eyes, spider-veined cheeks, and a forehead with the shine of alcohol sweat. His hair was dirty but combed, and he wore a barely serviceable brown suit that looked to be at least third-hand. He also had the beady eyes, thin lips, and small head Miles tended to associate with people who'd been born to drunk mothers.

"What can I do for you, Sheriff?" he asked in a tremulous voice.

"What is the meaning of this," came a much more authoritative voice from the back seat.

Miles leaned in for a look and saw a man in a clean three-piece suit, clutching a briefcase on his knees.

"I hired this man to drive me to Roche Harbor," he said. "Why have we been stopped?"

"Who are you?" Miles asked.

"James Daniels. Daniels & Warren Bookkeepers of Bellingham. I have just arrived by boat, and I am headed to Roche Harbor for an urgent business engagement."

"Well, Mr. Daniels. You're going to have to find another way to get out to Roche. We need to ask the elusive Mr. Hawkins here a few questions concerning a police matter."

They waited a moment as Hawkins, with obvious reluctance, handed the coins constituting his fare back to Daniels. Looking profoundly irritated, Daniels got out and set off for the steamship terminal on a quest for some other mode of transportation.

"I understand you've been going to church, Mr. Hawkins," Miles said.

"There a law against going to church?"

"Not at all. But in your case, it's unusual, isn't it? Is something weighing on your mind?"

"No," he answered too quickly.

"Confession eases the conscience, I'm told. Eases the soul. Isn't that right, Floyd?"

"So say the wise."

"But wait—do Methodists practice confession?" Miles asked, looking across the car at Floyd who shrugged in ignorance. "You *are* Methodist, right Mr. Hawkins?"

"I, uh . . ."

"You were praying in the Methodist church Wednesday night."

"Sure. Right."

"You know, Rupert, if Methodists don't practice confession, if something is on your mind, you can always tell us. We might even be able to help you out. Matter of fact, if you help us figure some things out, I'm sure we can help you out. With some money. With some protection. With immunity from prosecution. Who knows?"

Miles noticed that Hawkins's eyes were searching the interior spaces of his car, jumping from here to there, seeming to pause on places where a flask of booze could be stowed. A thin beading of sweat had emerged on his hairline.

"You seem uncomfortable, Rupert. Nervous, even."

"I just lost cross-island cab fare, thanks to you. I could have bought a sandwich and a tank of gasoline with that."

"Seems like you're doing alright for money, judging by that nice new pair of wingtips you have at your house."

"What were you doing in my house?"

"Looking for you. How did you afford those fancy shoes, if I may ask? Did you just come into some money? Some gold?"

"Gold? Ha. I wish I'd found some gold. But there's no gold on this island. None. You have to go east to the mountains to pan for gold."

"Isn't there supposed to be gold aboard the wreck of the *Empress of Burma*?"

"Is there?"

"You tell us."

"I don't know anything about that. Even if there was gold, how would I get it? It's underwater, right?"

"So what were you doing on the *Daisy* out near D'Arcy Island?"

"Keeping watch. Captain Cooper was below working on his engines. He paid me to stand watch on deck."

"Anyone else aboard?"

"I don't think so. Oh, wait. Yeah. That mechanic, Bronson or whatever. He was below deck."

"Brennan? Sean Brennan?"

"Yeah, that's the fella. He was helping Cooper install a new engine."

"And you didn't remember this when I first asked you?"

"Huh?"

"You said you didn't think anyone else was aboard. Seems a

big thing to forget, even if only for a moment."

Hawkins grinned stupidly. "My memory, you know . . ."

"I know what?"

"I don't know. Sometimes my brain is a little funny."

"A little funny, huh? Did you see the *Lucky Lena* out there?"

"No."

"That was a quick answer. Are you sure?"

"Yeah."

"But you know about it? About the *Lucky Lena*?"

"I know she's tied up on the wharf. The one they found adrift, right? I don't remember seeing her. Could have been out there I suppose. My vision isn't what it was."

"And with your bad vision, Cooper still hired you to keep watch?"

"Well, I can see if we're drifting toward a lee shore or a big reef. I'm not blind."

"But no *Lucky Lena*?"

"Not that I know of."

"Or any dark-gray painted boats? Say about 50-foot long?"

"I don't think so."

Miles paused to think.

"You picked up two Chinese from off the *Bangor* a few days ago. Well-dressed Chinese."

At this, Hawkins turned to look at Miles. His eyes had gone wide and the color had gone out of his face.

"I pick up a lot of people at the terminal."

"A lot of Chinese?"

"I guess."

"You pick up a lot of Chinese coming off the *Bangor*. Huh. Well, I suppose I could be utterly behind the times and out of touch with what goes at the steamship terminal a mere two blocks east of the station I sit in every working day. Are you saying you don't remember giving them a ride?"

"Sometimes my memory isn't so good, Sheriff."

"Like when you're drinking?" Floyd asked.

"Look, Rupert," Miles said. "I don't care about that. Have I ever hassled you about public drunkenness before?"

"You made me sleep in jail once."

"To keep you from dying of exposure on the park bench where I found you, Rupert. It was winter."

"Oh."

"Look, you need to tell me where you took those Chinese, or I'm going to take you in."

"I . . ." Hawkins froze up.

"What? What is it?"

"Nothing. I'm fine."

"You don't look fine. You look terrified. Did they threaten you?"

Hawkins stared back, mute.

"Did they say they'd cut your man parts off if you spoke with the law? Because let me tell you, if I put you in jail for a couple of days and then cut you loose—which might just be what I do if I don't start getting some answers here—those Chinese are going to *assume* you talked to me. Then where will you be? Or rather, where will your man parts be?"

"Sheriff, please."

"Decision time, Rupert."

"But I—damn. Damn. I don't know where they went *exactly*."

"What does that mean?"

"They had me drop them off out by nowhere."

"You aren't making sense."

"Sheriff, listen. They had me drive them out toward Roche Harbor."

"They went to Roche? Where? To the Smokehouse?"

"No, no. They had me turn south at the junction with West Valley Road, then drive another—I don't know—maybe two miles. Then we pulled over."

"By what?"

"That's what I'm saying. By nothing. There's nothing out there. It's where the road passes through the woods. East of

Mitchell Bay, I think. That's where I left them."

"But . . ."

Hawkins looked perplexed. "But nothing."

"Didn't they threaten you?"

"No."

"Then why were you reluctant to tell us."

"Look, Sheriff. I haven't done anything. That's the God's honest truth."

"I'll ask one more time, Rupert. Why didn't you want to tell us?"

Hawkins squeezed his steering wheel. "Because . . . "

"Because why?"

"Because they were assassins."

Miles and Floyd exchanged grave looks.

"Assassins?" Floyd asked.

"Oriental assassins," Hawkins said.

"Why do you think that?" Floyd asked.

"They both wore their braids up. Sean Brennan says that's how you know."

Miles glanced at Floyd, who gave a quick nod of affirmation.

"How did that come up in conversation?"

"With Brennan? I don't know. I guess I must have mentioned the Chinese when we were on the *Daisy*. Yeah, that was it. I'd never seen such well-dressed Chinamen in my whole life, you know?"

Miles thought for a moment. "Alright, Hawkins. Hop in the back of the truck. We're going to take you back out there so you can show us exactly where you dropped them. Tap on the roof when we get to the spot."

With Hawkins now in the truck bed and Bill headed back to the station, they drove across the island, eventually turning onto West Valley Road. Eventually, Hawkins knocked on the roof, Miles pulled over, and they all got out. As Hawkins had claimed, it was a stretch of road with nothing around but forest. Particularly dense, dark forest.

"You dropped them off here?" Miles asked. "There aren't any houses or driveways or anything."

"Like I told you."

"You're sure it was right here?" Floyd asked.

"I recognize that big fir," he said, pointing to a recently fallen giant that had come down alongside the road. "This is where they got out."

"Then what did they do?" Miles asked.

"Nothing. Stood here until I left."

"Didn't start walking?"

"No."

"Did they maybe tend to look in any particular direction?"

"They watched me until I was gone."

"Maybe they had arrangements for someone else to pick them up here," Floyd suggested while Miles looked up and down the road.

"Maybe."

Hawkins smoked a cigarette and fidgeted while Miles and Floyd walked a few hundred yards of the road, looking for footprints, a trailhead leading into the woods, or anything else that might give a clue as to where the Chinese had gone. They found nothing but a used tire, a decomposing roadkill possum, and half a dozen discarded beer bottles.

THIRTY-TWO

"I think we should have brought Hawkins in for interrogation," Floyd said as he and Miles sipped hot coffee back at the station. "He looked like he was going to have a coronary as you questioned him."

"But because of my questions, or because he's conditioned to fear police? Or because he just needed a drink?"

"A few more questions in the hot seat might have cleared that up for us."

"We don't have enough information to pin him down, Floyd. It's entirely possible that his involvement is innocent and coincidental."

"And he's going to church all of a sudden?"

"If we get a bit more information, we can take another stab at him," Miles said.

"Fair enough. But I have to ask it again—what about Brennan? He was on the boat with them out by D'Arcy Island. He didn't mention that to us before, did he?"

"I don't believe so. But I imagine he would have told us if he'd seen anything noteworthy."

"Unless he was involved."

"Unless he was a killer, you mean. Unless he was, to use your words, morally insane. Brennan."

"I understand your doubts. But look at it—he's desperate for money to save his business. To pay for his mother's care back in Bellingham."

"Desperate enough to murder people? A fellow with no criminal history? A fellow I've never even seen so much as jaywalk? Floyd, he's an engine mechanic. He was installing new engines on the *Daisy*. You'd expect to find him aboard, testing systems, checking his work."

"We can't rule him out based on what we know."

"Point taken."

"So, what should we . . . " Floyd paused, his eyes locking on something behind Miles. "What in the world is that?" he asked, pointing at a large glass jar on a shelf next to the stove. In it, something frothy and brownish and rotten-looking was gently bubbling away."

"That's Bill's sourdough starter."

"Sourdough starter?"

"For the flapjacks you've been eating. It's what gives them that extra bite."

Floyd's mouth fell open. "Is it sanitary?"

"Have you had any bowel issues?"

"No, but—"

"Then it's probably okay."

"Huh." Floyd did his best not to frown. "Anyway, now what should we do?"

"Good question."

As if on cue, Bill came in the front door. "*Arcata*'s taking on water at the pier," he said, referring to the U.S. Government's sole rumrunner-hunting revenue cutter in the region.

"The *Arcata* crew might know something," Floyd said.

"Unlikely," Miles answered. "They're usually the last to know anything about anything."

"It's worth asking."

"I don't think so."

"The ship is tied up barely two blocks away, Miles. What's the harm? Why the reluctance?"

Miles gulped the last of his coffee, sighed, and looked at the ceiling. "Let's just say the *Arcata*'s captain and I have philosophical differences."

"Over what?"

"Everything."

"Huh. I think I'm starting to see a pattern."

"With respect to what?"

"You versus everybody else."

"Hey, now," Miles said, giving Floyd a look. "I'll put it this way: the captain is another half-deranged temperance fanatic. And he has no compunction about crossing ethical lines."

"How do you mean?" Floyd asked.

"I mean he's more than happy to board the boats of every honest fisherman he can catch up with, cite them for their pencils not being sharp enough, or whatever other petty maritime misdemeanors he can trump up. More than happy to ransack their boats, knock their teeth in, and basically interfere with their livelihood until they have no choice but to turn informant—which puts them and their families at risk for retribution.

"I see. But still, if it's his job, his holy crusade, to interdict rumrunners, he might very well know something useful. Let's talk to him. What else are we going to do right now? Come on."

Miles sighed again. "Oh, Floyd. You're as stubborn as my mother."

*****

Miles and Floyd descended a broad ramp from the main pier to a floating service dock used by vessels taking on fuel and water. There, Miles noticed a red and white silkscreened flyer tacked to a piling. It advertised a meeting at the Odd Fellows Hall scheduled for the next evening—a meeting sponsored by the Knights of Labor and featuring labor leader Edward Callahan as keynote speaker. It invited *all white brother laborers* to a discussion of how to *abolish the wage system.*

"I wonder if Errol Buchannan's goons will try to break up that Callahan guy's meeting," Miles said as they strode down the dock.

"It would make for an exciting evening," Floyd said as they

arrived alongside the 85-foot USRC *Arcata*.

"Permission to come aboard?" Miles said to the only crewman he saw on the deck. The man was slouching against the railing, smoking, wearing a greasy tank top undershirt in lieu of his uniform shirt and jacket.

"What?" the man mumbled, flipping his cigarette into the water.

"Captain Eckart around?"

"On the bridge."

"Can we go up there?"

"Who are you?"

"Sheriff Miles Scott. And this is Detective Floyd of the Seattle Police Department."

"Need captain's permission to come aboard."

"Right. And seeing as how you're done with your smoke, seaman, maybe you could go ask him for me."

"Yeah. Alright. Wait here."

The vessel itself was filthy, from bow to stern. Its obsolete Hotchkiss gun was speckled with seagull droppings. The hull and vertical surfaces that had once been a glossy white were dulled by a residue of sea salt and grime, the teakwood decks oxidized and cracked.

"I've never been aboard a revenue cutter before," Floyd said.

"Prepare to be underwhelmed. This isn't exactly the USS *Arizona*."

"Hey you," the slovenly crewman shouted down from an open window on the bridge. "Captain says you can come up."

"Is there a gangway?"

"Are you injured or something?"

"No."

"Then just jump."

*****

Miles and Floyd ascended a short ladder to the small,

cramped bridge where they found Captain James Eckart and another seaman huddled over a radio set at a miniscule corner table. Eckart was at least as slovenly as the swab they'd met on deck, with pale skin, baggy eyes, greasy dandruff-speckled hair, and a paunch that strained his shirt buttons. The bridge itself smelled of marine paint and engine oil and was in need of a good mopping. A sawed-off coffee can serving as a makeshift ashtray sat full of cigarette butts next to the helm. The seaman sitting by the radio set held an ink pen at the ready, poised to make entries in a logbook. On the radio, a female voice with a French accent was telling a children's story involving a badger and a bear. Glancing at Miles, Captain Eckart held a finger to his lips.

"What shall we do today, Bear?" the voice on the radio said.

"Let's look for strawberries, Badger. Big and red and sweet."

"Strawberries?" Captain Eckart said. "Doesn't that mean Alexander Beach?"

"Yesterday you told me Alexander Beach is blueberries," the seaman answered.

"Blueberries? I thought blueberries meant Bowman Bay."

"Bowman Bay is a picnic of honey and warm biscuits."

"Oh, to hell."

"Don't mean to interrupt," Miles said. "We can go get you kids some milk and cookies and come back when story time is over."

Captain Eckart glared at him. "You have no idea about Bear and Badger, have you? *The Adventures of Bear and Badger* story time?"

"I'm sure it's delightful."

"It relays coded messages, broadcast from the most powerful radio station in Seattle," Eckart said.

"Coded messages."

"Don't take that tone with me, Miles. That Frenchy-sounding woman telling the story is married to Otto Stenersen, the biggest bootlegger this side of Chicago. The children's story contains coded messages to the rumrunners, telling them where to drop their shipments, where their lookouts have spotted revenue agents, and so forth."

Behind Eckart, the seaman at the radio rolled his eyes for Miles and Floyd's benefit, then mouthed the word *crazy*.

"Should we come back another time?"

"Just make it brief. And you," he said to the seaman. "Keep listening."

"We towed in a Deer Harbor-based boat that was spotted adrift Wednesday morning off Turn Point," Miles said. "Crew and anchor missing. Hold full of bullet holes and blood."

"What vessel?"

"*Lucky Lena*."

"A rumrunner. Relatively new to the business. One of Otto Stenersen's, as a matter of fact."

"*Lucky Lena* is a rumrunner for Stenersen? You're sure?"

"Caught him putt-putting around D'Arcy Island, in Canadian waters, more than once. No American fishing boats put-put around D'Arcy unless they're up to no good. Especially when it's barely an hour after the schooner *Malahat* is observed offloading liquor crates onto the island in broad daylight. The *Malahat*, as I imagine you know, is owned by Consolidated Exports Company of Vancouver, British Columbia, which is the single biggest supplier of smuggled liquor in the region. Stenersen's supplier."

"What did Jensen have to say for himself?"

"Who?"

"Hans Jensen. Captain of the *Lucky Lena*. What did he have to say when you caught him?"

"I meant that figuratively. We *saw* him. We couldn't catch him. Couldn't even get close enough to hail him. Almost did, one time a month or so back. But now he's got a new engine."

"Engines, plural," Miles said. "Twin Liberty gasoline engines, supposedly cannibalized from surplus warplanes parked down at Boeing."

"That would explain why he left us in his wake last week."

"You spotted him last week? Where? Were there any other

boats around?"

"It's always a one-way street with you, Miles. How about if you give me some information for once?"

"Like what?"

"I trust you were thorough in your search of the *Lucky Lena*."

"Of course."

"Did you find anything aboard that could have served as a codebook? Maybe some seemingly nonsensical notes about bears and badgers and blueberries? Maybe a little crib sheet jammed between the pages of a legitimate book?"

"We found a nautical text that had been hollowed out to create a hiding spot, but there wasn't anything in it."

Eckart nodded knowingly. "That's a pity." He coughed a phlegmy cough into his hairy fist. "On an unrelated matter, I'm obliged to make enquiries about a resident of your island, name of Akroyd."

"Why?"

"A routine matter."

"What sort of matter?"

Eckart looked equal parts reluctant and irritated. "I was expecting to hear from him concerning . . ."

"A routine matter. Yes. Thanks for explaining. As for whatever routine matter you were planning to discuss, it turns out Akroyd's dead."

"Dead?"

"Looks like he fell off a cliff and the impact crushed his skull in."

"Fell, or was pushed?"

"Interesting question, Eckart. There's no evidence to suggest that he was pushed, but no evidence to rule it out either. His body washed up at Smallpox Bay."

"And, presumably, no evidence to indicate that someone hit him over the head to crush his skull?"

"Not thus far."

"You'll get me a copy of the autopsy report?"

"Autopsy report? This is San Juan Island, Eckart. There's no real medical examiner. I had the town physician take a look at the body. You know as much as I do."

"Did you search his home?"

"Yes."

"Well? Did you find anything noteworthy? A logbook, perhaps?"

"Logbook?"

"Don't be obtuse! Do I need to spell it out? A logbook of ship observations. The man was in our unofficial employ as a watcher."

"Oh, he was, was he? Thanks for sharing that information in such a timely manner."

"Don't pretend to be offended, Miles. You know as well as I do that half the local police in this state are corrupt, if not actively working for the rumrunners. I couldn't compromise a source."

"Presumably you trust me."

"I wouldn't have told you about our relationship with Akroyd if I didn't."

"Unless you didn't think you had a choice once you lost contact with him."

"Well?"

"No, Eckart, we didn't find a logbook." The comment earned Miles a quick, perplexed glance from Floyd.

"You're sure?"

"Positive. My turn again. What do you know about a Trafton workboat called the *Daisy*?"

"The *Daisy*. Don't know that one. Why?"

"It disappeared around the same time we found the *Lucky Lena* adrift. Captain is missing."

"Could be a new player. We've been seeing a definite upsurge in aggressive, even bloody activity lately, across the whole Puget Sound region. An influx of previously unknown but very well-armed hijackers, as opposed to the established Seattle and Tacoma rumrunners who don't generally carry guns but rely on the speed of their superior boats. It could be random. It could be orchestrated. Like maybe someone trying to edge out the local syndicates for a bigger piece of the action. I'll tell you that for free."

"The *Daisy*'s captain is no cutthroat."

"If you say so. But he could have been another victim."

"I suppose," Miles said.

"Now let me ask you this, Miles: have you seen any local boat captains acting funny or installing new engines or painting their hulls dark colors? Or have you at least heard any rumors?"

"Rumors you can use to harass the people I'm sworn to protect?"

"I beg your—I thought this was a friendly exchange of information."

"You always cast too wide a net. It hurts good people and you don't care."

"The hell do you—"

"Save your breath, Eckart."

Eckart's face flushed. "You have your job, Miles, and I have mine."

"And what has your job done? What has Prohibition done to this country other than give rise to a vast criminal economy that corrupts politicians and police, turn the border region into a battleground, and make millionaires out of murderers? People are drinking more than ever."

"Prohibition is the law, Miles. And if it matters to you at all, my father and brother both died of cirrhosis."

Miles stopped himself. "I didn't know that." He held his palms up in front of him as if in surrender. "I'm truly sorry." He turned to leave, wondering how the country could ever move beyond its social civil war over alcohol. "But I still think we're all shooting at the wrong target," he said, looking back over his shoulder as he opened the door.

"What's that supposed to mean?" Eckart asked.

"Drunkenness is a symptom more than a cause."

"A symptom of what?"

"I don't know, Captain. But whatever it is, that's our real enemy."

THIRTY-THREE

Dwelling on what Eckart had said about the upsurge in bloody Puget Sound hijackings as they walked back to the station, Miles worried anew about the possibility of a full-blown rumrunner war breaking out, possibly in his own backyard. In his vulnerable islands. The fear so distracted him that he caught the tip of his boot on a sidewalk step and careened right into Floyd, running his shoulder into Floyd's hip and then hitting his forehead on Floyd's knee, knocking Floyd sideways so that his head hit the corner of the brick bank building. They both crumpled to the ground.

"Mind how you go, Miles!" Floyd said, holding a hand to the side of his head.

"Sorry," Miles said, holding his own forehead. "My mind was somewhere else."

"I wouldn't have guessed."

"You're bleeding a little. Not bad."

They both rolled onto their rear ends, sat up, and waited for the pain to subside—for the stars to go away.

"Do you think it's really getting as bad out there as Eckart was saying?" Floyd asked.

"It's probably worse."

"Why do you think that?"

"Because Eckart couldn't find his own rectum with both hands and a map. He and his crew of potbellied half-wits would be the last to know how things are really going out there."

"That isn't good," Floyd said as they slowly got up.

"No."

Floyd took a long look over his shoulder, back down the hill to where the *Arcata* was tied up. "Do you think there's any chance that Eckart . . ." He let his statement hang unfinished.

"Chance that Eckart what? Could have gone rogue? Could have killed the Jensens out of frustration and rage?"

"Well. He certainly sounds deranged."

"He is. And it wouldn't be the first time that law enforcement has crossed the line in these parts. But I don't see it. Not with Eckart. He's just too much of a slouch."

"Yeah. I'm probably inclined to agree with you."

Miles brushed himself off. "If I'm being honest, I feel like we've hit a sort of dead end. At least for the time being, I don't know what other leads we can pursue here in the islands."

"Are you suggesting we go to Seattle?"

"Angus Cooper seems to have flown the coop, there's no sign of the Cantonese, McCaskill won't talk to us, and Akroyd is dead." Miles shrugged. "If our top suspects are highbinders and rumrunners, then all roads lead to Seattle."

"Sheriff, come quick," shouted Lyle Miller, one of the better local fishing boat captains, as he ran down the road toward them.

"What is it?" Miles asked as Miller came to a stop and tried to catch his breath, hands on his knees, as if he'd been running all over town.

"Reverend McCaskill," Miller gasped. "He's beating the daylights out of Rupert Hawkins. Like he means to kill him."

"Where?"

Miller pointed. "Grocery."

Miles and Floyd ran up the hill and turned left on Harrison Street where, half a block down, Hawkins lay on his back in the middle of the road, unmoving, a torn grocery sack and three small tins of scrapple scattered to one side of him. McCaskill was nowhere to be seen.

"The reverend jumped him as he exited the grocer's and started beating on him with an axe handle," Fields, the dry goods shop owner, said very matter-of-factly as they slid to a stop over the bloodied, unconscious man. "Shouting about how Hawkins couldn't hide his drinking from God, or some such thing."

Floyd bent down to check his pulse. "He's alive."

Hawkins's lips and right eyebrow were split open, spilling blood. Blood also poured from both his nostrils.

"That son of a bitch," Miles muttered.

"Let's sit him up so he doesn't aspirate," Floyd said. "We can prop him against that," he added, pointing to a post that supported a corner of the barber shop's awning. When they tried to move him, he groaned and grabbed at his chest without opening his eyes. "He might have some broken ribs," Floyd said. "Let's just roll him on his side so the blood drains out of his nose and mouth."

"Run and get Dr. Boren," Miles said, as a gasping Lyle Miller finally caught up with them.

"Right away." He took two loud breaths, then ran onward.

"We had better lock up McCaskill," Floyd said. But Miles again looked lost in thought. "Miles? I said we had better go arrest the good reverend."

"McCaskill stopped himself," Miles said. "If he'd wanted to kill Hawkins, Hawkins would be dead."

"He may die yet, from internal bleeding in his organs or brain. Even if he doesn't, this is first-degree battery pure and simple."

"People get into fights all the time."

"This wasn't a fight. Hawkins's knuckles are unmarked. The poor guy was just getting himself a pauper's dinner of tinned meat when he got jumped. Beaten to a pulp in broad daylight, right in the center of the town you're sworn to protect."

"I know, Floyd. But . . ."

"But two county councilmen are members of his congregation," Floyd said, nodding as he remembered.

"Yes."

"Well, hell's bells."

*****

An hour later, Dr. Boren came down to the station with his diagnosis.

"Hawkins had his bell rung pretty good. But he isn't showing any lasting signs of a concussion, so he's probably in the clear. I stitched up his face, and he has one cracked rib on his right side that he's griping about. But I dare not give him morphine with as much alcohol as he already has in his system or he's liable to go into respiratory arrest."

"Thank you, doctor."

"Anything else I can help you gentlemen with?"

"Just please don't let His High Holiness, Reverend McCaskill, anywhere near Hawkins."

"I wouldn't be terribly effective protecting Hawkins from a goliath like McCaskill. And I can't force him to stay in my office if he wants to leave."

"I know, but . . . Forget it."

Boren gave a shrug and departed.

"Floyd, would you mind going down to the steamship office to get us two tickets to Seattle?" Miles asked.

"What about McCaskill?"

"We won't get any information out of him directly. But I'm going to have Bill shadow him while we're gone."

"First available ship, I assume?"

Miles considered the question. Marion was only going to be in town nine more days. A trip to Seattle would surely eat up at least three of them. And there were absolutely no guarantees they'd learn anything useful in Seattle. Still, if there was a chance their efforts could head off a bloody rumrunner war in the San Juan Islands, then they had to try.

"Miles? First available ship?"

"I suppose so," he answered without enthusiasm. "Yes."

*****

They spent the rest of the day canvassing the docks one more time, asking if anyone had seen the *Daisy* or any of the missing men. It got them nowhere.

Passing Marion's mother's house as he drove home in the twilight, Miles's attention was drawn to Marion's bedroom window. It glowed from within with a warm pink light. He'd sat in that very room on many occasions, the two of them playing cards or jacks or checkers in the glow of the lamp she always covered with a handkerchief of one color or another. Her room always smelled of the red cedar lining of her closet. Sometimes of beeswax when her floor or furniture had just been polished. He wondered why his memories involving scents were always so vivid. Like when he'd tried to kiss her at the fair and gotten close enough to smell the jasmine oil in her hair. He could still picture the side of her face exactly as it had looked in that moment. The curve of her neck. The delicacy. The smoothness. The perfection. He ached to return to that evening, if only to once again brush his cheek against hers for a fleeting moment.

With sudden violence, the right-side tires began to shimmy as the truck strayed from the road. Startled from his daze, Miles jerked the wheel to fix his course. Then, with reluctance, he turned his mind to what he needed to pack for the trip to Seattle. Marion's cheek would have to wait.

THIRTY-FOUR

Two Weeks Earlier

There were now long periods of violent motion. Long, long periods of darkness. Long periods of not knowing if it was night or day. Not knowing for certain whether I was awake or dreaming. I usually felt sick from the never-ending motion, the cold, the damp air, the sour smell. When I didn't feel sick, I was painfully hungry. We got very little food. I was getting weaker. And I was afraid. Always afraid. Every few days, when the fat Cantonese man came with rice and water, he took another girl. And every time the girl came back, she looked terrified. Looked as if she had lost her mind. No girl who came back ever spoke of what happened to her. One never spoke again at all. Thinking about it made me tremble.

There were only four of us left who the fat man had not taken away yet. I feared I would be next. I feared what he would do to me.

In this realm of darkness and confusion and misery and fear, I began to wonder if I was dead, unsure of how to tell. I found a small, sharp pebble on the floor and jabbed myself in the thigh with it to reassure myself that I was alive. I used it to scratch little marks in the rusting wall. Though I couldn't see, I did my best to scratch my name. After, I could feel my name with my fingertips. This comforted me. Reassured me that I existed. That I was still a part of this world.

*****

Sometime before our next rice bowl came, the girl who hit her head died. She had not eaten since the journey began. She got weaker and skinnier by the day, then finally rolled onto her back and stopped breathing. We were trapped with her dead body lying next to us for a long time, until the next time the fat man came. He cursed when he saw her, shouted at her to get up as if he did not believe us that she was dead. Then he cursed again, muttered something about his pay, and closed us back in with her body for another long time. Eventually, he returned with a small wheeled cart. He had us pass the girl's stiff, strange-smelling body through the hole where he wrestled it onto the cart and tied it down with a rope. Grunting and cursing as he crashed and banged the cart against the wall, struggling to get around a large pipe and a table, he rolled her across the next room to the bottom of the stairs. Then he came back and closed the hole.

I never learned the dead girl's name. She hit her head before most of us ever found the courage to start talking to each other. The fat man probably dumped her body overboard in the night. At least he didn't take any of us away with him that time.

*****

The last time I was able to sleep, I dreamt of snow. Not my mouse. Actual snow, coming down on my village. White, weightless flakes falling thick and soft on the ground. The whole village, the fields, the trees—everything blanketed in pure white. Everything quiet. Everything peaceful. Everything clean and beautiful. I was very happy while the dream lasted.

THIRTY-FIVE

The *Bangor* was already boarding when Miles and Floyd met at the steamship terminal the next morning.

"Is that what you're wearing to Seattle?" Floyd asked, seeing that Miles was dressed in his usual work clothes.

"Do you ask just to make a point, or do you really expect me to answer?"

"Well, it's just that—"

"Floyd, I find it a little strange that you worry more about my clothes than I do."

"I find it a little strange too."

Miles grinned. "Would it make you feel better if I told you that I packed a suit just in case we have to go to a fancy speakeasy?"

Floyd gave a curt nod.

As the *Bangor* slipped her moorings and steamed out of Friday Harbor in the calm and salty morning air, Miles found himself leaning against her stern rail and gazing back at the waterfront with a vague sense of loneliness, if not loss—much as he had when he left for the war on the very same vessel in 1918. His mind drifted to thoughts of Marion's looming return to New York, and it took considerable effort for him to refocus on what they might be heading for in the not-yet-entirely-civilized Western city of Seattle.

It was a clear day, so Miles roamed the sunny wrap-around deck, watching for eagles and orcas as the ship ran down the San Juan Channel, across the Juan de Fuca Strait, and into Admiralty Inlet—the busy shipping lane leading to Seattle, Tacoma, and beyond. As the buzzing maritime hub of Port Townsend came into view off the steamer's starboard bow—framed by a backdrop of the jagged, glaciated Olympic Mountains—Miles realized that they were passing into what locals referred to as the Triangle of Fire: an area within range of three massive U.S. Army Coast Artillery Corps bases built to protect the strategically critical shipyards and ports of the inner Puget Sound. Between the three bases, there were more than a hundred pieces of heavy artillery in bunkers and fortified emplacements, their great barrels trained on the very stretch of water the *Bangor* was steaming through. Not even the Imperial German High Seas Fleet would have dared try to pass through such a zone of destruction.

He stepped into the main passenger cabin to find Floyd, white-knuckled once again, sitting slumped in a chair that faced an interior wall. He seemed to be staring at the base of the wall, which offered nothing more interesting to look at than glossy white marine paint over riveted sheet metal.

"Hey, you doing alright?" he asked Floyd.

Floyd exhaled loudly. "Never better."

"Keep an eye on that wall. Make sure nobody tries to paint any Bolshevik slogans on it."

"Ha."

"Can I bring you a cup of coffee from the galley?"

"No. No thanks," Floyd said, shutting his eyes tight. "It defies logic. I fully understand the scientific principles of buoyancy. And yet . . ." His eyes still squeezed shut, he shook his head.

"Hang in there."

"Uh-huh."

*****

It was late morning by the time the *Bangor* passed the West Point Lighthouse and entered Elliot Bay—where the ever-growing skyline and bustling waterfront of Seattle at last came into view. Suddenly, there were vessels everywhere—some under way, some tied up at piers, some at anchor out in the bay. Ships bound for or arriving from heaven only knew what ports around the Pacific Rim and beyond. Large ocean liners. Cargo ships—most of them built of steel, some still built of wood and rigged for sailing. Stubby tugboats, their funnels churning out columns of black coal smoke. And numerous small passenger steamers of the so-called Mosquito Fleet, motoring between Seattle and various islands and hamlets all over Puget Sound. In fact, it was to the very epicenter of Mosquito Fleet activity that the *Bangor* was headed: the always busy Galbraith Pier, at the foot of Spring Street.

It took another twenty minutes for the crew to maneuver the ship into its berth, tie up, and secure the gangplank. Floyd was the first passenger to disembark, practically running down the ramp with relief, the color returning to his face. He and Miles waited for a porter to hand their bags through the vessel's cargo door, then made their way to the terminal exit leading out onto Railroad Avenue. There, Miles happened to make momentary eye contact with a man who was leaning against a utility pole on the sidewalk, holding an open *Seattle Post-Intelligencer* newspaper that flapped violently in the wind. It struck Miles as an odd place for the man to be trying to read given that the entryway to the Mosquito Fleet terminal offered ample shelter from the stiff breeze blowing down the waterfront. The man's eyes quickly dropped to his flapping newspaper. Respecting a gut feeling, Miles watched him for a moment. He was a big man. Not quite as big as Miles, but big enough to intimidate most people. He wore a diamond pinky ring and a striped suit Miles thought was just ostentatious enough to suggest the man might be a gangster.

Calm down, he thought. *You're being paranoid again.*

Then, as Miles was just about to ask Floyd where they should go first, the man's eyes lifted and locked on Miles once again. This time it was Miles who averted his gaze, not wanting to appear rude, worried the man would realize he'd been staring at him.

They set off to find Miles a decent but cheap hotel room, with Miles looking over his shoulder more than once to make sure the big man with the newspaper wasn't following them. A few blocks down the waterfront, they came across a five-story brick establishment called, quite simply, the O.K. Hotel. It was an unpretentious workmen's hostel fronting Railroad Avenue, adjacent to the waterfront and a new elevated trolley trestle. They got Miles checked in and dumped both of their bags in his Spartan third-floor room. Floyd took the opportunity to splash water on his face in the sink, hoping to shake off his jitters from their voyage south. Then, intending to go straight to Seattle Police Department Headquarters to gather information on where the King of Rumrunners, Otto Stenersen, might be found, they stepped back out the front door where, to their happy surprise, they spotted a large sign for the Deepwater Salvage Company attached to the front of a cargo pier directly across the street. It was the company that owned the *Deepwater Doubloon*—the professional salvage vessel spotted loitering near D'Arcy Island the evening before the *Lucky Lena* was spotted adrift. Since it was the middle of the business day, and since they'd intended to eventually stop in anyway, they went there first.

THIRTY-SIX

The pier in which the offices of the Deepwater Salvage Company were housed was long and broad, jutting well out into Elliott Bay. A rusty tramp steamer with Athens, Greece registry was moored to its south side. Miles and Floyd entered through a barn-style double door off Railroad Avenue that was big enough to drive a truck through. The entire first floor was a high-ceilinged and shadowy warehouse containing stacks of lumber, sacks of grain, coils of thick rope, and wooden barrels of unknown content. The air smelled strongly of timbers treated with creosote, like new utility poles or railroad ties. They found a thick-necked longshoreman leaning against a barrel and taking a smoke break, asked him for directions, then climbed a set of stairs against one of the interior walls. It led up to a long second floor hallway, one side of which was lined with doors to the offices of various businesses. A seafood trading company. A freight forwarder. A purveyor of marine equipment. Finally, they came to the door for Deepwater Salvage and gave it a knock. To their mild surprise, it was answered by a conservatively-dressed, entirely prim-looking secretary with her gray hair tied back in a tight bun.

"May I help you?" she asked.

"We'd like to speak with the owner," Miles said. "Is he in the office today?"

"Mr. Hauer is indeed in. May I ask what this concerns?"

"It's a police matter. One of Mr. Hauer's vessels may have been in the vicinity of an incident we're looking into. We're hoping someone aboard the vessel may have seen something that would be of help to us."

"I see." She showed them to an incredibly comfortable crushed velvet couch in an otherwise undecorated and windowless anteroom, offered them tea—which they declined—then asked them to wait while she went down a short hallway to make the necessary inquiries. Less than a minute later, she was back. "Mr. Hauer would be happy to see you. Right this way, gentlemen."

"Gustav Hauer," said the middle-aged blonde, barrel-chested man who came around the desk and extended a giant, heavily callused hand in greeting. Miles and Floyd introduced themselves. Hauer's desk was no simple pine affair of the sort Miles expected of a waterfront seaman's office, but was instead a large, custom-made work of art. Its edges inlaid with intricate decorative patterns, the whole thing appearing to be built of exotic hardwoods. His walls were decorated with trophies of his trade. A brass propeller. A shadow box of ancient Chinese coins. Another shadow box with a China plate bearing the logo of a lost ocean liner called the SS *Valencia*. Outside Hauer's wide office window, a curling wisp of coal smoke rose from the stack of the Greek tramp steamer moored alongside the pier.

The man himself was a Scandinavian giant in shirtsleeves, with giant forearms and giant shoulders to match his giant hands. He was impeccably groomed, which struck Miles as odd for someone in such a rough line of work. His only obvious flaws were thick scars on the knuckles of all his fingers, and a left ring finger that was missing half of its original length.

"Thanks for seeing us," Miles said as he and Floyd took the offered seats and Hauer returned to his leather desk chair.

"My pleasure," he said. "Estelle tells me you're here about a police matter. How may I be of assistance?"

"It's our understanding that one of your vessels was operating in Haro Strait last week, near D'Arcy Island."

"The *Deepwater Doubloon*. My flagship, if you will. Yes, indeed."

"May I ask why?"

"Why it was in Haro Strait? Of course. My firm was hired by the Canadian Pacific Steamship Company to locate the wreck of one of their ocean liners. The RMS *Empress of Burma*, which, as you probably already know, sank in Haro Straight in 1918 after tearing her hull open on a reef."

"Hired to locate, or to salvage?"

"For now, just to locate. By our estimation, the wreck is in deep water. Very deep. Too deep for mounting any sort of conventional salvage operation."

"So the wreck hasn't been located?"

"No. In addition to being awfully deep, the terrain on the bottom of Haro Strait is discontinuous, meaning that it's very hard for us to drag it for clues."

"Given that the wreck is probably in such deep water, why does Canadian Pacific want you to bother?" Floyd asked.

"They never said. But sometimes the families who lose loved ones in sinkings like this want to know the location of the wreck for memorial reasons. And I suppose there's always a chance—albeit a small one—that it's not that deep after all."

"If that were the case," Floyd asked, "then what would they want you to salvage from the wreck?"

"Usually it's something like the ship's safe. Sometimes a piece of secret military hardware. Sometimes the propeller. If the wreck is shallow enough, we can recover the hull metal to sell for scrap. When a wreck is very shallow, sometimes we can even patch her up and raise the whole ship. But that's a tall order, let me tell you."

"I'm sure," Miles said. "Is it odd that a Canadian steamship line would hire an American firm to search for a wreck in Canadian waters?"

"Not at all. We're by far the biggest and best equipped company north of San Francisco. And we arranged all the necessary permissions with the British Columbia provincial government, as well as the involved federal ministry in Ottawa. Plus, given her last known course, she could very well have come to rest on the American side of the border. Nobody knows for sure."

"I see," Miles said. "Well, to get to the point of our visit, we're making inquiries concerning two vessels—one, a semi-converted seiner called the *Lucky Lena;* the other, a Trafton workboat called the *Daisy*. Both boats were operating in the vicinity of D'Arcy Island the same evening the *Deepwater Doubloon* was there. Long story short, the crew of the *Lucky Lena* has disappeared, while the *Daisy* has disappeared altogether, along with its captain. Our hope is that your crew might have seen something that would help us in our investigation."

"The good news is that I was captaining the *Doubloon* that day, and I know exactly the vessels you're talking about."

"Is that right?"

"We observed the *Lucky Lena* out there at least a dozen times over the past month."

"Doing what?"

"Sometimes loitering very close to D'Arcy Island. Sometimes making a pathetic attempt to look like they were fishing when it was quite clear that they were watching us."

"Watching you?"

"Yes, sir. Observing our work through their binoculars. Tracking our every move."

"What for?"

"It's not unheard of for unscrupulous captains to try to steal the fruits of our labors. Plunderers. Thieves. They watch us until we locate a wreck, and then, when we inevitably have to put in for fuel or supplies, try to steal whatever they can from it."

"How on earth could a couple of fishermen like them reach the wreck of the *Empress of Burma*?"

"Well, I didn't say their plan made any sense."

"So you think the captain of the *Lucky Lena* had plunder in mind?"

"Don't know why else he would be spending so much time watching us."

"What about the *Daisy*?"

"The *Daisy* watched us too, but only recently. Watched us and the *Lucky Lena*, both."

"Last Tuesday?"

"Tuesday. Yes. In the late evening. Both vessels were out there. *Lucky Lena* showed up just before sunset and took up station off D'Arcy Island. The *Daisy*, not far behind, motored in circles about a mile to our north."

"Did you happen to see the *Daisy* approach the *Lucky Lena*?"

"No, sir. We left the area as dirty weather was brewing. But I can tell you that as we departed, both vessels were in roughly the same positions they'd been in since arriving on the scene. That was the last we saw of them."

"I have a question," Floyd said.

"Of course."

"Is the *Empress of Burma* supposed to contain anything of unusual value?"

"Not according to its manifest."

"What about something not listed on the manifest?"

"Such as?"

"Gold, for example."

"Gold." Hauer smiled and leaned back in his chair. "My favorite word. And as a matter of fact, Mr. Floyd, it just so happens that there is a rather fun if entirely crazy legend out there."

"Concerning gold?"

"A king's fortune in gold. Russian gold. So I suppose I should call it a tsar's fortune."

"Tsar Romanov's gold?" Floyd asked, his eyebrows arched. "What's the legend?"

"Mr. Hauer probably has things to do," Miles said, not wanting to waste time with such nonsense.

"No, no. It's no bother. It isn't a long story. But it's a good one. Yes, Mr. Floyd. The story—the fable, I should say—involves the lost gold of the Russian imperial family. Hundreds of tons, or so they say."

"One of the biggest reserves of gold in the world," Floyd said, sounding fascinated.

"That's right. Now then, as everyone knows, Tsar Nicholas, Tsarina Alexandra, and their five children were supposed to have been slaughtered in cold blood by Bolshevik savages in Yekaterinburg in the summer of 1918."

"Supposed to have been?"

"There are persistent rumors that one of the children—possibly Princess Anastasia—escaped."

"Escaped to where?"

"No one knows. But there are also persistent rumors that as the Russian civil war raged, the White Army—that is, those military units loyal to the tsar—moved the imperial gold out of the capital of St. Petersburg, to a place of safe keeping in Kazan, an ancient trading city on the Trans-Siberian Railway about 500 miles east of Moscow. Needless to say, the war didn't go well for the White Army. Kazan fell to the Bolshevik Red Army in 1918. But when the Bolsheviks took the city, there was no gold to be found. No sign of it. Some believe that Admiral Alexander Kolchak, the doomed supreme commander of the White Army, ordered it shipped to the Siberian city of Irkutsk where it was eventually dumped into Lake Baikal to keep it from falling into the hands of the Bolsheviks. But some say that in the last days before the fall of Kazan, Kolchak sent the gold east on the Trans-Siberian Railway, clear across Asia, to the Russian Pacific Coast port of Vladivostok, along with a small escort of loyal soldiers and an entourage of aristocratic refugees—one of whom was reportedly seen wearing a broach bearing the double-headed eagle of the imperial family's coat of arms."

"Princess Anastasia," Floyd muttered.

"And an elusive fortune in gold. Great story so far, right? That much of it could even be true."

"That much of it?" Miles asked, surprised to find himself engrossed. "What happened next?"

"Heaven knows. But guess what the *Empress of Burma*'s last port of call was before she sank near D'Arcy Island?"

"Vladivostok," Floyd said.

"Indeed. Vladivostok. The very city to which Kolchak allegedly sent the imperial gold and the mysterious entourage of aristocrats. The *Empress of Burma* stopped in Vladivostok barely a month before Red Forces took control of the city. From there, she sailed for Vancouver. As you know, she didn't quite make it. She probably sits in 700 feet of water at the bottom of Haro Strait."

"And people suspect the Russian gold was aboard."

"It's all conjecture. Hearsay. A friend of a friend of a friend knew some drunk stevedore in Vladivostok who claims to have helped load dozens of extremely heavy crates onto the *Empress of Burma*. Crates which, according to the actual, official Canadian Pacific cargo manifest, contained nothing more interesting than rife ammunition being shipped out as part of the evacuation of a legion of loyalist mercenaries."

"How do you know all this?" Miles asked.

"Well, for better or for worse, my line of work sometimes involves treasure maps and the chasing down of legends. Every once in a great while, one of them turns out to be legitimate, and you find a great chest of gold coins in the hold of a sunken Chinese cargo ship," Hauer said, pointing to the shadow box of Chinese coins on his wall.

"But you don't believe there's gold aboard the *Empress of Burma*?" Miles asked.

"No. There just isn't enough reliable information to make it likely. Of course, the fun thing about fables and ghost stories and conspiracy theories is that it's often impossible to disprove them. So they live on and grow like weeds. Are they true? Anything is possible, I suppose. But probably not."

Miles thought for a moment. "So the wreck hasn't been found, and you don't have a salvage contract with Canadian Pacific?"

"No. Not yet."

"Meaning there'd be no reason for you to have a confrontation with the crew of the *Lucky Lena*? To chase them off, or . . ."

"Or? Or what? Shoot them? Make them disappear? Those are wicked implications, sir. Mind you, we will defend our lawful and rightful claims from the likes of pirates and thieves. But as I mentioned, we have no salvage contract—just an agreement to find the ship—and it's probably too deep to allow for any meaningful recovery anyway. For that matter, even if we had salvage rights, and even if there were a fortune in gold aboard, the *Lucky Lena's* two-man crew of amateurs wouldn't have posed any threat."

"What if they had a Kretchmar diving apparatus?" Floyd asked, both lawmen watching Hauer's face intently.

To their surprise, Hauer smiled.

"Did they?" He laughed. "A Kretchmar suit?" He turned to gaze out his window, a look of boyish wonder on his face.

"Would it have made a difference?" Floyd asked again.

Hauer, still smiling, shook his head. "I don't know what the limits of that particular suit are. It's German. I've heard little about it and have never seen one myself. Regardless, past 160 feet deep, you need a special gas mixture that is very hard to come by. Less nitrogen and more helium than regular air. Even with that, the deepest I have ever, ever heard of anyone diving is about 50 fathoms—300 feet. And that was an elite U.S. Navy crew using a state-of-the-art Mark V dive suit to recover a submarine off Honolulu. A submarine built by Moran Brothers here in Seattle, as a matter of fact. I digress. I'll just say it again: given that the wreck is probably 700 feet down, the *Lucky Lena's* amateur crew didn't pose the least threat."

Unless the wreck has been found, Miles thought, *and isn't that deep after all.*

THIRTY-SEVEN

"You think Hauer might be holding out on us?" Miles asked as he and Floyd headed for Seattle Police Headquarters.

"I suppose it's possible. He seemed like a straight shooter though. Forthright."

Police Headquarters was in the Seattle Public Safety Building—a six-floor, triangular Beaux Arts style structure fronting Yesler Way. A near replica of New York's famous Flatiron Building, but in miniature. The research section was headed by a wiry, gray-haired but bright-eyed Sergeant named Robert Clark. He was the force's lone sexagenarian, born in Seattle in 1859—a time when Duwamish Indian villages still dotted the shores of Elliott Bay—to parents who were members of the pioneer Denny Party. The department kept Clark on, despite his age, because the man had an unparalleled knowledge of the city and its inhabitants. And though as a sergeant he was outranked by many men half his age, they all deferred to him.

"Young Detective Floyd," Clark said in welcome as Floyd and Miles came through the door of his poorly lit basement office. "I was expecting you a bit earlier."

"My apologies. We jumped at an opportunity to interview the owner of Deepwater Salvage."

"Ah, Gustav Hauer. Haven't heard much about that old villain in a few years."

"Villain?" Floyd said. "We found him rather affable."

"Ha. Don't let his Rainier Club manner fool you. He's a rogue, albeit a clever one."

"How so?"

"About fifteen years ago, he was a claim jumper in the Cascade foothills north of Ellensburg. Cut the throat of a competing gold miner and squatted on his placer claim on Williams Creek for more than a year before the law finally caught up with him."

"And now, fifteen years later, he's a thriving marine salvager?" Miles asked. "They didn't lock him up for good or hang him?"

"Illiterate Ellensburg jury acquitted him, heaven knows why. But take my word, he did it. Yes, he did. And you are?"

"Oh, my apologies again," Floyd said. "This is Sheriff Miles Scott from San Juan Island, which, as you know, I was dispatched to in order to help with a murder investigation."

"Yes, of course. Welcome, Sheriff Scott."

"Please, call me Miles."

"Welcome, Miles."

"Have any new bits for us?" Floyd asked.

"Matter of fact, I do. Concerning those triangular fragments you sent down—the ones with the burned edges that looked like remnants of money or official documents—turns out they're the upper left-hand corners of certificates of naturalization used by the U.S. Department of Labor. Put simply, they're immigration documents. But get this: they're forgeries."

"Forgeries?"

"What we have of their serial numbers don't match up with any genuine immigration records at the Department of Labor."

"Forged immigration documents?" Miles muttered, more to himself than anyone else. "Why on earth would the Jensens have those?"

Clark waited until it became clear that Miles had nothing else to say. "Anyway, that's all I have for you gentlemen at the moment. Is there anything else I can do for you?"

"As a matter of fact, yes," Miles said, giving Clark a rundown of their suspicions about two possible tong highbinders being on the island.

"Then I'm guessing you want a meeting with one of the tongs," Clark said with a huge grin.

"Yes, but we have no idea which one."

"Oh, that's even better."

"You sound amused."

"Trying to get a meeting with a tong is like trying to get a meeting with Santa Claus. They're rarely willing to speak with anyone, let alone acknowledge their own existence. And if, by some miracle, they grant you a meeting, you'd learn more by talking to the nearest fir tree."

"I see."

"Still, they might agree to meet with you if they think they can get something out of it. Like information. Like an idea of how far your investigation has progressed. Put another way, if they *do* agree to a meeting, you can bet they're involved, on some level, with the subject of your investigation. So if you meet with them, pay extremely close attention. They'll play disinterested good Samaritans. But they might accidentally give you a tiny clue as to their true interest or involvement."

"Understood."

"Now then, the fact that you don't suspect a particular tong adds another level of complexity. I think the best course of action would be to request a meeting with the Chinese Peace Society. It's a sort of board of directors, if you will, comprised of the leaders of each of the tongs. In theory, it's there to arbitrate disputes between the tongs, thereby avoiding bloodshed. Needless to say, it hasn't been terribly effective on that front. Regardless, if one of the tongs is involved, or if your case involves a feud between tongs, they will know as much as anyone. I'll pass your request for a meeting along to our so-called Chinese community liaison upstairs. Fella named Gong Gee. Supposedly, he has a contact at the Chinese Peace Society. Probably belongs to a tong himself, for all we know."

"We're also looking for Otto Stenersen," Miles said.

Clark gave him a long, hard look. "Is that right?" He exhaled.

"As young Floyd here probably told you, Stenersen is a popular man in these parts. And by these parts, I mean the police department. Has a lot of friends high up."

"He isn't a suspect," Miles said. "But the captain of the revenue cutter up our way says the men who disappeared off the *Lucky Lena* were a couple of Stenersen's guys."

"I see. In that case, I suppose you could try to convince him that you're only trying to bring the killers of his men to justice. Given how loyal he is to his men, he might approve of your efforts. Might even help. But he's wary of folks he doesn't know. Has this skulking, obsessed local revenue agent after him right now, name of Clifford Charles. A stumpy, ungentlemanly little creep. Fingernails always dirty. Lips always wet. His wife's a raving loon."

"Do you know where we might find him?" Miles said.

"Agent Charles? Probably lurking in the bushes outside the windows of the YWCA."

"No, I mean where we might find Otto Stenersen," Miles said, suspecting that Clark was being deliberately obtuse.

Clark looked reluctant.

"Sergeant, I'll swear on a stack of Bibles that Stenersen isn't anything remotely resembling a suspect. We just think he might have information we can use."

Before continuing, Clark glanced at Floyd, who nodded in reassurance. "He has an office in Smith Tower, just down the street. His company is called Amalgamated Imports."

"What about after-work hours?"

"There's no such thing for him. But he usually stops by to see a couple of his best customers at their establishments each evening. Ever the chummy salesman, Stenersen. Always with the smile and the glad hand. Tonight, I'd recommend trying the Bucket of Blood first. After 9 p.m., move to the Rose Room."

"How do you know where he'll be at any given time?" Miles asked.

"I don't know to a certainty. But those are his tendencies.

How do I know his tendencies? Because those are the places where I drink!" He laughed. "Just pulling your leg, Miles. Stenersen's a very public figure. You might even call him a media darling. He's careful, but he doesn't hide. Anyway, the nice thing is, if you *are* going to imbibe, if you go to one of the juice joints Stenersen supplies, you know you're getting good stuff. Top-quality booze. Nothing watered down by greasy wop bartenders. Nothing tainted with methanol compliments of carless hillbilly moonshiners out in Bellevue."

"Don't you need a password to get into the Bucket of Blood?" Floyd asked.

"Ah! I'm glad you asked. No. No password. You need a membership card," he said, opening and rifling through one of his desk drawers until he found two pale green cards. "Here." He handed them to Floyd. "Now your names are William Downing and Lee Scranton. Don't ask where I got those cards. Bit of a macabre story. Anyway, you'll knock and then hand those cards through a slot at the front door."

"What about for the Rose Room?"

"No. No membership card. No password. The Rose Room takes a different approach, hiding its real purpose in plain sight. You'll understand when you get there."

THIRTY-EIGHT

Miles and Floyd exited police headquarters and turned down Yesler way toward Smith Tower, where the offices of Otto Stenersen's ambiguously named company, Amalgamated Imports, were located.

"'I'll swear on a stack of Bibles,' says the agnostic," Floyd said.

"Did you like that?"

"It got you what you wanted. Then again, wasn't it Dante who said the eighth circle of hell is reserved for pretenders?"

"I'll be in good company."

"I'm sure."

*****

Miles swung open one of the heavy bronze doors at the main entrance to Smith Tower—the fourth tallest building in the world, at 484 feet. The lobby was remarkably cool, and remarkably opulent for Seattle, with marble walls, ornate light fixtures, and highly decorated, highly polished elevator doors.

"Ever been in here before?" Floyd asked.

"Never."

"It's a bit of a wonder, isn't it? Supposedly, on the 35th floor, there's a hall called the Chinese Room that was designed and decorated by Cíxī Tàihòu, the late Dowager Empress of China. Supposed to be all carved teak walls, gold paint, Chinese lanterns and whatnot. My mother says it's like something out of a dream."

"Your mother who you still live with?"

"Hardy-har-har. Yes, Miles. My mother who I still live with. Just like you."

They took a quick look at the backlit building directory, found that the offices of Amalgamated Imports were on the 38th floor, and stepped into the nearest elevator.

"Which floor, sirs?" the uniformed operator asked.

"Thirty-eight, please," Floyd said.

"I'm sorry, sirs. This elevator only serves the 22nd through 33rd floors. Elevator to 38 is the last one down the hall to your right."

When the men went down the hall to their right, they encountered a cordon and desk with a security officer blocking public access to the elevator they wanted.

"Headed to 38," Floyd said.

"Do you have an appointment, sir?"

"We do not."

"Floor 38 consists of private offices. Only visitors listed in the appointment book are allowed beyond this point."

"Of course," Floyd said, showing his detectives badge.

"Ah."

"We just need a quick word," Miles said.

"Still, sirs, with respect, I can't allow you to pass unless you have an appointment or a, uh—"

"A warrant," Miles muttered, looking at Floyd with a smile. "You're supposed to have a warrant, Floyd. How many times do I have to tell you?"

"It isn't at all that kind of visit," Floyd said to the man. "Still, we don't want to get you into hot water with your employer."

"No hard feelings," Miles added.

THIRTY-NINE

"Know a good place for lunch?" Miles asked Floyd as they exited Smith Tower. "The speakeasies don't open until after dark, right? We have some time to kill."

"As a matter of fact, my mother has invited us to lunch. Cold sandwiches, if that suits you."

"Sounds great."

They set off across downtown, heading for the trolley line that would take them north, to Queen Anne Hill. But before they got more than a block, they walked smack into a group of picketers, half of them wearing sandwich board signs. They stood in a fidgety cluster in front of a small deli.

"The Anti-Japanese League and the Seattle Culinary Union ask that you not eat here, sirs," one of the picketers said, blocking their way down the sidewalk. He was a short, fat man with red bulging eyes of the sort Miles associated with thyroid problems, his face contorted in a hateful sneer. Miles found him repulsive for more reasons than he could count.

"What's this all about?" Miles asked, looking at the man's sign. It read: *No Japs! No Chinks!*

"This restaurant employs Orientals."

"To wash dishes and mop the floor? So what?"

"It's on the Central Labor Council's blacklist. We're demanding that the owner quit his unfair labor practices, fire the Japs and Chinks, and hire whites to take their places."

"What's the issue?"

"The issue?" the man echoed, leaning forward and looking up into Miles's eyes. "The issue is that they'll work for nothing while the rest of us starve. The issue is that they're heathen animals."

You aren't in any danger of starving, tubby, Miles thought.

The man stood there staring with his angry, bulging eyes, as if daring Miles to offer a different opinion. Perhaps hoping Miles would. Miles had known several such men in the Army—men who just had to tell everyone what they thought. He found them a tiresome breed and tended to assume they hadn't gotten enough attention as children.

"Step aside," Floyd said as he and Miles pushed their way through the picket line and continued on their way, eventually jumping aboard a trolley as it crossed Cherry Street. Floyd sat down, seemingly disinterested. But Miles, who didn't come to Seattle all that frequently, stood by a window, craning his neck to see damn near every building, car, or person they passed along the way. It might have been his belief that cities bred ambition, greed, corruption, and crime. But it didn't mean he wasn't fascinated by them.

After a few minutes, the trolley began its long, steep climb up Queen Anne Hill, drawn by a heavy moving cable that ran under the road. About two-thirds of the way up, it came to a shuddering halt in the middle of the street.

"Everyone please remain seated," the trolleyman said, not offering further explanation.

Miles, who was now in a seat that faced backward, found himself staring straight down the very steep hill they'd been climbing and having to brace his feet to keep from sliding forward and falling to the floor. It was an unnerving sensation. His grip on the handrail next to him tightened as he began to wonder how often the clamps holding the trolleys to the underground cables failed—began to wonder what would happen if one did. Would the trolley go careening hundreds of feet back down the hill to sure destruction, its passengers torn and smashed into bloody debris? He glanced over at Floyd, who didn't look the least bit concerned.

"Floyd."

"What?"

"What's the problem?"

"With what?"

"Why have we stopped? What was all that jerky shuddering?"

"Cable probably popped off a pulley or something."

"Popped off?" he said, trying to mask his surging fear. Happily, a fancy yellow sports car roared past the trolley on its way up the hill, momentarily distracting Miles from his anxiety. "Floyd, get a look at that."

"Wow. That's a sight to behold."

"It's a Stutz Bearcat," Miles said. "Supposed to be able to go more than 70 miles per hour."

"You're joking."

"Probably costs more than you or I make in a year."

*****

It was more than ten minutes before the trolley resumed its climb and at last emerged atop Queen Anne Hill. They hopped off at Galer Street and walked a few blocks east, to the well-cared-for bungalow where Floyd lived with his widowed mother. A cedar trellis covered in old grapevines framed the entrance to the short walk to the front door. The walk itself was flanked by narrow beds of purple and white salvia. A tall maple shaded the house and its manicured yard from the afternoon sun. Behind the house, through gaps in the trees, Miles could make out the distant snowcapped peaks of the Cascade Mountain Range.

"I have to warn you," Floyd said, "my mother can be a bit preachy."

"Please. My mother was a schoolteacher for 32 years. Her baseline conversational style is to talk to you like you don't know how to wash your own backside. I'll be fine."

The dark hardwood front door opened before Floyd could knock. An elfin yet somehow imposing woman in an apron stood in the gap.

"I was expecting you some time ago," Beatrice Floyd said by way of a greeting. "The sandwiches are getting stale."

"I'm sure the sandwiches are fine, Mother. Trolley cable slipped a wheel or some such thing."

"Well, never mind."

Floyd introduced Miles, then Beatrice took them straight to the kitchen table. It sat in an alcove below a bay window looking down on a honeybee hive in the backyard. The air in the house smelled of baked pastry. With little in the way of preliminaries, they got straight to eating. A tower at the end of the table held three platters, each with half a dozen tiny sandwiches—cucumber, smoked salmon, and egg salad. There was also a large pot of Darjeeling tea and a tray of tiny seed cakes.

"Are you married, Miles?" she asked right out of the gate.

"Alas, no."

"At your age? Well. Ashton tells me you were in the war."

"Yes, ma'am."

"What a terrible waste."

"Mother, you shouldn't disparage anyone's military service," Floyd said.

"I don't refer to his service and sacrifice as an individual," Beatrice said. "I mean the war as a whole."

"It was the war to end all wars," Floyd protested.

"No, she's absolutely right," Miles said. "It was a waste. And if it was the war to end all wars, then I'm the King of Siam."

"I imagine you don't care to talk about your experiences over there," Beatrice said.

"Well, I wouldn't want to be rude at your table when you've—"

"Nonsense. We'll speak of other things. How are you liking your visit to the city?"

"It's a wonder. Someone mentioned that the population of the greater Seattle area just topped 300,000."

"We'll run out of room soon," Floyd said. "People will have

to start living all the way out in Bellevue, among the cows and hillbillies."

"I suppose it's exciting, in a way," Miles said. "Having people moving here from all different places—bringing their own styles of food and art and music. Though I will say that I was a bit taken aback by the anti-Asian restaurant worker picket line we ran into on the way here."

"The picketing is unchristian and disgraceful," Beatrice said, shaking her head. "I'll tell you boys something, it's always the lazy and uneducated who fear competition. The men who didn't pay attention in school or didn't put any effort into bettering themselves and who now have the low-wage jobs as a consequence. The hard truth is that they chose that path for themselves. And now, in pretending to be the victims, in blaming others for their predicament, all they're really doing is abdicating control of their lives, rendering themselves all the more subservient. It goes against the American spirit."

"Mother, I'm sure Miles doesn't need a lecture on—"

She held up an index finger. "I'll tell you boys something else—those Orientals are hard workers. They work a lot harder than your average Italian or Russian. They've put in as much blood and sweat into building this country as anyone. Letting them immigrate and come into contact with Christian Americans is good for them, too."

"Needless to say, you've hit on one of Mother's pet issues," Floyd said.

She lifted her cup as if to take a sip of tea, then set it back down and resumed her speech. "Really, Ashton," she said. "What has the Chinese Exclusion Act accomplished, aside from setting a new low for unchristian, unconstitutional legislation? Has banning Chinese immigration pushed the wages of white laborers up? No. All it has done is give rise to a new criminal underworld that smuggles, extorts, and sometimes murders desperate and starving would-be immigrants. And now the laborers who were already here can't bring women over, which means they can't marry amongst their own kind. So they turn to houses of ill repute, staffed by teenage Chinese slaves deceived by false promises of work or sold by desperate parents and smuggled into America by pirates and cutthroats."

"Mother volunteers with a Presbyterian organization that rescues young Chinese women from forced prostitution," Floyd said, by way of explanation. "The tongs call her and her group the white devils."

"A moniker we wear with pride," Beatrice said. She finally took a sip of tea, gazed out the window, and shook her head. "Chinese Exclusion Act, indeed. Meanwhile, every bloodthirsty Fenian, Sicilian gangster, or godless Bolshevik who wants into this country has a free ticket. It's senseless."

"Anyway," Floyd said, hoping to put an end to his mother's rant, "we saw the most extraordinary car on our ride up the hill, Mother. A Stutz Bearcat. Miles says it's capable of going over 70 miles per hour. A mechanical wonder."

"Your generation and its motor cars and gasoline engines," she said. "Always in such a big hurry. Wanting to get to everything now, now, now. Just turn on the engine and go." Miles had to stifle a laugh after taking a quick glance at Floyd and seeing him roll his eyes. "Nobody's willing to take care of horses or tack, or even bother to learn how to ride anymore," she continued. "Nobody wants to put in the work."

"Mother—"

"It's laziness. Sloth. One of the seven deadly sins. An unearned sense of entitlement to immediate gratification. But you know what? When this country runs out of oil in a couple of years, we'll be back to the horse, and none of you younger people will know how to use them. Then where will you be?"

The ring of Beatrice's telephone cut her short. As Floyd went to answer it, she began to pry into Miles's affairs, asking that most dreaded of questions concerning what his plans were for the future. Miles tried, in vain, to divert her by raving about her seed cake and asking if he could pass the recipe along to his own mother. Fortunately, Floyd returned before she'd been able to get too far into her cross-examination.

"Guess what?" Floyd said. "The Chinese Peace Society agreed to a meeting. It's this evening."

FORTY

By the time Miles and Floyd reached the address they'd been given for their meeting with the Chinese Peace Society, low clouds had rolled in off the Pacific, darkening the day and dropping a steady cold rain. To their momentary confusion, the address—on Jackson Street, near the Great Northern and Union Pacific train stations—turned out to be that of a small grocer. But before they had a chance to double-check the information they'd jotted down, a very old Chinese clerk who was tidying up a stack of jackfruit muttered, "police," then pointed down an aisle that led deeper into the store. The men followed his direction, eyeballing the seemingly disinterested handful of customers as they made their way past tables and shelves of unfamiliar roots, mushrooms, fruits, and dried fish. They arrived at the dimly lit rear of the store, by open barrels of aromatic loose-leaf teas, waiting for someone to offer further guidance.

"Now what?" Miles said, his gaze settling on a severed pig head that sat in a tub of ice.

"I guess we wait. Maybe they're watching for tails, making sure that we've come alone."

"That's a troubling thought. I mean, if one of the tongs had a hand in the murders and they think we know too much, what then? They cut our throats and feed our body parts to pigs?"

As Miles said this, a young but muscular Chinese man with a long cue braid appeared in the frame of a door leading further into the back. He nodded, then gestured that they should follow him. He led them down a narrow hallway, past a cramped office, past a storage room stacked to the ceiling with crates, boxes, and barrels, and right out a back door into a cobblestone alley that stank of the rancid gray effluent that was trickling its way toward a nearby storm drain. The man looked up and down the alley, then, without a word, led them half a block down to where another muscular Chinese man flung open the back door of a building on the opposite block. They led Miles and Floyd into a dark antechamber, closed the door, and then frisked them without any request for consent.

"We're not armed," Floyd said, having insisted, over Miles's objections, that they wouldn't be admitted to a meeting with the Peace Society if they brought weapons. But the Chinese men continued to search them as if they hadn't heard.

Done with their pat-downs, the Chinese picked up two lit lanterns, opened another door, and led the men down a vaulted stairwell into a basement containing nothing but a scattering of empty glass bottles. *A trap,* Miles thought as he clenched his fists and began breathing quickly, getting ready to fight for his life. But the Chinese men, looking nonthreatening and handing Floyd one of the lanterns, simply nodded to the far end of the empty basement space where Miles and Floyd could just make out an arched doorway in the semidarkness. They crossed the basement, passed through the doorway, and emerged out onto the sidewalk of an underground cobblestone street, complete with abandoned storefronts for a bakery, a printer, a boutique, a paint store, and a public bathhouse. The air was cold and damp, as that of a cavern. Steaming, hissing, dripping pipes ran along the dark ceiling.

Miles realized they were in what was called Underground Seattle—a man-made wonder created when, after the great fire of 1889, the city fathers decided to raise the level of the streets in the low-lying Pioneer Square business district by an entire floor to alleviate chronic problems with the city's sewers and toilets backing up during particularly high tides. An engineering feat, they'd built an elaborate frame system and then pushed an entire hillside down into the area as fill, entombing the former ground level of the city below the modern streets. The old ground level was still down there, of course, largely left to the rats and officially condemned out of fear of the bubonic plague. But small sections were still used for illicit storage. For gambling parlors. For opium dens. Still accessible via nondescript manholes or dusty, forgotten stairwells.

They crossed the underground street and entered the front of what was once a Western Union telegraph office. There, at a round table lit by a green glass fixture that hung from the ceiling, eight old Chinese men in dark three-piece business suits sat in chairs, waiting quietly, cups of steaming tea placed before them. Miles and Floyd were ushered to the only two empty chairs at the table, where they were both momentarily lost in amazement at finding themselves sitting with the kings of Seattle's secretive Chinese underworld. The old men stared at them, silent, expressionless.

"Thank you for agreeing to meet with us," Miles said. He got no response, so he gave them a very vague rundown of the situation—how the Jensens had vanished, how the *Lucky Lena* had been found adrift with a Chinese symbol written in blood in its forward hold. Remembering, too late, that silence is its own sort of power, Miles wound up his story and waited. An extended period of deep breathing and the quiet sipping of tea finally ended with the clearing of a throat.

"How can we help police?" said a man who looked to be the oldest of the group. Perhaps the chairman.

Miles considered the question, not wanting to be overly aggressive in his response. "It was our hope that someone in the community might have information that would help us find out what happened to the crew."

"Because of Chinese symbol on boat you think Chinese involved?"

"Possibly," Miles said, not yet wanting to reveal that they suspected two tong highbinders had come to the island.

"What symbol, please?"

Miles took a folded piece of paper from his jacket pocket, on which was a crude drawing of the symbol they'd found aboard. "Is this Chinese?" he asked, already knowing.

"Yes, Chinese."

"Cantonese?"

"Cantonese, yes."

"Can you tell us what it means?" he asked, playing dumb. "Is it someone's name, perhaps?"

"No name. Symbol for death."

"Death."

"Yes." The man appeared thoughtful for a moment. "Do you find other evidence of Chinese on boat?"

"Other evidence? Such as what?"

"Identity paper. Chinese clothing. Shoe. Chinese book. Personal thing, like Chinese would have."

It dawned on Miles that he was the one being questioned. "No, nothing else," he said.

Though the old men remained utterly stone-faced, Miles thought he sensed the slightest hint of collective relief in them. Irritated at this, he decided to poke at the hornet nest a bit.

"With respect, can you think of any reason why tong highbinders would journey to San Juan Island?"

The probable chairman's expression remained impassive, and his answer was a long time coming. "Highbinder, like in San Francisco? No. No highbinder in Seattle. Seattle tong are gathering hall. Benevolent club to support Chinese community. Find job and housing for immigrant. Play cards. Play mahjong."

Right. That's why we had to meet in this hidden underground room, Miles was tempted to say. *Because tongs are just social clubs. And housing and jobs for what immigrants? Immigration of Chinese has been banned by the U.S. Government for 40 years.* "So, no tong members were sent to San Juan Island?"

"Maybe for work in cannery," the man said, shrugging.

"Are there conflicts between any of the tongs right now?"

"Conflict?"

"Feuds. Wars."

"No. No war. San Francisco tong, maybe. No Seattle tong war."

"Do Seattle tongs use San Juan Island for transshipment of anything?"

"Trans—sorry, how you say? Trans . . ."

Miles suspected that the man understood just fine, and probably spoke perfect English. But he played along. "Transshipment. Movement of goods through the island."

"Ah. Ah. What good?"

"Opium," Miles said with a hardened tone. "Liquor. Illegal immigrants."

"Oh, no, no. Seattle tong benevolent."

"And you've had no conflicts with, for example, rumrunners?"

To Miles's surprise, the old man smiled. "No. No, officer. Seattle tong just club. Benevolent community club."

FORTY-ONE

"That old fella loved the word *benevolent*, didn't he?" Miles said as they made their way to the Stenersen-supplied, preeminent Seattle speakeasy they called the Bucket of Blood. He stopped in front of a shop window as a shining, star-shaped copper cake mold caught his eye. "My mother would love that," he said by way of answering Floyd's questioning look. "She makes fruitcakes for her circle of retired teacher friends every Christmas."

"Fruitcakes? Yuck," Floyd said.

"I know."

"Mine makes mincemeat tarts every Christmas. Chopped beef, lard, citrus peel, raisins. It's twice as awful. But she loves them."

Miles grinned.

"What?" Floyd asked.

"We just met with the high lords of Seattle's criminal Chinese underworld, and here we are, a few minutes later, gazing at cake molds and talking about our mothers' awful Christmas baking traditions."

"That is a bit funny."

"Well, the horrors of fruitcake aside, I definitely need to get my mother a gift before we go back to Friday Harbor. Little gestures like that mean the world to her."

"You should try that new Fredrick & Nelson flagship store at 5th and Pine. It's enormous."

As Floyd said this, Miles caught the reflection, in the shop window, of a man walking by, heading in the same direction they had been. Something about the man struck Miles as vaguely familiar. Then it hit him: he looked like the man with the ostentatious suit and diamond pinky ring who'd been reading the *Post-Intelligencer* by the entrance of Galbraith Pier. Miles turned for a closer look. But the man was already walking away from them, so Miles couldn't see his face. He had a pinky ring. And he seemed the right size. But it was impossible to tell if he was the same man from behind. And Miles had no real reason to chase him down. Even if it were the same man, it was probably just a coincidence. Still, it made him wonder.

*****

They arrived at the Chinatown address Sergeant Clark had given them for the Bucket of Blood speakeasy. It was on a seemingly deserted alley littered with discarded crates, refuse bins, and broken bottles. Two feral tomcats hissed at each other just across the way. The door was riveted steel with a narrow mail slot in its middle. Above it hung a broad sign with painted Chinese characters.

"You sure this is it?" Miles asked. "It's dead quiet."

"Clark has never steered me wrong. Give the door a knock."

Miles did. Nothing happened, so Floyd slid the membership cards partway through the mail slot and jumped back a bit when someone on the other side of the door pulled them through. A moment later, the door opened and a giant of a man—his head as big as a pumpkin, his hands like bear paws, and his face nearly impossible to see because it was partially eclipsed by a bright ceiling light—gave them each a long look as he held the membership cards at arm's length. In a moment of panic, Miles wondered if the former holders of the membership cards were personally known to this doorman-giant, and whether he might be thinking about how best to remove each of their heads.

"William Downing and Lee Scranton," the giant said at last, in what was quite possibly the deepest, slowest voice Miles had ever heard—though he'd expected nothing less given the man's sheer immensity. "Welcome."

The giant handed the cards back to the men, then flung the door all the way open and stood aside so they could pass into a dim stairwell leading down to the basement level. As they descended toward another steel door—behind which they could now hear music—Miles saw elaborate murals painted on the walls to either side. They depicted men in top hats and tails, women in pearl necklaces and furs, some of them smoking cigarettes, all of them looking as if they should be holding martinis. Reaching the bottom, they gave the second steel door a knock and were admitted, without ceremony, to a fancy underground nightclub. Dozens of patrons—dressed to the nines—sat at small tables, stood at the long bar, or danced to a band playing on a small stage at the far end. Waiters worked the floor with silver trays carrying big tin cups of beer and cocktails of all colors. The men took the only available table—a two-top in the dead center of the room.

"Let's order Glenfiddich and see what all the hubbub is about," Miles said.

"We're not ordering whiskey."

"We have to order something, or they'll think we're revenue agents. Might as well be Glenfiddich."

Floyd was shaking his head.

"Floyd, people may literally be dying to bring Glenfiddich to Seattle. Aren't you at all curious?"

"You don't have to actually order it. Just ask if they have it."

"And then, what, order a ginger ale? Don't be ridiculous."

"Miles, we're policemen. I don't think—"

"Can I get you fellas a drink?" a white-jacketed server asked, having appeared out of nowhere.

"Do you have Glenfiddich Scotch whiskey?" Miles asked.

The server smiled. "I wish, buddy. I wish."

"Let's make it a gin rickey, then. And my pal here likes, what, a sidecar?"

"That's my drink," Floyd said, having never even heard of a sidecar.

"Also," Miles said, handing the server a crisp new dollar, "we'd be grateful if you'd let us know if and when Mr. Stenersen arrives."

"Of course, sir."

As soon as the server was out of earshot, Floyd said, "And *that* won't make them think we're cops?"

"We could be anybody. Maybe a couple of restauranteurs with a business proposition."

"I don't know."

"On an unrelated note, I'll bet you're wondering what a sidecar cocktail is."

"Out of purely academic interest."

"It's made of cognac, orange liqueur, and lemon juice, served in a coupe glass with a sugar-coated rim. We had a few days off in Paris one time, and my buddies and I found this great little joint call the New York Bar. Anyway, the bartender there—Harry something or other, a Lowland Scot—was a bona fide genius cocktail maker. Supposedly, he invented the sidecar. Now it's world famous. And now you know the story."

Floyd started to look as if his mind had taken him somewhere else, far away. Then, all at once, he was back. "Speaking of Paris and your time in Europe, do you really think the war was a waste, like you told my mother?" he asked Miles. "Or were you just being agreeable?"

"Nine million soldiers and thirteen million civilians killed, Floyd. For what? Did the borders even move?"

"Well, we didn't start it. But we had to join the fight, didn't we? It was a battle of good versus evil."

"I hate to break it to you, Floyd. But no matter how desperate we are to believe otherwise, the world is never simply good and evil or black and white. It's gray. It has always been gray. It will always be gray. And the soldiers and civilians are all just pawns in some gray ruler's gray game."

"I have a feeling that I'll regret asking. But what's the gray ruler's gray game?"

"To get more," Miles said.

"More what?"

"More everything. If the war taught me anything, it's that there are just too many men in this world who have to have more. Always more. It's greed that drives men to take bribes, smuggle booze, murder folks like the Jensens, or lead entire nations into war. It's all just fundamental human nature played out at different magnitudes."

"If it's so fundamental, then how do we have civilized society?"

"Civilized men contain it. Civilized men have self-restraint."

"There you are. See? No reason to despair."

"Unfortunately, Floyd, it's my considered opinion that most men aren't civilized. So, we're probably destined to destroy ourselves."

Floyd forced a smile. "Let's change the subject."

*****

They spent the next two hours comparing stories of playing high school baseball, being pressured by their mothers to find suitable girls to marry before they got too old, and fishing for salmon with their fathers. It turned out they had quite a bit in common.

"Truth be told, I miss my father terribly," Floyd said at one point.

"Me too." Miles raised his glass. "To fathers."

"To fathers," Floyd echoed, eyeballing his own cocktail somewhat uncertainly. They clinked their glasses together. Then Miles took a tiny sip from his while Floyd pretended to do the same.

"Well," Miles said, setting his glass back down. "No sign of Stenersen here. Should we go try that other speakeasy, the Rose

Room?"

*****

Halfway along their walk to the Rose Room, they heard the unmistakable sound of gunfire echo across the night from somewhere to their south. Five shots, probably from two different pistols given the sounds. Probably at least two blocks away.

"Sounds like the hooligans are coming out to play," Floyd said. "When the longshoremen get off work, the area south of King Street can get a little bit . . ." He stopped himself as he noticed Miles slowing his pace and staring at a man in a flashy suit walking in the opposite direction on the other side of the street. "What is it?"

Without answering, Miles continued to watch the man.

"You know that fella?" Floyd asked, still getting no response. "Miles? You think we're being followed?"

Miles exhaled. "I think I'm just being paranoid," he said. But he continued to watch the man for another ten or fifteen seconds. "Yes, I think so. Paranoid."

FORTY-TWO

The Rose Room was on the main floor of Seattle's elegant Butler Hotel, barely three blocks from police headquarters. It was a much larger and more refined space than the Bucket of Blood, with ornate chandeliers, mahogany paneling, and plush carpeting. There was fine China and sterling silver on every one of the 100 or so white linen covered tables. A tall glass mirror ran the length of a massive bar that held no apparent liquor bottles but was nevertheless manned by busy, bowtie-wearing bartenders who set up trays of various cocktail glasses—some filled with ice, the others completely empty—and handed them over to tails-wearing servers. On a bandstand in a far corner, next to a busy dancefloor, the world-famous Vic Meyers Orchestra played a jazzy foxtrot Miles recognized but couldn't name.

"Good evening, gentlemen," their server said the very second they sat down. "May we offer you some refreshment this evening?"

"A double Glenfiddich, neat, with a small glass of water on the side, please," Miles said.

"Very good. And for you, sir?"

Floyd had to take half a second to collect himself. "Uh, the same."

"See?" Miles said as the server walked away. "That wasn't so hard, was it?"

A minute later, a different server dropped off two empty Scotch dram glasses and two short highball glasses of fresh water. Shortly after that, a busboy arrived with a shallow porcelain tub from which he extracted two brown glass bottles labeled ginger ale. He rolled back a corner of the tablecloth, then set the bottles in concealed holders attached to the side of the table.

"I'm going to take a wild guess that those bottles don't actually contain ginger ale," Floyd said.

"You don't think?" Miles said.

As the busboy disappeared, Miles wondered if they made the bussers serve the alcohol as a way of allocating the risk of arrest to the junior employees.

"This must be what Clark meant when he said the Rose Room hides its real purpose in plain sight," Floyd said.

"A smooth operation," Miles said, uncorking his bottle and pouring a measure of Glenfiddich into his dram glass. "This place does it right. Look, Floyd, they even use the proper tulip dram glass to concentrate the aromas."

"Where did you learn that?"

"I was invited to a New Year's Eve Scotch whiskey tasting by a British Army lieutenant stationed at our supply yard in Neufchâteau. He was from Edinburgh. That's in Scotland."

"I know that Edinburgh is in Scotland," Miles.

"I assume you're a Scotch neophyte."

"Of course I am."

"Just watch what I do. First, raise the glass to the light and give it a gentle swirl, appreciating the warm amber color as you release its vapors into the glass."

Floyd did as he was told.

"Now bring it up to your nose and give it a gentle smell," Miles said. "What do you get?"

"Grain."

"Good. Malted barley, to be specific. Maybe a bit of orchard fruit and honey. I'd say there's something floral too. A highland mountainside covered in blossoming heather. A Scottish glade in the springtime."

"With a dozen Scottish maidens fair, barefoot and dancing the reel?" Floyd said. "You should write advertisements for the

Sears Roebuck Catalog."

"Now we set the palate with a small sip that we swish around in the mouth for a moment before swallowing, getting it all over the tongue. The first sip can seem a little hot."

Miles sipped the Scotch. Floyd did not.

"What?" Miles said.

Floyd just shrugged.

"Floyd, this isn't your grandad's bathtub gin. You aren't even going to taste it? At these prices? It's just a sip."

"I'm a police officer. So are you."

"And so was the fella who probably smuggled this Scotch."

"That's his concern."

"Suit yourself. You'll change your mind when you hear my tasting commentary anyway. Speaking of which, the next sip is where the magic happens." He closed his eyes and took another sip. "Oh, glory. Smooth on the tongue. Flowers and spices. A hint of cinnamon."

"You sound like a pastry chef."

Miles's eyes were still closed, his face flushed in ecstasy. "Maybe a little bit of sweetness, a little bit of oak at the end. Yes, oak." He opened his eyes. "Now we add just a drop or two of water to open up the flavor even more, and taste again."

"How long is this going to take?"

"Floyd, I'm telling you, a sip of fine Scotch brings you a little closer to God."

"You don't believe in God."

"This Scotch may change my mind."

His mind drifting back to Miles's troubling comments about the war, instead of a sip, Floyd absentmindedly took a gulp. He nearly choked. He put a clenched fist to his lips as his face turned red. Then he grabbed his water glass and drained it.

"Not like that," Miles said with a grin. "But it's good, right?"

Floyd couldn't yet speak, so he just stared at Miles with angry, watery, bugged out eyes.

"Gentleman," said another server who appeared at their

table. "An invitation." He extended a white-gloved hand that held a small silver platter on which a fine, white, card stock envelope lay.

"An invitation to what?" Miles asked.

"I'm just a messenger, sir," the server said, setting the envelope on the table before disappearing into the crowd.

Miles looked at the envelope, then looked at Floyd.

"Are you going to open it?" Floyd asked after clearing his throat, his face still flushed.

Miles did. Inside, calligraphy on a simple white card requested the honor of the presence of Messrs. Miles William Scott and Ashton Donald Floyd for dinner at the home of Mr. and Mrs. Otto W. Stenersen, on Highland Drive, Queen Anne Hill, at 6 o'clock the following evening.

"I guess we can quit looking for Stenersen," Miles said, handing the card to Floyd. "He even knows our middle names."

*****

Disconcerted by Stenersen's dinner invitation, but relieved at being able to call it a night, they rose to go home—Floyd to his mother's house, Miles to the O.K. Hotel. As they did, the Vic Meyers Orchestra stopped in the middle of whatever jazz number they were playing and began a rendition of "How Dry I Am." The song change seemed to initiate a flurry of activity throughout the Rose Room, with every single bartender, server, and busboy grabbing a dish tub and frantically going from table to table, dumping each patron's cocktail. Getting rid of evidence, undoubtedly tipped off about an imminent raid.

Sure enough, as soon as Miles and Floyd exited onto James Street, three cars pulled to the curb and out jumped a dozen slouching and depressed-looking Prohibition agents who formed up around their apparent leader—the only man among them with a determined look on his face—and promptly marched in the front entrance of the Rose Room.

"Did you see that fella who led them in?" Floyd said. "That was Clifford Charles."

"Clark mentioned that name. What's his story again?"

"He's the regional assistant director of the Bureau of Prohibition. Least popular man in Seattle. A zealot."

"He and McCaskill and Eckart should form a sewing circle."

With that, they bade each other goodnight and parted ways. Miles's walk to the O.K. Hotel was uneventful, the city having quieted down. He checked for messages at the front desk, hoping for some sign of life from Marion. There was nothing, so with a heavy sense of emptiness, he climbed the stairwell and fumbled with his key before unlocking the door and stepping into his room. There, Miles stopped in his tracks, stood, and stared. Something was off. Perhaps it was an unnatural quiet, an item out of place, or a scent that hadn't been there before. He couldn't quite say. But he was utterly certain that someone was or had been in his room.

Taking a quick peek under the bed and in the wardrobe to make sure nobody was there to jump him, he began a slow and methodical examination of his things, checking the pockets of his clothing, making sure none of his tickets or documents were missing from his valise. The tickets and torn stubs could give a snoop a rough idea of the timing and general location of his movements, for whatever that was worth. But there'd been nothing in the room that would provide anyone with any material information about the investigation. What troubled him far more was the possibility that someone was keeping an eye on him. Perhaps someone with the Jensens' blood on their hands. Perhaps someone who'd be willing to spill more blood if they decided Miles was a threat.

FORTY-THREE

Strait of Juan de Fuca, British Columbia
(near the U.S.-Canada maritime border)
Seven Days Earlier

After a very long, very rough stretch of time closed off in the secret room, with no visits by the fat Cantonese man and no rice, things got suddenly calmer. We could stand without having to hold a hand against the wall. Soon, the fat man came and opened the hole. He gave us rice and water and told us we were nearing the end of our voyage. His rough, uncaring voice sent a shiver of fear through my body. What new suffering would the end of our voyage bring? What cruel treatment would we face next? Would we die like the girl who hit her head?

He reclosed the hole without waiting to take away the rice bowl and without taking any of the girls. We ate in darkness.

*****

Not long after our meal, the pounding thunder noise that had gone on for what felt like many days finally stopped and we felt the boat lean into a long, gentle turn. Things got quiet and still. Eventually, the fat man came back and told us to follow silently. I checked to make sure Snow was still in my pocket before I stood up. I had to blink my sensitive eyes many times as I climbed out of the hole and into the light of the next room. Weak and dizzy, we stumbled up the many stairs and emerged on the deck of the boat. It was night. I could see in the moonlight that we were in a wide bay. There were lights dotted along the distant shore. The fresh, cool air smelled faintly of woodsmoke and green trees.

We held hands as we were led to the very back of the boat where there were no windows looking down on us. The fat man told us to climb overboard, one at a time, down a heavy net that dangled over the side. I was afraid. It was very dark and I knew there was water below. I did not know how to swim.

One by one, we climbed over the side. When my turn came, I peeked over the edge and saw a very small boat waiting below. As we each climbed down, we were helped aboard by a friendly-faced, pale foreigner. A boy, but a very big and tall one with very round eyes. He silently nodded to each of us as we set foot on his little boat. Like all foreigners, he had an odd smell. Not bad. Just different. He looked nervous, which made me nervous too. Once we were all aboard, he gave a wave to the Cantonese man, pushed off from the big boat with one of his oars, and quietly paddled us out into darkness.

*****

After a lot of paddling by the foreigner, another larger boat appeared out of the darkness ahead of us. It was maybe a fishing boat. If it had lanterns, none of them were lit.

Pulling alongside, the boy tied ropes to the larger boat as an older foreigner—also big and tall, also friendly-faced, but also nervous-looking—came to the side and helped us climb aboard. As on the big boat, we were led below. But this time there was lantern light. This time we were given blankets, cold water so fresh it tasted almost sweet, and large pieces of very chewy, very heavy bread—not made from rice flour—with a yellowish, fatty, salty spread smeared over one side of it. And though they looked nervous, the men smiled at us, shyly, and with respect, before climbing back up to the main deck.

With a noise of pounding thunder like on the big boat, but louder, with a faster pounding rhythm, and with a hum that was not as deep, our new boat began to move. Though I couldn't see outside, it felt like it was going faster and faster. Faster than I had ever moved. Impossibly fast.

*****

Eventually, the thunder noise got quieter and the boat felt as if it slowed down and stopped. Then the thunder noise stopped. The foreigners came down the steps and made hand motions that I think meant they wanted us to stay quiet again. So we chewed on our bread, drank our water, whispered to each other, and waited.

I was still afraid, not knowing what was coming, knowing I was in a strange foreign land, far from home, far from family. But the friendly, shy faces and respectfulness of the foreigners, the fresh water and tasty bread, the cool, fresh air, and finally being out of the stinking, dark, secret room of the big boat had me starting to feel a tiny bit hopeful that maybe, after all the suffering and fear, things were going to be okay.

As I had done so many times since leaving home, and hardly aware that I was doing so, I put my hand into the inner pocket of my tunic to feel the warm, reassuring softness of Snow's fur. I felt my comb there. But as I probed the corners of the pocket, I couldn't find Snow. With growing panic, I felt all around, my hands checking every bit of space. I looked all over my clothes in case she'd climbed out and was hanging on. I patted down my clothing in case she'd crawled into a warm gap or fold. Then, as my heart began to pound, as my breathing began coming in gasps, I looked all around the floor. Snow was gone.

I fell to my knees, put my hands over my face so the other girls wouldn't see, and began to cry. I couldn't stop myself. I knew it was shameful given whatever horrors some of the other girls had been through on the ship. But I loved sweet little Snow. She was my comfort. My link to home.

What would become of her? If she made it off the boat, would she survive in this strange new land? Would she find good things to eat? Would she find a safe and warm place to sleep? If she made it to land, would the foreign mice be kind to her? Welcoming? Would she be able to speak their mouse language? Or would she be an outcast? Would she starve? Would a foreign snake or bird catch and eat her?

I sobbed. Tried to take deep breaths. Dried my eyes. Sobbed more. I'm sure the other girls had by now noticed I was upset. None of them asked me what was wrong. They looked preoccupied with fear. This was understandable. But I was so deeply sad that my own fear, strong as it was, felt suddenly unimportant. I was sure I would sob all night.

Then I heard a faint, low, far away sound that I guessed was more boat thunder noise. Not from our boat. From another. We all heard it at once, then looked at each other with new uncertainty, new dread, as the deep thunder sound slowly grew louder. Whatever it was, it was coming closer.

FORTY-FOUR

The next morning, with nothing to do until their dinner with Stenersen, Miles and Floyd went their separate ways. Floyd returned to police headquarters to take on a backlog of paperwork from his other cases, while Miles rode a trolley out to explore the University of Washington campus that was slowly taking shape on the grounds of the 1909 World's Fair, then visited the new Frederick & Nelson department store downtown to buy his mother a bolt of jade green silk that he pictured her using to make pillows.

As he waited for the clerk to package the silk up, he wandered the main floor out of curiosity as to what was considered fashionable in the big city these days. His eyes were drawn to a dazzling cobalt blue dress of a style similar to the one Marion wore to the Odd Fellows. Hip-length, adorned with blue glass beads, and priced at more than a month's pay for a sheriff. As he stood staring at it, wishing he could afford to buy it for Marion, it occurred to him that she had grown to be so much more than the simple local girl she was when he shipped out for the war. She was educated. She had a taste for fashion. She followed world events, went to jazz clubs, and heaven knew what else. With a cold feeling in his stomach, he wondered if, having spent years out east, she had, on some level, come to view local islanders such as himself as rubes—unlearned, unsophisticated, uninteresting. He wondered if she was secretly appalled by his plain work clothes, his simple life, the indelicate way he played his saxophone.

*****

Reconvening near the Butler Hotel at 5:30 p.m., they boarded the Queen Anne Hill trolley, then sat utterly silent, their faces serious, as they rode back across downtown. When they reached the base of the steep climb up Queen Anne Hill's southern slope, a white-knuckled Miles sprang to his feet and said, "Let's walk from here."

"Walk? Up the hill? Why?"

"Trolley will probably break down again."

"Unlikely."

"Come on. We have time. A little exercise is good for the mind."

They hopped off the trolley and began their ascent. Ten minutes later, sweating and breathing hard, they turned onto Highland Drive—a tree-lined street of tall hedges, gated driveways, and big, architecturally unique houses with sweeping views out over Downtown Seattle and the maritime bustle of Elliott Bay. A couple more blocks on foot brought them to a semicircular drive and a meticulously landscaped yard that fronted a massive Arts and Crafts-style house. The same sleek yellow sports car they'd seen from the trolley on their way to lunch with Floyd's mother stood in the drive.

"Look, it's that Bearcat again," Miles said, pointing to it, forcing small talk, unable to fully disguise the tension in his voice. "Maybe Stenersen will let us take it for a spin."

"So we're really doing this?" Floyd said.

"Doing what? Voluntarily walking into the home of Seattle's answer to Johnny Torrio and Al Capone?"

"They say he's nothing like them," Floyd said, sounding uncertain.

"*They*, huh? Do you believe what *they* say about him not letting his men even carry guns? The biggest bootlegger on the West Coast?"

"It's probably true." Floyd looked at Miles and smiled a weak smile. "Still, it's hard to believe someone could be top dog in the rumrunning business without burying a few bodies. So, if we go in there, I suppose there's always a chance that we never come out. That we end up feeding tulips in his back yard. Ha-ha."

"Then again, if he wanted to kill us, he could have already," Miles said.

"Maybe he wants to know what we know *before* he kills us."

"Thanks for putting my mind at ease, Floyd."

They climbed to the front porch and gave the glossy black door a knock with an ornate brass knocker. It opened to reveal a young, well-dressed woman in glasses.

"Good evening, gentlemen. I'm Stella, Mr. and Mrs. Stenersen's secretary. You must be Mr. Scott and Mr. Floyd."

"Yes, ma'am," Floyd said. "That's us."

"Won't you come in?"

"Thank you."

"Mr. Stenersen should be here shortly. Can I fetch either of you gentlemen a glass of lemonade?"

"Lemonade?" Floyd asked as they passed an open doorway to a room in which two giant men in suits sat smoking and watching the street through a large window. "No. No, thank you."

"I'll show you to the parlor, then. Mrs. Brill, our chef, will serve dinner promptly at 6:30 p.m."

Stella left them in a large room decorated with fine leather furniture, maritime oil paintings, and Tiffany lamps. But what really drew the eye was a large window framing an unobstructed view of the Seattle skyline and waterfront, with the great glaciated volcano, Mount Rainier, looming in the background, its 14,000-plus foot summit lit brilliant white by the evening sun.

"What do you suppose this is," Floyd said, gazing at an ornate maple wood cabinet that stood four feet tall against one of the walls.

"Maybe one of those contraptions that opens up into a small bar?" Miles said.

"It's a gramophone," said Otto Stenersen, striding into the room. "Good guess though. I'm Otto. I'm going to guess that you are Sheriff Scott," he said, offering his hand to Miles.

"Yes, sir."

"And that makes you Detective Ashton Floyd of my beloved Seattle PD."

Stenersen was a tall, imposing man—at least as tall as Miles. Yet he bore an utterly disarming smile and aura of welcoming charm. His suit was well-tailored but simple, his shoes well cared for but common.

"Where's the crank?" Miles asked, returning his attention to the gramophone cabinet.

"I'm glad you asked," Stenersen said with a beaming smile, opening the cover to reveal a recessed turntable and a slot housing half a dozen records. "Have a look. This thing is my pride and joy. A prototype. Not available to the general public as yet. There's no crank."

"No crank?"

"You just plug it into the wall, and a little electric motor does the rest."

"You're joking."

"See for yourself." Stenersen pointed to a power cord leading from the bottom of the cabinet to an outlet in the ochre-painted wall. "The tone arm has a big horseshoe magnet in it. They call it an electromagnetic pickup. There's no sound box or amplifying horn." He drew a record from the slot, placed it on the turntable, positioned the tone arm, and turned a knob. "I'll tell you something, fellas, we live in an amazing modern world." A few seconds of scratching were followed by the first soprano saxophone notes of a jazz tune emanating from speakers hidden behind a wicker screen on the side of the cabinet. The sound was exceptional. "Like it? It's a fella named Sidney Bechet, the latest jazz maestro out of New Orleans. A genius, my view."

Miles's mouth dropped open. "Amazing."

"Isn't it?"

"I don't recognize this one."

"That's because it was recorded in New York City just last week. Came in on yesterday's Oriental Limited. I take it that you're familiar with Sidney Bechet."

"He's something of an inspiration to me."

"You play saxophone, then?"

"A Buescher."

Stenersen smiled. "Same as Bechet. Wish I had one here that you could play for us."

"I hardly do the instrument justice."

"Nonsense. I mean, there's only one Sidney Bechet, right? But I'm sure you play just fine."

"My mother says I play like a bull moose."

Stenersen laughed out loud. "My mother once told me I played piano like Genghis Khan. True story."

"Well—there's only one Genghis Khan."

"Ha! Anyway, I've heard Bechet's music described as emotional and reckless. Like his personality."

"His personality?"

"Unfortunately, yes. For all his talent, he's supposed to be a real no-goodnik. A cad with a short fuse. Smacks women around. He's even been known to shoot at his fellow musicians."

"Maybe they were lagging behind the beat," Miles said.

"A capital offense! Well, fellas, I appreciate you coming by. We'll try to make it worth your while. Mrs. Brill is cooking up one of my favorite dishes for us tonight. Beef Wellington."

"What's that?" Floyd asked.

"Do you like beef?"

"Very much."

"Then you'll love it. It starts with a center cut of tenderloin we got from a rancher out in Redmond. Then Mrs. Brill coats it in layers of pâté and mushroom and shallot duxelles, wraps the whole thing in buttery pastry dough, roasts it to a juicy medium rare, then serves it in thick slices topped with a truffle cream sauce. We'll be joined this evening by my wife, Marie, along with

Deputy Mayor Royster. Havana cigars in the garden after, if you care for them."

And that's the part where the security gorillas I saw in your front room will knock me over my head and bury me under the tulips, Miles thought, half seriously.

*****

They made small talk about wretched Seattle weather and wretched Seattle traffic until the deputy mayor arrived, at which point Stenersen's wife, Marie, slid open a double pocket door separating the room they stood in from the dining room and invited the men to come to the candlelit table. She was adorned in an evening dress of ivory silk with tiers of scalloped beadwork. All of a sudden Miles felt horribly underdressed in his threadbare suit wrinkled from travel. But Marie's warm smile and easy French-accented greeting quickly alleviated his discomfort.

As they took their seats, Miles was mildly surprised to see the table set with nothing more to drink than tall glasses of ice water with mint leaves and small cubes of frozen watermelon floating in them. There were no wine glasses. No cocktail glasses. Nothing of the sort.

It was immediately clear that Marie ran the show at the dinner table, leading conversation, politely asking about each of her guest's families, backgrounds, and interests. "Now, do either of you gentlemen have children?" she asked Miles and Floyd. "Neither of you? Two handsome men already well into their twenties? You need to start having children."

"She's only giving you a hard time because she's always looking to grow her fan club," Stenersen said.

"Pardon?" Miles said.

"She has a children's radio show that broadcasts on a station we have set up in the basement here. The big antenna is on the hilltop just east of us. We have the most powerful signal in the region."

"A radio show?" Floyd asked.

"The Adventures of Bear and Badger," Marie said. "It's a story reading."

"Ah yes!" Miles said with a hair too much volume.

"I take it you're familiar with the show?" Stenersen said, his face suggesting he was just barely able to suppress a smile.

"I mean—I don't have children. But I've heard of it."

"Indeed."

They ate what to Miles was one of the most delicious meals he'd ever had as new Sidney Bechet music played on Stenersen's state-of-the-art gramophone in the background. The beef Wellington was served with a crusty country bread and tomato basil salad. The plates were cleared for a dessert course of custard topped with sugar-coated blueberries, served with hot black coffee.

"Otto tells me you were in the war," Marie said to Miles as Stenersen leaned across the table to light the cigarette she'd stuck in her long ebony holder. "In France, I assume?"

"Yes, ma'am," Miles answered, wondering how Stenersen had come by that bit of information, let alone his middle name.

"May I ask what you thought of my home country?"

"Well, the horror of the war aside, I loved it. All the little villages. The cheese. The wine."

"Wine?" Stenersen half shouted. "But you have no scales, sir. No forked tongue. Do you mean to tell me that the wine didn't turn you into a demon?" he said with a wink.

"Don't interrupt him," Marie said. "Apologies, Miles. Please go on. You were saying the cheese, the wine . . ."

"The bread. The city of Paris."

"Ah, you went to Paris."

"On leave. My whole detachment spent a week there."

"Where did you stay?"

"A small hotel in the 5th District, on Rue de Buci."

"A lovely street."

"You know Rue de Buci?"

"I grew up nearby. A block from Luxembourg Gardens, in fact."

"My wife, the Parisian," Stenersen said with obvious pride.

"What were your favorite things about the city?" she asked.

Miles took a moment to consider her question. "In a way, it was an odd experience. Being in Paris, I mean. On leave from the war. Witnessing normal life again, all of a sudden. It's like coming in out of a windstorm."

"That's quite an analogy," the deputy mayor said, making one of his few contributions to the conversation.

"But I suppose my favorite things about Paris were particular moments in time."

"Such as?" Marie asked.

Miles took a moment to think. "There was this one day. This one morning, rather. I woke with the dawn, grabbed a tin mug of coffee at the front desk, and took a long walk. We were there in the winter, and it was snowing. A breathtaking thing to see in that ancient city. In a bit of a trance, I wandered all over, just walking the streets, watching the shop owners open their doors and sweep snow from the sidewalks. Watching them load their produce racks and bread bins. I remember coming across a lone street vendor who was already out with his cart at that early hour, roasting chestnuts over a small brazier down by the Seine River. You could smell their aroma from half a block away. Then I crossed a minor bridge, stopping midway to watch the current for a minute, then went a block or two up the far side when all of a sudden I found myself standing in the gently falling snow in front of a small cathedral. It was behind a wall with a gate. But the gate and the cathedral were both open and nobody was around, so I went in." He took a breath. "I'll never forget that moment as long as I live, walking in out of the snow. It was quiet and I was all alone. The air smelled of incense. Devotional candles glowed in iron racks in the corners. And in place of walls, the cathedral had hundreds and hundreds of little stained glass windows built into panels several stories high, supported by a mere framework of stone. All colors of glass, but dominated by this one brilliant blue. An otherworldly cobalt blue. And all of it backlit by the morning sun. It's impossible to adequately describe. It was easily the most beautiful manmade thing I'd ever seen."

"Sainte-Chapelle," Marie said. "Chapel of the Kings."

"Yes. That was it."

"A Gothic architectural wonder in the Palais de la Cité, home of the Kings of France until the 14th century."

"I'll tell you what," Miles said. "I'm not a religious or spiritual man. Not at all. But I remember feeling a sudden, odd lightness in my chest as I gazed at that stained glass, smelled the candles and the traces of incense, all the while listening to the soft echo of my own breathing."

"A policeman and a poet," Stenersen said.

Miles could have added that just as suddenly as the sense of lightness had come on, it died with his realization of how odd and tragic it was that humanity could create such an incredibly beautiful thing as that cathedral, but could also create the horrors of the trench lines that began barely 60 miles east of Paris, where millions upon millions of young men had been slaughtering each other for years.

"You paint quite a picture," Stenersen said.

"It was quite a moment. One of those rare ones that's perfect, but also sad because you know that you can never quite go back to it."

*****

The deputy mayor departed just after dinner, Marie went upstairs to work on the script of her next radio show, and Stenersen, Miles, and Floyd retired to wicker chairs on the wide back porch where they smoked cigars with a twilight view of Seattle. The waterfront had grown relatively quiet with darkness falling and most of the vessels now moored. The largest ships stood at anchor out in the bay, with white anti-collision lights shining high up on their superstructures or rigging. Countless windows of the city skyline glowed from within.

"Well, gentlemen," Stenersen began. "I'm told you were hoping to have a word with me. How can I be of service?"

Seeing no point in faltering now, Miles dove in. "We're informed that you are in the, ah, international trade business."

"Strictly imports."

"Yes. In short, we've been given to understand that a boat crew from my jurisdiction who disappeared last week might have been a couple of your importers."

Miles gave him a brief summary of the *Lucky Lena* situation, all the while having the distinct impression that Stenersen already knew everything Miles was telling him, and then some. He waited as Stenersen nodded, then lifted his legs up on an ottoman.

"I see. Well, I have importers, and then I have *importers*. The crew you speak of were more along the line of freelancers. That being said, we don't want anyone getting hurt out there. I say this to my men over and over again: nothing we import is worth a single human life. It just isn't."

"I couldn't agree more," Miles said. "It concerns me that the import business is growing more dangerous here in Puget Sound, and that this may have been a factor in the possible murder of two citizens I was responsible for protecting."

"I empathize." Stenersen looked thoughtful. Thoughtful and worried. "Needless to say, one-off acts of piracy aren't unheard of in these parts. Usually, they involve a high-speed boat chase. Occasionally, an importer gets his nose bloodied or his eye blackened before his cargo is taken from him. But this? A crew vanished, presumed murdered? Bullet holes and blood everywhere?"

"A mess," Miles said.

"It was exceedingly rare to see anything like it around here—until very recently, that is," Stenersen said, puffing on his cigar. "I'm obliged to tell you that I've had people make a few discreet inquiries over the very matter you speak of."

"Oh?"

"It's like this, fellas. The main importers in this region are, by and large, very decent men, and they know they have a good thing going. Believe it or not, they cooperate. Business is thriving, and everything is usually peaceful. In general, nobody gets hurt, and a lot of good men are able to put food on the table and keep their kids in decent shoes. Nobody wants to see things go back to the way they were under Mayor Gill, when you had daylight shootouts between the unprincipled henchmen of guys like the Billingsley Brothers and Pirate Jack Margett. With innocent civilians and police officers getting caught in the crossfire like it was bloody Chicago. Those were dark times here." His face went grim. "That being said, did either of you read about the murder in Tacoma two weeks ago?"

The men shook their heads.

"You've heard of Pete Marinoff? Legitimate Pete, as the papers call him?"

Miles shook his head again. Floyd nodded.

"A fellow importer and personal friend of mine," Stenersen said. "Anyway, a truck driver who happened to be in Pete's employ was robbed of his cargo and murdered in a parking lot off Commerce Street. Shot through the ear with a .32 at close range. No witnesses. But a little bird told me there is a fair bit of, shall we say, circumstantial evidence that the murder was perpetrated by an associate of Clancy Donovan."

"The San Francisco mobster?" Floyd asked.

"The San Francisco mobster who covets the Pacific Northwest import trade. Exactly." Stenersen shook his head. "That poor truck driver of Pete's was a family man who left behind a widow and two tots. It makes a man's heart ache to hear that sort of thing. Now, this wasn't the first time someone hijacked one of Pete's shipments. But it was the bloodiest time, at least as far as we know. Unfortunately, there are also rumors that Clancy's goons hijacked one of Pete's boats somewhere in

Admiralty Inlet, probably north of Bainbridge Island. Nobody is 100-percent sure because the boat, its cargo, and its crew simply disappeared from the face of the earth three weeks ago after last being seen running south past Kingston. The thing is, the two-man crew were veteran seamen with a very sturdy boat. And it wasn't like them to not at least call their wives at home if they were delayed. So needless to say, we're fearing the worst." Stenersen stubbed out his cigar. "In my mind, this all signals an escalation. An incursion by outside forces who don't necessarily share our local importers' concern for human life. Obviously, our worry is that Clancy Donovan's gang is making moves to gain a toehold in the Puget Sound import market, using whatever means necessary to do so."

"So the disappearance of the *Lucky Lena* crew might be the work of the same gang," Miles said.

"Exactly. Needless to say, my fellow importers and I don't want to see some sort of war break out between our people and Donovan's. Plus, he's a very clever man, known for orchestrating false flag incidents, making it look like someone else did the hijacking or killing, turning importers or their people against each other, playing one importer against the other, like we saw last year down in Portland. His deceptions starting wars where the locals kill each other off until Donovan can just traipse on in, crush the leftovers, and take over. We want to nip this thing in the bud, for everyone's wellbeing, including the folks up in the San Juan Islands who you're obligated to protect, Sheriff. To that end, as I learn anything of the matter, I'll be sure to pass it along to you without delay. I know I can't ask you to do the same. But rest assured, we're on the same page with this. The last thing any of us here want is blood running in the streets."

"Or in the water," Miles added.

FORTY-FIVE

They'd gone more than two blocks before Floyd broke the silence of their walk from Stenersen's house to the trolley stop.

"That was weird."

"You think so?"

As they rode a clanking trolley back downtown under the yellow glow of streetlights, it struck Miles that Stenersen was a man of unusual contradictions. Though his outfit probably generated more revenue and employed more men than C.D. Stimson's lumber empire and William Boeing's airplane company combined, he drove a Stutz instead of a Rolls Royce and lived in a Craftsman house—albeit an impressive one—instead of a mansion. And although he was involved in an often-bloody line of business dominated by avaricious egomaniacs, he had no apparent desire to seize territory from his regional bootlegger colleagues and didn't allow his men to carry guns. Against his better judgement, Miles was inclined to like him.

And yet Stenersen had arranged the hand-delivery of dinner invitations that included their middle names. What was that about? Letting them know that he knew where they were and what they were up to? Knew all about them? Was it supposed to be intimidating? And why had the deputy mayor shared their dinner table?

Then again, Stenersen hadn't tried to bribe them. Perhaps that simply meant he'd done enough background checking on Miles to know he had a history of turning down attempted payoffs, perhaps even from Stenersen's own organization.

"You're looking a bit pensive," Floyd said. "Something on

your mind?"

"Too many things. Things that don't seem to go together."

"Such as?"

"First of all, I've decided that it wasn't Stenersen's goons who searched my room. Not unless he and his lovely wife are two of the best actors in history. So, if we assume, which I'm inclined to do, that he's being straight with us, not attempting some sort of misdirection, then he's letting us know we don't have to waste our time pursuing leads that involve his organization. Helpful. But I also find it interesting that he had the deputy mayor dine with us. That fella didn't say much, did he? Wasn't there for his contribution to the conversation, was he? Just there to show the flag. Just there as a message. A living, breathing message that Stenersen's operations have city hall's unofficial blessing. Mind you, I'm no apostle of Prohibition. But the fact that the king of the local bootleggers is in tight with local government has some interesting implications with respect to our investigation, doesn't it?"

"I'm not sure I follow you."

"Lenora Street!" the trolleyman shouted as they screeched to a slow, momentary stop.

"If Stenersen really doesn't let his men carry weapons," Miles continued, "and assuming Clancy Donovan's gang is behind the recent bloodshed, then how does Stenersen plan on stopping them? Left that bit kind of vague, didn't he?"

"Well, Stenersen has a pretty strong track record of buying people off. Paying to get what he wants. Paying instead of shooting. So maybe he'll just pay Donovan's goons to join up with him."

"What are the chances of that working, do you think?"

"Probably not great. So maybe one of the less pacifistic local bootleggers will make Donovan's men disappear."

"That's certainly one possibility. And seeing as how all the local bootleggers cooperate—meaning they probably share information with each other—we shouldn't share information with Stenersen unless we want to be complicit in whatever measures the less pacifistic local bootleggers take to keep Clancy Donovan out of the Pacific Northwest. Like maybe scalping his men."

"He wasn't asking you to share information."

"Yeah, but let's not be naïve."

"I beg your pardon?"

"Look, Floyd. You're a smart guy. Why were you sent to Friday Harbor?"

"Orders."

"Well, sure. But why *you*?"

"Because of my expertise in modern forensics."

"We have crime scene guys we summon from Bellingham or Port Townsend as a matter of routine. Those towns are a lot closer than Seattle. So again, why you? I didn't call for you. No offense."

Floyd gave him a blank stare.

"Pike Street!" came the shout for another stop.

"How about this?" Miles asked. "Where did your orders come from?"

"The chain of command."

"Your lieutenant?"

"Well, actually no. From Chief Severyn's office."

"Orders direct from his royal highness, Chief of Police William B. Severyn himself. Is that normal?"

"No."

"So your orders came from the top, concerning a crime in our remote corner of the state. From the chief himself. And who does the chief answer to?"

"The mayor."

"The mayor, whose trusted deputy was just staring at us across the dinner table at Stenersen's house."

"Yeah, but—"

"And who does the mayor answer to?"

"The citizens."

"Sure, Floyd. Right. But who does he *really* answer to?"

Floyd looked thoughtful. "Probably to whoever makes the big donations to his reelection campaign war chest."

"There you are. Follow the money, right? Like that crazy Bolshevik Lenin says. And where is the big money in Seattle these days?"

"I see where you're going with this."

"I'll say it anyway. The big money is with the bootleggers."

"So you're saying we're actually working for the bootleggers?"

"The bootleggers. Maybe the Chinese tongs, with their money machine speakeasies and underground gambling clubs. Who knows?"

"But if it's the bootleggers," Floyd said, "if it's Stenersen, then maybe he's planning to have the Seattle Police help him fight Donovan."

"Maybe."

"Madison Street! All off for Madison!"

"Let's get off here," Miles said.

They walked down First Avenue, more or less in the direction of Miles's hotel, until Floyd drew to an abrupt stop.

"What is it?" Miles asked.

"Are you sleepy?"

"Sleepy? No. My mind is so spooled up right now that I'll be lucky to sleep at all tonight."

"Feel like a walk?"

"Why not."

Floyd led Miles down through Pioneer Place, turning left at the boisterous Merchants Café—rumored home of yet another basement speakeasy—and eventually zigzagging up into Chinatown. As they walked along, discussing the evidence and information they'd collected to-date, they passed businesses, blocks, and alleys that smelled, alternately, of baking bread, Asian herbs and produce, cheap perfume, and old urine. The people they passed tended to be Asians going about their work as if

Miles and Floyd didn't exist, or white men in suits ducking in or out of unmarked doors, looking furtive and entirely unwilling to make eye contact. Down one alley, they could hear a couple of drunks yelling at each other in some foreign language. Danish, Miles thought. Then, for a brief moment, they caught the unmistakable smell of opium seeping through the crevices of heaven knew what nearby building.

"Where are you taking me?" Miles asked.

"Place called the Alhambra."

"Another speakeasy?"

"A jazz club."

"You're kidding."

"Hottest jazz club in town."

"Floyd, you're alright."

"Just don't tell my mother I was out this late."

The Alhambra was in the basement of a building at the corner of 12th and Jackson Street, in the very heart of the burgeoning Seattle jazz scene. There was a line of black men and women in striking cocktail attire waiting outside the guarded door to the basement stairs. A few of them stood reading a newspaper Miles had never heard of called *The Seattle Enterprise.* A highly-polished red sports car with extravagant cream upholstery was parked just outside the front door.

"Is that another Bearcat?" Floyd asked.

"I think it's a Mercer Raceabout," Miles said. "Incidentally, I'm feeling underdressed again."

"You and me both."

"Are we, uh, supposed to wait in line with the colored people?" Miles asked under his breath.

"I don't know for certain. But I say, when in Rome . . ."

"I thought it was St. Augustine who said that."

"How would an agnostic know?"

Miles smiled. "Good question."

As they waited in line, whenever the door opened, jazz music floated out into the night air, causing Miles's heart to lift. When finally admitted, they made their way down the narrow stairwell to a lower level crowded with people dancing to a black-suited five-piece band—drums, piano, trombone, trumpet, and saxophone—jammed onto a small stage. A placard on an easel by the stage read *The Odean Jazz Orchestra*. They wound up a variation of "Ja-Da," then began "Beale Street Blues," at which point the visibly sweating folks who'd been dancing dispersed for a break.

"This is fantastic," Miles said, smiling from ear to ear. "Best jazz club I've been in since London."

"And would you believe it's colored-owned?"

"You're kidding."

"Fella by the name of Harry Legg."

"That's a hell of a name."

"Isn't it? But everyone thinks Legg is just the straight arrow front man. That it's really run by a couple of dubious but very clever businessmen named Blackie Williams and Noodles Smith. Ever heard of them?"

"I'm sure I haven't."

"Notorious, street-hardened club owners who know how to bring in the best bands. The music here is so good that nobody wants to bother investigating them."

The music *was* good. And as it began to carry him away, Miles realized, with no small measure of surprise, that there were colored folk, Orientals, and whites all rubbing elbows. Men and women. Businessmen and laborers. All welcome. All enjoying jazz—to Miles, the most quintessentially American genre of music—without any apparent care about the skin color, line of work, or gender of the people they stood next to, behind, or in front of. The seeming harmony, however temporary it might have been, filled him with a sense of warmth that stood in stark contrast to the unease he'd felt bearing witness to the naked hate of the anti-Japanese protestors they'd walked past two days earlier, barely a mile away. And for a brief but joyful moment, Miles had genuine hope for the human race.

*****

"That was a treat, Floyd. I thank you," Miles said as they made their way to the nearest trolley stop. "These colored jazz joints are really developing their own West Coast sort of sound, aren't they? I mean, that trumpet player was hands-down one of the—"

"Hey, Miles!" someone shouted from close behind them as they were cutting down a dark and narrow alley, looking for a shortcut to Yesler Way. The man who'd shouted, and a companion, were jogging up to meet them. "It's Miles, right?" the man said, extending his hand in greeting. But then his face came into the anemic light of a naked bulb over a nearby alley door and Miles saw that the man had an aggressive look in his eye. So did his companion.

"Do I know you?" Miles said.

The man retracted his hand when Miles refused to take it. "A bit outside of your bumpkin jurisdiction, aren't you, pal?"

"What do you want?" Miles asked, and hearing the scuffling of shoes behind them, he turned to see four more men hotfooting it up from the opposite end of the alley.

"What do I want?" The man said. "I want what everybody wants. For you to go back to your little seagull shit island and mind your own business."

"Is that right?" Miles said, subconsciously rising onto the balls of his feet, looking around and taking the group's measure, confident he could take out at least two of them, maybe three—provided they weren't carrying weapons. "And who the hell are you, chummy?"

"Never mind who I am. Let me tell you what's going to happ—"

The man was cut off, mid-sentence, when Miles's enormous fist plowed right into his mouth, caving in several of his teeth, driving the man backward and dropping him flat on his back. At that, the rest of the group pounced—two of them on Floyd, three taking on Miles. Ducking and moving as he kept his hands up, Miles did his best to keep any of them from landing a solid blow. He took out another with a quick uppercut to the jaw. But as he was spinning on his heels to keep one of them from grabbing his arms from behind, he momentarily lost track of another, and that was all it took. A blinding white light exploded from the right side of his head. Then all went dark.

*****

"Miles? Can you hear me? Miles?" he heard Floyd ask in a faint and distant voice just before he felt cold water pour onto his face.

He gasped and choked, clearing his nose and throat. "Hey! What gives?" he asked, overcoming a stabbing pain in his head to just barely open his eyes. Floyd and two uniformed Seattle Police Officers were bent over him. One of the police was trying to hold a bloody rag to Miles's head. The other held a now empty, upturned water flask.

"Easy does it, sir," one of the police said as Miles forced himself to sit up in the middle of the alley. "You took a good crack to the noggin. Hoodlum son of a bitch had a blackjack club. Opened up a good gash here next to your eyebrow. Might want to have Swedish Hospital take a look at it."

"How long have I been out?" Miles asked, accepting the rag and pressing it to his head wound as he spotted two of someone else's teeth on the pavement next to him.

"Couple of minutes," Floyd said. "Lucky for us, Denny and Maynard here happened by on their beat. Chased off our assailants."

"Who were they?"

"No idea. Someone who doesn't want us poking around asking questions."

"Clancy Donovan?" Miles asked.

"Maybe. Or maybe Gustav Hauer, or even one of the tongs."

"Would tongs hire Caucasian thugs?"

"Seems unlikely, unless they wanted to hide their tracks." Floyd chuckled. "You really pummeled one of them, Miles. Guy ran off with blood pouring out of his mouth. Forgot to take his teeth with him."

Miles took stock. In addition to his gashed open head, the knuckles of both his hands were thoroughly bloodied. And though he didn't remember it happening, both his trouser knees were ripped wide open, and the right shoulder seam of his jacket was torn out. "Looks like I need a tailor." Out of belated concern for his de facto partner, he looked at Floyd, only to discover that he was utterly unscathed. "You don't have a scratch on you."

"Guess I'm just a better fighter than you."

"I guess," Miles said, noticing that even Floyd's knuckles were unmarked. Then he began to wonder how the two men he'd knocked for a loop had managed to run away from Floyd and two able-bodied patrolmen.

The officers helped Miles to his feet, and once they were sure he wasn't going to fall back down, bade him and Floyd goodnight.

"I'm a little dizzy."

"I believe you," Floyd said. "You want to go up to Swedish Hospital?"

"No."

"Let me at least walk you back to your hotel to make sure you don't pass out in the gutter."

They took their time, with Miles holding the bloody rag to his head wound and periodically stopping to lean against a building or brace his hands on his knees as he caught his breath and regained his bearings. As they at last walked through the front door of the O.K. Hotel, a United Parcel Service delivery boy entered behind them, took an envelope from his satchel, and, handing it to the front desk night clerk, said, "Express delivery for a Miles Scott."

"I'm Scott," Miles said, eyeing the delivery boy with perplexity as he was handed the envelope. Hoping against reason that it might be a letter from Marion, he tore it open and read the brief telegram within, his jaw going slack as he did so.

"What?" Floyd asked. "Something wrong?"

"Two more bodies washed up."

"Two bodies? On San Juan Island?"

Miles just nodded his bloody head.

"The Jensens?" Floyd asked. "Angus Cooper?"

"Girls."

"Girls?"

"Two Chinese girls."

FORTY-SIX

Miles and Floyd caught the first steamer to Friday Harbor the next morning—which that day happened to be a vessel called the SS *Rhododendron,* running an irregular route that included stops at Langley and Coupeville on Whidbey Island. It was a longer ride, but would still get them to Friday Harbor a full hour before the later-departing *Bangor.* As always, Floyd sat facing an inner wall and tried to imagine that he was somewhere else.

They made good time as far as Coupeville. But their luck ran out with the steamer entering a dense fogbank as it skirted Swinomish tribal waters and began its turn westward toward the Juan de Fuca Strait. A sudden softening of the engine noise got both men's attention as the captain slowed the vessel down.

"Fog," Floyd muttered, having allowed himself a brief and fearful glance over his shoulder and out the window. "Holy hell."

It was the worst possible spot to hit fog, as they were approaching Deception Pass—a treacherous, narrow channel in which countless vessels had wrecked throughout the years. So named by the great British explorer George Vancouver himself, it was barely 400 feet wide, lined on both sides with jagged cliffs and submerged reefs. The ever-dark, ever-cold ebb and flood tides raced through it with such speed that there were visible rapids, roiling eddies, and whirlpools one might expect to see on a wild river pouring out of the Cascade Mountains. In short, Deception Pass could be a challenge to navigate even on a clear day.

Miles's wounded skull still throbbed with a pain made worse by the deep vibrations of the ship's engines. He was still light-headed, and his mind whirled with dark and anxious thoughts of the two young Chinese girls whose corpses awaited their examination, of who might have sent the men who'd attacked them in Seattle, of the imminent danger of a foggy passage through Deception Pass, and of Marion's looming departure to New York. His heart suddenly pounding, he felt an overwhelming need for fresh air. He rose, slow and ponderous, to his feet, then made his way to the nearest door to the outside deck, leaving a visibly terrified Floyd doubled over on a bench with his hands clasped over the back of his head, no doubt praying for a swift end to their predicament.

The steamer had slowed to a crawl, with crewmen taking up lookout positions on either side of the bow and flying bridge. The captain began to sound the ship's whistle every twenty or thirty seconds. Miles knew that in doing so, a captain who was familiar with the route could, in theory, determine his position through echolocation. He also knew that, in general, Puget Sound steamship captains were renowned for their great skill in navigating blind. But echolocation wasn't an exact science—given variations in how echoes bounced off cliffs, low shorelines, trees, and whatnot—and ships trying to navigate by it were wrecked in the Pacific Northwest every year.

The whistle blew and Miles counted in his head—one, two, three—knowing that sound travelled at just over 1,000 feet per second at sea level, so that an echo that took two seconds to return meant the shore was roughly 1,000 feet away. So far, so good—the echo took over three seconds to bounce back. But as they steamed on, the echoes came back fast and faster. Two seconds. A second and a half. Miles strained his eyes to see through the dense fog, but couldn't make out a thing through the wall of white. That meant the crewmen couldn't either.

All at once, Miles realized that he'd completely lost his bearings. The vessel could be heading north, south, east, or west—toward a beach, a reef, or open water. He had no idea. It was an unnerving sensation, and he realized, with a surge of despondency, that it more or less mirrored how he felt about the investigation. It seemed everything that happened—every witness interview they conducted, every scrap of evidence they found, every bit of news they received—brought confusion instead of clarity. No answers. Only more questions.

In a brief telephone conversation with Bill that morning, he'd come to learn that the two dead Chinese girls had washed ashore at Hanbury Point, near Roche Harbor and just across Haro Strait from D'Arcy Island. According to Bill, Dr. Boren's initial examination of the bodies indicated that they'd been in the water for several days. Each had been shot in the chest and had their bellies slashed open with some sort of blade.

So now they had three men and a mentally deranged child gone missing, as well as three bodies washed ashore, all in the span of a single week. It was beyond unprecedented in Miles's knowledge of San Juan Island history. It was freakish.

His focus was shattered by indecipherable shouting between an officer on the flying bridge and the port side bow lookout. The *Rhododendron*'s whistle rang out once more, and was this time answered by an echo barely half a second later. More shouting. Louder shouting. And the vessel turned hard to starboard.

"Holy cow," Miles said out loud, grabbing for the deck railing to steady himself as the ship listed with the turn. He stared and stared, expecting to see a massive rock formation looming in the fog. A reef that might tear the hull open and sink the ship. Might end his life. Might send his remains to the cold, dark bottom to slowly decompose or serve as food for Dungeness crab. Then, as suddenly as they'd seemed destined for disaster, the ship emerged from the fogbank and into the clear air of a sunny autumn day. A small rocky island stood a couple hundred feet off the port side. And the chasm of Deception Pass itself loomed maybe half a mile off their bow. The tide was slack. The water calm. The ship's engines rumbled as she resumed her normal speed.

Realizing he'd live to see another day, Miles took a deep and satisfying breath of the crisp marine air and returned to the passenger cabin where he found Floyd still doubled over on his bench.

"Floyd, you doing alright there, buddy?"

"Yuh."

"See that little island off the port side? That Seattle-Bellingham boat, SS *Kulshan*, ran aground there about ten or twelve years ago. Remember? What a mess that was."

His story drew a miserable glare from Floyd.

"For that matter, you ever heard of Ben Ure or Pirate Kelly?" Miles asked.

"Nuh."

"Years ago, Ure and Kelly used that island as a base for their notorious smuggling operation. They made a fortune bringing in illegal Chinese laborers."

Miles recalled that Ure, in particular, was known to be a cold-hearted son of a bitch who would tie the Chinese up in burlap sacks, claiming it was to hide them in case they were boarded by the Coast Guard. But in truth, if pursued, Ure would just toss the bags overboard to get rid of the evidence. A few days later, the drowned Chinese, still in their burlap sacks, would start washing up on the nearby islands.

Miles gazed out the windows at Deception Pass. "*Plus ça change, plus c'est la même chose.*"

"Whuh?" Floyd mumbled.

"It's an expression I learned in France during the war. 'The more things change, the more they stay the same.'"

FORTY-SEVEN

The next thing Miles knew, he was blinking to clear his blurry eyes, laying on his back in what appeared to be a doctor's examination room, his head cradled in Sylvia Rosen's lap.

"Hold still," she said, bent over him, seeming to concentrate on his forehead.

"Where am I?"

"You don't remember getting taken off the boat?"

"What boat?"

"You're in Dr. Boren's office."

"What?"

"Ashton says you started looking pale and dizzy while you were crossing the Juan de Fuca Strait. Then, when you stood up to go to the lavatory, the ship rolled on a big swell and you fell on your face. Out cold. You had to be carried off the boat, while the aquaphobic Floyd, looking like he was going to have a coronary, nearly knocked an old lady off the gangplank trying to get to dry land. An impressive pair, you two."

"What's that smell?"

"They wheeled you up here in a fishy wheelbarrow."

"Jeez!"

"All the while, your bug-eyed, terrified populace was shouting questions at you about the bodies that washed ashore."

"While I was being carried home in a dirty wheelbarrow. How considerate."

"They're just scared. Anyway, I don't suppose you remember repeatedly asking me what Marion's *issue* was as we rolled you up here."

"Oh, no!"

"Oh, yes. *What's her issue, Sylvia? Tell me, Sylvia. Please. What is it?* Over and over again, like a drunk."

"Just let me die here."

"I'm afraid you're destined to survive. But you lost a fair amount of blood out of this head wound. And you probably have a mild concussion from your dramatic fall, if not from your tussle in Seattle. Anyway, I'm sewing you up, so stay still unless you want a needle in the eye. If you're a good boy, you can have a cookie afterward."

"Really?"

"No."

Miles moaned weakly. "Please don't tell Marion."

She smiled. "I won't. But listen—when we're done here, I actually do recommend you eat something with a bit of sugar. And salt. Then drink water. We can't have your blood pressure dropping on you again. Heaven knows what compromising position we might find you in the next time this happens."

"At least they didn't find me *in* the lavatory."

"That would have made for a good story. *Sheriff Scott found on the pot*, the *San Juan Islander* reports."

If he weren't so troubled and miserable, Miles might have smiled. "Where does Boren have the two bodies that washed ashore?"

"As a matter of fact, they're in tin livestock watering troughs full of ice in the next room, patiently awaiting your examination. But you're not going anywhere until I finish closing this wound, so just hold your horses. How did you get into a tussle, anyway? Insult one of those barrel-chested longshoremen?"

"We got jumped by goons."

"Whose goons?"

"An excellent question. Unfortunately, circumstances dictated that we race home before being able to investigate."

"You've had quite a week, Miles."

"You said it." Miles tried to relax as she pulled another stitch through the loose flaps of skin on his head. Her face hovering directly over his own, he found himself studying her. He wasn't a fan of short hair on women. And there was nothing he would describe as particularly delicate about her features. But her face nevertheless exuded something he could only think to regard as lovely strength. Indeed, she was, in her way, undeniably beautiful. Strong, poised, and beautiful. It might have been her poise that most impressed him.

"Sylvia, are you real?" he asked.

"What on earth do you mean?"

"You seem so normal."

"Ha. Wrong."

"And undisturbed."

"Well, thanks, I think. But I'm not quite sure I understand what you're—"

"You worked in a surgical field hospital during the Battle of the Marne."

"Oh, now I get it. You're wondering whether I'm pretending that I'm not a traumatized, shattered soul. Well, for similar reasons, I could probably ask the same question of you."

"Definitely an act in my case."

"It makes you feel so utterly powerless, doesn't it? Seeing it up close. War and disease and death in such magnitude. You feel so completely insignificant in the face of it all."

"And yet, having seen the worst of war, how is it that you're so—I don't know—sound?"

"Women have stronger minds than men. Everybody knows that."

Miles smiled. "I don't doubt it. But that doesn't really help me."

"You're asking for my help?"

He shrugged. "Why not?"

"I told you before, you should talk about it."

"What do you mean? Talk about it how?"

"Articulate exactly what happened. Tell the story of your

trauma."

"Why? Why would I ever want to revisit it?"

"Because, Miles, every time you tell the story, the memories lose a little bit of their power over you. They become a little less overwhelming. A little less frightening. A little less painful. This is an oversimplification, but you can sort of think of it like diving from the high platform at the pool. At first, it's terrifying. But do it enough times, and it becomes less and less of an ordeal."

"You're desensitized," he said.

"In effect, yes. And you don't even have to tell the story to people. You can tell it to the wind. You can tell it in your mind. But tell it, every day. Then one day you'll wake up and realize that it doesn't have quite the same grip on you as it once did. That you're starting to feel better. Starting to feel human again."

"It's just that easy, huh?"

"Easy? No. It takes a long time. It takes courage and dedication. But it works. It worked for me."

He looked doubtful. "You come up with this on your own?"

"No. My father is a professor of psychology at Brandeis."

A quiet moment passed as Sylvia put two more stitches in his head.

"When I was giving you the tetanus serum injection the other day," she said, "you were about to tell me about something that disturbed you profoundly."

"Was I?"

"It was about unloading a box and carrying it to an enclosure out behind a field hospital, wasn't it? Out the back door, by the garbage bins and incinerator?"

Miles met her eyes, then gave a reluctant nod.

"Well?" she asked. "What did you see?"

A crate, he thought without speaking.

The room seemed to darken around him. As if he'd entered a long tunnel.

A crate, he thought again as his memories took flight.

The image was crystal clear in his mind's eye. A muddy,

roofless area enclosed by a tall, leaning wood plank wall. A distant column of black smoke rising into the darkening orange-grey sky. Air that smelled of blood, burning wood, kerosene, black mud, and rotting garbage. A blood-smeared leather apron of the sort used by butchers, hanging on a hook by the back door. A half-empty can of fuel oil on the ground below the open hatch of the incinerator that glowed red from within. A hospital window smashed out and boarded over. The wood at the bottom of the back door frame already rotting. Everything in a state of decay. Especially the contents of the crate. The large wooden crate standing next to the incinerator. The crate full of amputated body parts. So many that they were overflowing. Mutilated arms and legs. Hands. Feet. Smashed and shattered and torn. All of them covered with swarming blackflies. Thrown away like offal in a butcher shop. Like garbage. Waiting to be burned in the incinerator. And there was one, in particular—a colorless, amputated arm, its hand leaning out from the top of the crate, its index finger extended and pointing at the ground. At the deep, dark, soggy mud. As if it were trying to tell him something. Warning him that inevitably, one day, his own remains would be burned and scattered upon or buried under the mud. Or that maybe, in the end, all he was was mud.

Then, a dirty, gaunt, expressionless orderly had come out the back door. And with a brown cigarette hanging from his mouth, wearing his own bloody brown leather butcher's apron, with no apparent emotion at all, he'd started throwing the limbs, one-by-one, into the incinerator like it was nothing to him.

Miles had seen human carnage before. But this time it had been different. He didn't know why. He remembered not being able to breathe. Feeling as though he'd just been told some dark and terrible and undeniable secret. A secret that he'd always known, deep down, but had been able to ignore until then. And with it had come a terrible surge of anxiety, so powerful and enduring that it still haunted him, years later.

"Don't want to tell me?" Sylvia asked, still waiting.

He smiled a sad smile. "Maybe another time."

She nodded. "Okay."

He looked away from her, then said, "I'm glad to know you, Sylvia."

"I'm glad to know you too, Miles."

FORTY-EIGHT

"You sure you want to do this right now," Floyd asked as Miles, holding a small cloth-wrapped block of ice to his head, lumbered into the examination room where Floyd and Dr. Boren were already scrutinizing one of the girl's bodies on a stainless steel gurney while the other waited in a tin trough full of ice. Bill stood back in a corner of the room, looking disgusted but doing his best to stay out of the way.

"At least take a chair, Miles, won't you?" Dr. Boren said.

"I'm fine. A little dizzy is all."

"You look like death," Floyd said.

"That makes three of us," he said, nodding at the bloated and colorless bodies as he approached for a closer look, grabbing the corner of the gurney for support. Both bodies still had fragments of seaweed stuck in their long, dark hair. Their mouths were trussed with cheek retractors to reveal poorly cared for teeth and blackened tongues. The eyelids of the body on the gurney were held wide open by ophthalmic speculums. Its irises were clouded over. Milky.

What struck Miles first was how young they were. And how slight and fragile-looking. They were just girls. Boney, malnourished girls. He wondered what sort of diseased slum or starving village they might have come from. Wherever it was—assuming they hadn't been kidnapped or sold into slavery—the poverty or hardship or terror had been bad enough to drive them from their families, friends, and country, clear across the vast and merciless Pacific Ocean, in an attempt to settle in a completely foreign and sometimes hostile land on the far side of the world.

Probably not unlike what drove Miles's own ancestors to the New World. But now here they were, shot and sliced open, discolored and rotting. They hadn't made it. Everything they and their descendants could have been in America was lost.

"My thoughts drift back to our interview with the Chinese Peace Society," Miles said in a slow and somber voice. "Those old men staring at us. Impassive. Feigning ignorance. Feigning *innocence*. Playing us for fools."

"A deceitful race," Bill muttered from his shadowy corner.

Miles took a deep breath. "Fill me in, Doctor Boren, if you'd be so kind."

"You're looking at two East Asian girls in their mid-teens," Boren said. "Their bodies were spotted out near Hanbury Point by the crew of a workboat heading into Roche Harbor. They'd washed up about forty yards apart. Dead at least three days. Probably longer. Assuming they've been in the water most of that time, the colder temperatures would have slowed the rate of decomposition."

"Any evidence of other bodies?" Miles asked. "Shoes? Clothing? Remains?"

"I pressed Lyle Miller and Jacob Fields into helping me search the nearby rocks and beaches," Bill said. "We covered about a half mile in either direction. Didn't find anything else."

"Both girls were shot in the chest," Boren continued. "And, as you can see, both had their meager bellies slashed open."

"Seems excessive," Miles said.

"Bodies will initially sink in water," Floyd said. "But after a few days or weeks, depending on water temperature, their insides will decompose to the point that their abdomens bloat with methane, carbon dioxide, hydrogen sulfide, and ammonia. Then they float back up to the surface."

"Well, sure."

"My point is that the killer or killers knew this," Floyd said. "So someone slashed open their abdomens so that the gasses of decomposition could escape and not build up buoyancy."

"Then why didn't these two stay on the bottom?"

"Maybe they got caught in kelp in the warmer surface waters," Boren said. "Maybe a strong current or storm surge drove them ashore. Maybe the killer's blade didn't slash deep enough to rupture the peritoneum."

"The what?"

"The membrane lining the inside of the abdomen. The skin of the balloon, if you'll pardon the expression. I'll be able to tell you if it was ruptured in just a minute, not that it matters now."

"He knew to slash open the abdomen," Miles mused. "A knowledgeable killer, then. Experienced."

"Maybe," Boren said, sounding thoroughly disgusted with humanity. "Also, for what it's worth, both girls were poor."

"What makes you say that?"

"Look at their teeth. No hint of modern oral hygiene or dentistry. Bone structures indicative of undernourishment. And their garments are of poor cloth."

Beatrice Floyd's comment about Seattle brothels being staffed by indigent Chinese slave girls smuggled into America rang in Miles's ears. As did Sergeant Clark's mention of the scraps of official-looking papers they'd found being fragments of forged immigration documents. "You suppose the girls were destined for one of the tong-run West Coast whorehouses?" Miles asked no one in particular.

"Yes," Floyd said. "And I imagine they were being smuggled in aboard the *Lucky Lena*."

Miles nodded. "So, we're looking at human trafficking."

"At least in part," Floyd said. "The Jensens may have had their hands in more than one pot. Illegal immigrants, booze, opium, lost Russian gold. Who knows?"

"Who would want to kill a boatload of teenage girls from China?" Boren asked.

"A rival tong?" Miles said. "Wanting to eliminate the competition?"

"Tongs have certainly gone to war over control of the

pleasure trade." Floyd said. "Even over claims to specific women."

"Helen of Troy, the Chinese version," Dr. Boren said. "The face that launched a thousand highbinders."

Miles glanced at the doctor, surprised at his seeming levity, then figuring it was just how the man coped with the macabre unpleasantness of examining corpses. With the unsettling proximity of death.

"Something like that," Floyd said. "Still, I'd think a rival tong would just steal the girls and use them for their own purposes. Or sell them. Not slaughter them."

"Anti-Asian vigilantes, then?" Miles said.

"Wouldn't be the first time that vigilantes have mass-murdered Chinese in this country," Floyd said. "Off the top of my head, I know there were massacres of mostly male laborers in Rock Springs, in Hells Canyon, even in Issaquah. But to deliberately target and murder defenseless *girls*? Even the Knights of Labor have never gone that far, have they?"

"Heaven knows," Miles said. "I suppose it's safe for us to assume that the forged immigration certificates we found fragments of on the *Lucky Lena* were for the girls."

"Meaning it's also safe to assume there were eight girls aboard the *Lucky Lena*, since there were fragments of eight individual certificates."

"Mercy," Miles whispered. "Eight girls."

"In any event, we need to find those tong highbinders before they leave the island," Floyd said.

"And that anti-Chinese agent provocateur labor activist from Seattle," Miles added. "Isn't he with the Knights of Labor?"

"Edward Callahan," Floyd said. "Yes. I'd half forgotten about him."

Miles shook his head as he gazed upon the poor, dead Chinese girls, thinking again on how very fragile human life was, wondering what sort of monster would do such a thing and where that monster was hiding.

FORTY-NINE

Miles, Floyd, and Bill went back to the station, armed themselves with handguns, and headed out. But barely ten feet from the door, they were chased down from behind by Jacob Fields.

"Sheriff! I say, Sheriff! I hear you found two more bodies. Girls this time. Murdered, right?"

"I'm not at liberty to discuss an ongoing investigation, Jacob."

"Oh, come on. Everybody's already talking about it," he said, gesturing to the group of onlookers rapidly gathering around from up, down, and across the street.

"Then ask *everybody*."

"Well, Sheriff, I mean, do you have any good leads? Does evidence point to anyone yet?"

"Why, Jacob?"

"Well, of course we'd all sleep a whole lot better if we knew you were closing in. Isn't that right?" he asked the circle of mute, spooked-looking onlookers.

Miles looked at each of their faces—male and female, young and old—but found himself more irritated than empathetic. "I didn't realize you were so sensitive, Jacob."

"Well, Sheriff, come now."

"Rest assured, Jacob, we'll let you know as soon as we arrest anyone."

With that, Miles turned his back.

*****

Because of a cold north wind, they crowded into the cab of Miles's truck. Their first stop was China House, where Bill, unwilling to abide the Chinese, opted to have a cigarette and wait in the truck while Miles and Floyd had another word with Henry, the proprietor. This time, there weren't any Chinese men loitering on the railing. In fact, there were none to be seen. The place felt deserted. Miles opened the front door without knocking and found Henry sitting at his desk. A look of terror flashed across the man's face before he mastered himself.

"Ah, Mr. Miles. And Mr. Floyd. Good to see you again. Yes. Welcome."

"Didn't mean to frighten you, Henry," Miles said. "Were you expecting someone else?"

"No. No. Just startle. Come in, yes, come in," he said, taking a quick look over his shoulder, through the open doorway between his office and the kitchen.

"Quiet around here today," Miles said.

"Quiet. Yes. You want chair?"

"No. We're only here for a moment. Did you hear about the bodies that washed up at Hanbury Point?"

"Bodies. Yes. Very bad."

"Look, Henry, my friend, I have to ask again. Have you heard anything that might help us? Or do any of your boarders maybe know anything?" As he said this, Miles strode up to Henry's desk, friendly as could be, and sat on the corner of it. The spot afforded him a view through the door to the kitchen. There was nobody there.

"No," Henry said. "I just hear you find body. No more."

"What about the Cantonese men who came up on the *Bangor*? Anyone see them?"

Henry looked terrified. "No."

"No?"

Henry just shook his head.

"Floyd here thinks they might be tong highbinders."

"High?"

"Boo how doy," Floyd said, interpreting even though he was sure that Henry understood.

Henry pretended to think. It struck Miles as an exceedingly poor acting job.

"No, I no know boo how doy," he said, a thin line of perspiration appearing on his hairline.

"Henry, listen," Miles said. "We won't tell anyone that you spoke with us. You understand? You have my word. But the sooner we find these men, the sooner we can all sleep better at night."

"Ha. Yes. But I no know anything," he said, with another quick glance over his shoulder toward the kitchen.

"Nothing, huh?" Miles said, leaning over to take another peek into the kitchen for himself. Still empty. "Nothing at all?"

"Sorry, Mr. Miles."

FIFTY

With their search for the phantom highbinders leading nowhere, Miles, Floyd, and Bill drove to the far southern shore of the island, out beyond the windswept, grassy slope where American soldiers had built their garrison during the so-called Pig War with Britain in 1859. Eventually, they came to a long dirt drive that led through pasture to a small white farmhouse just off the beach—precisely where Friday Harbor's International Longshoreman's Association representative, Manny Goldstein, said they would find Edward Callahan, the Knights of Labor bigwig and alleged ringleader of the Seattle General Strike of 1919, who was freshly released from prison.

"I'm a bit surprised that Goldstein was so forthcoming about where we could find Callahan," Miles said.

"The Longshoreman's union is part of the American Federation of Labor," Floyd explained. "And there's no love lost between the AFL and the Knights."

"Is that right? It isn't one big happy brotherhood of reds?"

"Most unions think the Knights are too radical."

"Shades of gray."

"Shades of red."

"Good one."

Miles brought his truck to a squeaking stop where the dirt drive opened into a weedy parking area next to the house, leaving the truck in such a position that it would block any attempted getaway by car. There were no vehicles to be seen. But there was a closed-up, whitewashed barn next to the house that was certainly big enough to contain one.

As the three of them got out, they checked the magazines of their guns to make sure they were fully loaded. Then they spread out, line abreast, and walked toward the house.

It seemed an odd place to find a red-toothed Bolshevik. The yard featured a dwarf tree loaded with ripening apples, well-tended rose bushes, and a zinc table like something from a Paris sidewalk café. A handful of friendly goats gazed at the men from the other side of their fence, one standing on its hind legs and leaning against the fence as if it wanted to get their attention and start a conversation—which would no doubt include a request for food.

As planned, Floyd and Bill took up positions at opposite corners of the front of the house while Miles marched up to the door, gave it a loud knock, then stepped back a few feet so that he could keep an eye on the greater area. After a moment, the door opened wide to reveal a small, slight man—neither old nor young—who had the good sense to have his hands hanging still and visible to either side of his hips. He wore a dull green Soviet-style worker's tunic with a matching cap; he couldn't have been more than five feet tall.

"Can I help you?" he asked in an East Coast accent Miles couldn't quite place.

"Police. We're looking for Edward Callahan."

"I'm Callahan," he said, his voice soft.

"You're Callahan?"

"Yes."

"The Knights of Labor leader?"

"That's me. Were you expecting an ogre?"

"We need you to come with us."

"Why?"

"We'll explain that at the station."

"Am I under arrest?"

Miles thought about lying to speed things along, then thought better of it. "No."

"Then I'll meet you at the station," he said in the same soft voice as two very large men appeared behind and to either side of him in the doorway. Bodyguards, Miles assumed.

"Just get in the back of the truck, Trotsky," Bill shouted from his corner of the yard.

"The back of the truck," Callahan echoed. "I'll have you know that, if necessary, these two men will serve as witnesses to offer sworn testimony as to my uninjured condition prior to being taken into your custody.

"We just want to talk," Miles said. "But we *will* talk, one way or another. And without your pet gorillas."

Impassive and utterly still, Callahan stared at him, seeming to take his measure. Then he acquiesced, signaled for his bodyguards to back off, and followed Miles to the truck.

*****

"Nice outfit," Miles said, facing Callahan across a table at the station. Floyd and Bill sat close by, listening, Floyd taking notes.

"It's the latest in Bolshevik fashion," Bill said from his desk. "Gotta look the part, right?"

"With respect," Callahan said amicably, "the Knights of Labor aren't Bolsheviks. As a matter of fact, we utterly reject the tenets of communism."

"Is that a fact?" Miles said.

"You might be thinking of the IWW. The Wobblies."

"You're wearing a Bolshevik worker's tunic," Bill said.

"They're work clothes. Cheap and durable. It's what we wear down on the docks."

"You were jailed for promoting Bolshevism after the 1919 Seattle strike," Floyd said.

"Excuse me," Callahan said, holding up a finger to emphasize his point. "I was jailed on the basis of trumped-up charges brought by the corrupt minions of former Mayor Ole Hanson, a militant anti-labor fanatic. We were protesting the continued use of wartime wage controls even though the war was over."

"What are you doing here?" Miles asked

"You brought me here."

"What are you doing on San Juan Island?"

"I've been invited to speak at the Odd Fellows Hall tomorrow evening."

"Invited by whom?"

"I'm not at liberty to say. Nevertheless, I welcome your attendance."

"If you're speaking tomorrow, why did you come up from Seattle last Saturday?"

"To visit my aunt Fanny."

"Your aunt Fanny. You playing with me, little man?"

"No, Sheriff. I'm not playing with you. Fanny is short for Stephanie."

"Stephanie what?"

"Miss Stephanie Bennett. She owns the farm you just took me from. If you don't believe me, I encourage you to send someone to check a tax assessor's plat map at the county clerk's office."

The name rang a bell with Miles. Miss Bennett was a reclusive spinster, if memory served. "What sort of man visits his aunt for a week?"

"Her farm is a nice place to read and take walks. Do a bit of gardening."

"Gardening. Right. And were you gardening Tuesday night?"

"No, I don't think so."

"What were you doing?"

"Reading, I should think. At Aunt Fanny's."

"Can anyone corroborate that?"

"Aunt Fanny can."

"Aunt Fanny can confirm that you were there all night? Let me guess, she checked on you every half-hour."

Callahan didn't bother to respond.

"What's the nature of your relationship with the Jensens?"

"The Jensens? I know one man named Jensen, and he lives

in Licton Springs, north of Seattle. Is that who you mean?"

"You're telling me you don't know anything about Hans and Leif Jensen, or their boat, the *Lucky Lena*?"

"I don't know the first thing about boats. And I'm quite sure I have no idea what you're talking about. You have to give me more."

Callahan's face didn't change in the least. Miles decided he was either the most stone-cold serpent he'd ever come across, or his public image as a union hothead and provocateur was a complete fabrication.

"You are a labor agitator."

"I am a member of the Knights of Labor."

"He's one of the guys we can thank for a single cup of coffee now costing ten cents in Seattle," Floyd said.

"Ten cents?" Miles said. "That only gets you *one* cup? Must be some damn good coffee."

"And the stevedore who unloads the sacks of coffee beans from the Columbian freighter can afford to put food on his family's table and buy shoes for his children," Callahan offered as a counterpoint.

"Are you here to unionize the workers at the Roche Harbor lime works?"

"All are welcome to hear me speak."

"Who are you working for?"

Callahan sat back in his chair. "The real question, Sheriff, is who are *you* working for? You're surely somebody's marionette, whether you're conscious of it or not."

You got that right, Miles thought.

"I work for a cause," Callahan said. "I fight for the dignity of labor."

"Of *white* labor, you mean," Miles said. "We saw one of your flyers specifically inviting *white* brother laborers to your talk."

"Is there anything wrong with a white man looking out for his own? Surely, the yellows look out for their own. The Jews look out for their own. The Sicilians."

"Do you have a problem with non-whites?"

Callahan shrugged.

"How about Chinese?"

"Not as long as they stay in China. China is for Chinese and America is for Americans."

"Sounds simple enough," Miles said, catching Bill nodding to himself out of the corner of his eye.

"Oriental immigrant workers have no dignity, Sheriff. They'll work for less money, so white workers are forced to accept lower wages in order to compete. They undercut the white man's standard of living." He said this without rancor. It seemed that it was, for him, a mere recitation of data.

"I thought the big unions, like the IWW, were bringing Asian laborers into their ranks," Floyd offered.

"A decision I continue to oppose."

"By means of violence?" Miles asked.

"By means of public discourse."

"Public discourse. Right."

"What are you getting at, Sheriff? And what does any of this have to do with people named Jensen or their boat—whatever its name was?"

"The *Lucky Lena*," Miles said, watching Callahan's face.

"If you say so."

"It's a local boat two men disappeared from. We found it adrift, full of bullet holes and blood. Seems it was carrying a load of Oriental immigrants, as you call them."

"I take it the immigrants were killed."

"At least two of them."

"I'm fighting against wage slavery, Sheriff. I may be angry, but I'm not a murderer."

"Really? How many unarmed Chinese did your Knights of Labor brothers gun down or burn alive in Rock Springs? 20? 30? Remind me."

"That was half a century ago. And a thousand miles from here."

"Same union, same creed."

"I'm sorry, but that's flimsy reasoning. Like me judging you for police excesses during the Chicago Haymarket Riot. I can only answer for myself, Sheriff. And I fight for the dignity of the working man."

"The white working man, to whom the Chinese laborer is a threat, in your view."

"If the unions are bringing Asian workers into their ranks and insisting that they be paid union wages, then what's the problem?" Floyd asked.

Callahan gave a slow blink, as if weighing his response, then turned to Floyd and smiled a mirthless smile. "The problem, detective, is that they are racially inferior godless heathens who eat dogs and rats. They are a major source of crime. They'll never assimilate into American society. They don't share our values. They have no moral compass. They strip America of her wealth by sending their earnings back to China. These are facts."

"Now we're at the bone," Miles said.

"I have nothing against the Chinese—"

"Clearly."

At this, Callahan paused. His eyes had opened just perceptibly wider. He took a deep breath in through his nose and then let it out slowly. It was the biggest rise Miles was going to get out of him. "America is for Americans," he said softly. "China is for the Chinese."

"Or, as you just described them, racially inferior heathens," Floyd said. "You make these poor Chinese girls sound subhuman. Like animals. And what's wrong with killing animals? We do it all the time, right? Why not kill a few to set an example. Let the story serve as a deterrent. Let the consequent fear help stem the tide of illegal immigration. Of cheap Chinese labor."

"Did you say *girls*?" Callahan asked. "The victims were girls?"

"You didn't know, huh?" Miles said. "Yes, Callahan. Girls. Teenage girls."

"Destined for whorehouses, then." Callahan muttered,

nodding to himself. Then he sat up straight in his chair. "With respect, Sheriff, your implication that I would murder a boatload of Chinese girls to discourage further immigration of cheap laborers is absurd."

"Why?"

"Because white men aren't competing to be Asian whores."

Miles just stared at him, irritated at the way the man could serve up wretched hatred with such a calm demeanor.

"I assume we're done here," Callahan said. "May I trouble you for a lift back to my aunt Fanny's house then?"

"I don't think so."

"Very well. I'll call for a ride."

"No, I think we're going to keep you here for a little while."

"Here? You mean in jail?"

"That's right."

"You have no constitutional basis for doing so."

"We need to check out your story. Bill, put him in the cell for me, will you?"

"I'm scheduled to speak at the Odd Fellows Hall tomorrow."

"Not my problem, mac."

"You are violating my constitutional due process rights, Sheriff. You're making a grave error."

"Grave? You threatening me, pal?"

"This is fascism," he said with so little feeling in his voice that Miles had to wonder whether they were having an argument at all.

"Call it what you want," Miles said. "But I encourage you to shut your cold-blooded trap before we shut it for you."

Bill, looking conflicted, escorted an unresisting Callahan to the cell in the back of the station building as Miles and Floyd rose to leave. But when Miles reached for the front door, he saw a folded-up scrap of paper slipped under it.

"What's that, an anonymous tip?" Floyd asked facetiously.

Miles picked it up and opened it. It bore a crude sketch with a number of curving lines, a few relatively straight lines, and an arrow pointing to an "X." There were no words.

"I'll be damned," Miles said.

"What?"

"It's a map."

FIFTY-ONE

After comparing the crude sketched map that someone had slipped under the front door to the official surveyor's map of San Juan Island that they kept at the station, Miles and Floyd came to the mutual conclusion that the "X" marked a spot a couple hundred yards west of the same forested stretch of West Valley Road that Rupert Hawkins had led them to a few days earlier. Leaving Bill behind to keep an eye on Callahan, Miles and Floyd headed for Miles's truck.

*****

They reached the west side of the island as the evening sky was beginning to darken.

"You alright?" Floyd asked Miles. "You look troubled."

"I'm embarrassed to say that that pipsqueak Ed Callahan got under my skin." He shook his head. "All these bastards. Callahan. Nosy, callous Jacob Fields. Errol Buchannan. Reverend McCaskill. Captain Eckart. The Anti-Japanese League. The Seattle Culinary Union. The accursed Knights of Labor. I tell you, Floyd, sometimes it feels like this whole damned country is going to burst into flames. Between the racial tension, immigration issues, labor disputes, the war on alcohol. So damned much crime and anger. So damned much mindless hate."

"Yes. Well, you can take a modicum of comfort from something my mother always tells me."

"What would that be?"

"It's never as bad as the papers make it sound."

They parked in the same place on West Valley Road where they'd parked with Hawkins.

"You think it was Henry who slipped us the map?" Floyd asked as they got out of the truck.

"Could be. He sure didn't seem to want anyone overhearing him talking to us. But he's a good man. I'm sure if he knew something helpful, he'd find a way to get it to us." Miles looked up and down the road, as mystified by the seeming ordinariness of the location as ever.

"Any path to the where the 'X' is on the map would have to intersect this road somewhere," Floyd said. "But if there is a path, maybe it's deliberately concealed. Why don't we conduct our search parallel to the road again, but this time following a line a couple dozen yards into the woods."

They walked straight into the woods from where they parked the truck, having to claw their way through the first few yards of dense ferns, brush, alder saplings, and maples before the forest floor opened up into a cathedral of great tree trunks. After getting about 50 feet in, they took a hard right turn to the north and began paralleling the road. Slowly, their eyes glued to the ground, they made their way nearly a quarter mile before deciding they'd gone beyond the area highlighted by the mysterious hand-drawn map. Doubling back, they reached the point where they'd turned north and continued onward to the south. It was at least another ten minutes before Miles saw something.

"Floyd," he said, pointing.

It was a slight, barely visible, mostly linear compression on the soft forest floor. Like the very beginnings of a footpath. A trail running away from the road. Eyes focused on the ground, they followed it west, further into the forest. It was slow going. Neither Miles nor Floyd were trained as trackers, and they had to back up several times to reacquire the faint path.

"Should we go back and grab your lantern?" Floyd asked.

"Light is fading pretty quick."

"Let's press on. And let's keep our voices down in case anybody else is out here. Don't want to spook the quarry."

Just as Miles said this, a small cabin began coming into view in a glade up ahead of them.

"Look," Miles whispered, pointing. They drew their guns and slowed their approach. It soon became obvious the cabin was very small indeed—probably a one-room structure. No smoke rose from its crooked chimney. All was quiet. It was situated a few yards from the shore of a large pond.

"I'm having déjà vu," Floyd said.

"You and me both."

The cabin, which appeared very old, was built of large logs. Miles figured that it had been built by a long-dead homesteader. Its north face was green with algae, and the surrounding area was largely overgrown. But a new-looking laundry line hung between two stout maples near the pond's edge. Clearly, it wasn't anyone's full-time residence. Still, the well-trod earth leading to and from the only door indicated it had, at the very least, been visited recently.

The men snuck up to either side of the door. Miles reached for the handle, mouthed the words *one-two-three*, and threw the door open. Both men pointed their pistols into the dark interior and sprang inside. There was nobody there. As Miles had guessed, it was a single-room structure. The interior contained very little. A river rock fireplace, clean and cold. Four sets of smallish bunk beds, two each against opposing walls. A cistern fed by a pipe that came in through a low section of the roof. A crude shelf stacked with Army surplus blankets, tin cups, a half-empty burlap sack of rice, and a single cast iron pot. A broom and feather duster leaning in a dark corner. Two single beds set apart from the others, situated to either side of the door. These two beds were the only two with pillows. They also had much better mattresses than the bunk beds did.

The men holstered their guns and began a search.

"A lot of beds," Floyd said.

"But not much else. Seems like it isn't set up for anything but sleeping."

"It's clean, too. Recently cleaned. Very little dust on anything."

"Clearly someone is using this place. But for what?" Miles said.

Miles now wished they'd gone back for the lantern. The cabin had no windows, and what light came through the door was already inadequate, fading with the approach of night.

"Miles," Floyd said, holding up several papers he'd pulled from under the mattress of one of the single beds. Stepping over for a closer look, squinting, Miles saw that there were three separate documents, each bearing decorative borders like those of U.S. dollar bills, each inscribed with red serial numbers and the words *United States of America*, *Department of Labor*, and *Certificate of Naturalization*. The upper left-hand corners of the documents looked exactly like the fragments they'd found aboard the *Lucky Lena*. Each was filled in with a hand-written Chinese name, the person's sex, age and height, hair, eye and skin color, and the name and city and state of residence of their spouses. After that came pre-printed official language. *Be it remembered that* Mrs. so-and-so*, then residing at* such-and-such address in Los Angeles, California*, who previous to her naturalization was a subject of* the Republic of China*, having applied to be admitted as a citizen of the United States of America on* such-and-such a date, *the* such-and-such *federal district court, having found that the petitioner has resided in the United States continuously for a period of five years . . . and that said petitioner intends to reside permanently in the United States, and has in all respects complied with the law in relation thereto, therefore ordered that she be admitted as a citizen of the United States of America.* Each certificate bore different signature dates spanning the past eighteen months. The first was for a girl named Mei Liu. A beautiful name, Miles thought.

"Figure these are forgeries too, with fictitious spouse

names?" Floyd said.

"Probably. But why are they here? And where are their owners? For that matter, how could anyone expect these to pass inspection by a federal official? I mean, they're dated the past year or two. But there's been a total ban on Chinese immigration since the 1880s, right?"

"Not total."

"No?"

"There are limited exceptions for workers with certain skills. Which probably means there are exceptions for their wives, too."

"I suppose that would explain why they have spouses listed on these certificates," Miles said, looking around the room. "So, what do we think this is? An abandoned homesteader's cabin being used as a transit point? A safe house for illegal Chinese immigrants?"

"Young Chinese girls, it would seem."

"Destined for brothels, like Callahan said?"

"I hope not," Floyd said. "But wherever they were going, I'm guessing the Jensens were smuggling them in from Canada aboard the *Lucky Lena*."

"The Jensens. Holy mackerel. Who would have guessed?"

"This seems an odd place for a safe house," Floyd said, "well-hidden and forgotten though it may be."

"Not so odd, really. By my estimation, we're just south of Mitchell Bay, which would be a good, sheltered place to offload illegal immigrants. And Mitchell Bay is maybe two miles from Canadian Waters. Four miles from D'Arcy Island, for that matter."

"But where on earth do they go from here?" Floyd asked. "Have you ever seen packs of Chinese girls lining up for tickets for the *Bangor*?"

"I sure haven't. And I'm sure that's something I would have noticed."

They finished up their search of the cabin, finding nothing else of particular interest, then went back outside to search the surroundings. They'd barely taken three steps out the door when Floyd spotted a raised patch of recently turned soil. "Miles, look."

"Oh, no."

It was a roughly three-by-six-foot rectangular patch of disturbed earth that couldn't have been more than a month old.

"A fresh grave," Miles muttered, wondering if the body of Mei Liu might be rotting a few feet down.

"And look over there," Floyd added, pointing.

There were two more very similar patches of upturned earth a few feet away. Judging by how much the soil had settled and been covered with fallen leaves and fir needles, Miles took a guess that one of them was maybe six months old, the other a year.

"Girls who didn't survive the journey," Miles suggested, thinking that somewhere along the way, they'd succumbed to bad fortune in the form of disease, starvation, accident, or perhaps violence. Forces of a universe that was utterly indifferent to their struggle. Though he knew nothing of these girls, it made him sad to stare at their graves in the fading light and contemplate all the deprivation and suffering they may have endured, only to end up buried in an unmarked hole, left to decompose in anonymity in a dark and forgotten patch of forest far from home.

"You know, it could be the Jensens under there," Floyd said. "Or Angus Cooper."

Miles hadn't thought of that. "Maybe under the newest one. The other two patches have been there a while. Still, I suppose we had better have someone exhume the remains so we can find out. But not just yet. I have an idea."

*****

It took Miles and Floyd more than half an hour to find their way through the darkened forest and back out onto West Valley

Road. They lost their bearings numerous times before at last emerging, scratched up, dirty, and grumpy, a good quarter mile south of where the truck was parked.

It was after 10 p.m. by the time Miles dropped Floyd at his hotel and got back to the station. There, he found Bill asleep in his chair, his feet propped up on Miles's desk. He woke with a start as Miles came through the front door. "Damn. Sheriff. Sorry. Nodded off."

"Not to worry, Bill. You're going above and beyond staying this late. How is our guest?"

"Callahan? Asleep now. We played a few games of cribbage through the bars. He's an interesting fella."

"Is that so?"

"I'm no leftist," Bill said. "But it's hard to argue with his opinion of Chinks."

"Speaking of Chinese," Miles said, and he filled Bill in on their discovery of the cabin in the woods. "So now I'm afraid I have to ask another favor of you. A big one. Is there any chance I can talk you into staking out that same stretch of West Valley Road that we visited with Hawkins?"

"No problem."

"Bless you, Bill. There's a stub of dirt road that leads to the back fence of the Wilson dairy pasture. You can park there, and nobody will see you until it's too late. Question anyone who loiters around there. Let's see if anything crawls out from under a rock."

*****

Miles passed Marion's house as he drove home under a canopy of bright stars, only partially aware that his foot was drifting toward the brake pedal as her driveway approached. But it was far too late for a visit. She was surely in bed asleep. Indeed, there was no warm pink light glowing in her bedroom window. The house was dark.

As he drove on, all he could think about was the fact that there were only six days until Marion would depart for New York, and if the *Lucky Lena* investigation kept going as it had, he'd never get a chance to spend time with her. Would never have a chance to convince her to stay.

FIFTY-TWO

"Morning, Sheriff," Bill said as Miles came through the front door. The predawn sky was just beginning to lighten and Bill was already brewing a pot of coffee.

"You're here awfully early, Bill. How was your night? Get any sleep?"

"I was too busy."

"Busy?"

"Got a little yellow surprise for you."

Bill took Miles back to the cell where a Chinese man wearing a fine suit sat on the bench. His nose was swollen, his nostrils crusted with dried blood. He also had a substantial gash over one of his cheekbones. Edward Callahan stood against the wall on the far side of the cell.

"Get this slant-eyed serpent away from me!" Callahan said with far more emotion and animation than he'd ever shown them before.

"What's the problem?" Miles said.

"Cutthroat's been staring at me all night. Staring with those dead eyes of his."

"Calm down."

"Found him on West Valley Road, right where you told me to be," Bill said.

"Out walking?"

"When I caught up to him, he was walking. But he'd just been dropped off. I didn't get a good look at the car racing off in the dark. Anyway, look what I took off of him," Bill said, opening a footlocker against the wall opposite the cell and picking up a large and well cared for meat cleaver that was so flawless and polished that Miles could see his reflection in its steel. Miles touched the edge of the blade. It was razor sharp. "Son of bitch was wearing it against his side in a sort of leather sling holster type of thing."

"Holy smokes," Floyd said, entering the room. "That's a big cleaver. Good morning, by the way."

"This thing could split your skull in half with no effort at all," Bill said. "Like a samurai sword."

"He probably just uses it for cooking," Floyd said, grinning.

"Floyd, didn't you say that tong highbinders like to use meat cleavers as street weapons?" Miles asked.

"I did, indeed. You might even say they're famous for doing so."

"Could you imagine someone pulling one of those on you in some dark alley of Chinatown?" Miles said.

"It'd be hard to forget."

"Any identification on him, Bill?" Miles asked.

"No, sir."

"What happened to his nose and face?" Floyd asked. "Callahan do that to him?"

"I didn't come within ten feet of that heathen," Callahan said. "Don't try to pin it on me."

"He didn't want the free ride to the station I was offering," Bill said. "Took a bit of convincing."

"Oh—I, uh," Floyd muttered.

"What is it?" Miles asked.

"A moment of your time?" Floyd said, ushering Miles and Bill into the front room. Once they were out of earshot of their prisoners, looking troubled, he asked, "On what basis are we holding the Chinese man? Ignoring, for the moment, that Bill isn't a sworn law enforcement officer with arrest authority."

"He's a Chink," Bill said, sounding irritated. "What other authority do we need?"

"Certainly we can question him," Floyd said. "But really, do we have authority to have him in custody?"

"He matches the descriptions we've gotten."

"Because he's Chinese and he's wearing a suit?"

Miles shrugged. "What more do you want?"

"At best we have grounds for a non-custodial—"

"Floyd, please," Miles said, holding up his hands.

"I'm just saying that if a court of law is eventually reviewing statements of—"

"Look, Floyd. I'm sorry. But I don't have the time or the patience for this right now. Bill, cuff the Chinaman to the table. And cut Callahan loose."

"Wait—cut Callahan loose?" Floyd almost shouted. "We haven't even verified his alibi yet."

"Can you really imagine him—one little jerk—slaughtering the Jensens and eight Chinese girls?"

"I can't imagine anyone doing it. It doesn't mean they didn't."

"I don't think he did it."

"You're going to cut a suspect loose on nothing more than a gut feeling? We have a damn sight more justification for holding Callahan than we do for holding some random Chinese fellow."

"Look at our new guest, Floyd. Look at his eyes. Then look at Callahan's. Which one is a killer? Which one was carrying a meat cleaver, for Pete's sake?"

"None of our victims were killed with a meat cleaver, Miles. And it's a huge mistake to let Callahan go. One we may come to regret. Don't do it."

"We need the space."

"The space?"

But Miles didn't explain. Bill went back to the cell and handcuffed the Chinese man to a heavy-duty eye bolt that was screwed into the middle of the heavy table they used for playing cards and questioning suspects. Then Bill set Callahan free.

"You need a ride back to Aunt Fanny's?" Miles asked as Callahan headed for the door.

"Go piss into the wind, Sheriff."

"Oh, Edward. What happened to your mild manner?"

Callahan slammed the door shut behind him.

"I hope you're right," Floyd said.

"I told you before, I'm always right."

*****

Miles took a seat opposite the Chinese man, who sat quietly, his hands cuffed to the table, staring at Miles without any trace of emotion. Floyd and Bill stood in the wings.

"What's your name, friend?" Miles asked.

Nothing.

"Wong Chun Ting, is it? No? How about Kwan Ping? You both came up from Seattle on the SS *Bangor* last Saturday."

"Your name *is* Cantonese," Floyd added, his tone loaded with suggestion.

"What are you doing here?" Miles asked.

The man continued to watch Miles, impassive.

"I'm sure you have a legitimate purpose for being here. So why don't you just tell us what it is and you can be on your way." Silence. "Look, you're probably just here to pick up the girls, right? That's not our concern. We're local police, not immigration agents. If that's all it was, we can work with you. Explain yourself, and we'll let you walk right out that door there. Help us, and we'll help you." More silence. "Look, fella, if you don't give us something, we'll be forced to assume the worst." He waited, then stood up, stretched his arms, cracked his knuckles, and began rolling up the sleeves of his shirt. "And if you force me to assume the worst, my friend, you will also force me to get whatever information I need out of you by whatever means it may require."

The man's eyes seemed to go even more blank, as if his consciousness had somehow up and left for quieter pastures.

"Have it your way, pal," Miles said. "We'll proceed under the assumption that you are a tong highbinder."

"Boo how doy," Floyd said.

"A hatchet man. A killer. How does that sound? Are we on target? While we're at it, let's go ahead and say that you killed two local fishermen and a boatload of Chinese girls last Tuesday evening. Maybe your tong wants to take over the brothel business in Seattle, or is already in it and wants to suppress new competition, so you got rid of another tong's girls. You had Rupert Hawkins arrange for Angus Cooper to take you on his boat, the *Daisy*, out into Haro Strait. Then you boarded the *Lucky Lena*, shot the crew, shot the girls they were smuggling, slashed the bodies open and chained them to the anchor or just threw them overboard."

The man's eyes never left Miles's. He didn't look the least bit intimidated. In fact, he still showed no emotion at all. No remorse, no anger, no fear. He just stared like a man brain damaged.

The only thing I can't figure is why you're still here, Miles thought. *Unless you're waiting to jump another boatload of girls.* "Where is the *Daisy*? Where is Angus Cooper? Or did you get rid of him to cover your tracks?"

Nothing.

"Which tong are you with?"

Nothing.

"How do you know Rupert Hawkins?"

Still nothing.

Miles took a long breath, came around the table, and loomed over the Chinese man. "Give me your name," he said, leaning down until they were nearly eye to eye. "Name," he said again.

Miles stood up straight and then, in the blink of an eye, backhanded the man so hard it split both his lips. Miles waited a moment. "Name," he said again. Again he smacked the man across the face, smearing blood that poured from his lips across his left cheek. But the man said nothing. He turned and stared up at Miles as if nothing had happened. As if he hadn't just been struck. As if he didn't feel pain.

"Alright, pal," Miles said. "You asked for it." This time he punched the man in the gut with a closed fist. The man doubled over for a brief moment, then resumed his zombie stare.

"Name," Miles said again.

"He might not speak English," Floyd said, looking hugely uncomfortable.

"He doesn't live in Shanghai. He lives in Seattle," Miles said, giving Floyd a warning glance just before he punched the man again, this time in the jaw. "Name." Miles hit him again. "Maybe you found the girls there by accident. Were you looking for opium? For liquor? For gold? Answer me, you little bastard, or I'll beat your face to—"

"Miles!" Floyd shouted, gesturing to the door.

Miles glared at him, looking incensed. They left the cell and went into the office area.

"Floyd, don't raise doubts in the prisoner's presence," Miles said, clearly angry, once the door to the holding area closed behind them.

"Apologies. But look, a fair number of these guys really don't speak English."

"Maybe not fluently. But the guy knows what the word *name* means."

"Let's call an interpreter up from Seattle."

"That's a long time to wait. And the other highbinder is still out there. Heaven knows what he's capable of doing in the meantime. We're in a race against time here, Floyd."

"If I call headquarters right now, they might be able to get an interpreter on the afternoon ship to Friday Harbor."

"Still. Time is of the essence."

Floyd wondered if Miles's main concern with time had to do with Marion's looming departure for New York. But he had the good sense not to voice his suspicions.

"Maybe some of the girls are still alive somewhere, " Miles continued, "being held for ransom or heaven knows what, facing some bloodthirsty, short-fused highbinder cut-throat who won't respond well when his partner here fails to return from whatever errand he was on."

"We have no constitutional justification for holding him—certainly none for torturing him."

"Don't be melodramatic, Floyd. He's Chinese."

"So what?"

"Exactly."

Floyd shook his head. "Miles. You're a moral man."

"Don't patronize me."

"Fine. But is this really how you do things up here?"

"It depends on the circumstances."

"What circumstances?"

"How about three bodies, and at least four people gone missing in a single week, not to mention the unmarked graves? How about the likelihood that there'll be a lot more bodies washing ashore, a lot more unmarked graves, if we don't find the perpetrators?"

"Alright. But look, the tongs have a lot of money, which means they typically hire really good lawyers. However this turns out, we want our prosecution to stand up to appeal. Because trust me, they will appeal any conviction that isn't airtight. And if we *coerce* a confession, well . . ."

"Depends on the judge."

"True. But which judge ends up being assigned to the case is a crapshoot in and of itself, isn't it?"

Miles huffed and turned to look out the window. "This is frustrating. I want this case closed and done with." He jammed his hands in his pockets. "Fine. Make the call to Seattle. But if we can't get an interpreter up here today, we're taking this son of a bitch to the woodshed."

FIFTY-THREE

Floyd called his headquarters and arranged for an interpreter. They promised one would arrive that same afternoon. But that still left them with several hours to wait. Miles tried to call Marion, but got no answer at her mother's house even though he let the phone ring for the better part of two minutes. She was probably visiting her ailing grandfather. Hanging up, he stared at the still, silent phone for another half minute, willing it to ring, longing to just hear Marion's voice.

At a temporary loss for what to do with the investigation, Miles and Floyd decided they'd go to Morgan's Inn for the herb and garlic butter steamed clams Miles had raved about. "You can't leave my island until you've tried them," he told Floyd. "They're the best in the world."

But as they were about to step out the door, the phone rang. Miles rushed back to it, hitting his kneecap on the corner of a desk as he sprang forward to pick up the handset. "Police," he said, rubbing his knee, his heart pounding.

"This is Errol Buchannan." He paused, waiting for a response. "Of the lime company at Roche Harbor."

"Oh, *that* Errol Buchannan?" Miles said without enthusiasm.

"Sheriff, you are to keep that unhinged temperance fanatic McCaskill off company property. Do you understand me? If I catch that maniac out by the Smokehouse dock harassing my workers again, I'll shoot him for trespassing."

"Trespassing is a capital offence in Roche Harbor now, is it?"

"I'm asking politely, and I'm telling you as a courtesy. Do your job."

With that, he rang off.

"Everyone is telling me to *do my job* these days," he said to Floyd. "First McCaskill, now Errol Buchannan. And here I thought I was already doing it."

"What's the issue this time?" Floyd asked.

"Seems McCaskill is lurking out near the Smokehouse again, giving its patrons the evil eye or what have you."

"Should we warn Rupert Hawkins?"

"Would it stop him from going there?" Miles asked.

"Probably not."

"Yeah." He reached for the phone again. "All the same, I suppose I should place a call to that squirrelly bartender and tell him to give Rupert a heads-up if he sees him."

Eustace Hampton connected the call. The bartender promised to pass word to Hawkins if and when he came to drink.

"There," Miles said. "Now we're morally secure."

*****

Ten minutes later, they were seated at a window table at Morgan's, devouring huge bowls of steamed clams with wedges of warm, crusty sourdough bread. As he always did, Miles was using his bread to soak up every last drop of the buttery broth—with its bits of garlic, shallots, and thyme. He fought the urge to lick his fingers clean, knowing that if his mother were there, she'd whack his knuckles with a spoon for such unmannerliness. He could almost feel the pain, though she was miles away.

Floyd was telling a story of discovering a severed human scrotum in an alley off Yesler Way back when he was a foot patrolman in Seattle, and of how he'd had a recurring castration nightmare ever since. "It made quite an impression on me."

"Sure," Miles said, only half listening, lost in his own thoughts, watching for Marion's mother's car out the window.

"Did you even hear my story?"

"Yeah. Severed scrotum."

"I find a man's precious sweetbreads discarded in an alley, and all you have to say about it is *sure*?"

"Sorry. I was just pondering something strange."

"What?

"Something I heard a couple of locals say. That if the Jensens had turned to smuggling, then they were fair game, having freely chosen to cross that proverbial line. Having gotten greedy. No longer content to live simply like most folks in these islands. In short, that we shouldn't waste our time."

"Wait—the Jensens were fair game for murder because they weren't, as you say, content to live simply? Come on, now. Surely some of them—the rumrunners, I mean—are driven to their trade by genuine need. Financial pressure. Unusual challenges. I mean, look at Angus Cooper, assuming his acquisition of a big Liberty engine means he was going into rumrunning. Poor widower just trying to take care of his invalid daughter? There's a difference between greed and need, isn't there?"

"Like I said, it wasn't my idea. It was just something I heard."

"Why are you pondering this?"

"I don't know. Maybe because it feels like this job is taking over my life."

And taking away from your precious limited time to woo Marion, Floyd thought. Wisely, he kept his thoughts to himself.

FIFTY-FOUR

That afternoon, Miles and Floyd met at the steamship terminal well ahead of the interpreter's arrival so that they could take a more extensive look at the passenger manifest records. After a bit of pushback from the head clerk, they were led to a back room—more of a coat closet—where the manifests were archived and organized in boxes arranged by year. It didn't take them long to find what they were looking for.

"Here," Floyd said, jotting names down in a notebook. "Just last month. Seven Chinese girls departing for Seattle on the *Bangor* on Tuesday the 7th."

"And here's a group of six on a Wednesday in April," Miles said. "I can't believe I haven't noticed this before, these big groups of Chinese girls departing on the steamer."

"They probably sneak them into the terminal out of the back of a van or something," Floyd said.

"I suppose."

"Now the key question is when did the girls get here?"

Over the next two hours, the men searched the weeks, then the months prior to the dates of the girls' departures, going over thousands of names—entries for every single inbound and outbound passenger on every one of the mosquito fleet steamers. They went back as far as eleven months. They were able to find several more groups of Chinese girls *leaving* the island. But there was no record whatsoever of any of them ever arriving.

"Smuggled in, one and all," Floyd said.

"So it seems."

*****

They found the interpreter just as he got off the boat. Being the only Asian aboard, he was easy to spot.

"Well met, gentlemen," he said. "My name is Li Guozheng. But I go by William."

"I'm Miles. This is Floyd. It's our understanding that you specialize in Cantonese."

"That's correct. I'm fluent in prestige Cantonese, and, more specifically, the Guanbao, Guangfu, and Zhongshan dialects. I'm also fluent in Taishanese, of course, and conversational in all other major Yue dialects."

"Thank you for coming on such short notice," Floyd said.

"It's my pleasure. I love travelling by ship. And on a day when the weather is like this, it's a genuine treat."

"You're very articulate," Miles said.

"Thank you, Sheriff. So are you," William said, drawing, to Floyd's secret amusement, a thoroughly perplexed look from Miles.

*****

As they walked back to the station, Miles asked Floyd for a private word, so they dropped back from William the interpreter.

"Listen, Floyd. The highbinder is obviously a hard man. I know you have reservations. But we're going to run this interrogation my way, alright? Your objection is noted. But this is my jurisdiction."

"Wasn't it William Hazlitt who said that violence ever defeats its own ends?"

"Floyd."

"Very well. But I'm telling you, Miles, we're going to end up reaping the whirlwind for this."

*****

Back in the jail cell, Floyd and the interpreter leaned against the back wall while Miles and Bill stood to either side of their prisoner, still seated and handcuffed to the table, his face already bruising and swollen from the earlier session.

"Even though we know you speak English, we got a Cantonese interpreter," Miles said. "How about those apples? Now you don't have an excuse for not answering our questions. And if you don't, well . . ."

The man still stared at Miles without expression.

"So let's try again. What is your name?"

The interpreter repeated the question in Cantonese. Getting no response, he tried two other dialects. Still nothing. Miles stepped back and gave Bill a nod. Bill, whose fist was wrapped in a wide leather strap, punched the Chinese man in the gut.

"Name," Miles repeated. When the man failed to answer this time, Miles let Bill go to town on him. Over the next couple of minutes, he took a dozen blows to his abdomen and face.

"Name!" Miles shouted, slamming his palms on the table as Bill continued taking the man apart. He was beginning to think this Chinese man had some sort of sensory deficiency. Either that or he was made of iron. He was taking the sort of beating that brought most men twice his size to tears. But aside from the occasional, uncontrollable sound of air being forced, violently, from his lungs, he didn't make a peep. And he never looked distressed. More bored than anything.

The interpreter, William, on the other hand, looked very uneasy. "Gentlemen, gentlemen," he said. "Pardon my interruption. But this seems, ah, irregular."

"It *is* irregular," Miles said. "This whole week has been irregular. Very irregular. And we've gotten to a point where we need some damned answers."

"I see," William said, sounding doubtful if not alarmed.

"You're going to knock him unconscious," Floyd

complained. "What information will we get out of him then?"

Miles gestured for Bill, who seemed to be thoroughly enjoying himself, to stop. He tossed Bill a towel to wipe off his blood-covered knuckles. There was blood everywhere. On the table. On the man's clothes. Pooling on the floor beneath his feet. "He's a tough little bastard," Bill said. "I'll give him that."

"Let's try a different tack," Miles said. "Tell him we know the tongs run illegal immigrants through San Juan Island, and that it's therefore a perfect spot for them to hijack and destroy the property of a rival tong. A tong they're feuding with. Tell him we already have the names of the girls right here," he said, unfolding a sheet of paper and pointing to the names he'd copied from the steamship passenger manifest logbook of seven Chinese who'd departed together on the *Bangor* a month earlier. "See? Right here. Seven girls. Seven girls who aren't on any arriving ship's manifest, meaning they were smuggled onto the island."

"Ah, pardon me," William said. "Not seven girls."

"What? Look—one, two, three, four—"

"No, no. That's five girls and two men," William said. "These two names, here," he said, pointing, "are male."

"Two men? What about here?" he asked, pointing to the names of the six Chinese individuals who'd left the island together in April. "All girls?"

"No. Four girls. Two men."

Suddenly, it seemed all the more possible that the highbinders had come to simply rendezvous with and escort the young girls to Seattle or wherever they were bound. Not to kill them. Indeed, it seemed to Miles an entirely plausible explanation. After all, presumably, the immigrant girls wouldn't know how to get from San Juan Island to Seattle. They'd need guides. For that matter, how on earth would one tong have discovered the route and timing of another tong's human trafficking operation—one that had, to his considerable embarrassment, evaded Miles's own notice all this time even though he was the head of law enforcement on the very island being used as a transit point? It seemed an unlikely thing.

But why were the highbinders still on the island? Were they waiting to see how the investigation shook out? Waiting to find out who killed their girls and who to target for revenge?

Miles didn't have long to think about it. The station telephone rang, as if on cue. It rang twice before the group of them seemed to realize a call was coming in.

"Floyd, would you mind?" Miles asked.

"Of course." Floyd went to answer the call. A moment later, he reappeared in the doorway. "It's for William."

"For William?" Miles said.

"Ah," William said. "Pardon me." He disappeared into the office section of the station, but was back in a flash. "Forgive me. I must go."

"Go?" Miles said. "You just got here."

"I'll return as soon as I can. Is the steamer to Seattle still here?"

Miles looked at the clock on the wall. "For another three minutes. You'll have to run for it."

"Forgive me."

"What happened?"

"My mother—I'm sorry, I must go."

*****

Ten minutes after William the interpreter had left them in a cloud of dust, Floyd was, via three different telephone calls to headquarters, able to find out why he'd had had to rush back to Seattle.

"His mother was reported missing," Floyd told Miles as he hung up. "Probably abducted," he added with a sinking heart

"What?"

"Abducted by a tong."

"What makes you say that?"

"They left a basket of oranges on her bed. Her sister

discovered it earlier today."

"I don't follow you, Floyd."

"It's some sort of tong message. It can probably be interpreted to mean that they've taken William's mother hostage to see that he doesn't help us anymore. Or else."

"Or else his mother meets the business end of a meat cleaver?"

"Something like that."

"Judas H. Priest. What the hell is going to happen next?"

The door flew open and a tall white man in what might have been the flashiest suit Miles had ever laid eyes on sauntered in, chin high, body language screaming that he owned the place.

"Help you, pal?" Miles asked.

"A. Harold Dewey, attorney at law."

"Good for you."

"You are holding my client, Kwan Ping, in your jail."

"I am?"

"Illegally, in fact. That is to say, without cause."

"Ping, you say?"

"Kwan Ping."

"Huh. This is news to me. Nice pocket watch, by the way."

"He's a Chinese man.

"With a name like Ping? You don't say."

"You sound confused, Sheriff. Do you have a lot of Chinese men in your holding cell? Perhaps, despite holding him in violation of his rights, and probably—shall we say—*encouraging* him to speak, you still don't know his name. No matter. You'll take me to him at once."

The phone rang. "Hold on a second, A. Harold Dewey," Miles told the lawyer. "Sheriff's office," he said into the phone.

"Miles, it's Jon Boren."

"Hey, Doc."

"I've had a chance to take a preliminary look at the three bodies exhumed from out by the settler's cabin. Three young females in Oriental clothing, each in a different state of decay, so

I would guess they were buried at different times over the past year or so."

"Different shipments of girls?" Miles muttered to himself.

"Pardon?"

"Sorry—nothing."

"Though my assessment is of obviously limited value given that the bodies are decomposing, none of them have any apparent signs of trauma. No bullet holes or broken bones. So it's quite possible that they died of illness and not by violence."

"I suppose that will have to suffice for good news today," Miles said before hanging up. He wondered how many different groups of smuggled Chinese girls had been temporarily housed in that old cabin.

"You were taking me to my client, Kwan Ping," Dewey said, breaking Miles out of his trance.

"Look, mac—"

But Miles was cut off, mid-sentence, by the lawyer thrusting a document in his face. It was a San Juan County court order commanding Kwan Ping's immediate release, signed by his honor, Judge Carl Angstrom—an octogenarian Miles thought was far too forgiving and soft with his gavel.

"Unless you wish to be held in contempt, you will release my client at once."

"You want for me to throw this city peacock out into the street?" Bill asked, glaring at the lawyer as Miles continued to read through the court order.

"I do. Very much. But I don't think we had better."

Miles took Dewey to the cell and, with deliberate slowness, released Kwan Ping. The lawyer didn't bother with any expressions of outrage at Ping's battered and bloody condition. He merely waited as his client gathered up his things.

Just another day at the office for these two, Miles thought.

As they made their way out, Kwan Ping stopped and turned to Miles. "If you would be so kind as to give me back my hat, please," he said without the least trace of an accent.

Miles's eyebrows rose. "So," he said. He shook his head and almost smiled. "Do you have his hat, Bill?"

Bill, looking venomous, nodded at the coat rack. An unfamiliar bowler hat hung from an upper hook. Bill made no move to get it, so the lawyer did it for him. Then they watched, frustrated and helpless, as lawyer and suspect walked right out the door.

"Well, that's just great," Floyd said. "Now what?"

"Go back to Seattle and re-interview the Chinese Peace Society?" Miles said.

"Why? So they can sit there and stare like a bunch of mute zombies again? So they can laugh at us the moment we leave?"

"Yeah, maybe not." Miles plopped down in his desk chair and put his feet up on his desk. "Well. Who are we marionettes for now?"

FIFTY-FIVE

Miles used the unexpected lull to call Marion again. This time, to his instant joy, she answered. In an oddly stilted conversation, Miles asked her to dinner. Of course, Sylvia had to come along too. So with a glimmer of hope that it might help him find a moment to be alone with Marion, he invited Floyd to join them.

They met at a cozy place on Harrison Street called Kelly's—the only alternative to Morgan's for a sit-down dinner. It had been a thriving pub before Prohibition. But its Irish-influenced menu, including its hugely popular lamb stew, kept it alive.

Miles and Floyd arrived wearing the same suits they'd had on all day—Floyd's pressed, Miles's rumpled. But Marion and Sylvia came looking as tony as ever, sticking out like a couple of fashionable sore thumbs in an unfashionable one-horse town. They all ordered the stew, split two rounds of brown soda bread served with salted local butter, then lingered over fresh blackberry cobbler and coffee as Miles caught them up on the basics of their investigation.

"In sum, as of a few hours ago, we had two tong highbinder assassins, a rabidly racist labor agitator, an assaultive temperance fanatic, and heaven only knows how many murderous rumrunners, opium smugglers, human traffickers, pirates, and deranged revenue agents loose on and around the island," Miles said.

"And let's not forget our cutthroat salvager-maybe-turned-treasure hunter lurking in the surrounding seas," Floyd added, apparently no longer concerned about discussing an investigation with two civilians.

"And no promising leads," Miles said with emphasis.

"You should write a book about this case," Marion suggested.

"My mother would say the story is too complex for the impatient, lazy modern mind," Floyd said.

"And it has no ending," Miles added. "Yet."

They fell quiet as their server refilled coffee cups.

"So how long does it take you to travel out here from New York?" Floyd asked.

"Four days," Sylvia said.

"Holy cow. I'd lose my mind, sitting in a train seat for four days."

"Oh, no—the long-distance trains are really quite elegant. There's a restaurant car, a lounge, a game room. And we get sleeping berths. The bedding is Egyptian cotton."

"Oh. How many times did you have to change trains on the way out here?"

"Only once. We rode the Broadway Limited from New York to Chicago, then the Oriental Limited from Chicago to Seattle. I'll tell you, that Oriental Limited is a gorgeous train with a gorgeous route. The Rocky Mountains. The Cascades. Indian lands of the golden plains."

"Sounds romantic," Miles muttered.

"It is, indeed," Sylvia said, with a covert glance at Marion.

"And you're from Boston, Sylvia?" Floyd asked.

"I am."

"I would love to go to Boston. So many great universities. So much science and education and enlightenment."

"Enlightenment?" Miles said, giving Floyd a dubious look. "I'd always heard it was a town full of drunk Irish Catholics."

"Who says alcohol isn't the path to enlightenment?" Marion asked. "And my mother is Irish, you insensitive ass."

"Some neighborhoods—the Jewish ones—are more enlightened than others," Sylvia added with a wink.

As the weather was good, they took an after-dinner walk,

making a rough circuit of town. Marion and Sylvia smoked aromatic brown cigarettes jammed into the ends of long cigarette holders. Before long, with each of them pausing in different places to peek through darkened shop windows or gaze out over the quiet harbor, and with Miles doing a bit of surreptitious maneuvering, the group split in half, with Miles and Marion bringing up the rear, a block or so behind Sylvia and Floyd who were laughing and chatting away. The sun had set and the town and harbor glowed in a magical pink light. Miles kept sneaking glances at Marion. She was as beautiful as ever.

"How is your grandfather?" he asked.

"Still hanging on. He's a strong old man."

"Maybe that's where *you* get it."

"It's hard on my mother though. Sometimes I think it would be better for her if he'd just let himself move on."

"You mean pass away? Can a person decide that?"

"I'm sure you can. Think how many stories you hear of people with broken hearts willing themselves to die just after their spouses pass away."

Miles figured such stories encompassed coincidence and only seemed commonplace because they were so memorable.

"So you may be staying in town longer then?" he asked, his heart leaping in his chest.

"Good question. We have engagements back in New York."

"Engagements?"

"Sylvia teaches at Mount Sinai Hospital, and I'm enrolled at Barnard College."

"You're in college? I'll say it again: you amaze me."

"And I'll say it again: I am amazing. Still, it's hard to imagine leaving my mother alone in this situation. Maybe I'll just send Sylvia home."

"Yes?" Miles said, trying to keep the surge of joyful hope from showing on his face.

"It's just that I hate the idea of her travelling alone."

"She's been to war, Marion. I'm quite sure she can handle

first-class train travel."

"Do you care for her?"

"For Sylvia? Yes. Very much."

"I'm so glad. That means quite a lot to me."

"Really? You've never struck me as the type to care what anyone else thought about who your friends were."

"Well. She's a very good friend. And so are you. It's different."

They walked half a block in silence. Twice, Miles caught Marion sneaking quick, cautious glances at him. Was this really happening? Was she attracted to him? Was she working up the nerve to say so? His heart began to pound.

"Sylvia told me something of your conversations," Marion said, her tone confusingly reluctant.

"Yes?"

"About the war."

"Oh." Miles deflated. "What did she tell you?"

"Nothing specific. She tends to speak in metaphors when it comes to this sort of thing—at least when she talks to me. Probably because I'm such a delicate flower."

"Ha-ha."

"But she said that you've gazed into the abyss."

"Hmm."

They walked a few more steps, then Marion stopped in her tracks and looked at him. "Life has more to offer you, Miles. I know it's easy for me to say. But I miss the happy, spirited boy I grew up with. I want you to find a way to reconnect."

"Yes." He swallowed hard. "Actually, along those lines, it would mean the world to me if—"

"Sheriff!" Bill shouted, jogging up the street. The commotion got Floyd and Sylvia turned around. "Just got a call from the RCMP in Vancouver."

"You were still at the station?" Miles asked.

"Just tying up some loose ends. Mopping blood out of the cell and so forth."

The mention of blood drew a troubled look from Marion.

"You're a dedicated man," Miles said, not quite able to conceal the irritation in his voice. "What's up?"

"They found Angus Cooper's boat."

"The *Daisy*? Where?"

"Mouth of the Fraser River, run aground on a sandbar just off Steveston."

"In British Columbia?"

"Sounds like Cooper ran for it to Canada," Floyd said.

"I got the number for the RCMP constable handling the case. He said he'd wait up for your call."

Miles's jaw tightened in frustration. He turned to Marion, aching to pour his heart out to her, restraining himself in the presence of everyone else. "Listen, we should continue this conversation," he said to her.

"I know. Call me tomorrow. I'll be at home all morning."

She leaned in close and, for the first time ever, kissed his cheek. For a split second, he caught the scent of jasmine in her hair, and his mind reeled in the dazzling light of a thousand happy memories from their shared past. He felt as if his whole body were suddenly filled with a sustaining warmth—the formerly hollow parts of him brimming over with a sensation he instinctively recognized as eternal, pure, and good. He yearned to wrap his arms around her. To hold her. To keep her.

Instead, he had to content himself with a longish hand squeeze and one more look at her smiling face framed by the otherworldly backdrop of a dusk-lit Friday Harbor and a sky filling with stars.

FIFTY-SIX

Miles woke from a poor and restless night's sleep, irritated and stupefied at how many times he'd been thwarted in his pursuit of Marion. As he'd half expected, the phone conversation with the RCMP constable hadn't been worth cutting his evening short for. All he'd learned was that someone had attempted to scuttle the *Daisy* by chopping a hole through the inside of her hull with an axe. If Miles had to hazard a guess, he'd have said that Angus Cooper fled across the border with his daughter to escape the law or whatever killers he'd gotten himself mixed up with. Then, in an effort to cover his tracks, he'd tried to get rid of his boat once they'd reached the Fraser River Delta, hoping the *Daisy* would drift out into the Strait of Georgia and sink. Instead, the *Daisy* managed to beach herself on one of the many sandbars that made the entrance to the Fraser River shipping lanes so treacherous. Unfortunately for Miles, the wreck of the *Daisy* had been swamped and tumbled about in at least a dozen tides since its abandonment, so there was, predictably, no useful evidence found aboard. In fact, the vessel was already half buried in tidal muck. And Cooper was probably well on his way to the Alaska Territory by now. Or perhaps headed east on a Canadian train. Out of practical reach, at any rate.

Happily, Miles was able to reach Marion by phone when he got to the station just after 9 a.m.

"That was a lovely evening," she said.

"It was, wasn't it? Good food. Good company. But I believe we ended things with the mutual understanding that we'd had to break our conversation off prematurely."

"It was rather an abrupt ending."

"And that we should resume our discussion, perhaps, today. Which is part of why I'm calling. So I'm wondering if I might talk you into meeting for lunch."

"Today?"

"Say a picnic at Mulno Cove. I know you're reluctant to leave Sylvia by herself with your mother. But it would mean a lot to me if I could have you to myself, alone, for just a bit."

"Alone?"

"Yes. I'd very much like to speak with you, but without an audience."

"About what?"

"I'd rather tell you in person."

"Ah. I see. Well, I'm sure it would be lovely. But between my family obligations and duties as a host to Sylvia, it might not—"

"It wouldn't be long. I promise. Just a quick lunch. Maybe a game or two of Sink the *Deutschland*," he said, referring to a game they'd invented as kids—named after the one-time flagship of the Imperial German High Seas Fleet. It involved setting a log of driftwood afloat and seeing who could score more hits with rocks as the tide slowly carried it away. "Or maybe a quick blackberry fight, like in the old days."

"Ha."

"I'll have you back before anyone misses you."

"Oh, Miles. I really . . ." The line was quiet for a moment. "Alright. Alright."

"Fantastic. When should I pick you up?"

"I'll meet you there."

He hung up and, with a wide smile on his face, got a fresh percolator of coffee going on the stove just as Floyd and Bill arrived.

"You look happy this morning," Floyd said.

"Yes. I suppose I feel rather good."

"What's on the agenda for today? It seems we're running out of options."

"The only thing I can think to do is take another run at Rupert Hawkins."

"You really think he knows something?" Floyd asked.

"Probably not. But what else are we going to do? Callahan and the highbinders are surely gone by now."

"They're not," Bill said.

"You're joking."

"No, sir. I checked the outbound passenger manifests at the steamship terminal not ten minutes ago. Unless they found private transport, which I doubt, they're all still here."

"Still here? Why?" Miles asked of the ceiling. "Callahan already gave his speech at the Odd Fellows. And the highbinders know we're onto them. In their shoes, I'd have been on the first boat out of here."

"Maybe Aunt Fanny bakes a mean apple pie," Floyd said.

"Maybe Callahan did kill those girls after all," Miles said. "Maybe he heard the *Lucky Lena* was going to be full of Chinese, but didn't know they were going to be women. Then, in a panic, he killed them because they were witnesses to his murder of the Jensens."

"Along similar lines," Floyd said, "maybe Reverend McCaskill thought he was going to make an example of some rumrunners, and then killed the girls for the very same reason Callahan might have. Though it's hard to imagine a self-professed man of God slaughtering innocent girls."

"Apparently you've never opened a history text."

As Miles said this, two weathered, frightened-looking fishermen came through the door in an obvious rush. They looked like they'd come straight from their boat, still in coveralls and rubber boots.

Please, no, Miles thought. *Not something else. Not before lunch.*

"Sheriff," one of them said, his eyes big.

"What is it, Charlie?"

"We was running back from Sidney this morning after buying a new net and, anyway, a girl. We saw a girl."

"A body?"

"No, sir. Live girl. Oriental. On Halibut Island," he said, referring to an insignificant landmass Miles hardly thought of as an island—a narrow, 1/3-mile-long rock with a small stand of trees on its crest, about a mile inside of Canadian waters, and only three miles north of D'Arcy Island.

"We spotted her on the northeast part," the old fisherman said. "Then George took a look with the binoculars. Looked like she was gathering oysters. But something wasn't right with her."

"Not right, how?"

"First off, she tries to run and hide when she spots us motoring around the point. But she runs funny. Lurching, sort of. Like she's hurt."

*****

Utterly dejected, Miles called Marion back to cancel their lunch date at Mulno Cove, noting, with unease, what he took to be a hint of relief in her voice. "What about tomorrow evening?" he asked with a sudden sense that a door was closing—that he was fast running out of time.

"Tomorrow?"

"Please. It would mean a lot."

After another minute of unabashed coaxing, she finally agreed.

"I promise you, cross my heart, that I'll be there no matter what comes up," he said before hanging up.

FIFTY-SEVEN

Haro Strait, British Columbia
(near D'Arcy Island)
Ten Days Earlier

I have lost a lot of blood. On the boat, I could see a large puddle on the deck under me when I dared to open one eye. And even though I held my hand against the wound—tried to hold it shut—I am sure much blood has leaked out of my body since they threw me overboard into the water. The coldest water I have ever felt.

At first I thought it was a miracle when I saw the floating wood plank after I drifted away from the boat. But the pain became so much worse when I struggled to clamber onto it, sliding back into the water on my first three tries. Pain like fire. Cold fire. So bad I almost wanted to die to escape it.

And then more cold. I shivered so hard and for so long, my teeth chattering, my free hand barely able to hold onto the metal spike in the wood that I have been using to keep myself from slipping into the dark water again. But finally, the shivering stopped and the pain was not as bad. And I grew very tired. Very sleepy. I tried to stay awake, knowing I might roll off the plank if I fell asleep. But sleep—the escape, the peace, the warmth and comfort of sleep—was so tempting. I imagined dragging my sleeping mat over by the stove back home in my village. I imagined the wonderful warmth.

Through a break in the clouds, I could still see the seven stars of the Northern Dipper, so I knew I had not yet left the earth. But the stars had grown brighter. The gateway to heaven had grown closer. I prayed for forgiveness. I prayed that I might see my family again one day, in this world or the next.

FIFTY-EIGHT

Miles had the old fishermen run him and a petrified Floyd up and around the north end of San Juan Island, past Roche Harbor, and across thoroughly choppy waters in Haro Strait to tiny Halibut Island, where they claimed to have seen a skittish and possibly injured Asian girl that very morning. As they approached the Canadian maritime border, they caught sight of the USRC *Arcata* patrolling near D'Arcy Island, to their south, its funnel pouring thick black coal smoke into the sky such that every rumrunner within ten miles would know exactly where she was. Miles pictured Captain Eckart sitting on its bridge, grumpy, slouching, and constipated, squinting through binoculars and obsessively searching for rumrunners like some modern-day Captain Ahab.

"There she is," Charlie, the elder of the two fishermen, said, pointing straight off the bow. The low form of Halibut Island was just now distinguishable against the backdrop of much larger Sidney Island behind it.

"Shouldn't we at least radio the Canadians?" Floyd asked from where he cowered in the very middle of the wheelhouse, his eyes glued to the deck.

"After the fact," Miles said. "The girl could be mortally injured. Last thing we need is cross-border bureaucratic processes slowing us down."

"Point taken."

They motored to the northern tip of the rocky islet, where a tiny cove afforded the only sheltered and relatively safe landing point, then drifted forward until the hull just touched beach gravel. Charlie dropped an anchor off the stern to keep the boat from turning sideways against the shore. Then, having asked the fishermen to stay onboard, Miles and Floyd hopped off into knee-deep water, carrying a medical kit, food, and a wool blanket.

"I'm going to have to take up drinking if this job is going to have me riding in boats this frequently," Floyd said.

As the narrow island was barely 60 yards across at its widest point, by keeping about 80 feet apart, they were able to view its entire breadth as they slowly made their way south. It didn't take them long to find signs of life. A few feet into the island's one small stand of trees, in a nook of rock offering shelter from the prevailing winds, Miles came across a small, crude, recently constructed shelter—more of a cocoon—made of branches wrapped in bull kelp. It was stuffed with dry madrona leaves and tall grass. He pictured the girl crawling inside and surrounding herself with a thick layer of debris to keep warm. Simple and moderately effective protection from the elements.

Downwind of the shelter, he found a scattering of cracked mussel and oyster shells—undoubtedly the girl's main form of sustenance. At least she wasn't starving. Miles did, however, wonder where she got water to drink, until he came upon a series of small, stale puddles in a shallow fissure in the island's ice age glacier-scoured rock.

He and Floyd came together as they neared the narrowing southern end of the island. Given that the girl had no doubt seen the boat approaching, Miles guessed that she was retreating further and further down the island as they advanced. But she was running out of land. Soon, they'd have her cornered and there would be no place for her to hide.

Indeed, a couple of minutes later, Floyd froze in place and, without a sound, raised his hand to signal for Miles to stop. He pointed to a small boulder, just large enough to conceal a child or very small adult. Miles nodded, then quietly sidestepped over to where Floyd stood. He could just see the top of the girl's head. Her hair was black and disheveled.

Without coming any closer, and in the softest, most sympathetic voice he could muster, Miles said, "Girl, we're not going to hurt you." He knew she probably didn't understand his words. But he hoped his tone would carry the gist of his message. "We know you're afraid. But we're here to help. We'll wait for you by your shelter. I'm going to put a blanket and food here for you," he said, taking the wool blanket from his satchel and setting it on the ground at his feet. He took out an apple, a piece of smoked salmon, and a canteen of fresh water and set them on top of the blanket. The girl didn't move a muscle. Miles and Floyd slowly withdrew.

Back near her cocoon-like shelter, the men got a big bonfire going. Floyd warmed himself by the fire while Miles went to update the fishermen and beg them to stay put. When he got back, Floyd asked if he really thought the girl would come willingly.

"I don't know," Miles said, staring into the fire. "But if she's badly injured, we don't want to risk trying to physically force her unless it's absolutely necessary." Then he looked up into the treetops. "The breeze is coming from the northwest."

"So?"

"She's downwind of us. I have an idea." Miles found a long stick, sharpened the end with his knife, then extracted several strips of bacon from the food bag they'd brought along and began roasting them over the fire. The air filled with their aroma and the gentle breeze carried it down the island toward the girl.

"You may be a genius," Floyd said.

"I can't argue with that."

*****

Men have come. Always men. I saw their boat approaching the island and moved to the far end to hide. But to move hurts so much. Takes so much energy. I just want to sleep. I have wanted to sleep since I spotted this little island in the moonlight and slowly paddled my plank of wood toward it with one hand. Why do I still try to stay alive? I am so tired of trying.

The men have lit a fire. I can smell the smoke. They are cooking. A warm fire and warm food. They want to draw me out of hiding. The aroma is delicious. Something both salty and sweet. How I long for something warm, something salty and sweet to fill my stomach. Or even just to taste it after these long, miserable days of being in pain. Of being cold. With nothing to eat but cold shellfish and cold seaweed. Nothing to drink but cold, foul-smelling water. I would do anything to be able to drink—to even just sip—a warm cup of tea.

But there will be no tea. This time they will find me. I have no more energy to run. This time they will make sure I am dead like all the other girls.

*****

They spent a couple of hours roasting bacon, strip by strip, eating most of what they cooked. But the smell didn't lure the girl. As the shadows were growing long, they gave up on Miles's plan and walked back down the island, seeing no sign of her until they got all the way back to the boulder she'd tried to hide behind earlier. The wool blanket, food, and canteen sat exactly where they'd left them. Desperately hoping the girl wasn't dead, Miles picked up the canteen and blanket and slowly sidestepped until he could see her leg sticking out from behind the boulder. "Hey there," Miles said, again in his softest audible voice. "It's alright."

He stepped forward until he could see most of her body—could just make out that her chest was rising and falling with her shallow breathing—then opened the canteen and held it out to her.

"Are you thirsty?" he asked, creeping around the edge of the boulder. The flat, fading light revealed an emaciated apparition—a frail ghost of a girl. Filthy, shoeless, and clothed in nothing more than the torn and tattered remnants of a simple Chinese peasant's tunic. But alive.

He gestured for Floyd to come help and unfolded the

blanket to wrap the girl up. It was then that he noticed her injuries. A probable bullet wound between her breast and shoulder, and what looked to be a foot-long slash to the left side of her belly. Both wounds were covered in some sort of poultice made from what looked like ground up seaweed. As he draped the blanket over her, an edge of it caught on the poultice covering the longer wound, causing it to fall off, revealing a deep cut with a portion of intestine bulging through it.

Miles gasped. He'd seen his share of wounded during the war. But this wasn't a soldier. It was a child. "Jesus wept," he whispered, meeting Floyd's eyes. "She's just a girl. Somebody's little girl."

FIFTY-NINE

Back in Friday Harbor well after nightfall, Dr. Boren and Sylvia—who Miles had called in because of her battlefield hospital experience—did their best to clean, sanitize, and stitch up the Chinese girl's bullet wound and the deep slash in her belly. They had to remove a bit of necrotic tissue, but were amazed at how little there was given how long the girl had probably been wounded and without medical care. It made them wonder at the possible healing secrets of the pulverized seaweed poultices she'd self-applied.

She yelped when they flushed her wounds with antiseptic, but was otherwise an unflinching and compliant patient—this despite the fact that nobody could communicate with her, including Henry, whom Miles had practically dragged from his bed. Henry's best guess was that she spoke a lesser-known Cantonese dialect.

Meanwhile, Miles and Floyd waited in Dr. Boren's reception room.

"Never in my life," Floyd said, letting the statement hang.

"I know," Miles said, shaking his head. "It's just beyond imagination."

Miles wondered how the girl had managed to survive. The *Lucky Lena* was probably smuggling her to San Juan Island from some rusty, rat-infested steamship anchored in Canadian or international waters after crossing the Pacific from Shanghai or Hong Kong. From there, she'd have been escorted to Seattle, Portland, or maybe San Francisco, probably to work as a prostitute in a tong-run brothel. Instead, hijackers had taken over the boat, shot and sliced everyone open right before her eyes—shot and cut *her*—then thrown the bodies overboard. Only, in all the madness, blood, and fading light, they didn't notice that their handiwork hadn't quite finished off one of the girls. That when she'd gone overboard, she'd pretended to be dead, treaded water, maybe climbed onto a log or wooden plank drifting by, and then ridden it north on the tide, through the cold darkness, to Halibut Island. There, she'd somehow managed to recover from certain hypothermia, done her best to treat her own wounds, then hidden—subsisting on raw oysters, seaweed, and maybe wild berries, with little hope of survival and little idea of what to do next—for more than a week.

"The one bit of good news," Miles said, "is that if she survives, we now have a live witness. Someone who can positively identify the gunman."

Floyd looked up at him, his face grim. "Yes. Good news."

"But I'm sure word is out about her rescue. Needless to say, if the killers are still on the island, they'll come for her. We have to keep her safe."

Sylvia came out of the examination room. "I think she'll make it," she told them.

"Thank goodness," Miles muttered.

"We have her about as fixed up as we can get her. Both wounds are deep. I'll have Swedish Hospital send up another tetanus serum tomorrow. For now, she just needs to rest. Anyone around here speak her language?"

"No. But we'll summon another interpreter from Seattle in the morning. Listen, Sylvia, I can't thank you enough. Dr. Boren is a fine physician. But, well, with all your experience with combat wounds—"

"No need to explain."

"And I'm so sorry for dragging you out of bed in the dark of night."

"Don't be silly."

"You've just, I mean, for you to—"

"Miles, do I need to slap you? The situation is as under control as it is going to be. Go home and get some sleep. You're too tired to even form a sentence."

"I can't leave her here undefended."

"Bill is going to be outside all night."

"We don't know how many killers there are. Someone needs to be inside too."

"Then give me your pistol," she said. "Really, give it to me. I'm wide awake."

"You can shoot?"

"Like Annie Oakley. Springfield and Lee-Enfield rifles. The Colt 1911. Browning Auto-5. You name it." When Miles looked doubtful, she went on. "One of my patients in Château-Thierry was a range master from Camp Benning. I made him teach me while his foot was healing. Seven weeks of private lessons."

"You astonish me, Sylvia."

"So you keep saying. I'll close the curtains, bar the door, and read my book on the couch here. Anybody tries to bust in, I'll turn them into a colander. Give me your gun, go home, get a few hours of sleep, and relieve me in the morning."

"It's a .45 semiautomatic," he told her, unbuckling his gun belt and handing it over to her.

"I can see that," she answered, un-holstering the gun and deftly popping the magazine out to check the load. Then she slid the magazine back into the gun and drew back the slide to put a round in the chamber. "Go to bed, Miles."

"Can I see her first?"

"She isn't conscious at the moment. We gave her a bit of morphine."

"I'd still like to."

"By all means then."

Miles nodded to himself, went to the door, took a deep breath, and turned the knob. The examination room was dimly lit by a small lamp in the corner, the main overhead lights having been turned off. The girl, half of her scrawny abdomen covered in bandages, was asleep on the bed with a blanket pulled up over her legs. Dr. Boren was putting instruments, medicines, and gauze back in a chest of shallow drawers against the wall.

"Just wanted to see her again, Doc," Miles said in a hushed voice.

"I understand. But please let her sleep."

"Of course."

"Goodnight, then," Boren said, grabbing his cloak from a hook on the wall.

"Good night."

As Boren closed the door behind him, Miles pulled a chair over to the head of the bed, sat down, and stared at the girl. She was a sorry sight, her face drawn, her skin ashen. An innocent, fragile, helpless creature a million miles from home.

So tired that his ribs ached with the effort to sit upright, Miles slumped his chair, rested his chin on his propped-up palm, and gazed at the girl's face. Curiously, in looking at her, the first thing that popped into his mind was his memory of the rabid anti-Asian restaurant worker protest in Seattle. And not for the first time, it struck him as tragically absurd that men could get so worked up over people having different languages, religions, nationalities, or colors—things that were so utterly trivial next to the measureless, inescapable shadow of mortality. It seemed to him such a waste of valuable time in light of how fleeting a person's existence really was. After all, what did such differences really mean? Everybody was reduced to the same colorless dust sooner or later. Indeed, the pathetic and broken creature before him might have been a slit-eyed yellow heathen on paper. But all Miles could see at that moment was a little girl.

He let his heavy eyelids drop for what seemed like a brief moment. Then he heard a small sound. Hardly a squeak, like the mew of a thirsty kitten. Opening his eyes, he discovered that the girl was looking at him through barely opened lids.

"Hello," Miles he softly, reaching out to touch her hand, then stopping himself, not wanting to startle the girl. "You're safe, little girl. Safe."

Blinking slowly, she again squeaked what might have been the fragment of a word.

"What?" Miles asked. “Did you say something?”

The girl stared at him with an expression he could only guess might mean she was summoning the last of her energy in order to speak again.

"Do you speak English?" he asked, knowing the question was futile. "Who did this to you?" He waited for a half a minute, listening to her shallow breathing. Then her lips parted.

"How tong, " she whispered, just audibly. "How tong."

"Your tongue? Are you thirsty?" he said, knowing that what he heard was phonetic—not real English words—but so desperate to communicate that he asked anyway.

"How tong."

"Wait—something about the tongs? Did a tong highbinder do this to you?"

"How tong," she said again.

"I don’t understand."

She went quiet and let her glassy eyes close for a moment. When she opened them again, she shifted her focus from Miles to the top of a small cabinet next to the bed. Following her gaze, Miles saw what looked like some sort of comb.

"You want the comb?"

With her mouth hanging open, she began to lift an arm as if to reach for it—which gave Miles hope that her will to live was intact. Then, changing her mind, she settled for raising a finger to point at it.

"This?" he asked, reaching over to get it for her. It looked to be made of jade, with an almost luminescent marbling of various shades of green. Its teeth were long, its wide shaft carved with elaborate flower designs. He placed it in her open hand. As her fingers closed on it, Miles heard her sigh with what he took to be relief as she once again let her eyes fall closed.

He felt an aching need to provide comfort. He looked

around the room, thinking he could give her an extra blanket or pillow. There were none. He considered combing her hair. But she obviously wanted to hang onto the comb. Plus, her hair was dirty and horribly tangled, and he knew he'd hurt her no matter how gentle he tried to be. Instead, he reached out and softly enveloped her small hand in his own. The cold of her skin shocked him. He reached out with his second hand to sandwich hers between both of his, trying to warm her. But the cold persisted. As the cold was absorbed into his own palms, a deep and powerful shudder rolled through his entire body. And it struck Miles that this helpless, weak child was, in a way, an embodiment of innocence. That her condition was, in microcosm, a representation of a dark truth of human nature—of what unchecked greed could do.

For the first time in many years, he wept.

SIXTY

Miles, armed with a Colt revolver and Winchester pump-action shotgun, relieved Sylvia first thing in the morning, sending her home with so many expressions of gratitude that she grew annoyed with him. Then he called Floyd at his hotel to ask if he had any idea what *how tong* meant—it had been nagging at him since he woke up.

"I have no idea what it means," Floyd said. "Why?"

"It was something the girl kept saying last night. She was trying to tell me something. Maybe something about a tong or the highbinders."

"We can ask the interpreter when he gets back."

Miles hung up and took stock of the situation. The room in which the Chinese girl slept was windowless and secure. Yet it would be a strain on his already meager manpower to post a continuous guard, and he didn't give old Dr. Boren good odds in a shootout. Thus, it seemed to Miles that the best option was to get the girl out of there and hide her. So, when Dr. Boren arrived, Miles asked how soon it would be safe to move her. Boren was adamantly opposed to the idea until Miles explained that someone would almost surely try to kill her, and that if Boren was around when they came, he'd end up with a second navel.

"I see your point," Boren said. "But if she absolutely has to move, I'd rather she move to Swedish Hospital in Seattle than to some hiding place on the island." He shoved his hands into his lab coat pockets and appeared to deliberate. "Then again, a journey by steamship would probably be worse than a short drive. The critical thing is that she not try to get up. She can put absolutely no strain on her abdomen. None whatsoever. So we would need to remove her on a litter upon which she could stay horizontal and immobile. But let's wait until afternoon."

"Better to get her out of here immediately."

"No. I want to observe her for a bit after she wakes up. And I want her to sleep as long as possible. Anyway, we need to wait for the tetanus serum coming on the boat from Seattle."

Miles considered arguing. But his subconscious had already directed his right hand to the reassuring bulk and coldness of the giant gun holstered at his hip. For the time being, he'd protect her personally. "I guess we'll wait then."

"Good. Also, where are you going to take her?"

"Somewhere nobody will find her. A place where her presence won't expose anyone else to danger."

"That's rather vague."

"It's probably better that I not tell you, Doc."

"What if I wish to check on her wellbeing?"

"We're balancing risks."

"As a medical man, I have an ethical responsibility. I'm afraid I have to insist on access."

"If you're going back and forth to her hiding place, someone could follow you."

"Then I'll stay with her."

"Doc—"

"I insist."

*****

After observing the Chinese girl all morning, satisfied that she was at least stable for the time being, Dr. Boren helped Bill and Miles fashion a litter out of a thick wool blanket, a wooden plank, and a couple of two-by-fours Miles retrieved from his mother's house. They secured the girl to it and carefully loaded her into the back of Miles's truck. Then, at very slow speed and with tremendous caution, Miles drove Bill, Boren, and the girl to the remote and sparsely populated southwestern part of the island where they moved her to a vacant fishing shack at the extreme edge of a place unofficially known as Grandma's Cove. There were several other shacks and plank houses in varying states of disintegration around the shores of the cove. Vanishing monuments to a dying culture, all but one of them abandoned. But Miles knew the bent old man who lived, part time, in the most intact of them at this time of year. Known to locals as Indian John Tse-nah-talc, he was the very last of a once numerous group of natives who would come to the same cove each year to reef net for salmon in their traditional manner. Though the shoreline reef netting fishery had long since collapsed with high-capacity commercial fish traps and purse seiners decimating the local salmon runs, Indian John still came each year. But, as there was little to catch close to shore anymore, he rarely bothered to fish. Maybe he just needed a break from his half-dozen grandchildren who lived next door to his permanent home on Lummi Island. Whatever the case, having known and liked Miles since Miles was a young boy exploring the island with his fishing rod, and with the understanding that Bill or Miles would be checking in on a daily basis and that Boren would be there taking care of the Chinese girl, Indian John was happy to help by keeping a quiet eye on the shack. It was on the far side of the cove from his own, but in clear view. He could walk to the nearest house and place a call to the station if anything was urgently needed or seemed amiss. In the meantime, they were leaving the girl and Boren with plenty of food, water, medicine, and soft cots with warm blankets.

*****

"Where have you two been?" Floyd asked as Miles and Bill got back to the station.

"Hiding the girl," Bill said.

"Where?"

"In the boondocks," Miles said. "Rest assured, nobody will find her."

"Including me, apparently."

"Sorry. She's in a shack on the southeast side of the island. It's hard to explain how to get there. The place doesn't even have an official name."

"Huh. Well, four things," Floyd continued. "First, I'm afraid Li 'William' Guozheng, our Cantonese interpreter from the other day, is unavailable."

"For how long?"

"For forever. He's dead. His landlady found him in bed with his throat cut."

"A tong murder?"

"Undoubtedly."

"Bastards must have abducted his mother to compel him to break off helping us and go home. Then they killed him. We'd better go find those damned highbinders again. They just jumped back to the top of our list of suspects."

"Actually, his murder might not signify all that much with respect to our investigation."

"Meaning what?"

"William may have been punished for merely being involved in the interrogation of a highbinder in general. Not necessarily because the particular highbinder we had in custody might have been involved in the *Lucky Lena* hijacking."

"He was an interpreter, not a snitch."

"The tongs may not appreciate the distinction. They're rather a disciplined bunch."

"I still think we should lock up the highbinders until we know more."

"I agree."

"I imagine it'll be difficult for your headquarters to find us another interpreter when word spreads that William had his throat cut over the same job."

"Believe it or not, they've already found one for us," Floyd said. "Young fella from Hong Kong who works with a professor of anthropology at the University of Washington."

"Young fella who doesn't read the *Seattle Times* murder column, apparently."

"Our gain. His name is Kuang. Albert Kuang. He'll arrive on tomorrow's 10 a.m. steamer from Seattle."

"Great. Let's make sure we meet him at the dock to give him an armed escort."

"Amen. And by the way, I had headquarters ask Kuang what *how tong* means."

"And?"

"*How tong* means *it hurts*."

Miles closed his eyes. "Oh, mercy."

"I know."

A silent moment passed.

"What were the other things?" Miles finally asked.

"Huh?"

"When we came through the door, you said there were four things."

"Oh—sorry. The lawyer who came to spring Kwan Ping—headquarters says he's known to work for the Sun Wui tong. So now we at least know Ping is a highbinder, as well as which syndicate is operating in the area."

Miles looked at the clock. "Oh—I have to run."

"I have more for you."

"Walk with me. I'm heading to the grocer."

Miles and Floyd went out the door. "The last thing was that a man named Bruce Anders, who said he plays bridge with Dr. Boren, came by the station and told me he saw Rupert Hawkins going into the Methodist church again last night. That Hawkins was weeping, looking like he was losing his mind. Anders thought you should know."

"Maybe Hawkins needs a confessor," Miles said. "Sean Brennan!" he shouted as they were walking up the block on the opposite sidewalk. Brennan looked up, then crossed over to their side.

"Hey there, Sheriff. Detective."

"You coming from the docks? You seen your pal Rupert Hawkins around?"

"That drunk is no pal of mine, Sheriff. Why?"

"You're looking for Hawkins?" Jacob Fields, the dry goods shop owner said, peeking out from under the hood of his car ten yards down the block. "He was just here."

"Just now?" Miles asked, looking up and down the street.

"About five minutes ago. Right when I started trying to replace this drive belt," he said, holding out the frayed black band as if to prove he wasn't making the story up. "Matter of fact, I thought he was going into your station. Stood outside it for a good minute, muttering gibberish to himself. Even reached for the doorknob at one point. Then he staggered off."

"Sounds like he wants to tell us something," Floyd said.

Brennan huffed. "Good luck. By this time of day, that wino imbecile is usually too drunk to put a coherent sentence together."

"It's barely after four," Floyd said.

"He's usually sober in the morning," Brennan added, "if you catch him before ten or eleven o'clock."

"Which direction did he go?" Miles asked.

"Got in his car right up there," Fields said, pointing, "then headed northwest on Second Street."

"The direction of Roche Harbor," Floyd muttered. "And the Smokehouse."

Miles took a step toward his truck, then stopped in his tracks. "Let's pick him up at his house in the morning, when he's relatively clearheaded," Miles said. "We'll pump him full of coffee and withhold his booze until he talks."

"We're not going to get him now?" Floyd asked.

"No. Brennan's right. He'll be incoherently drunk by this hour."

"If he can drive himself to Roche Harbor, I'm sure he can talk."

"It'd be like talking to a three-year-old. Trust me. It's not worth the trouble."

"Then let's at least lock him in the cell until he sobers up."

"And have to clean vomit tomorrow? No. We'll pick him up in the morning."

Floyd gave him a long, hard look. "Tell me this isn't because you're desperate to see Marion."

"Easy does it, Floyd."

"You're making a mistake."

"Floyd, we have another interpreter coming from Seattle tomorrow, an eyewitness survivor who's going to tell us everything, and we know exactly where Hawkins will be in the morning. Take a deep breath. We're almost home."

SIXTY-ONE

Despite Floyd's reproach, Miles grinned, then whistled—actually whistled—the tune of Paul Whiteman's "Whispering" as he walked up the street to the grocer. In all likelihood, the case would be solved the next day, and he was, at long last, going to be able to spend real time with Marion. With only Marion.

At the market, he gathered sausages, bread, and mustard, then deliberated over whether to get ginger or raisin cookies, wondering which Marion would prefer. He put two ginger cookies in paper, began wrapping them, then reopened the paper and put them back on the baker's shelf, opting for the raisin cookies instead.

"You going to touch every single cookie before you make up your mind, Miles?" the old shopkeeper said with a smile. "Some things never change."

Nearly half an hour early, he parked his truck on the shoulder of the main road above Mulno Cove and set off down the short trail to the beach—a trail he and Marion had created in innumerable trips to the cove throughout their youth—picking a quart of ripe blackberries as he went. The trail—still faintly visible though they hadn't used it in years—emerged onto a small sandy beach, at the top of which the remains of their old fire pit still sat. He gathered dried grass, twigs, and small logs of driftwood, got a fire going, then dragged larger logs around it for seating. He found a big sun-bleached plank and set it across two of the big logs to serve as a table for two. Topping it all, he found a log that was the perfect size to serve as the battleship should he talk her into a game of Sink the *Deutschland*.

In a hopeless attempt to occupy his excited and impatient mind, he began skipping rocks out over the cove, never getting more than five skips in a row. He wondered what he'd say to Marion when she arrived—how far he'd be willing to go to convince her not to go back to New York. Probably as far as it took. As he reflected on his feelings in the days since her arrival, he realized that the mere possibility that he might make a life with her had filled his imagination with warm visions of the future. Filled him with a renewed sense of purpose.

As if it were a sign, he spied a fist-sized, emerald green blown glass float of the sort Japanese fisherman used with their nets and droplines. They were Marion's favorite thing to find when beachcombing. Like treasure to her. For his own part, it had always fascinated Miles that such a thing could break loose in a storm, float—for months or even years—all the way across the Pacific Ocean, and wash up intact on a beach of San Juan Island. He wondered what life was like where it came from. Probably simpler.

Tiring of skipping rocks, he took the glass float back up by the fire and wiped it clean with a handkerchief, then occupied himself setting out plates and napkins. Among the jumbled scraps of wood that were always to be found at the high tide line, he found and sharpened a pair of long, thin sticks they could use to roast their sausages over the fire.

Shadows of the tallest trees began to creep out onto the top of the beach as the evening sun slowly descended in the west. Checking his pocket watch, Miles saw that Marion was now twenty minutes late. No matter. She was probably helping her mother and Sylvia clean up from their dinner. He strained his ears, trying to hear if any cars were motoring along the road out by the trailhead. He heard nothing but birdsong.

A large ship steamed into view, running north, up the San Juan Channel. Taking a second glance, Miles realized that it was the Deepwater Doubloon. He wondered if Gustav Hauer were aboard, and whether his crew had had any luck locating the wreck of the *Empress of Burma*.

Another ten minutes went by. He added wood to the fire. Perhaps Marion's mother had needed the car to visit her ailing grandfather, so Marion had chosen to walk. That would triple the amount of time it would take her to get to the cove. But they'd still have plenty of daylight. Not the end of the world.

Miles decided to start playing Sink the *Deutschland* on his own. He dragged a driftwood log to the north end of the cove, tipped it up on end, and let it fall into the water with a huge splash. Then he gave one end of it a shove with his foot to get it out into the tidal current. As it floated along, he noticed, for the first time, that was an unusual log, with curving, irregular bands of light and dark brown wood. Not from any tree that grew in Washington State. Maybe from some faraway tropical rainforest. It was exotic. Beautiful. It had probably broken loose and rolled off the heaving deck of a barge or cargo ship in some long-forgotten Pacific storm.

He threw stone after stone at the log as the outbound tide slowly drew it south and away from shore. But he was out of practice and most of his throws missed badly, falling short, even at relatively close range. The further away the log drifted, the fewer hits he scored. And soon the log was so far offshore that he was throwing rocks as hard and high as he could, just hoping he might come close. Desperate throws. 'Hail Mary's, as they called them in football. Eventually, it was beyond his range no matter how hard he threw. But it still took him a while to give up.

As he walked back up the beach, he heard light rustling in the brush to his left. *At last.* "It's not like you to get lost in the woods," he said. But then, to his disappointment, a young doe emerged from the trees, froze in its tracks, and stood staring at him with its big, innocent brown eyes. "Sorry," Miles said out loud. "You weren't who I was expecting." The doe wandered off and disappeared.

He stoked the bonfire once again, stretched out on a patch

of relatively clean sand, crossed his hands behind his head for a pillow, gazed up into the clear evening sky, and took a deep breath of fresh air through his nostrils. How he loved this place. This island, this cove. His mind once again drifted, this time back to memories of smiles and laughter on other Indian summer evenings with Marion at this very beach. Blackberry picking that always degenerated into blackberry fights, each of them in turn attacking or retreating, ducking behind giant logjams of driftwood. Both of them knowing their mothers would be furious because of the dark juice stains all over their clothes, the pulp of smashed berries stuck in their hair and smeared on their skin. Neither of them caring a bit.

An idea came to him: they could build a house here, on Mulno Cove. Why not? After all, it was their mutual favorite place when they were kids. Their stomping ground. Why not raise their own children here?

You're getting a little ahead of yourself, big guy, he thought.

Still, he could picture it. A small, simple house with a barn and workshop. A vegetable garden. Fruit trees. A view out over the water, framed by grand old Douglas firs and maples. Kids running around. Boys. Two fair-haired boys. He'd teach them to fish for trout and salmon, just as his own father had taught him. Teach them to dig for clams. To forage for mussels and oysters and wild berries. Teach them to work on car engines. They'd grow up capable but without destructive ambition. Maybe they would study at the University of Washington. Maybe they would design the next great automobile. Whatever they did, wherever they went in life, Miles and Marion would be proud of them.

Miles had to laugh. He usually found such sentimentality hugely annoying in other people. Yet here he was, his mind unwilling to let the vision go. It filled him with a degree of optimism and joy he hadn't felt since before the war. He saw himself and Marion on their back porch, watching the boys play catch with a football in the shade of a great willow. He could hear them talk, could smell their sweat. He saw snow-covered pastures and the family gathered around a Christmas tree. He saw Marion and their sons catching flounder from the shore of False Bay. He saw a graduation ceremony at the school playfield on a sunny June day. Saw his younger son congratulating his older brother who wore a cap and gown and stood proud on the front steps of the school. From where he and Marion stood by the waiting car, Miles tried to call out to the boys, but his voice caught in his throat. Then, to his horror, he realized that he couldn't remember their names. Couldn't call to mind the names of his own sons.

He woke with a start. He'd been dreaming. A dream so joyful and glorious that it was painful to leave behind. He sat up and looked around. The sky was dark. The fire had burned down to a handful of dying embers. He was still laying on the sand. The temperature had dropped and the cold had penetrated his clothes to the point that he was now chilly. The beach was still deserted. He was alone.

With a deep breath and a heavy heart, he slowly got to his feet. He kicked sand over the embers to extinguish them, kicking harder than he needed to. Not bothering to gather the picnic things, he groped his way through the dark, back up the trail and on out to his truck.

*****

Arriving at home, he kicked off his boots, drank a large glass of water, and tiptoed upstairs to his room, not wanting to wake his mother. Switching on the light, he found a fine stationary envelope atop his bedspread. His mother had probably left it there for him to find. There was no address or stamp. Just his name, written with a fountain pen. He recognized Marion's penmanship. *Ah, an explanation*, he thought, tearing it open. *Dear Miles,* it read. *By the time you read this, I'll be gone.*

The world capsized like a top-heavy ship—rolling sideways, then upside down. He read something about Marion and Sylvia catching the eastbound Oriental Limited out of Seattle that night. Something about Marion not belonging in Friday Harbor anymore. Something about always loving him like a brother. It was at that point that Miles paused and sat down on the corner of his bed to catch his breath.

The bottom dropped out of his stomach. He felt cold. He'd been a fool. Delusional. A part of him knowing, all along, that she would never end up with him, living on a quiet cove just down the road from their childhood homes, following the pattern of their parents' lives. The signs had always been there, after all. Her enduring interest in venturing beyond the horizon. The arm's-length way she'd dealt with him. The subtle but unmistakable distancing. His longtime sense that she was holding back some essential part of herself.

Not bothering to change into pajamas, Miles flopped over in bed, fully clothed, and stared out his window into the darkness.

SIXTY-TWO

Miles spent a wretched and largely sleepless night trying to cope with a profound sense of loss and rejection. With wave after wave of sadness and emotional pain. To his great irritation, he also found himself thinking about things his mother had said—for example, that he was, perhaps, getting too old to find someone to share his life with.

Were things already as good as they were ever going to get for him? Would he spend the rest of his days in a job he disliked and living with his mother? He felt as if he'd missed some eminently important train. One that bore away his rediscovered sense of meaning in life. In a way, of course, last night's eastbound Oriental Limited had done just that.

Wide awake sometime after 3 a.m., he considered going on a night watch. He could play a little Sidney Bechet when his arms tired of holding the binoculars. It would kill time, if nothing else. But he couldn't muster the motivation to sit up, let alone get dressed. He fell asleep an hour later.

He woke with the sun, but with no desire to get out of bed. For more than an hour, he lay there imagining Marion on the train to Chicago, passing the great peaks of the Rocky Mountains, their summits lit pink in the predawn Montana light, Marion and Sylvia waking up to a breakfast service of hot scones and jam with a pot of gourmet coffee. The vision made the inside of his rib cage feel empty but for a few butterflies, while an odd tingle radiated down his arms, hands, and fingers, making them feel weak. He wanted nothing more than to go back to sleep.

At least the investigation was nearing closure, thank heaven.

The investigation. Ugh.

He remembered that he needed to meet the new Cantonese interpreter dockside when he arrived on the morning boat from Seattle. With a groan, he dragged himself out of bed and shuffled his way to the bathroom where the simple task of brushing his teeth somehow took him more than five minutes.

"Sleeping the day away?" Nellie asked when he found her in the kitchen preparing to can a batch of string beans from her vegetable garden. He didn't bother to answer. "Much as I did when you were still a *child*, Miles, I'll remind you to please close the windows when you go to bed at night so that we don't get flies and mosquitos in the house."

"What are you talking about?" he asked, irritated, as he reached for the coffee can, Monsieur Rousseau glaring at him from his cat pillow in the corner.

"You left the window open last night."

"I did not."

"You certainly did."

"Which window?"

"The one next to the back door."

Miles walked to the back of the house for a look.

"I've already shut it," she called after him. "You needn't trouble yourself now."

But I didn't open it either, Miles thought.

It was an ordinary 12-pane sash window next to their back door. It wasn't latched—but then, they usually only latched their windows if they were leaving home for an extended absence. Everything appeared normal from the inside. However, when he opened the back door, a foot-long splinter of wood came off the doorframe and fell at his feet.

What the hell?

The doorframe had a huge crack in it, and in the part of the frame just below the latch there was a deep square impression in the wood—like that of a pry bar being used to try to force the door open. Peeking out, he saw that the outside of the window frame had a similar mark and similar damage. The lilies of the valley below the window were trampled.

He tried to raise the window from inside the house and found that it stopped after about five inches—not enough of a gap for a man to squeeze through. He lowered the window, then tried to raise it again with the same result. It jammed, solidly, five inches up. The frame must have warped over the years, and they'd never noticed before because they almost never opened this particular window.

Miles stepped outside and scanned the surrounding area—the yard, the orchard, the edge of the nearby forest—hoping to spot a meaningful clue. Then he made a quick circuit of the house, examining each first-floor window and the front door. Everything else looked normal.

"Someone tried to break in last night," he said, returning to the kitchen, explaining his findings to his mother.

"What of value would someone expect to steal from here?" Nellie asked. "Some bent silver forks? The old clock?"

"They were probably looking for me, Mother."

"Looking for you?"

"With bad intent. Pack an overnight bag. I'm taking you to stay with Meredith Bailey until this is over."

"I'm not going anywhere."

"Don't be ridiculous. What if they come back? Are you going to run away? You can hardly walk with your bad hip." He pictured her limping, fleeing for her life in midnight darkness.

"Miles—"

"Having you here means *both* of us are in danger. And having to worry about you makes me more vulnerable."

"Miles, I am not about to let some unknown scoundrel force me out of my own home. Who will look after Monsieur Rousseau?"

"Monsieur Rousseau? Who gives a . . ." Stopping himself, Miles wiped his hands over his face. "Look, you can bring your cat, alright?"

"No."

"Why on earth not?"

"A person has to draw a line, Miles. What if I don't stand up for what's right? Where will I be then?"

"You'll be alive, mother! How does that sound?"

This seemed to startle her for a split second. But she reverted to her initial rigidity in the blink of an eye. "No, Miles. You're either a part of civilized society or you're not. I refuse to enable chaos and bad deeds by thinking only of myself."

"For heaven's sake! You really think that by . . . You know what? Never mind."

Instead of moving his mother to a safe house, he spent the next half hour nailing all of the first-floor windows shut with a hammer and a box of ten penny nails.

"You're going to ruin the window frames."

"I'm being careful not to hit the wood."

"You'll ruin them."

"It's either this, or I bind, gag, and drag you out of here."

The windows secured, he went back upstairs to his bedroom closet and took from it the old, lightweight .410 double-barrel birding shotgun he'd used as a kid, loaded it, and took it back downstairs to his mother. "You remember how to use this?"

"Of course."

"It's only birdshot, so aim for the face."

"I'm not an idiot."

"I can have Bill bring you a revolver when—"

"Miles, go to work. Quit worrying about me. I'll be fine."

He insisted that she bolt both doors and wedge chairs against them after he left. "And don't open the door to anyone—I mean *anyone*—you don't know. Or anyone you *do* know, for that matter."

"I'll say it again. I'll be fine."

SIXTY-THREE

Miles found Bill waiting on the street in front of the steamship terminal. The *Bangor* was just tying up in a hard, steady rain. "Morning, Bill. Didn't think you abided Chinese where it wasn't absolutely necessary."

"Figured you could use an extra set of eyes while we escort this Chink interpreter to the girl. Someone to watch your back."

"I appreciate it."

"By the way, that salvager you guys have been talking about. The Deep, uh . . ."

"Deepwater Doubloon."

"That's the one. I saw its tender tied up on the wharf about an hour ago. Thought you might want to know."

"Was anyone aboard?"

"Two crewmen. They looked to be loading crates of food and a coil of heavy cable."

"No officers? A middle-aged, barrel-chested blonde guy, maybe?"

"No officers that I saw. Crewmen were lanky and pretty young, I'd say. They loaded their stuff and motored back out into the channel. I didn't see the salvage ship itself."

Probably just provisioning, Miles thought. Still, it would have been good to find out exactly what they were up to.

It took a few minutes for workers to secure the ship to the pier and maneuver the gangplank into place. Then the passengers from Seattle started to stream off, scurrying in all directions once they passed through the terminal and emerged onto the rainy street. Miles glanced over the crowd, looking for an Asian face.

There were fishermen, tradesmen, businessmen, a handful of women—some of their faces partially obscured by the umbrellas, hats, or folded newspapers they were using to keep dry. All Caucasians. No Chinese. A couple more lollygaggers trickled off, bringing up the rear. And that was it.

Damn it. "Bill, go ask the office for the inbound manifest, will you? I'm going to check onboard. Maybe the guy fell asleep on the toilet or something."

"Will do."

Miles had to flash his sheriff's badge and threaten to toss people into the water to convince the crewmen to let him aboard the ship without a ticket. He made a quick stop on the bridge, assuring the captain he wouldn't detain them for more than a few minutes and confirming the vessel hadn't made any unscheduled stops between Seattle and Friday Harbor. Then, as a couple dozen Seattle-bound passengers began boarding, and with the help of two crewmen, he did a quick sweep of the passenger areas to make sure the interpreter wasn't, for whatever reason, still aboard. He wasn't.

Miles met Bill back at the main entrance to the terminal. "Here's a strange thing," Bill said. "There *is* a Chinese name on the manifest."

"Kuang?"

"Kuang. Yes. That was it. They have him down as boarding in Seattle."

"But he never disembarked," Miles said, more to himself than to Bill.

"Should we stop the boat?"

Miles turned to watch as crewmen began unmooring the *Bangor* from the pier. "No," he said at last.

"Could be the guy got cold feet and is hiding somewhere onboard."

"No," Miles said again. "He's not on there. Someone threw him overboard. He's dead."

"What makes you—"

"How was your picnic with Marion?" they heard Floyd shout as he approached from up the street. His voice carried an uncharacteristically disapproving tone, which immediately got Miles and Bill's attention.

"Uh—"

"The picnic you went on when we should have been interrogating Rupert Hawkins."

"Good morning to you too, Floyd."

"I hope it was worth it."

"What is your issue?"

"Just got a call from the lime works. Hawkins's body washed up in Roche Harbor this morning."

SIXTY-FOUR

Miles, Floyd, and Dr. Boren squatted over the body of Rupert Hawkins, face-up on a tarp in an unused storage shed at Roche Harbor. Lime kiln workers had pulled his body from the shallows near the Smokehouse pier after a morning shift stevedore spotted it.

"He wasn't in the water very long," Dr. Boren said. "As you can plainly see, he's still in his street clothes, and they appear to be in relatively good order considering the man's standard of attire. So he probably drowned right here in the calm waters of Roche Harbor."

"*Did* he drown?" Miles asked. "Or did he die before going into the water, like Akroyd?"

"There is blunt force trauma to the back of his skull. Looks like a single whack from some sort of small club. An axe handle, maybe. But it looks like he did indeed drown. His lungs were full of seawater. I'll be able to tell you more once I cut into him."

"Someone clubbed him unconscious and tossed him into the water," Floyd surmised.

"So it would seem," Boren said. "Unless he slipped, fell backward, hit his head, and fell into the water all on his own. But given the angle of the injury to his skull, that strikes me as rather unlikely."

"He was probably drinking at the Smokehouse, as was his habit," Miles said. "His assailant probably waited until Hawkins was thoroughly soused and heading home, then rang his bell and tossed him off the pier. Easy work."

Miles and Floyd went to the Smokehouse to take statements

from the customers. But there were only two people there—a bartender and a carpenter from the lime works—neither of whom had been in the speakeasy the night before. Or so they said.

Next, they looked for Hawkins's car. It hadn't been parked up on the main road, so they searched the lime works property. Happily, they didn't run into hotheaded Errol Buchannan. But they didn't find Hawkins's car either.

"Maybe someone gave him a ride out here," Floyd said.

"Maybe the same someone who sent him to his reward," Miles said. "Maybe Reverend McCaskill. Maybe a tong highbinder. Maybe whoever enforces the collection of Smokehouse gambling debts."

"We'll probably never know, thanks to your careless—"

"Hey, now!"

"Hey now, what?"

"You forget yourself, Floyd."

"No, Miles. It's *you* who forgot *yourself* yesterday evening."

"I don't need you to—"

"Hawkins was a suspect and a critical witness."

"Floyd—"

"As important as Hawkins was, for you to simply—"

"Alright, already! I take your point. I made a bad decision."

"A very bad decision."

"Yes, Floyd. A very bad decision."

*****

Miles and Floyd drove straight from Roche Harbor to McCaskill's homestead, intending to arrest him if he didn't have a viable alibi for the previous night. Though both men had serious doubts that McCaskill had killed the Jensens and the Chinese girls, he'd certainly demonstrated a willingness to hurt Hawkins.

They came to a skidding halt in the gravel of McCaskill's

drive, hopped out, drew their guns, and ran straight for the front door of his cabin. Miles gave it a loud knock while Floyd stood back with his pistol up and ready in case the man came out fighting.

"McCaskill!" Miles shouted. "Come out of there."

There was no response.

"If you don't open this door in five seconds, we're kicking it in."

Still no response.

"Hell with it," Miles muttered, raising his foot and smashing the door in with one mighty kick. He and Floyd burst in, ready for action. But McCaskill wasn't there. They repeated the same act over at the chapel, but found it to be empty too.

They did a quick search of the property, not even sure of what to look for. The cabin and chapel were, predictably, monastic. They found bibles, hand-carved Latin crosses, handmade cups and plates, homespun clothing, and very basic furnishings—but nothing to suggest that McCaskill had killed Hawkins or anyone else. In fact, there was nothing there to indicate that McCaskill had any interests beyond his religious beliefs. No books, no musical instruments, no artwork, no flowers. Just bare necessities and Christian paraphernalia.

*****

They drove back to Friday Harbor in silence.

"Drop me at my hotel, if you would," Floyd asked as they approached town.

"What for?"

"Hawkins is as dead as a doornail. McCaskill is in the wind. I'm assuming it isn't feasible to swear in a posse and search your entire godforsaken 50-square-mile island for the highbinders. And we can't communicate with the surviving girl until headquarters hoodwinks or browbeats another Cantonese interpreter into coming up here and helping us. According to my reckoning, aside from going back to the Smokehouse and canvassing possible witnesses this evening, that leaves us dead in the water, if you'll pardon the expression. I'm going to have myself a proper lunch and then maybe take a nap."

*****

Miles dropped Floyd at his hotel, then went on to the station. A small crowd was gathered at the front door.

"Sheriff, is there a maniac loose on the island?" someone yelled.

"Whose body did you find this time?" yelled someone else.

"Should we stay locked up in our homes?"

"Will you swear in a posse?"

"Do you think we should send our women and children off the island?"

Miles dismissed the crowd brusquely, shouting over the din that everyone should just go about their business and let him do his job, that he was doing all he could, but that people should be mindful of their surroundings.

"Mindful of our surroundings?" someone shouted back. "The hell does that mean?"

But Miles was done with them. He pushed his way through the throng to the front door. Bill was waiting for him with a fresh percolator of strong black coffee. "Bless you, Bill," Miles said, gladly accepting a cup. "What a morning." He filled Bill in on how things went at Roche Harbor as Bill made him a sourdough flapjack without bothering to ask if he was hungry.

"Where does Floyd get off?" Bill asked. "City boy telling you your business like that."

"No, he's absolutely right. Irritating, but right. If I hadn't been so stubborn about meeting Marion, we'd be sweating Hawkins for all he's worth right now. Maybe cracking the case wide open. Instead, Hawkins is dead, our interpreter is probably dead, a killer is now almost certainly active on the island, the local population is terrified, and Marion is gone. I struck out, Bill."

"Don't be too hard on yourself," Bill said, setting the buttery, honey-glazed flapjack down in front of Miles. "A lot of what's been happening is out of your hands."

"I struck out. Plain and simple." He took a sip of hot coffee.

Bill's face had a troubled expression.

"You alright?" Miles asked him.

"Maybe. I don't know. I hate to be paranoid," Bill said.

"About what?"

"Well, I'm sure he had legitimate reasons. But I noticed Floyd hiring a car ride from down near the steamship terminal yesterday, just after you left for your picnic. I happened to be heading home and, by sheer coincidence, ended up following right behind him."

"So?"

"His hired car turned north on Tucker Avenue."

"Which turns into Roche Harbor Road."

"Exactly. It's probably nothing. I just thought you should know."

"Thank you," Miles said, staring into his coffee cup, feeling the walls falling in around him. That was all he needed—another reason to be suspicious of Floyd. Questions began to assault his mind. Why would Floyd have hired a ride out toward Roche Harbor? Maybe he was just exploring. Why did he look so worried when they were motoring out to recover the surviving witness from Halibut Island? He was probably just terrified of riding a small boat across the choppy Haro Strait. How did he come out of their fight with six roughnecks in Seattle completely unscathed? Perhaps he really was that good a street fighter. Perhaps he fought with his elbows. Maybe, probably, perhaps. And topping it all was the as yet unanswered question of who told Seattle's chief of police to send Floyd up to Friday Harbor in the first place, and why? Miles had no sure answers.

Could Floyd actually be a cold-blooded killer? Could he have murdered Hawkins, then used feigned outrage over Miles keeping his date with Marion in order to cover his own tracks? There was just no way. Floyd's mother had seemed so virtuous. She couldn't possibly have raised a cold-blooded killer for a son.

Could Floyd be a corrupt cop? Sure. There were plenty of corrupt cops out there. Paid to look the other way. To inform. To be someone's marionette. But corruption was one thing, murder something else. Floyd couldn't be a murderer. No way in hell. An accomplice, perhaps? An accessory?

The uncertainty was driving him to distraction. He had to settle the issue for himself, one way or the other, once and for all.

*****

Miles drove back out to Roche Harbor and the Smokehouse speakeasy. "Everybody just go about your business," he told the only four people there. "I'm just looking for someone who might have some information I need. Nobody is going to get hauled in for having himself a drink."

He seated himself at a table in the far corner from the bar and began dealing himself a hand of solitaire with a grimy deck of cards he found there. He only played three hands before Jane Hill—the hotel dishwasher, drinking buddy, and reluctant occasional girlfriend of Rupert Hawkins—shuffled in and took a stool at the bar.

"Miss Hill," Miles said, causing her to look over her shoulder at him.

"I ain't seen Rupert today," she said, turning away again.

"I believe you. When was the last time you did see him?"

She took a moment, probably pondering the consequences of not answering. "Saw him yesterday."

"What time?"

"I'm not for sure. Afternoon."

"Here?"

"Sure, here."

"Who left first, you or him?"

"Him."

"What time was that?"

"Maybe four. Five. I don't know. He usually comes back later in the evening, around nine or ten."

"And when did you leave?"

"Maybe an hour after him."

"Do you remember detective Floyd, the other police officer I came with last time we saw you here?"

"City boy. Fancy suit. Sure, I remember."

"Was *he* here yesterday?" Miles asked with new gravity in his voice.

"He's *your* partner."

"I'm asking you."

She gave him a worried look. "Yeah, he was here. I seen him coming down the pier as I'm leaving."

"On his way to the Smokehouse?"

"Yeah."

"Did he say anything to you?"

"He asked if I knew where Hawkins was. What else? Somebody is always looking for Hawkins."

SIXTY-FIVE

Floyd didn't return to the station until just before the dinner hour. "Any updates?" he asked as he came through the door.

"Not yet," Miles said.

"Really? You didn't get a call from headquarters? They still haven't found an interpreter?"

"Not a single call all day. Where have you been? Not napping this whole time?"

"I walked the trunk line."

"You mean the main cable for the island telephone service?"

"That's right. All the way to where it comes ashore near Pear Point."

"What for?"

"Looking for taps. Looking for clues that someone might be listening in on our phone calls. You said yourself that it seems like we're always a step behind. An eavesdropper could be one explanation."

"Did you find anything?"

"Only a yellow jacket nest in the hollow of a log I was climbing over. Got stung five times. Then, on the walk back here, it dawned on me—the switchboard operator, Eustace, uh . . ."

"Eustace Hampton."

"Yes. Her. Can you see her taking payoffs to report on our telephone conversations?"

"No."

"Everyone has a price."

"Everyone but Eustace Hampton. Did you walk the trunk

line alone?"

"Yes."

"Did anyone see you?" *Anyone who could verify your alibi*, he wanted to ask.

"I don't know. What difference would it make?"

"Investigative confidentiality," Miles offered lamely.

"What?"

"It's best that the general public doesn't know what we're up to. What leads we're pursuing. That sort of thing."

"Okay."

"Did you go back out to Roche Harbor last night?"

The question seemed to catch Floyd off-guard. "Yes."

"Why?"

"Why did I go back out there? Why do you think? To find Hawkins and bring him in."

"Did you go alone?"

"You were with Marion, if you'll recall."

Actually, I wasn't.

"What about Bill?"

"Bill was fixing to go home. And I didn't think I needed backup."

"Why didn't you at least tell me you were there last night? It would seem relevant, especially given that it's approximately where Hawkins's body turned up."

"Am I being cross-examined?"

"It just seems odd."

"I didn't mention it because I guessed—correctly, it seems—that it would irritate you to know that I did so. That I didn't wait for you. That I took independent action even though this is your jurisdiction and your community. Your turf. It didn't make any difference in the end anyway."

"Did you see him?"

"Hawkins? Yeah, we shared a bottle of Glenfiddich," Floyd said. "Of course I didn't see him. If I had, he'd be here, alive, wouldn't he? We'd be questioning him."

Miles gave Floyd a good, long stare, trying to read his mind through his body language. "Sorry," he said at last. "I think I'm overtired. Frustrated and overtired. Forgive me."

"It's nothing."

"Also, Marion stood me up. She's gone. It seems she left for New York before I even went to meet her. Snuck off, I supposed you could say."

"Oh. I'm sorry, Miles. I'm truly sorry."

"You don't sound terribly surprised."

"It isn't really my place to—"

"No, I'd welcome your thoughts."

"My thoughts." He took a moment. "It's just that you seemed a lot more interested in her than she did in you, and that, well..."

"What?"

"You know, she seemed, I guess, close with Sylvia. Very close."

"What do you mean?"

"Like Alice something-or-other and Gertrude Stein."

"Gertrude Stein again? Who the hell is Gertrude Stein?"

"What I'm saying is that maybe they have a sort of Wellesley marriage type of arrangement. A Boston marriage. You know?"

"No, I don't know. What on earth is a Boston marriage?"

"Cohabitation by two women. Two committed women."

"You mean—"

"Yes, I mean. Perhaps Marion is turning into, you know, a lesbian."

Miles's jaw hung open. His blink rate increased. "That's absurd."

"Is it?"

"How does someone turn into a lesbian?"

"Hell if I know. Maybe it's the company they keep. I know of one rather peculiar lay minister in Seattle who blames the occult. And some Arab scholars say it has something to do with lactating mothers eating too much celery when breastfeeding their daughters, or something to do with hot vapors."

"Hot vapors?"

"Whatever that means."

Miles stood dumbfounded. "This damned job. If I'd just had a little more time with her, maybe I could have convinced her to change back."

"I'm afraid I've never heard of it working like that."

Miles shook his head. "Well, damnation," he muttered. "Damnation. I'll tell you, sometimes this world makes no damned sense to me." He took a deep breath, trying to redirect his thoughts back to what he needed to do.

"On an unrelated note, what's on the agenda?" Floyd asked. "And if you need a bit of time alone, I understand."

"I'm fine." He strategized for a silent moment. "Actually, could I trouble you for a favor?"

"What would that be?"

"Tired as I am, I'm worried that if I go for much of a drive, I'll fall asleep at the damned wheel. Could you go and check to make sure our witness is alright?"

"Isn't Dr. Boren with her?"

"He had another emergency to attend to. She probably needs more food and water too."

"Of course. Just tell me where you have her hidden."

Miles took a few minutes to draw a map to the trailhead to Grandma's Cove and describe which old fishing shack the girl was in. Then he gave Floyd a canteen, a bag of fresh fruit and vegetables, and the keys to his truck.

"I'm much obliged," he said as Floyd headed out the door.

SIXTY-SIX

As soon as Floyd was out of sight, Miles ran to Luke Gruden's brand-new REO Speedwagon truck parked just around the corner, found the keys where Gruden promised they'd be, fired up the engine, and raced out Cattle Point Road to find a spot where he could watch Floyd pass by. Knowing that Floyd wouldn't recognize Gruden's truck, Miles parked in the driveway of a random cottage fronting the main road and waited. Less than a minute later, Floyd came rolling by, looking solemn, oblivious to Miles's presence. After waiting half a minute, Miles backed out onto Cattle Point Road and, keeping a healthy distance, began following Floyd down to Grandma's Cove.

His plan was simple. If Floyd was working for whoever hijacked the *Lucky Lena*, then he'd surely have been instructed to kill the girl—the only living witness—if the opportunity presented itself. Floyd's actions here would either incriminate or absolve him, once and for all.

*****

Once he got within half a mile of the cove, Miles slowed to a crawl, watching for his own parked truck. He found it, empty, exactly where he'd told Floyd to leave it. Floyd was nowhere to be seen, meaning he'd probably already walked on down the fishing trail that led to the cove. Taking to the trail himself, Miles paused at each bend, doing his best to peek further down the way to make sure he wasn't going to overrun or be spotted by Floyd. Eventually, the trail opened up at the head of the cove.

The waves of a high tide were churning against the rocks below, drowning out most sound. The tiny fishing shack was in view a few dozen yards to his right, around the length of the cove. Miles began to crouch as he went, ducking behind bushes and trees wherever he could, getting closer and closer to the shack. When he was no more than 50 feet away, he heard a single gunshot from inside.

What the hell?

He sprinted forward, drew his gun, threw open the plank that served as a front door, and, his eyes not yet adjusted to the darkness within, sprang forward and tripped, falling face down onto Floyd. He jumped to his feet as if burned by fire, then scrambled backward, his gun all the while trained on Floyd.

"What—what in the hell!" Miles shouted. "Explain yourself!"

Floyd, who was flat on his back, said nothing. Instead, he held a hand flat against his upper chest as a bloodstain quickly grew beneath it. He was wide-eyed and appeared to be gasping for air. The canteen, fruit, and vegetables he'd brought were strewn about the floor of the otherwise empty shack.

Miles knelt at Floyd's side. Floyd looked up at him, his face a painting of shock and suffering. "Floyd, can you hear me? Floyd? What happened? Who shot you?"

Floyd shook his head weakly, leaving the question unanswered.

His gun up and his finger on the trigger, Miles crossed the floor of the shack, threw the back door open, and raced outside. A dense thicket of brush and small trees began a few feet from the back door, providing perfect cover for anyone fleeing the area. Aside from that, the surrounding land was vacant. Whoever shot Floyd was gone.

SIXTY-SEVEN

"Relatively speaking, he's quite fortunate," Dr. Boren said to Miles back in the all-too-familiar waiting room of his office. "None of his vital organs were hit. The bullet went clean through, un-fragmented, missing the top of his left lung by a hair, then ricocheting off his scapula and exiting his back. There is no major vascular damage. And I don't think he has any nerve damage, but time will tell. Still, he's going to be in an awful lot of pain."

"May I speak with him?"

"You're welcome to try. But I'd recommend waiting until morning. We gave him a lot of morphine. He probably won't respond."

But if he does, his guard might be down, and he might not even remember what we talk about, Miles thought. Moving toward the door of the examination room, Miles realized Dr. Boren was in lockstep behind him. "Ah, Doctor, if you could give me a few minutes alone. We'd be discussing confidential matters concerning our investigation."

"Oh. Yes. Yes, of course."

*****

"Floyd?" Miles said, looking down at him. His shirt had been cut from his body and a large bandage covered the upper left-hand corner of his chest. "Floyd? Can you hear me?"

One of Floyd's eyelids twitched. "Muh?"

"Floyd, who shot you?"

Nothing.

"Floyd," a little louder. "Who the hell shot you?"

"Uhn."

"What?"

Floyd blinked slowly but said nothing else. Miles deliberated for a moment before asking his next question.

"Who do you work for, Floyd?"

Floyd's eyes opened a crack, then closed back up.

"Clancy Donovan? One of the tongs? Floyd, wake up. Floyd! Do you work for Gustav Hauer? For Stenersen?"

It was no use. If Floyd was conscious of Miles's questions at all, then he was ignoring them.

*****

Miles spent the night in Boren's office guarding Floyd, concerned that his assailant might return to finish him off out of fear that Floyd could identify him. He worried, paced, and drank far too much coffee as he reasoned through what had happened, at last coming to the conclusion that he'd once again been a fool. While Floyd could—via Stenersen's influence over Seattle City Hall—be the unwitting minion of rumrunners who wanted to know what had happened to one of their crews, it was highly unlikely that he was anything other than what he claimed to be. If he'd meant to kill the girl, he wouldn't have bothered to carry the canteen, fruit, and vegetables from the truck out to the shack. And he probably would have taken his gun, which he hadn't. Then, of course, there was the fact that he'd been shot—probably by someone who *did* intend to harm the girl. Thankfully, Miles had moved the girl and Dr. Boren out of the shack beforehand—taking them to his mother's house.

Miles was furious with himself. Because of his selfishness, his stupidity, they'd lost the chance to question Hawkins. Because of his paranoia, he'd sent Floyd into harm's way. The man could have been killed. He could end up crippled.

Not even two full days earlier, an end to the investigation had seemed within reach, and Miles had thought himself on the brink of a life-changing reconnection with Marion. Now a key suspect was dead, their sole remaining witness couldn't communicate with them, Floyd had been shot, and Marion was gone. He felt utterly defeated.

SIXTY-EIGHT

Miles was startled awake by the sound of Dr. Boren closing the door to the examination room. Having slept on a chair in the waiting area, his body was sore, his neck stiff.

"Sorry to wake you," Boren said.

"I didn't even hear you come in," Miles said, yawning. "How is your patient."

"Doing well, all things considered, but said he's still in a lot of pain."

"Can I talk to him now?"

"Oh, shoot, Miles. I just gave him another shot of morphine. I should have checked with you first. I apologize."

"When will he be coherent again?"

"Maybe late afternoon."

Damnation! "I see."

"Listen, I'm heading down to Morgan's for breakfast," Boren said. "May I bring anything back for you?"

"No, thank you."

"Well. Coffee is in the cabinet. Please feel free to help yourself."

*****

Struggling to get his mind working after his thoroughly inadequate sleep, Miles was just finishing his third cup of Dr. Boren's awful coffee when Bill threw the front door to Boren's office open, looking spooked. "Sheriff!"

"Bill."

"I just heard. Floyd. Is Floyd okay?"

"He'll live."

"Thanks be to God. And the girl? Is she safe?"

"Yes. Good thing Luke Gruden and I moved her to my mother's house."

"Did Floyd see who shot him?"

"I don't know yet," Miles said. "He went into shock right after I found him and he's still sedated." But then he sat bolt upright, and his eyes popped wide. "Hell's Bells," he whispered.

"What is it?" Bill asked.

"I just . . ."

"What?"

"Something just occurred to me. Look, I have to run. I'll explain later. Listen, do me a favor, will you?"

"Anything. Name it."

"With all due respect to Dr. Boren, I think I'd sleep a whole lot better tonight if actual surgeons took a look at Floyd down at Swedish Hospital. Can you go find Gruden and ask if he can run Floyd to Seattle in his fast workboat this evening? Tell him it's a medical emergency. I'll pay him whatever he wants."

"Right away."

Miles watched Bill go. Once he was out of sight, Miles double-checked that the key to the gun locker was in his pocket, then headed for the station.

*****

As soon as Dr. Boren got back to his office, Miles handed him a double-barreled shotgun.

"Do you know how to use this?" Miles asked.

"Of course. Are we going duck hunting?"

"If anyone comes through your front door without a good reason for being here, shoot them."

"Miles!"

"I'm sorry, but you're my only option, Doctor. Don't let

anyone get to Floyd. I'll return as soon as I can."

*****

Miles returned to Dr. Boren's office just after three. "Is your mind clear?" he asked a very unhappy-looking Floyd, who had a mountain of pillows stacked behind him on the sick bed. His left arm was in a sling and he was gritting his teeth.

"A little too clear," he said slowly and with great effort. "Morphine's wearing off."

"What the hell happened?"

"I remember knocking on the door of the shack. Nobody answered, so I opened it and stepped inside. As I waited for my eyes to adjust to the darkness, someone shot me."

"A highbinder? McCaskill? Anyone we know?"

"Didn't see him. The muzzle flash blinded me just long enough for whoever it was to escape out the back door."

"Damn it to hell! Not your fault, Floyd. But damn it to hell just the same."

"How did you get down there so quickly?"

"Well, ah—"

"Is the girl alright? I don't think she was in there, Miles."

"She wasn't."

"What! Did someone take her?"

"She's alright. Bit of a long story."

"Tell me."

"I'll explain when you're feeling a bit better."

"Miles."

"She was, she'd been . . . I'd already moved her."

"What do you mean? You'd already moved her out of the fishing shack? Before I went there?"

"Yes."

"Then why did you send me to bring food and . . ." He closed his eyes. "You thought I might be the killer."

"I'm sorry."

"Well, well."

"It's my fault that you were shot." Miles swallowed hard and looked away. "You could have been killed."

Floyd gave him a hard look. "Yes. Yes, Miles. I could have been killed."

"I'm so sorry, Floyd," Miles said, taking a seat on Dr. Boren's stool and staring through the floor, reluctant to meet Floyd's eyes. "Heavens above, I'm so sorry."

A quiet moment passed between them. Then Floyd tried to take a deep breath, cutting it short as pain shot through his wounded shoulder. "Look, Miles," he said, wincing. "Maybe if I'd been in your shoes—"

"No, no. You've been nothing but a tremendous help. It was stupid of me."

"A bit stupid. But I'll tell you what. I'll forgive you if you go right now and tell the doc I need another shot of morphine. A big one."

"Oh, boy," Miles said, turning his gaze to the ceiling. "I'd give anything for your forgiveness, Floyd. I really would. But, uh . . . "

"But, uh, what?"

"Let's hold off on the morphine. You have to keep your wits about you."

"What for?"

"Luke Gruden is down at the docks, getting his boat ready to run you down to Seattle."

"The hell are you talking about? Another damned boat ride?"

"I'm sorry."

Floyd groaned. "Someone *shot* me, Miles. Put *a hole* through my body. I could use a little something for the pain. And that something doesn't involve getting in another boat. Plus, the doc said I should stay right here. So, if you please, go tell him I'd like more morphine."

"I'm afraid I have to insist."

"And I'm afraid I might *kill you* if I don't get some morphine *right now.*"

*****

That same evening, Bill got hold of a wheelchair from the widow's rest home on Second Street, and he and Miles rolled Floyd down to the docks where Luke Gruden was warming up his boat. There were a lot of troubled looks on the faces of the townsfolk and fishermen who saw the wounded policeman being sent home. By now, everyone knew who Floyd was—knew he'd come to help solve the tragic, frightening case of the *Lucky Lena* hijacking. But now here he was—a police detective, a trained gunfighter—grievously wounded, having barely escaped with his life, being evacuated. Leaving the rest of them behind to face the unavoidable question that if a policeman was vulnerable to whatever hidden and dark forces were at work there, then who wasn't? And who would be next?

A small crowd gathered and followed them as they rolled Floyd down the dock, some wishing him well, some just staring, looking spooked. At Gruden's slip, a couple of men helped Miles and Bill hoist Floyd—slumped in his wheelchair and wincing with pain from the jostling—over the gunnel of the boat and onto the stern deck. Floyd looked like death, his skin pale, his expression miserable. Gruden rolled him into the wheelhouse and lashed his chair to a post, securing it upright in case they ran into rough water out in the Straits.

Miles and Bill took a minute to wish Floyd a quick recovery and good health. "Tell your mother that my mother wants her recipe for seed cake," Miles said. "You can mail it to me at the station, and I'll see that she gets it."

"Yes, Miles. That will be my absolute top priority the moment I arrive in Seattle," Floyd said, looking like he'd rather gouge Miles's eyes out.

Bill's farewell was physical instead of verbal, as he stood silent and grave, patting Floyd on his good shoulder with his giant paw of a hand.

"Bill, please," Floyd said. "Everything that touches me hurts right now."

"Sorry. I'm sorry this happened to you."

With that, Miles and Bill hopped back onto the dock, untied the lines securing Gruden's boat to the dock cleats, and gave a wave as the boat motored out across Friday Harbor, finally turning south into the San Juan Channel and disappearing around the point as half the town stood and watched.

"Bill," Miles said.

"Sir?"

"I have yet another favor to ask. An important one."

"Anything."

"I have my mother staying at Meredith Bailey's house, out of harm's way, while I have the Chinese girl hidden at ours. I'd feel a whole lot better if you were out there at Meredith's house keeping watch. I just don't want anyone going after her to get to me, you know what I mean?"

"They wouldn't do that."

"I'm not so sure."

"Well, if it would make you feel better."

"Maybe if you just parked at the end of Meredith's drive. Hopefully you'll be able to sleep in your car."

"No problem. I sleep in my car all the time."

"Try not to let the ladies know you're there. I'd never hear the end of it if my mother thought I had someone watching over her."

They parted ways in front of the station as the evening sky began to darken, Bill heading off to gather what he needed for his vigil and Miles standing on the sidewalk for a moment, looking out across the calm, beautiful harbor as if committing the view to memory. As if saying farewell.

"And then there was one," he muttered.

SIXTY-NINE

On his way home, Miles couldn't help taking a long look at Marion's bedroom window as he passed her house. It was, of course, dark. The curtains were open as if to drive home the point that the room was vacated. Empty. It made him sad.

Arriving home, he parked his truck in the barn and closed the doors so that nobody could tell it was there. Walking to the house, he realized that the evening was unusually silent and still. There were no frogs or crickets singing. Not even a breeze. It made him uneasy. He glanced over his shoulder, then scanned the immediate area. Everything appeared normal.

Anticipating a long night, he went into the house and made himself a large pot of coffee. Considering the layout of the house with an eye to defense, he decided he'd surely hear if anyone tried to break through the nailed-shut windows. There was a back door by the pantry, but nowhere to keep an eye on it without being visible through the windows to somebody outside. He thought about covering the windows with bedsheets. But covered windows could make a man suspicious that the house was defended—especially a man who'd been there before, in an attempt to break in, and knew the windows hadn't been covered previously. It was critical that everything look relatively normal—secured, but undefended—so there was nothing that might turn a potential intruder away. Instead, Miles nailed the back door to the outside of its frame, leaving enough of each heavy nail exposed that an intruder would see the nails and, hopefully, attempt entry through the front door instead.

He left one light on in his mother's bedroom on the second

floor, which was normal, then went around turning off all the other lights in the house. Back in the living room, he slid a chair into an alcove where it couldn't be seen from the outside but had a direct view of the front door. He set up a side table next to it, put his loaded gun and his coffee on the table, and took a seat. It was a comfortable chair—his favorite chair in the house. An old velvet wingback in which his father used to bounce toddler Miles on his knee while playing a game they called Rodeo Bronco. A chair in which his mother used to read him stories like *Captains Courageous* and *The Call of the Wild* as he sat on her lap under the warm wool blanket she'd knitted for him just before he was born.

After an hour or so of sitting in the darkness sipping his coffee and periodically rechecking that there was a bullet in every last chamber in the cylinder of his gun, Miles tiptoed to the kitchen and picked up the telephone receiver only to discover that the line was dead. He rocked the cradle a few times in case the mechanism was stuck. Still nothing. No Eustace Hampton. No night operator. No sound at all.

Damn.

It wasn't unusual for the phone service to go out. But it usually happened when a windstorm blew trees or big branches down onto the lines. Tonight, it was dead calm outside.

He made another quick check of the main floor doors and windows, then sat back down in the wingback and began to wonder whether his new hunch was correct. Began to wonder whether anyone would actually show up, and if so, who. Would it be someone who'd hijacked the *Lucky Lena* with a premeditated plan to kill young Chinese girls, like highbinders from a rival tong, or Edward Callahan the anti-Chinese bigot? Or would it be someone who'd been after a load of liquor, opium, or even gold, had been surprised to find the girls aboard, and had killed them to eliminate witnesses to the murder of the Jensens? If the latter, it could be damn near anyone. Thugs of Clancy Donovan, the San Francisco mobster. Associates of Gustav Hauer, the cutthroat marine salvager and treasure hunter. Reverend McCaskill, the violent, deranged Prohibition zealot. The tong highbinders. Or even some as-yet-hidden local pirate. Whoever it was, to be willing to gun down a boatload of defenseless girls took something Miles was beginning to think might be beyond his understanding. Something that went far beyond the human tendency toward destructive greed he'd been preoccupied with since the war. Far beyond the terrible but familiar extremes of human nature. Indeed, if there was such a thing as true evil, then this killer was it.

He finished his cup of coffee and poured another. With nothing to do but wait in silent darkness, and despite his efforts to focus on other things, he once again began to dwell on how badly things had gone over the past several days. Began to feel sorry for himself. It was such an oppressive thought pattern that he considered screaming into the darkness—despite the obvious stupidity of doing so—wondering if it might somehow relieve the pressure.

Then he pictured the grievously wounded Chinese girl with her hopeless eyes staring up at him in Dr. Boren's office. Pictured the dead and bloated bodies of her fellow would-be immigrants. All his own gripes shrank to insignificance and were swept away in a wave of disgust over his self-pity. His problems were nothing compared to the hardships those little girls had endured. Things had been going badly, yes. But now he had a plan. Now he'd taken proactive steps. They might turn out misguided. But at least he'd taken control and set a well-reasoned course.

Taking what comfort he could from this small ember of optimism, he reminded himself that there were still things worth fighting for here. Many good people. A good community. A good way of life.

*****

Over the next couple of hours, he drank his entire pot of

coffee, then started doing jumping jacks—hoping to shake off sleepiness and get his heart pumping—before deciding that it made too much noise. At one point his head jerked so violently that he wondered if he'd fallen asleep. He couldn't be sure, but he suspected that he had since his mind felt a bit fuzzy. He sat still for half a minute, listening for any signs of trouble, not hearing anything but his own breathing. Needing to piss, he tiptoed to the bathroom, taking his gun with him, peeking out the windows as he passed, seeing nothing suspicious. Then, squinting in the darkness as he stood over the toilet doing his best to take aim, he decided that the noise of his urine falling into the water might be loud enough for someone outside the house to hear. So he set his gun on top of the tank, turned around, and sat down on the toilet seat. Afterward, knowing that the bathroom pipes made odd wailing noises when water ran through them, he neither washed his hands nor flushed the toilet.

The air in the house was growing cool. But he didn't want more coffee, and didn't want to bother with a fire in the stove, so, back in the comfortable wingback chair, he pulled a heavy Navajo blanket over his legs. He wanted to read to pass the time, but didn't dare light a candle or electric lamp. It was starting to feel like the longest day of his life.

He wondered where Marion was right now. Perhaps crossing the golden vastness of the Dakota grasslands and barley fields, or passing between the thousands of gemlike Minnesota lakes. He imagined being in her compartment, sipping coffee on a plush red velvet couch as the train rolled east along some untamed river, sounding its lonely horn as it went along. His head cradled in a feather pillow, his face turned so that he could watch the wild country pass by outside the windows, his body perfectly comfortable under fine first-class bedding. Warm. Content. Heading for the bustling city of New York, with its jazz clubs, its restaurants, its unfathomable mix of peoples. Marion smiling at him in the mirror as she sat at the vanity putting on the brilliant red Montana garnet earrings he'd bought for her from an old Kootenai Indian woman when he'd stepped off to stretch his legs at the Kalispell train station.

Dozing and lost in what had become a dream, Miles didn't hear the soft footsteps coming around the front of the house. Didn't hear them coming up the porch stairs and approaching the front door. Nor did he hear the gentle click-clicking of a set of picks slowly and patiently working at the cylinder of the lock.

He jerked awake in the darkness when his head fell forward. It took him a minute to sort out where he was. When he did, a deep sadness washed over him—all the worse because he'd been torn from such a vivid and happy dream. A taste of a future that had felt real. But one that would never be.

He blinked to clear his eyes, but still didn't notice that anything was amiss. Didn't notice the door lock's thumb turn slowly rotating counterclockwise. Didn't notice the door slowly opening. It wasn't until the door was halfway open that his eyes were drawn to the bright outdoor light mounted above the barn door on the other side of the driveway, and his mind, at long last, caught up to the present and told him that things weren't quite as they should be. That he shouldn't have been able to see the barn door light from where he sat—unless the front door was open. And suddenly, he realized that there was a silhouette in the doorway. The silhouette of a large man. A man raising a gun.

With a surge of adrenaline, Miles grabbed for his own gun on the side table and, not finding it, leapt from the chair, diving to his left just as the room exploded in a flash of blinding light, a loud bang, and a cloud of feathers bursting from the back of the chair he'd just vacated. A second bang, and the glass door of his mother's China cabinet shattered a few inches above his back, raining shards down upon him. Crawling on hands and knees as fast as he could go, praying for his flash-blinded eyes to readjust to darkness, for his ears to stop ringing, he reached temporary safety behind the kitchen wall.

Holy Mary!

In a fraction of a second, he realized several things. First, his gun was probably still sitting on the toilet tank in the bathroom, which was on the far side of the house—on the far side of the intruder's line of fire. Second, it wouldn't take long for the intruder to realize that Miles didn't have his gun. Third, there was no way out of the kitchen aside from smashing out one of the windows he'd so thoroughly nailed shut earlier in the day. And he'd never be able to do so quickly enough that the intruder wouldn't be able to turn the corner and shoot him at close range. In short, he was trapped.

Standing up against the wall, Miles grabbed the nearest thing he thought he could use as a weapon—in this case, his mother's big clay sugar jar—and lifted it high, hoping to bring it crashing down on his assailant's head if the man should turn the corner. He strained to hear breathing or footsteps over the ringing in his ears. He couldn't hear the man, but sensed he was drawing near. Feeling he needed a better weapon, he scanned the kitchen, his eyes settling on his mother's rolling pin. It was on the opposite side of the entrance to the kitchen. Miles shouted as he hurled the heavy sugar jar into the parlor, hoping to cause distraction or confusion, then jumped across to the opposite wall, turning for a quick glimpse of the intruder as he did so. A man was indeed there, in shadow, barely five feet away, and as Miles jumped he opened fire, taking two more shots that missed their mark but smashed through a cupboard and window and filled the kitchen with acrid gun smoke. Miles grabbed the rolling pin from the counter, turned, and crouched low, readying himself to spring at the intruder if he entered the kitchen, knowing he was probably going to die. But the next shot that rang out had a deeper tone. And it was louder. A different gun. A bigger gun. As Miles realized this, a man stumbled into the kitchen in front of him and crumpled to the floor, face down, before Miles could even hit him. Frozen in his own confusion, Miles gawked at the fallen man.

"Miles!" a familiar voice called. "You alright?"

"What? I . . . yes. Yes!" He took a few quick, deep breaths, trying to calm himself.

"I'm coming in. Don't shoot me."

"Right."

Miles, still in a crouch, reached up to switch on the kitchen light, then sprang forward to take the prostrate intruder's gun from his hand. He jammed the gun into the belt of his pants, then, in turning the intruder over, yanked the man's arm backward so hard that he probably dislocated his shoulder. Floyd, his left arm still in a sling, his right hand still aiming a gun at the intruder, stepped into the room where he and Miles beheld the ashen face of Sean Brennan, the boat engine mechanic. He was staring at the ceiling, expressionless but alive.

"Brennan?" Miles said, not yet trusting his own eyes. "I can't believe . . ." He left his statement unfinished, trying to sort through his thoughts.

The killer wasn't a dead-eyed tong hatchet man, a fire-breathing temperance fanatic, the bloodthirsty minion of an ambitious rumrunner, nor a venomous hater of Chinese. He wasn't the tool of a big syndicate or conspiracy or movement. He wasn't even an outsider. He was a seemingly ordinary, modest, mildly awkward local man. A man from San Juan Island itself. A place with no gold to be mined nor oil to drill for. No great cities. Nothing much to fight over. A place Miles had thought more or less immune to the forces that seemed to be driving the rest of the world toward oblivion.

"You're going to hang, Brennan," Miles said, still breathing hard, his disbelief turning to anger. To outrage.

Brennan took a shallow breath before answering in a labored voice. "No—no, I don't think so," he said, glancing at the bullet wound in his chest, the blood quickly soaking into his shirt all around it.

"Well, you'll burn in hell, at any rate."

Brennan took another labored breath and flashed a brief, weak smile. "No. Not that, either." A breath. "I thought you knew, Sheriff," he said, sounding almost disappointed. "I thought you understood. There's nothing out there waiting for you. Just darkness. Cold, uncaring darkness." Brennan's eyes seemed to be losing focus. "I can't feel my legs," he muttered, not looking the least bit troubled by the fact. And when he stopped breathing a moment later, he was a picture of serenity. It was as if the man hadn't a care in the world. No pain. No fear.

"Are you hurt?" Floyd asked, holstering his gun.

"No. Well, maybe," Miles said, realizing that he was bleeding from a deep cut in the side of his right hand, but having no idea how or when he'd injured himself. He grabbed a kitchen towel to stem the bleeding. "No big deal."

"And the girl?"

"Safe at Marion's mother's house. I snuck her over there after I dropped you at the docks. No need to use her as actual bait when the rumor of her being here would work just as well."

"Pretty good shot for a guy with a bullet hole in his own shoulder, right?" Floyd said, gritting his teeth, nodding at Brennan's body.

"A great shot, Floyd. And a great job of acting back at the docks. Anyone who saw you when we were loading you onto Gruden's boat would have guessed you were totally out of commission, if not at death's door. Maybe you should move to Hollywood and be in the movies. It's a safer line of work."

"No joke. On top of everything else, I twisted my ankle jumping off the bow of Gruden's boat down on your cove in the dark. It was mighty painful limping up here through your orchard and standing guard over your house. I'll tell you, between my shoulder pain and ankle pain, I was just about angry enough to shoot someone."

Miles half smiled. "I'm sorry."

"You've been saying that a lot today."

"Having Gruden drop you on the beach was the best way I could think of for getting you here without being seen, and for creating the illusion of your incapacitation and departure. Everyone had to think you'd gone back to Seattle and left me on my own."

"Of course."

"And look on the bright side: maybe the ankle pain will distract you from your gunshot wound."

Floyd gave him a withering look.

"That reminds me," Miles said. "Your morphine from Dr. Boren is on the counter there."

"Thank heaven," Floyd said, lurching straight for it.

"Want me to inject you?"

"I think I'll manage."

"Needless to say, I'm grateful for you enduring so much pain to keep a clear head. And I'm very glad you came. I thought you might change your mind and let Gruden actually take you home to Seattle."

"And miss all the fun?"

"I owe you my life, Floyd."

"Let's not be melodramatic. Anyway, I should have stopped Brennan before he got inside. Didn't even see the sneaky son of a bitch approach the house. Didn't know anybody else was here until I heard the gunshots."

"It was dark out there."

"Still."

Floyd pulled a chair from under the kitchen table, plopped his shot and battered body down, and prepared the morphine syringe.

"There's rubbing alcohol in the bathroom, and cotton balls in the—"

"Don't care," Floyd said, injecting himself. "Ohhhhhhhhh."

"Better?"

"Ha-ha-haaaaaah, yes. Better." He melted out of the chair and joined Miles on the floor next to Brennan's body, leaning his back against the wall.

"Sean Brennan," Miles muttered. "Quiet, polite, hard-working Sean Brennan. I just don't see it."

"He was under financial pressure," Floyd said. "Remember

how he was ripped off in his boat engine deal. Remember how he can't pay for his mother's care."

"Everyone's under financial pressure. I'm under financial pressure. But it doesn't occur to me to slaughter fishermen and Chinese girls. And Brennan had no body language or signs of feeling guilt. What the hell? A regular guy turns into a mass murderer like he was changing his shoes?"

"Was he a regular guy?"

"Wasn't he? What are you saying—that he suffered from moral insanity?"

"Remember the sea lion pups?" Floyd asked, starting to sound thoroughly groggy.

"Yeah, but . . ." Just then, Miles recalled that on the very day the *Lucky Lena* was towed in, Brennan asked him why he would bother to investigate murders if they were of mere rumrunners. And it occurred to him, too late, that Brennan had tipped his hand by saying such a thing. That, as Floyd had already believed, the man had a cold heart. Or no heart. Which meant that when it came to doing things most people considered evil, he was capable of anything. Miles wondered what terrible forces could have shaped such indifference in a man. And he shuddered at the implications. "What am I supposed to make of this, Floyd?"

"What do you mean?"

"Is Brennan a product of our modern times? Is he some new type of killer?"

"No," Floyd said through a yawn. "I think he's a very old type of killer. A type we're only now beginning to recognize."

"How do you recognize them?" Miles looked over when Floyd didn't answer and saw that his eyes were closed. "Floyd."

"What?"

"I asked how you recognize them."

"That's the big question. The morally insane are very good at pretending to be normal. At hiding their true unfeeling nature. It's one of the things that makes them so frightening."

"Heaven help us."

"Amen." Floyd took a deep breath. "I'll tell you something strange, Miles," he said, blinking slowly.

"What?"

"That's the first time I've ever killed a man. Yet I feel calm. Remarkably calm."

"You just injected yourself with morphine."

"Nah, nah—before that. I felt calm. Remorseless, even. Isn't that odd?"

"Maybe you're morally insane."

"Not funny."

"You'll feel differently tomorrow."

"It already is tomorrow."

SEVENTY

"Morning, Sheriff. Coffee's on," Bill said, as Miles came through the station door a few hours later, followed, after a moment, by a still somewhat morphine-dulled Floyd. "Floyd! What are you doing back here?"

Neither Miles nor Floyd bothered with pleasantries or explanations. They simply walked up to the desk Bill was resting his feet on, their faces hard, both of them wearing guns.

"You fellas want some flapjacks?"

"No," Miles said.

"You sure? I'm fixing to make a batch with butter and some good, dark molasses I bought this morning. A man has got to eat."

"No flapjacks, Bill."

"Okay. Is everything alright?"

Miles took a deep breath. "Brennan's name is on the passenger manifest for the same boat that was bringing our vanished interpreter up from Seattle."

"Pardon?"

"You saw Brennan's name on the manifest and you didn't tell me. That's the start of my working thesis, Bill. Stop me if I get anything wrong."

Bill took his feet off the desk and sat up straight.

"You told Brennan when the new interpreter was due to arrive," Miles said. "After that, he probably paid someone with a fast boat to run him down to Seattle in the night, then caught the *Bangor* home the next morning, on the same sailing our interpreter was taking. Somewhere along the way, our interpreter went out on deck for a breath of fresh air, or maybe a cigarette, and Brennan took the opportunity to knock the poor guy over the head and tip him overboard. Probably did the same thing to his vicious drunk of a father all those years ago—but that's another story. Probably did the same for Akroyd, shoving him off a cliff near Sunset Point. And for Hawkins, whacking him on the head and knocking him off the Smokehouse pier."

"Sheriff?"

"It's hard to believe that Brennan could have found the time to do so much. But then again, good mechanics are nothing if not methodical and efficient. Apparently, Brennan was methodical enough—heartless enough—to shoot both Jensens to death, then corral eight terrified and defenseless young girls into the aft end of the *Lucky Lena's* cargo hold where he took careful aim and shot each of them, one by one, before slicing open their bellies and dumping their bodies overboard."

"Sheriff, I don't know what you're—"

Miles held up a hand. "Don't bother, Bill. I checked in with Eustace Hampton this morning. I would have done so last night, but someone cut the phone line just south of Argyle."

"That's right by your house," Bill said.

"Yes, it is. And as I was saying, right after you went to find Luke Gruden yesterday evening, I finally convinced Eustace to jot down the content of some calls for me. Want to know the trick? The old biddy is willing to listen in and tell you what she hears, without a warrant, as long as it's on *your own* phone line. Like the line for our station here. Guess what she told me. Actually, again, don't bother. I only ask rhetorically. She told me that right after I told you I'd moved the girl to my mother's house, you tried to call Brennan. Tried three different times over the course of an hour. He didn't pick up, of course. He was busy by then, having already guessed at where I had the girl hidden. Fortunately, he guessed wrong. Smelling a rat, I'd already moved her again, this time to Marion's mother's house. But that's beside the point. What all this means is that you were probably trying to tell him where the girl was."

"No, I—"

"That you probably also told him where I had her hidden at Grandma's Cove. Told him what boat the interpreter would be arriving on. Told him that poor old Akroyd had seen the *Daisy* intercept the *Lucky Lena* near D'Arcy Island. Told him heaven knows what else. Meanwhile, I'd been suspecting poor Floyd here, to the point of accidentally sending him into harm's way. And all the while I wondered, with maddening frustration, why we always seemed to be a day late or a step behind with damn near everything we did."

Bill just stared at them. Eventually, he turned away.

"Why, Bill?"

For a few moments, Bill sat frozen—as if he hadn't heard the question. Then he nodded and turned to face them, looking grim. "Chinks took my job at the cannery. Took my father's job, too." A deep breath. "A month later, he had his stroke. For a while, there was no money coming in to pay for his medical care."

"There was nobody else you could turn to?"

He shook his head slowly. "No, sir."

"Still, how could you do it? How could you tell Brennan where to find that poor little girl?"

"I didn't know he meant to hurt her. He said he was going to stakeout the shack at Grandma's Cove and wait for the tong highbinders to show up. He told me it was the Chink gangs who hijacked the *Lucky Lena*. Told me he knew for sure."

"Did Brennan say *how* he knew for sure?"

"No. But it made sense, what with us finding that Chink symbol aboard."

"What about the Bible verse?"

"Just the Chinks trying to throw us off. Frame McCaskill, maybe. Brennan knows they're a sneaky race. Said they'd probably get away with it if we didn't help each other."

"Help each other?"

"He said he'd help us if I helped him by telling him what we were looking into. That way we'd stand a better chance of solving the case. And exposing the Chinese for what they are. Maybe get them run off our island."

"And then you'd get your old job back, assuming it hasn't been eliminated by that new salmon processing machine."

Bill shrugged.

"Quite a price, Bill. Was it worth it?"

Bill didn't answer the question.

"Brennan came for her again, last night, at my house," Miles said. "Tried to kill *me*."

Bill's eyes grew large. "Sheriff, I tried to find him last night. Searched half the island. To stop him. Once I knew he meant to kill the girl. Once I realized he'd shot Floyd. That's why I tried to call him. Not to tell him the girl was at your mother's house. I swear! You have to believe me."

Miles took a long time to answer. "Actually, I do believe you, Bill."

"I had no reason to think he killed Akroyd or Hawkins or the new interpreter."

"I'm not quite as sure about that."

Bill nodded to himself and rose from his chair. "I suppose you'll be wanting to lock me up, then."

Miles was quiet for a good long while. "No, Bill," he said at last. "I'm not going to arrest you."

"You're not?"

"You're not without blame. But I believe you were duped."

"I'm responsible, Sheriff. I helped a murderer."

"If you're in prison, who will take care of your father?"

Bill had no answer.

"Still," Miles said, "I think you should leave the islands."

"Leave the San Juans? They're all I know, Sheriff. They're my home. Where would I go?"

"The Alaska Territory."

"Alaska?"

"The salmon still run so thick up there that you can cross the rivers without getting your boots wet, just like it used to be here."

"The canneries are desperate for workers," Floyd added. "A man with your expertise ought to be able to write his own ticket."

"You could build yourself a nice cabin on some uninhabited cove like you've always said you dreamed about," Miles said. "Grow giant tomatoes for your father under that crazy midnight summer sun up there. Hunt elk. Mill your own cedar. Nobody would bother you."

"Alaska," Bill muttered.

"It'll be like going back to the Garden of Eden."

SEVENTY-ONE

Miles and Floyd stood on the steamship pier next to the *Bangor*. People were trickling up the gangway for the journey to Seattle.

"I'm still flabbergasted that Bill was tipping our hand to Brennan," Floyd said. "He seemed like such a decent man."

"He is a decent man," Miles said. "But he was angry, desperate, and maybe a little bit ignorant. I'm beginning to think that those three things are enough to make decent men lose their minds."

"I think you're right. Unfortunately, I also think a lot of men share those characteristics."

"Probably doesn't bode well for our species."

"Five minutes to sailing! All aboard!" a deckhand shouted from the top of the gangway.

Floyd looked over his shoulder at the *Bangor*. "Another boat ride. Lucky me."

"Go well, Floyd. And thank you."

"Take care, Miles. I'll give you a call if I ever hear that Sidney Bechet is coming to Seattle."

With that, Floyd turned, eyeballed the gangplank with a deeply reluctant look on his face, took a deep breath, and boarded the steamer for his journey home. He didn't look back.

SEVENTY-TWO

Three weeks later, Miles let it be known around town that he'd be away all day, taking the mostly healed Chinese girl—who an interpreter was finally able to tell him was named Yin—to the deportation station in Port Townsend, as was his duty. Yin was, after all, an illegal immigrant, since federal law explicitly and specifically banned the immigration of Chinese.

First thing in the sunny morning, he retrieved Yin from Meredith Bailey's house where she'd been convalescing, drove her to the docks, and took her aboard Luke Gruden's waiting boat. Then the three of them motored out of Friday Harbor, witnessed by half a dozen fishermen and dockworkers who were there going about their business.

Miles gazed at her as they motored out into the channel, wishing he could learn more about her. About the place she'd come from, and why she'd come to America. He could only fill in the blanks with guesses. Everything he knew of her came from a very brief and somewhat comical telephone conversation she'd had with a Cantonese interpreter in Seattle. She'd never seen a phone before. And when Miles tried to put the receiver to her ear, she'd recoiled in terror, as if the phone were some sort of torture device—which, to Miles, who hated talking on the phone, it was. When he finally pantomimed how to use it, finally convinced the wide-eyed and utterly mystified Yin that it wouldn't hurt her, she was able to answer a handful of questions from the interpreter, who then passed the answers on to Miles. What he learned was that she came from a small village on the Pearl River. That she was a farm girl. That her family was very poor. Her older brothers conscripted into the army. Her baby brother sick. Her father hurt—too hurt to work the land by himself. She did not know why she'd been sent away. She did not know her intended destination.

As far as anyone in Friday Harbor knew, she was now being sent back to China. But once Gruden's boat cleared San Juan Channel and entered Juan de Fuca Strait, instead of continuing south to Port Townsend, they turned east, motored past Lopez Island, then turned north—just as they had when they'd taken Sean Brennan's mother, Clarice, back to the Bellingham senile folks' home, where Miles had already prepaid for three months of care from funds he'd been saving to one day build a house.

They motored up Rosario Strait, past Anacortes, past Lummi Island, toward the small village of Point Roberts. There, Miles and Henry had arranged for Yin to be met by a Cantonese speaking family who ran a small restaurant and laundry. They had two daughters who were roughly her age and were willing to take her in and see to her education, provided she helped out with the family business. Henry assured Miles that they were good people—despite what Henry continued to describe as their Cantonese willingness to "eat anything"—and that Yin would have a good life there.

SEVENTY-THREE

In mid-October, Miles received a rumpled and grimy envelope at the police station. Marked *personal and confidential for Sheriff Miles Scott*, it bore no return address. But it was postmarked St. John's, in the British dominion of Newfoundland—a port city on a rugged, wild island jutting out into the Atlantic just east of the Canadian province of Quebec. Miles had a good idea of who it was from even before he opened it. When he did, he found tiny, poorly punctuated script filling both sides of a single sheet of paper.

Dear Sheriff Scott, it read. *By now I am sure you know that Sean Brennan murdered any number of souls aboard the* Lucky Lena. *You also probably know that he used my boat to do his dirty work. I feel I got to tell you what happened. For starters you may know that my boat the* Daisy *had an old diesel engine that was slowly giving out and making it hard for me to make a living. I did not have money for a new one. One day Brennan comes to me and says maybe we could help each other out and says he has a spare Liberty L-12 and that if I helped him ferry some tools and equipment from Anacortes sometimes then he would install the engine in the* Daisy *free of charge. I could not believe my good luck. We set to work installing the engine. Once it was in he said we needed to take it on a few shakedown runs out to D'Arcy Island and back to make sure it was running cool and proper. We brought Rupert Hawkins along for help.*

The first such day Brennan had me shut down and drift once we got out near D'Arcy saying he wants to see how fast the oil temperature drops. But the whole time we sat and drifted he watched the Lucky Lena *anchored off D'Arcy through his binoculars. He was not really interested in the oil temperature gauge but I was getting a free engine so I kept my trap shut and did not say anything. It was the same the next day with Brennan watching the* Lucky Lena *for two hours while we supposedly waited for the engine oil to cool. On the third such day Brennan asks if I knew anything about the wreck of the* Empress of Burma. *I said everyone knows she went down in Haro Strait. I said that was all I know. He looked at my nautical charts for a while and then went back to watching the* Lucky Lena *through the binoculars.*

All of a sudden he's excited. Says he wants me to take him over to the Lucky Lena *to have a word with its captain Hans Jensen from Deer Harbor. I told him it was getting dark and that a storm was blowing in and that we should head for home. He gets pushy. Says it's important. I asked what's so important it can't wait until tomorrow. He says the* Lucky Lena *was carrying liquor and Russian gold from the wreck of the* Empress of Burma. *He says I would get a cut for helping him and would never have to worry about money again and nobody would find out it was us because we would wear masks. I said I did not want no part of stealing someone else's cargo. He said it was already stolen and there was nothing wrong with stealing from thieves. I sure could have used the money but I knew in my heart that it would be wrong.*

I was thinking it through when I look up and see Brennan and Hawkins staring at me with crazy wolf eyes like they have maybe gone mad. Then I thought they might kill me if I did not do what they said. Afraid for what would become of my helpless daughter if they killed me I went along. Brennan told me to drive him around the back side of D'Arcy to come at the Lucky Lena *from the west. We come up alongside her and secured our lines and Brennan and Hawkins jumped aboard. They didn't wear masks. I do not think they had any. I think they just told me we would wear masks to get me to go along.*

I heard Brennan ask Hans Jensen where the gold was. Hans said he didn't know what Brennan was talking about. Then Brennan shot Hans's son Leif in the leg. Brennan kept asking where the gold was and the Jensens kept saying they did not know what he was talking about. They shouted back and forth louder and louder until all of a sudden Brennan up and shoots both Jensen men dead. I could not believe my eyes and I thought my heart would stop. The Jensens were good people and Brennan shot them down like they were just a couple of stray dogs. Then acting like nothing happened Brennan raised the Lucky Lena's *anchor and he and Hawkins cut the line and chained the Jensen's bodies to the anchor and dropped them overboard. Then they both went below deck looking for gold I guess.*

Just as soon as they went down the companionway I started to untie the line holding the Daisy *to the* Lucky Lena. *Then I heard the sound of unholy screaming. I will never forget that sound. It was like hogs screaming. Or lambs. Or children. And then there was more gunshots. Each shot came a couple of seconds apart like somebody was taking careful aim between each one. I undid the line and shoved off and waited until I drifted too far for one of them to jump back aboard before I started my engines. Last I saw of the* Lucky Lena *was Hawkins on her stern heaving a small body overboard and Brennan dropping what looked like a liquor crate and aiming his gun at me. Thank God none of his shots hit home.*

Amen, thought Miles, wondering how on earth Brennan and Hawkins got off the *Lucky Lena* and back to Friday Harbor after dark and with a storm rolling in. He'd probably never know. Mystified, he turned his attention back to Cooper's letter.

Fearing for my life I raced back to town and grabbed my daughter Milly and ran for it. I know I should have come to you instead. But as you and the whole town know Dr. Boren has declared Milly a certified idiot and lunatic. She cannot care for herself. Seeing as how her mother died of Spanish flu I could not risk going to jail or the gallows as an accomplice and leaving Milly to the care of the state or some church we don't hold with. She deserves better. I promise that if you do not come after me that she will have a proper Christian upbringing. You probably would not find me anyway. It is a big world. Also I am sure you have more important things to do than chase down an old fool like me. I do hope that Brennan and Hawkins face justice. I am sorry for being yellow. I hope those terrible men did not hurt anyone else. But a father's first responsibility is to his daughter.

God bless,

Angus Cooper

Having finished the letter, Miles sat back in his chair and thought for a moment. So Brennan and Hawkins had been after liquor and gold after all. Finding the girls aboard had been a surprise. Then Brennan, seeing the risk of leaving any witnesses alive, gunned them down in cold blood. Angus Cooper, who was by all accounts a decent man, had been duped and intimidated into helping hijack the *Lucky Lena*. All because he didn't have the money for a new boat engine, which meant that he was facing financial ruin.

Miles opened a drawer in his desk, took out a Ronson lighter he kept for the occasional cigar, then rotated Cooper's letter over its flame until most of it was on fire. He held a corner, repositioning his fingers more than once to avoid being burned, until barely a third of the paper remained. Then he tossed it into his metal wastebasket and watched as the last fragment turned to black ash.

SEVENTY-FOUR

Shortly after their dinner of herb roasted chicken and cornbread, Miles took a walk with his mother. The weather was particularly good—cool but comfortable, with the scent of turning leaves and wood smoke in the air. A few cirrus clouds spread their wispy tendrils east toward the Cascade Mountains in an otherwise clear sky. They walked out the driveway and turned south on the road, stopping to feed a dozen old carrots to a pair of chestnut horses named Cocoa and Cookie that lived in a fenced pasture across the way. The pasture was abuzz with bumblebees drawn to the small purple flowers of a sage-like weed that seemed to be everywhere. Probably the last flowers of the season.

Further along, they passed the trailhead to Mulno Cove.

"Been to your old cove lately?" Nellie asked.

"As a matter of fact, yes."

"Hasn't changed much, I imagine."

"No."

"You spent so much time there as a boy. I always thought that as an adult, you'd end up buying the land, building a house, and starting a family."

"There are lots of coves out there."

"Oh?"

"It wasn't the same. When I visited recently, I mean."

"No?"

"Physically, it was. But it felt different."

"How do you mean?"

"I suppose it just didn't have the same draw. Didn't have the same hold on my imagination that it once did."

"How sad."

"Yes. But, like I said, there are lots of coves out there."

As he said this, his ears caught an echo of laughter and the sound of feet tromping through the woods. To his astonishment, when he looked over his shoulder to seek out the source of the commotion, two children emerged onto the road from his and Marion's old trail and headed for town—a boy and a girl who couldn't have been more than ten years old, each carrying fishing rods and wearing boots half-coated with beach sand and fragments of seaweed. He didn't recognize them. But their innocent smiles and their sanguine, untainted joy struck a distantly familiar chord that launched him into fading but cherished memories of autumn evenings of his own childhood. Lost in thought for a blissful moment, he barely heard his mother suggest that they head back to the house as darkness would be falling soon. When he turned around, the children were gone.

*****

The stars were coming out when they finally got home, and they could just hear the lonely hoot of a distant owl carried across the chilly evening air. Instead of joining his mother for the offered game of cribbage by the warm wood-burning stove, Miles went out to their barn. A field mouse went scurrying across the floor as he opened the door and switched on the lights. The air inside was still, the aromas of hay and chicken feed as familiar as ever. Against the far wall, under its dusty canvas cover, sat the old Peerless Raceabout, untouched since Miles and his father had set down their tools one sad and fateful day back in 1918.

Miles first went to the workbench. There, he stared down at his father's old tools, their handles stained from use. Stained with sweat and grime from his father's own hands. Slowly, with a certain reverence, he picked up a mallet by the head and brought the handle to his nose, hoping there might be some trace of the scent of his father. It smelled only of beeswax and scorched engine oil.

Disappointed, he set mallet back down, turned to face the car, and took a deep breath. He approached the shrouded car tentatively, reaching out a hand and touching the canvas as if to make sure that it was actually still under there. He felt the resistance of hard, stamped steel. Taking great care not to fling years' worth of accumulated dust into the air, he rolled the cover back to reveal the car's polished black body, its brass headlamps, its ruby red upholstery. Then he took a step back to gaze upon its beauty.

He and his father had come so close to finishing its refurbishment. So close to actually taking it for a drive together. But life was like that, Miles had learned. Sometimes you got to where you wanted to go, and sometimes you didn't. Still, as he stood there, he began to recall happy summer days working on the car, him and his dad. Learning how to weld. Learning how to replace axles, gaskets, brakes, and cylinder heads. Getting dirty and greasy and laughing and drinking ice-cold lemonade that his mother brought them by the pitcherful. All of it good. All of it still a part of him.

With a faint smile and a nod to himself, he went to the workbench, grabbed a box of wrenches, and dusted each of them off with a rag. Then he walked to the front end of the Raceabout, opened the metal hood that covered its massive, magnificent engine, and got back to work.

SEVENTY-FIVE

Point Roberts, Washington
Two Months Later

Mei says I am getting good at using the iron. I have twelve more shirts to press and then a box of cabbage to chop up for the restaurant. But when we are done with our work for the day, Mei and Shu said we get to share the rest of the sweet lychee fruit their father brought back from Vancouver.

I share a big room with Mei and her twin sister Shu. They are my age, I think. They are nice to me. Like sisters. We work together, go to school together, and play together. Their bedroom is like a dream. It has glass windows and an electric light.

Their parents are from Taishan, so they are hard for me to understand. But they are very kind. They own their own restaurant and laundry business in this small village called Point Roberts. They used to live in a nearby city called Bellingham until white mill workers chased all the Asians away. But here in Point Roberts we are welcome. Mei says many of the people here are from a country called Iceland. They like the Cantonese food we cook for them. I want to learn English so I can ask them all about their country. Mei and Shu are teaching me.

Yesterday, for the first time in my life, I saw snow. Real snow. It snowed all morning. It did not collect on the ground. Mei said it was too warm for it to stick. But just watching it fall was the most beautiful thing I have ever seen. We took a break from schoolwork to run around outside and try to catch the flakes on our tongues. The flakes are smaller than in my dreams. But beautiful all the same. I hope it snows a lot someday. That it collects on the ground and builds up deep—so deep that they cancel school and we can just play in it all day.

We ate steamed gaau ji dumplings after playing in the snow. It was the biggest platter of gaau ji I have ever seen, each dumpling full of ginger and scallions and pork, served hot with black vinegar to dip them in. Gaau ji and as many cups of strong, hot tea as we wanted. Filling, warming, delicious. And it wasn't even for a special holiday! But eating the gaau ji made me sad too. It was always a special dish for my family. Something we had when things were very good. When we were happy.

On some nights, when the sky is clear, I look up at the Northern Dipper and I wonder if my family is looking at it too. If we can both see it, maybe we are not so far apart. I wonder if I will ever see my family or my village again. My father's smile. My mouse. I do not think I ever will. My heart tells me there will be no going back. It makes me sad. Sometimes, during the night, I cry. I miss my home. But I am not hungry anymore.

ACKNOWLEDGMENTS

Many, many thanks for the advice and/or hands-on assistance of Holly Pemberton, Sarah Haskins, Steven James, Jim Harris of the Pacific Northwest Writers Association, Lizzy Rolando at Salmonberry Books, Brandy Bowen at Watermark Book Company, Katrine at Griffin Bay Bookstore, Jenny Pederson at Darvill's Bookstore, Suzanne Selfors at Liberty Bay Books, Jane Danielson at Eagle Harbor Book Co., Karen Emmerling at Beach Books, Erin Ball at Third Place Books, Brian Juenemann, Larry West, Tiffany LaSalle, and Greg Holmes of the Pacific Northwest Booksellers Association, Diane Quayle, Dr. Cynthia Rigby, Nancy Overton, Jamie Woeber, "EditorNancy" on Fiverr.com, "Grandma Alexander" and her crack Seattle marketing team, and, of course, "Mango." This story would never have made it onto bookstore shelves without their invaluable help.

For more information about this era of San Juan Islands, Seattle, and Pacific Northwest history, see:

The History of Stuart Island
by James Bergquist
available from
Turn Point Lighthouse Preservation Society (www.tplps.org)
P.O. Box 243
Orcas, WA 98280

The Case of the Beryl G
by Eric Newsome
ISBN: 978-0920501290

Images of America - Friday Harbor
by Mike and Julia Vouri, the San Juan Historical Society
ISBN: 978-0738558691
(https://www.sjmuseum.org/)

Images of America – San Juan Island
by Mike and Julia Vouri, the San Juan Historical Society
ISBN: 978-0738581477
(https://www.sjmuseum.org/)

Once Upon a Time in Seattle
by Emmett Watson
ISBN: 978-1941890240

Seattle Prohibition: Bootleggers, Rumrunners & Graft in the Queen City
by Brad Holden
ISBN: 978-1467140201

Seattle 1900-1920: From Boomtown, Urban Turbulence, to Restoration
by Richard C. Berner
ISBN: 978-0962988905

Seattle from the Margins: Exclusion, Erasure, and the Making of a Pacific Coast City
by Megan Asaka
ISBN: 978-0295751863

Native Seattle: Histories from the Crossing-Over Place
by Coll Thrush
ISBN: 978-0295741345

Seattle Now & Then
by Paul Dorpat
ISBN: 978-1933245539

Archives of The Seattle Times and Seattle Post-Intelligencer newspapers:
(https://www.seattletimes.com/)
(https://www.seattlepi.com/)

Liquor flows and blood spills in 'Seattle Prohibition: Bootleggers, Rumrunners & Graft in the Queen City'
by Brad Holden, *The Seattle Times*
(https://www.seattletimes.com/pacific-nw-magazine).

The Rebel History Podcast
by Andrew Veith
(*https://www.rebelhistory.com/*)

Hidden Jazz Era Speakeasy Found Inside Old Building Was Known As "The Bucket of Blood"
by Rachel Heichelbech, *Dusty Old Thing*
(https://dustyoldthing.com/prohibition-era-speakeasy-found/)

The Louisa Hotel, Seattle, Washington: Remnants of a forgotten 1920s speakeasy and Prohibition-era murals were discovered in its basement.
by Amy Bonaduce, *Atlas Obscura*
(https://www.atlasobscura.com/places/the-louisa-hotel)

The 1st Record Ever Cut in Seattle
by Peter Blecha, *Northwest Music Archives*
(http://nw-music-archives.blogspot.com/2013/05/the-1st-record-ever-cut-in-seattle-1923.html)

D.C. Alexander's
"Clams Friday Harbor"

(4 entrée-sized servings)
4 strips of thick-cut bacon
4 tsp. olive oil
6 Tbs. salted butter
1 1/3 cups minced shallots
1 1/3 cups chopped fresh tomatoes
1/2 cup chopped fresh basil
8 minced garlic cloves
4 cups dry white wine (don't worry—Prohibition was repealed in 1933)
4 tsp. fresh chopped thyme or 2 tsp. dried thyme
2 Tbs. sherry
4 dozen fresh Manila or other small steamer clams.
A warm loaf of crusty sourdough or other rustic bread.

In a Dutch oven or heavy pot with lid, fry bacon strips over medium heat until crispy, turning them once. Remove the bacon to a platter to cool. Add the olive oil, butter, and shallots to the hot bacon fat. Sauté the shallots for three minutes. Add the tomatoes and basil. Sauté for another two minutes. Crumble the cooled bacon and return it to the pot. Add minced garlic and sauté for one more minute. Add the white wine, thyme, and sherry. Give the mixture a quick stir. Add in the clams. COVER and cook for 7-9 minutes, or until most of the clams have opened wide. Ladle the cooking broth all over the clams. Serve with warm crusty bread for dipping in the broth. DO NOT PRY OPEN and DO NOT EAT any clams that do not open wide on their own during cooking (unless you want to lose weight VERY quickly, speak in tongues, and possibly die a horrible, thoroughly inelegant death).

Go to bed.

Milton Keynes UK
Ingram Content Group UK Ltd.
UKHW011940010124
435297UK00001B/48